THE COWBOY'S
CHRISTMAS PLAN

by
Shanna Hatfield

The Cowboy's Christmas Plan
Copyright © 2011 by Shanna Hatfield

ISBN-13: 978-1467954976
ISBN-10: 1467954977

For permission requests, please contact the author, with a subject line of "permission request" at the email address below or through her website.

Shanna Hatfield
shanna@shannahatfield.com
shannahatfield.com

This is a work of fiction. Names, characters, businesses, places, events and incidents are either the products of the author's imagination or used in a fictitious manner. Any resemblance to actual persons, living or dead, or actual events is purely coincidental. Quotes were taken from http://brainyquotes.com

DEDICATION

To my favorite Sherman County redhead -
Thanks for your encouragement, support and friendship.
You are amazing and a source of continual inspiration!

Books by Shanna Hatfield

FICTION

The Women of Tenacity Series
The Women of Tenacity - A Prelude
Heart of Clay
Country Boy vs. City Girl
Not His Type

Grass Valley Cowboys Series
The Cowboy's Christmas Plan

><><

NON-FICTION

Savvy Holiday Entertaining

Chapter One

Everyone has a plan 'till they get punched in the mouth.
Mike Tyson

"I don't think I heard you correctly, Neil. Would you please repeat that?" Cadence Vivian Greer asked, looking at her boss in disbelief.

He has to be wrong, her mind screamed, while her body morphed into a consistency quite similar to watery oatmeal.

Neil Dumont took her by the elbow and steered her into one of his plush leather office chairs. Ordering her to put her head down between her knees, he released a long sigh.

"Cadence, I know this is a surprise, but it really shouldn't come as a shock," Neil said, sitting down next to her as he expertly patted her shoulder. Cadence absently wondered if he had a lot of practice comforting hysterical young women, since his daughter was her age.

"I know, Neil, but I need you to tell me exactly what happened," she whispered, sitting up and dabbing at her eyes with her finger. She couldn't fully wrap her head around the notion that all her carefully crafted plans for the future were falling around her like a crop of bad apples knocked from the tree.

Neil, one of the founding partners of the prestigiouslaw firm where she worked in Seattle, was well-respected. A family man with a wife of 32 years and two great kids, he was someone Cadence admired. Normally, she heeded his advice. When it came to Bill, however, she had blocked out his warnings and done as she pleased.

Nodding his head, Neil handed her his pristine white handkerchief and cleared his throat, just like he did before stepping before a judge in the courtroom. Cadence knew what that sound meant. After working as Neil's personal assistant for the past four years, she was familiar with all the sounds he made when he prepared to do verbal battle and win.

"Cadence, I warned you when you began working here to stay away from guys like Bill. I warned you when you two started dating that it wouldn't end well. I even warned you when you announced your engagement to be careful. I know you, Cadence. You are a no-nonsense kind of girl, so don't make me sugarcoat this. Bill sent an email out last night to all the attorneys in the office stating he had called off his engagement to you and was eloping with Miss Roberts."

"But Bill said…" Cadence was cut off before she could finish her thought.

"I'm sure he said he loved you, that you were the best thing that ever happened to him, that he'd spend his life making you happy. What he failed to mention was that he has chased after every skirt in this office while you two were supposedly engaged and Miss Roberts didn't even try to make it hard to be caught. You really shouldn't be surprised that a guy like Bill would run off with his secretary."

"How did I not see this coming?" Cadence said, starting to move on the emotional scale from devastated to angry. "How could he do this a week before our wedding?"

Cadence was more than flattered when Bill Aimes continually sought her out on breaks, walked her to her car after work, and invited her out for coffee. The hot-shot attorney was tall, handsome, successful and charming.

With a sigh of disgust, she thought about where that charm had gotten her.

For the first time in her life, Cadence felt like an idiot and a failure. If Bill had punched her in the face, she couldn't feel any more abused, violated, and hurt than she did right at this moment.

Bill definitely pulled the rug out from beneath her. Refusing to move in with him until after the wedding, Cadence had given notice on her tiny apartment and sold off all her furniture. Bill owned a beautiful condo with posh furnishings and made it clear he didn't want her hand-me-downs or second-hand finds in his sleek and modern environment.

And now Cadence had nothing.

"What am I going to do?" Cadence said, staring at Neil with a look of despair in her hazel eyes.

"Take a few days off, let your thoughts clear and give your heart time to mend, then come back to work with your head held high," Neil said in his commanding voice. "You didn't do a thing wrong, Cadence, except fall for a man who is completely undeserving of your love."

"Be that as it may, I can't keep working here. Not with him and his new bride coming back. I just couldn't do it, Neil."

"Now, Cadence, don't be hasty," Neil said, growing more alarmed by the look of determination on Cadence's face than by anything that had happened so far. "Once the dust settles, tongues will be wagging about another juicy bit of gossip and all will be forgotten."

"Maybe by the others, but not by me," Cadence said, getting up and pacing across Neil's office. "I can't keep working here knowing I'll run into him every time I turn around. It would be like rubbing salt in a wound on a daily basis. I don't have a choice, Neil. I have to leave."

Rising from his chair, Neil studied Cadence. She was the best assistant he'd ever had. If she wanted, she could have made an excellent attorney. Her mind was sharp, her demeanor cool and professional, and she quickly picked up on even the most infinitesimal details, except when it came to Bill.

Releasing another sigh, Neil knew Cadence was correct. Having to work in the same office with her former fiancé would be a form of torture. He'd love to see Bill kicked to the curb, but the fact that Bill's uncle was one of the firm's partners insured good ol' Bill would still have a job when he returned from his honeymoon.

"Cadence, maybe I can make a few calls and find you a position elsewhere," Neil offered as he walked up behind her where she stared out the window into the gray, rain-laden sky.

Turning, Cadence gave him the barest hint of a smile.

"Thanks, Neil, for the offer. But no thank you," she said, shaking her head. "I've made up my mind. I'm leaving. I'll start over somewhere else."

"Where will you go? What will you do?" Neil knew she grew up in a middle class home in the suburbs. Her parents had worked hard to help put her through college. As an only child, Cadence had been utterly alone since her parents announced a year ago they were moving to southern Mexico, where they could live inexpensively and enjoy an early retirement. They'd been saving their pennies for years to live out their dream. Still, Cadence never thought they would actually go and leave her behind. Alone.

Maybe that was part of the reason she had been in such a rush to marry Bill. She needed to fill the quiet left by the departure of her parents. Cadence talked to her parents once a month or so and she often spoke of an aunt who lived out in the sticks.

"What if you go spend some time with your aunt in Oregon? I bet she'd take you in until you can decide what your next step should be," Neil suggested with fatherly concern.

"Aunt Viv?" Cadence instantly warmed to the idea. Of course! She could go spend some time with Aunt Vivian and Uncle Joe in Grass Valley before she made any further mistakes or decisions.

Cadence smiled at Neil. "That's perfect, Neil. Thank you for the suggestion. I hate to leave you without an assistant, but I feel like the sooner I can cut my ties and leave town, the better off I'll be. Besides, I only have my apartment for another three days. I was going to stay at the hotel with my parents until the wedding."

"You know I hate losing you, Cadence. You've been a top-notch assistant and if there is ever anything I can do for you, you let me know."

Sticking out her hand, Cadence offered Neil a handshake, but he pulled her into a warm hug. "You've become like a daughter to me and all I get is a handshake? I think not."

Letting out a shaky laugh, Cadence hugged him back and again brushed at her tears.

"Now, I better go pack up my desk and get out of here."

Before Cadence finished cleaning out her desk, Neil walked by with a wink and a smile, dropping an envelope into the box she was filling with her personal belongings.

"You be sure and keep in touch," Neil said as he stood in his office door. "I want to know you landed on both feet and are doing just fine."

"I will, Neil, and thanks again."

Cadence picked up the box and her purse, hurrying out to her car. Waiting until she was back at the apartment, she opened the envelope to find her wages due plus a hefty bonus that would help her start fresh somewhere else. A note from Neil simply said, "You've more than earned it."

Sagging onto the one chair left in her apartment, Cadence let the tears flow. When they subsided, she straightened her shoulders, picked up the phone and began calling people to tell them the wedding was off, starting with her mom and dad.

><><

Watching the city's skyline recede to a blur in her rearview mirror, Cadence let out another sigh. Things could not get any worse unless she suffered the same fate as Lot's wife for looking back and ended up as a pillar of salt. And with the sky pouring down a steady drizzle of rain, the salt would quickly wash away and leave no trace behind.

She wished once again that her white-knuckled grip around the steering wheel was instead around Bill's neck.

What kind of man runs off with his secretary days before his wedding?

The kind who isn't worth crying over, as Aunt Vivian had told her multiple times during the last few painful days.

At 27, she was homeless, jobless, and jilted.

In her worst nightmares, Cadence would never have pictured herself in her current predicament. She was too serious, too organized, too grounded to let something like this happen.

And yet it had.

At least the last three days had passed in a blur. By the time she notified all her family and friends of the situation, returned the gifts, and reclaimed what funds she could from the canceled wedding plans, she was ready to leave and forget she had ever heard the name Bill Aimes.

As she drove south on the freeway toward Portland, she contemplated her journey to the middle of nowhere to stay with her Aunt Vivian in a self-imposed exile until she could figure out what she wanted to do with her life.

Casting one more glance in the mirror, Cadence mentally waved goodbye to the only life she'd ever known, resolved to face an entirely new one with tenacity and courage.

><><

Cadence stopped in Portland to do a little shopping before she finished the drive to Grass Valley. Her aunt assured her there were no malls, and suggested she might want to pick up a few things before heading east on the freeway.

When Cadence got back on I-84, she was the owner of six pairs of jeans, a handful of t-shirts, a dozen cotton blouses, a few sweatshirts, a warm waterproof coat and a pair of sturdy hiking shoes.

Growing up in the city and working at the law firm, Cadence's wardrobe consisted of power suits, silk blouses, and high heels. Her casual wear included slacks, ballet flats and cashmere sweaters. Nothing that would be very useful in a country community as Aunt Viv had pointed out.

Pulling off the freeway a couple of hours later, Cadence turned south on Highway 97 and drove through the small towns of Biggs and Moro before she came to Grass Valley, population 170.

A sigh escaped as she stopped the car in front of her aunt's pride and joy, Viv's Café, and went inside.

Goodbye Seattle, Starbucks and Nordstrom.

Hello greasy spoon.

Chapter Two

*The method of the enterprising is to plan with audacity
and execute with vigor.*

Christian Nestell Bovee

Timothy Andrew Thompson III, known from the day he was born as Trey, removed his dirty Stetson and wiped the sweat from his brow. Running a hand through his sun-streaked hair, he settled the hat back in place.

"Do you remember it ever being this warm in September?" he asked his brother, Trent, who was leaning over his horse's bent leg, hammering on another horseshoe.

Removing the last nail from his mouth and tapping it into place, Trent squinted through the bright afternoon sunlight at his older brother. "Nope, but I reckon it won't last much longer. Supposed to drop off cold in a few weeks."

"Well, I think I might be ready for some cooler weather," Trey said, as he put away their farrier tools and cleaned up the mess left behind from trimming and shoeing their horses.

"Sure you are," Trent said, a teasing gleam in his blue eyes. "As soon as it freezes, you'll do nothing but complain about how cold it is until the spring thaw sets in. You've got to learn to live in the moment and enjoy it, bro."

Trey grinned at his brother. "And when did you go and get all philosophical? You been hanging out at the school trying to get a date with Miss Lindsay again? You've really got to stop mooning over that girl."

Trent turned a narrowed gaze to Trey. "I do not hang out at the school and I certainly don't moon over any female." Trent rubbed the nose of his horse, "Except maybe this one. Lass is worth her weight in gold, aren't you?"

The horse answered by bobbing her head and rubbing it against Trent's chest.

Trey couldn't help but laugh. "You're pathetic."

"Look who's talking. When was the last time you had a date?" Trent questioned as he turned the horse loose in the pasture. "And escorting Mom and her cronies around does not count."

Trey refused to take Trent's bait and changed the subject as they walked toward the house.

"I think we should get cleaned up and head in to Viv's for dinner. I don't think I can stomach any more of your cooking or mine," Trey said, holding open the back door for Trent to walk in ahead of him. Pausing inside the mud room, they removed their dusty boots, hung their hats on pegs and brushed at their dirty jeans. Old habits die hard.

Looking at each other, they grinned.

"Guess we'll never forget to remove our boots before going inside after Mom and Lois drummed that lesson through our thick skulls," Trey said as they walked through the mudroom into the kitchen. Washing up at the sink, Trey pulled two cans of Mountain Dew out of the refrigerator and slid one over to Trent. Wiping the cold rivulets beading down the can onto his jean-clad leg, Trey popped the top and took a sip.

"Why did Lois have to go and retire on us?" Trent asked, taking a deep drink of the soda. "It was bad enough when Mom up and moved to The Dalles, but to have Lois abandon us too left us in dire straits."

Trey leaned against the counter. "I don't think we're exactly in dire straits, although we could definitely use another housekeeper and cook. But it isn't like they grow on trees out here."

Some people might refer to Grass Valley as the middle of nowhere. The sticks. Last stop before the edge of the planet gave way to a black abyss.

Trey and his brothers preferred to call it God's country.

The Thompson family settled into Grass Valley back in the late 1800s and had been there since. Located in the central Oregon high desert country, the rolling hills of wheat and pastures filled with cattle were about as close to heaven on earth as Trey thought anyone could find. Especially on a day when blue sky stretched as far as the eye could see, interrupted by the occasional fluffy white cloud.

When his father passed away six years ago of a heart attack, Trey wasn't sure how he and his brothers would keep the ranch going. He was only 24 at the time, Trent was 21 and their youngest brother Travis was 18. But they "put their backs into it" as their father taught them and kept things rolling along just like Drew Thompson would have done.

Their mother, Denni, was heartbroken when their father passed away and just couldn't stay on the ranch where they had lived and loved for nearly 30 years. So she moved an hour away to The Dalles, went to work for one of her friends in a quilt and crafts store, and started a new life. The boys tried to visit her every other Sunday. Sometimes she drove out to meet them at the little country church in Grass Valley and came out to the ranch with them on the weekends when they didn't drive into The Dalles.

Trey often wondered if it hurt their mother to see them. All three brothers looked like their father, muscular and solidly built. People knew better than to mess with one of the Thompson boys.

Although Trey was the shortest at 5'11", Travis came in at 6'1" while Trent topped the charts at 6'5". What Trey lacked in height, he more than made up for with broad shoulders, thick chest, and a commanding presence.

A few people had even been known to say he was the best looking of the Thompson boys. With a square jaw, thick wavy hair the color of fresh honey and a strong chin, he knew he had more than a few admirers among the female population. The fact that he inherited his grandmother's striking aquamarine eyes didn't hurt one bit either when he set out to charm the ladies.

His charm had gotten him nowhere with Lois. He finally came right out and begged her not to leave. Lois had been a housekeeper and cook for the family for as long as Trey could remember. When she became a grandmother in July, she decided she was ready to retire and moved to Boise to be close to her one and only daughter. At least she waited until after the wheat was harvested to pack up and leave.

So for the last month, Trey and Trent did the best they could at housekeeping and cooking. Their few hired hands had realized right away they could do better fending for themselves in the bunkhouse kitchen and had not been back to sample a meal at the main house since Trent set a pan of pre-made lasagna on fire. They were really going to have to get serious about looking for a cook.

The ringing phone brought Trey out of his musings. Taking two steps across the floor, he answered on the second ring.

"Thompson Ranch," Trey said politely.

"Trey! How's it going?" asked a familiar voice that sounded a million miles away.

"Great! How are you doing? Where are you at?" Trey was surprised to hear the voice of his youngest brother on the line. Travis was on his second tour of Iraq and they hoped he would be home in time for Christmas.

"You know I can't give you specifics, but I wanted to let you know I'm doing fine and I got the package you sent. Everything was appreciated," Travis said, his voice echoing across the line.

"You're welcome," Trey said, a smile lifting the corners of his generous lips. "You're sure you're okay?"

"Yep. The only way I could be better is if I was there to give you and Trent heck for letting Lois leave. Who is going to feed me when I finally do get home?"

Trey laughed. "We were just discussing that when you called. I'm working on some ideas."

"Work faster," Travis joked. "I don't want to come home and have to eat your cooking. That is a guaranteed death sentence. Now let me talk to Trent."

Trey passed the phone off to Trent and listened to the one-sided conversation.

They all were proud and scared when Travis came home and told them he had enlisted in the Army. The day he left state-side for Iraq, Trey wasn't sure their mother would be able to handle her baby heading to a war zone. She surprised them all by calmly wishing Travis well, reminding him to wear clean underwear and call home when he could.

As Trent said goodbye, he passed the phone back to Trey.

"You be careful, Trav. We expect to have you home for Christmas."

"I plan on being there, but you get busy finding a new cook. I'm not coming home if you two are doing the cooking."

Trey laughed. "And just where do you get off being so bossy?"

"It's all part of my job. Bye, Trey. Give Mom and Nana a hug for me."

"Will do. You take care."

Trey hung up the phone when he heard Travis disconnect. Turning to Trent he gave him a thoughtful look.

"Well, you heard our little brother. We better find a new cook and housekeeper before he gets home. It's time to get busy planning where we're going to find one."

Occupied out on the ranch, it had been a few weeks since the Thompson brothers made a trip into town to eat. They walked in the doors of Viv's Café during the dinner rush hour. It took them a few minutes to wander to an empty booth, stopping to chat with neighbors and catch up on the local news.

Taking a seat, they hung their cowboy hats on the hooks at the end of the booth then picked up the laminated menus that were kept in a wire holder between the ketchup and mustard bottles on the surprisingly shiny table. Viv didn't usually worry about keeping a high shine on anything. She figured if it was sanitized, it was good enough.

"What do you think?" Trey asked, surveying the menu that hadn't changed since Viv took over the café fifteen years earlier. "Chicken fried steak or meatloaf?"

"Hmm. Good question," Trent said, his stomach already growling as he thought about eating a decent meal.

The sound of ice and water glasses hitting the floor quickly drew their attention to the table across from them.

A flustered looking woman bent to pick up the tray of water glasses she had dropped. Her dark brown hair was caught up in a severe bun and her face was a fiery shade of red.

17

"I'm so terribly sorry," she said in a quiet voice to the family seated at the table. "Please accept my apologies." She hustled around the table with the tray of glasses firmly in hand only to slip on a chunk of ice and slide right into Trey. The one glass that hadn't yet spilled tipped over and ran down his front, soaking his shirt and jeans.

Sensing her humiliation, Trey reached out an arm to steady her. A flash of fire shot through his fingers and up his arm. Jerking his hand away, the woman drew in a gasp.

"I beg your pardon, sir. I'm so sorry," she whispered as she took a step back, looking horrified by what she'd done.

"Well, I reckon its fine," Trey said, a slow grin spreading across his handsome face. Although one side of his shirt was ice cold and clinging to his chest and it would look like he couldn't hold water if he stood up, he was incapable of wiping the smile from his lips. "I'll dry out by the time I'm finished eating. Don't worry about it. I…"

Trey's words were cut off when Viv hustled out of the back to see what all the commotion was about. Coming to a stop, she rested a hand on the woman's shoulder and gave it a squeeze.

"Well, if it isn't the Thompson boys, come to grace my fine establishment," Viv teased. "I haven't seen you two in a coon's age. You get tired of your own cooking?"

Trent laughed. "Yes, Ma'am, we did."

"That's just what I thought," Viv smiled. "Now, did you meet my niece Cadence? She's helping me out for a while."

Trent and Trey shot each other a look, but neither one said anything.

Trey nodded his head in the woman's direction and continued to smile.

"Nice to meet you Mrs…"

"It's Miss Greer," Viv said, looking between Trey and Cadence. "But you can call her Cadence. No need to be formal out here, is there?"

"No, Ma'am," Trent agreed. "No need at all."

Trent stood up and stuck out his hand. "I'm Trent Thompson and this is my brother Trey."

Cadence looked up and then looked up some more to see Trent towering above her 5'6" frame. She managed to work up a small smile and take his hand without dropping the tray again. Turning her head, she stuck her hand out to his brother. He stood up, and she was glad to see he wasn't quite so tall.

Darting a glance at his face, she was surprised by his eyes. Their color was the exact same brilliant shade as the Sea of Cortez, or at least how the water looked in the photo her parents had emailed her yesterday. Laugh lines crinkled at the corners of his eyes and his lips parted to show even, white teeth. She felt her own lips curl into a smile as she studied the cowboy named Trey. To say he was handsome would be making a gross underestimation of the truth. He was steal-your-breath-away gorgeous.

When he took her hand in his warm, callused one, she felt hot tremors shoot up her arm again and forced herself not to yank her hand back.

Angry for feeling attracted to any man, Cadence slammed the brakes on her emotions and put her cool demeanor back in place.

"It was very nice to meet you both," she said politely before returning to the kitchen.

Trey and Trent both watched her hurry away, gawking at how well she filled out her jeans. Viv pushed Trey back into the booth, handing him a napkin.

"What's that for?" he asked as she pushed the paper square into his hand.

"To wipe the drool off your chin," she said with a wink. "Don't you two go getting any bright ideas about my girl. She came here to get away from one of the most despicable examples of manhood you'd ever hope to meet and I don't need either one of you breaking her heart in any more pieces."

"Yes, Ma'am," Trent said, looking at Trey with a raised eyebrow.

Viv motioned to Trey to scoot over and slid beside him, fanning herself with her apron.

"As much as I love that girl, she is going to be the death of my diner," Viv whispered to the two boys she had watched grow up and become fine men. "She can't wait tables to save her life. She's broke more glasses in the last week than I've broken in a lifetime. Just today, Cadence spilled hot soup on Ermil Wright and dumped a platter of Buffalo wings on Fred Noder. I don't know what I'm going to do with her."

"Can she cook and clean?" Trey asked, surprised when he heard himself blurt out the question.

Viv slowly turned her head to look at him and took a moment before answering. "Can she cook and clean? That girl is fanatical about cleaning. She keeps running around with bleach wipes and a mop scrubbing anything that doesn't move. Have you ever seen the front windows so spanking clean?"

Trey and Trent looked at the windows. They were so clean they actually held a bit of sparkle from the fading evening light.

"Well, what about cooking?" Trent asked, picking up on the direction where Trey's thoughts were leading.

"She can cook, but it's fancy pants food," Viv said, sitting a little straighter in the booth. "She says all that grease I use to fry food is going to kill you all graveyard dead. One thing the girl can do fine is bake, though. You've never had pie like she can make. My Joe said her berry pie the other night was the best thing he'd ever eaten. Old coot!"

Trey smothered a laugh and patted Viv's hand.

"Well, you know we've been left high and dry since Lois moved to Boise," Trey said, hoping to play off Viv's sympathy. "What do you think of Cadence coming to work for us?"

"As your cook and housekeeper?" Viv asked, as she considered the possibility. "I don't know."

"What's not to know, Viv?" Trey said, liking the idea more by the minute. The girl might be a terrible waitress, but she wasn't hard to look at, that was for sure. "We'd give her room and board and a wage on top of it. She'd be out of the café but still close enough you can see her anytime you want and keep an eye on her. We wouldn't let anything happen to her, would we Trent?"

"No, Ma'am," Trent said, liking his brother's plan more by the minute. He could almost smell bread baking in their oven. "We'd treat her just like we would our own sister."

"See, right there is the problem," Viv said, shooting Trent a wary glance. "You don't have a sister and you three hooligans are too much for even your own sweet mama to handle. I just don't know if it would be proper for her to be living out there with all you bachelors. None of your hands are married are they?"

"No, Viv, they aren't," Trey said, starting to feel edgy under Viv's resistance to his plan. "But this isn't the Stone Age and we aren't a bunch of cavedwellers. She could have the whole north wing of the house to herself and we'd be clear over in the south wing. Come on. What do you say?"

Viv was about to say no, but turned just in time to watch Cadence upend a breadbasket in old Mrs. Henkle's lap.

"If she agrees, you boys can hire her," Viv said, getting up from the table with a shake of her head. "But no funny business or you'll answer to me."

"Yes, Ma'am," Trey said with a nod and a smile.

Trey and Trent watched Cadence spill, drop and fumble her way through the dinner service. Viv personally hand-delivered a brimming plate of chicken fried steak to each of them. They had just finished mopping up the last bit of gravy off their plates with a warm dinner roll when Cadence approached with two pieces of pie smothered by a crown of melting vanilla ice cream.

Although he had eaten his fill, Trey's mouth began to water as she carefully slid a plate in front of him then set one down in front of Trent. Keeping her aloof façade in place, she said "enjoy" then walked back to the kitchen.

Unable to talk while they were devouring the best piece of apple pie to ever cross their lips, Trey and Trent communicated by raising eyebrows, grunting, and nodding their heads.

When the pie was gone, they didn't care how much "fancy pants" food they had to eat, they'd do anything to be able to enjoy pie like that on a regular basis.

Waiting until the café was nearly empty, Viv came out to their table and motioned for Cadence to join them.

"Cadence, these two gentlemen have a business proposal for you," Viv said as she gave Cadence's shoulders a reassuring squeeze. Her aunt was tall and lean with a head full of short gray curls and pale blue eyes, a near replica of Cadence's own mother. Cadence leaned into her hug and tried to keep her heart from pounding. She knew she had to be the world's worst waitress and wondered how long it would be before Aunt Viv sent her packing.

"Miss Greer," Trey said, deciding Cadence might prefer to keep things a bit more formal. "We are in need of a housekeeper and cook. Your aunt thought you might be interested in the position. You would prepare breakfast and dinner for us and our hired men and keep up the ranch house. The hired hands take care of the bunk house and do their own laundry. We'd pay you $1,000 per month in addition to your room and board."

Cadence was quite surprised by the offer. The wages were more than fair considering they were in the middle of nowhere and to have room and board included was a bonus she had not expected at all. She would be close to Aunt Viv and Uncle Joe and would no longer have to be mortified every time she spilt something on a paying customer. She just wasn't sure the idea of living close to two bachelors, especially two extremely good looking cowboy bachelors, was the very best idea.

"How many men would I have to cook for?" Cadence finally asked in her best business tone. She looked at Trent as she asked the question. Looking at Trey seemed to scramble her thoughts and she had to fight to keep from getting sucked into those ocean blue eyes of his.

"Generally, there are eight of us, although right now there are only seven. Our youngest brother is finishing up his tour of duty in Iraq," Trent answered.

"Oh," Cadence said, realizing from Trent's tone how much their younger brother must be missed. "I hope your brother is safe."

"I don't know how safe he is, but when he called earlier today, he sounded just fine," Trey said, giving Cadence a crooked grin.

"You mean you two sat here this whole time and didn't even think to mention that Travis called?" Viv said, taking them both to task and pumping them for details about their brother. It gave Cadence a chance to study the two men seated before her. She decided they didn't look cruel or unkind, just dangerously handsome. Her aunt seemed to genuinely like them and she was pretty sure Aunt Viv wouldn't agree to send her anywhere that wasn't reputable. She still wasn't convinced this was a great idea. Cadence wasn't nearly as worried about being around Trent as she was Trey. Just standing close to him she could feel a shimmer of something magnetic and mysterious pass between them.

"Well, Miss Greer, what do you say?" Trey finally asked. "Will you put us out of our misery and come be our cook and housekeeper?"

"Could I give it a bit more consideration and let you know tomorrow?" Cadence asked. She wanted to check with Neil before she made any decisions. She had contacted him a couple of times for his opinion and he had given her solid advice. She could shoot him a quick message and see what he thought.

"Sure, we'll check with you after breakfast," Trey said as he took out his wallet and paid for their meal, leaving a generous tip on the table.

As he and Trent sauntered toward the door, Trey turned back for one more look at Cadence and offered her a warm smile.

He didn't know what had happened between them and was pretty sure he didn't want to find out. If he was smart he'd forget about asking her to work for them and ignore the jolt that shot through him when he touched her. That is exactly what he would do if he was smart.

But every man had a weakness and it looked like Trey's was, quite possibly, delicious pie.

Chapter Three

For I know the plans I have for you, declares the Lord,
plans to prosper you and not to harm you,
plans to give you hope and a future.
Jeremiah 29:11 - NIV

Cadence and Viv turned the café sign to closed, wiped off all the tables and finished cleaning up the kitchen. Viv was amazed, as she had been every evening, to watch how quickly and efficiently Cadence worked when it was just the two of them. She didn't drop, spill or break anything. It was when the café was packed that Cadence got nervous and the wake of disaster hit high tide.

"Cadence, honey, do you have any questions about the Thompson boys or their job offer?" Viv asked as they scrubbed down the counters and finished putting away the clean dishes.

"Not really, Aunt Viv. They seem nice enough," Cadence said, as her thoughts tumbled through her head. Most of them kept coming back to rest on Trey and those blue eyes of his. "So there are three brothers?"

"Yep, that's right," Viv said, stopping her scrubbing to lean against the counter. "All three of them look like their daddy, God rest his soul. Now there was a fine man.

Miss Denni couldn't have picked a finer husband, unless she had chosen my very own Joe."

"What happened to Mr. Thompson?" Cadence asked as she hooked her arm through her aunt's and they started out the back door.

"He had a heart attack six years ago. We thought Denni was going to die of a broken heart right alongside of Drew," Viv said as they walked slowly down the street and up a block toward home. "Those boys rallied around her and took over the ranch like their daddy taught them to do. Travis, he's the youngest, had a real hard time with his daddy dying. He got into a bit of trouble, but he eventually came around and the next thing we all knew, he joined the Army and was gone to be a soldier." As they stepped onto the well-lit porch, Viv pulled Cadence down beside her on the swing.

"Trey is the oldest. He is the third generation to be named Timothy Andrew Thompson. Denni said that was too big of a handle for any boy of hers and decided to call him Trey from the start. He's a fine man, honey, and an honorable one. All the Thompson boys are well-liked and the Thompson name goes back for more than a hundred years in these parts. They are good, dependable folks."

"Yes, Aunt Viv," Cadence said, taking in the information her aunt was sharing. "So where does their mother live now?"

"Denni lives in The Dalles," Viv said with a smile. "After Drew died, she just couldn't stand to be out at the ranch where his memory floated around every corner. She packed her suitcase, drove her car to The Dalles, got a job managing a quilt and craft store and rented a sweet little house. She seems very happy to be there. The boys go to visit her every couple weeks and when they don't make it, she comes here to see them."

Cadence listened to the quiet of the evening and pulled her sweater tighter around her.

"Aunt Viv, do you really think it is a good idea for me to take their job offer?" Cadence asked. "I know I've been about the worst help you could possibly have in the café, but I could find a job in Portland if I need to."

Viv gave Cadence a warm, motherly hug. "Now, honey, why would you go running off to Portland when you just got here? I love having you around. Even if you don't take the job with the Thompson boys, I bet I could come up with something else for you to do. I know waitressing isn't exactly your ideal career."

Giving her aunt's cheek a kiss, Cadence swiped at her tears.

"No more tears, honey. I thought after you cried yourself dry last week you were all done," Viv teased.

"I know, Aunt Viv. But I really appreciate you and Uncle Joe taking me in like this. I can't tell you how much it means to me."

"I'm as happy as a heifer with a new fence post that you're here. If you do go work for the Thompsons you aren't that far away. Now, I'm going to take these old creaky bones inside and head for bed. Sleep tight, honey, and give some thought to what the Thompson boys offered."

Cadence watched her aunt go into the house and remained on the swing until the cold chased her inside. Uncle Joe said it would start getting chilly and feeling like winter in another month, right after Halloween. She hoped he was wrong. These hot, sunny days of the past week had been so welcome after the cold, drizzly gray skies of Seattle. Having never ventured anywhere except along the coast for weekend trips, Cadence didn't realize the weather could be so different just a few hours to the east and south.

Going to her room, Cadence turned on her laptop and logged into her email account. Grateful her aunt had cautioned her that both internet and cell service could be erratic in Grass Valley, Cadence purchased a wireless internet card for her computer at the mall in Portland. So far, she hadn't had any problem connecting.

Ignoring the new messages in her inbox, she quickly typed a message to Neil, asking his advice on the Thompson's job offer. She then read through messages from her mom, some friends and the junk mail offering her special deals, discounts and items she couldn't possibly live without. She was just getting ready to turn off the computer when a reply arrived from Neil.

Cadence smiled when she read it.

Are you kidding me? Room and board plus $1,000 a month, surrounded by good looking cowboys? You can't pass this one up, Cadence! Go for it.

"I never said they were good looking when I mentioned the cowboys," Cadence said aloud, as though Neil could hear her. "How could you know that?"

Cadence climbed between the cool sheets, tossing around the idea of working for the handsome Thompson brothers. As she closed her eyes and drifted toward sleep, it was Trey's smile and bright eyes that filled her thoughts, along with a picture of how good he looked in those Wranglers and boots.

><><

The breakfast crowd was winding down when Cadence looked up to see Trey Thompson swagger through the door and sit down at a booth.

Managing not to smile and attempting to keep her run-away emotions in check, she brought a mug to his table along with a pot of hot coffee.

"Good morning, Mr. Thompson," she said in her crisp, business-like tone. "Would you care for a cup of coffee?"

"Sure would," Trey said, beaming a friendly smile that she found impossible to ignore. Using all her concentration, she managed to pour his coffee without spilling it. "Anything you recommend for breakfast?"

Taking a step back from the table Cadence made the mistake of looking into his eyes and getting tugged into their depths. "Well, I, um…"

Trey raised an eyebrow her direction and smiled encouragingly.

"I made cinnamon rolls this morning. Would you like one?" Cadence finally managed to say.

"Sounds great," Trey said, smiling like a fool and feeling like an idiot. For some reason, Cadence Greer seemed to have that effect on him. He couldn't stop smiling when he was around her and it was making him positively crazy. "Can you throw on a couple of fried eggs and some bacon, too?"

"Certainly, Mr. Thompson," Cadence said, stepping away from the table and right into one of the departing patrons. Her cheeks flushed a deep red as she hurried back into the kitchen with his order.

Trey sat watching her exit and shook his head. He didn't know if it was safe to bring her into their home. After that pie last night, he and Trent were almost willing to risk life and limb to get some more.

He also wouldn't mind having Cadence around to watch on a more permanent basis. At first he thought she must be in her thirties from her severe hair style and cool demeanor, until Viv mentioned she was 27, same age as Trent. For some reason, that thought made him nervous and fidgety. It shouldn't matter to him how old she was or what she looked like. At least he tried to convince himself of that.

Watching her lean over to clean off a booth, Trey got a great view of her backside and decided he was really going to have to keep his thoughts on a tight rein. She wore classic style blue jeans, a soft cotton blouse and flats. Nothing glamorous or big city about it, but with her hair pulled back in a bun and the aura of professionalism she exuded when she wasn't spilling or breaking something, it made her seem more mature and different somehow.

He didn't have time to contemplate his thoughts further as Viv came bustling out with his breakfast. One plate held a warm cinnamon roll with sweet icing running down the sides and puddling into delectable circles on the dish. The second dish held two eggs cooked to his idea of perfection, five strips of bacon and a generous scoop of hash browns, fried to a beautiful golden brown.

Inhaling the scent of cinnamon, Trey closed his eyes in bliss for a moment before sending up a prayer of thanks and picking up his fork.

When Viv sat down across from him, he quickly cut off a bite of the cinnamon roll and rolled his eyes in pleasure as the delicious pastry filled his mouth.

It was as good, if not better than the pie. If he hadn't been sitting down, Trey wasn't sure his legs would have held him. To be able to eat like that every day, he'd be willing to pay twice what they'd offered Cadence.

Viv sat with a knowing smile lighting her face.

"Did you talk to her yet?" she asked as Trey forked another bite of cinnamon roll.

"Nope, but I'll ask her to marry me right this minute if she'll make another batch of cinnamon rolls tomorrow," Trey teased.

Viv grabbed his plate and pulled it away from him.

"Now you listen here, buster, and listen good," Viv said, her eyes shooting sparks and her lips set in a thin line. "Don't you joke like that with my girl. She got left at the altar a week before her wedding and that's a sore subject with her. So don't you be teasing her like that. You understand?"

"I'm sorry, Viv. I had no idea," Trey set down his fork and looked properly scolded. "I promise the subject of marriage, weddings or matrimony will not come up at all, in any conversation. Now, may I please have that cinnamon roll back?"

Viv scooted the plate back across the table with a smile. When Cadence passed by, Viv grabbed her hand.

"Why don't you tell Trey what you told me this morning, honey," Viv said, giving Cadence an encouraging pat on the back.

Trey looked up from taking the last bite of his cinnamon roll and hoped Cadence was about to make him a very happy man.

"Mr. Thompson, after giving your proposal due consideration, I will agree to your offer. If it would work for you and your brother, the other Mr. Thompson, I could drive out this evening and be ready to start tomorrow morning with breakfast."

Trey studied Cadence, who stood with her hands clasped primly in front of her. She was a comely girl, with clear bright skin, big hazel eyes, rosy lips and, from what he could see around her waitress apron, a nice shape. He knew it was more than nice from the back view he'd snuck a glance at no less than half a dozen times this morning.

But he was willing to bet his best hat that if she learned to smile a bit more, loosen up those tight stays and have some fun, she'd be downright beautiful.

Not that he would notice or care.

"Well, Miss Greer, I reckon that would be just fine. Viv can give you directions. Please call me Trey and my brother Trent. All this Mr. Thompson business could get downright confusing. Do you need help moving any of your things?"

"No, but I would like to pick up some supplies before I come out, unless your kitchen is well stocked."

Trey let out a laugh. He was pretty sure the uptight Miss Greer would not think mac-and-cheese, boxes of cold cereal and microwave popcorn comprised a well-stocked kitchen. The only thing they had in abundance was beef and potatoes.

"I think you'll probably find the kitchen supplies sadly lacking," Trey said, pulling out his wallet. He dug out three crisp $100 bills and handed them to Cadence. "We've got a freezer full of beef and about fifty pounds of potatoes, but beyond that, you won't find much else in the kitchen. Why don't you run into The Dalles and get what you need before you come out this evening? Would that work?"

"That would be more than satisfactory," Cadence said as she stuffed the bills into her jeans pocket. What kind of man handed a perfect stranger $300 and sent them off shopping? One that was impressively trusting. Or impressively stupid. Or just plain impressive.

Viv stood up and threw an arm around Cadence. "You know, honey, it gets dark pretty early these days and since you don't know the area well, I think you better get packed up right after breakfast then head into town to get supplies. You can be back early afternoon and out at the Triple T before it gets dark. Don't you think that's a better idea, Trey?"

"Yes, Ma'am," Trey said as he stood up from the table, left money for his breakfast and settled his hat on his golden head. "I don't want the maker of the best cinnamon rolls I've ever eaten to get lost somewhere out in the hills."

Trey pulled a business card out of his shirt pocket and handed it to Cadence. "If you get lost on your way out, you can call the house phone, my cell phone number is on the back, but it doesn't always get great reception. See you this afternoon." With that, he tipped his hat and walked out the door.

><><

Helping Aunt Viv clean up after breakfast, Cadence went home and packed her suitcases and the few belongings she'd brought with her, loading them into her car. Giving Uncle Joe and Aunt Viv a hug, she travelled north toward the freeway and drove into The Dalles where she spent some time exploring and ate a leisurely lunch.

Proceeding to a grocery store, she filled not one but two shopping carts to overflowing with basic cooking and baking supplies. She added in plenty of fresh and canned fruits and vegetables as well as some cleaning supplies.

She felt pretty smug as she rolled the carts out to her car, having spent $249.63 for all the groceries and supplies.

Opening up the back of her silver PT Cruiser, Cadence looked from her already full car to the full carts and decided it might take a bit of work to get everything loaded. Dropping down the back seats, Cadence worked quickly and efficiently. In no time at all, the car was completely loaded and she was headed back toward Grass Valley. She programmed the address on Trey's business card into her GPS system and hoped it knew where it was going because she wasn't sure. Driving through Grass Valley, she stopped for a minute to say goodbye to her aunt and give her a hug before heading out to the Triple T and the Thompson men.

Cadence should have listened to Uncle Joe and followed him out to the Thompson Ranch. Instead, she had to be her independent, stubborn self and now she was sure she was never going to find the ranch. Following the detailed directions her uncle wrote out for her, and listening to the GPS, she drove just a few miles south of town before taking a left turn onto a gravel road. Driving down a dusty, winding road for what seemed like forever, Cadence hadn't seen a thing except bare fields, wheat stubble, and pasture being grazed by a sea of black cattle.

33

She was certainly glad she had listened to Aunt Viv and made this trip in daylight. Out here lost in the dark would really cause her to panic. Just when she was about ready to call Trey and ask where she'd taken a wrong turn, she topped a rise and saw a sprawling ranch ahead.

The rustic farmhouse, while one story, seemed massive. A porch ran the length of the front of the house and wrapped part-way down the sides with chairs placed in inviting clusters. Off the main section of the house on each side was a long wing that gave the house a definite "U" shape. Driving up the long driveway, she was impressed with how neat and well-kept the place looked. There was a large barn, corrals, a shed with machinery parked inside, a building that she assumed was the bunk house, a carport and garage, as well as several other assorted sheds. Continuing past the circle drive at the front of the house, she followed the driveway around to a side door she hoped was the kitchen.

Pulling to a stop, she appreciated how tidy and friendly the house looked with its split cedar shakes on the roof, light tan siding and warm brown and white trim. Just as she was ready to step out of the car, two rambunctious dogs came running down the porch steps and over to her door.

Never owning a pet and not spending time around dogs, Cadence didn't know if she should be afraid. Deciding the dogs probably weren't any more vicious than their owners, she opened the door carefully, stuck out her hand and talked softly to the dogs. Both dogs yipped and wagged their tails, then proceeded to lick her hand as she got out of the car.

Having not had that experience before, she wasn't sure she liked the feel of their slobbery tongues on her fingers.

"Bob, Bonnie, you two get back," a friendly voice rumbled from behind her. Cadence spun around to see

Trey walking toward her with a smile. "Wasn't sure you were going to make it," Trey said as he walked up next to her and gave each dog a pat on the head. "I was about ready to call out the posse when I saw the dust from your car coming up the road."

"How did you know it was me?" Cadence asked, curious.

Trey laughed as he walked to the back of her car and opened the hatch door. "Anyone else who would be coming out here is already here."

As he pulled the door fully open, grocery bags shifted and started to slide out.

"Be careful," Cadence said, grasping the handles of two bags before they tumbled out of the car. "I've got a pretty full load."

Trey looked into the car and whistled. "I think that might be an understatement." Grabbing as many bags as he could carry, he led her toward the door on the side of the house. "Did you leave anything in the store for anyone else to buy?"

Cadence didn't hear the teasing in his voice and went on the defensive. "I most certainly did. In fact, I brought you back $50.37 in change. I've got it right here in my purse."

"Miss Greer, I trust you," Trey said, setting the bags down on the kitchen counter. "If I didn't, I wouldn't have given you the money in the first place. Looks to me like you did a good job of shopping."

Trey walked back out to the car to get another load, wondering what had made Cadence so touchy.

Cadence let out a deep breath and walked back to the car. Bill, for all the money he liked to flash around, was a penny-pinching tight-wad. Any time he gave her money to pick something up, he wanted a receipt and the exact change, right down to the penny, accounted for. She was going to have to get used to people trusting her and trusting them in return. She stopped suddenly as she realized she nearly married a man she didn't trust. That should have been a big warning sign to her. Nearly as big as the one she failed to notice that said Bill would never trust her.

"You okay, Miss Greer?" Trey asked as he walked by on the way into the house with another load of groceries.

"I'm fine, thank you," Cadence said, hurrying to the car to help unload.

By the time they had all the groceries and supplies unloaded and Cadence's belongings in the house, Trent arrived and helped carry in the last box.

"Well, this might take some time to put away," Trey said looking around. "Trent, why don't you go park Miss Greer's car in the garage for her while I take her luggage to her room. Miss Greer, if you don't mind, we'll let you put the groceries away where you like, that way you'll know where to find everything when you jump into cooking tomorrow. Is that satisfactory?"

Cadence was once again caught off guard. They were going to allow her to waltz into their home and completely rearrange the kitchen to suit her? Who were these people?

"Yes, that would be just fine," she said, picking up a bag full of frozen items. "Do you have a big freezer?"

"Yes, Ma'am," Trent said, opening the door to the mud room where a chest freezer along with an upright freezer filled one wall. "The chest freezer is full of beef, but the upright is mostly empty."

Trent ran outside to move her car while Trey hauled suitcases and her few boxes to her room. When they both returned, they helped her put away the groceries and supplies. Cadence decided they must have left the kitchen much like their mother and their former housekeeper had set it up because the arrangement was both functional and sensible.

"I don't see a need to move anything. Everything is very well organized," Cadence said as they put away the last bag of groceries. Running her hand over the granite countertop, she smiled. "It is a beautiful kitchen."

"Would you like a tour of the house?" Trey asked as he watched her take in the large country kitchen complete with a double oven, commercial-sized fridge, two dishwashers and expansive counter tops. The big farm table easily seated twelve and light from a bank of windows brought in welcome sunshine on cold winter days.

"I'd like that very much," she said, following Trey and Trent to the front door. There was a partial wall to the right which kept the dining area from being visible to visitors. Straight ahead was another partial wall with a mirror, coat rack and small bench. It looked welcoming and inviting. On the left of the entry was a room they called the "ladies parlor" where a set of lovely Victorian furniture resided along with an upright antique piano. Next to it was a large office and library area. From there, she could see a long hallway in what the men called the south wing.

In the office, one wall was completely covered by an immense bookcase full of books. "It can get kind of boring in the winter out here when the weather hems us all in, so some of us like to read," Trent said. "Help yourself to any of the books."

"Thank you," Cadence said, looking around the masculine room. The wall behind the large desk had a variety of metal objects hanging on it. Walking closer to get a better look, Cadence tipped her head and studied the display. There were matching pairs of each object, but she still wasn't sure what she was looking at.

"Admiring my spur collection?" Trey asked, stepping beside her. "Are you familiar with spurs?"

"I know cowboys wear them, but I don't think I've ever seen a pair. I'm guessing some of them are more than a few days old," she said, pointing to a pair that looked ancient.

"Metal spurs date back to around 2 B.C. The first ones were most likely made of wood or bone," Trey explained, taking a pair off the wall and handing them to Cadence. As she held them, he pointed to various parts.

"Spurs are made up of some basic components with variations. This part is the heel band. It goes around the back of the boot. The metal bar coming away from it is the neck and that spinning piece on the end, shaped like a star, is called the rowel."

"Oh," Cadence said.

"The phrase 'earn your spurs' came from a time when knights earned their spurs," Trey continued his history lesson. "A disgraced knight would have his spurs taken away and his sword broken. Over in Spain, influenced by Northern European large rowels, and heel plates from Moorish spurs, they developed a spur that travelled to America with the conquistadors, which evolved into Latin American spurs to the south. They traveled north with vaqueros where the styles evolved yet again, based on climate and terrain of a region, into the shape of today's western spurs."

"Interesting," Cadence said, impressed with Trey's historical knowledge. "And what do they do, exactly?"

"They help your horse know what you want him to do," Trent added, stepping up on the other side of Cadence. "It gives the rider another tool to guide the horse in the direction he should go."

"It doesn't hurt them?" Cadence asked, suddenly thinking some of the spurs looked like they could poke a hole through concrete, let alone the tender side of a horse.

"Not the spurs we wear," Trey said, hanging up the spur she was holding and taking down another pair with spiked ends instead of rowels. "These would definitely have caused some damage."

"How old are some of these?" Cadence asked.

Trey pointed out a pair from the 17th century he had managed to find at a Portland auction, a pair from the 1880s, and a set that traveled with Teddy Roosevelt's Rough Riders.

"These belonged to our great-grandfather," Trey pointed to an old rusty pair. "Then there is our granddaddy's pair, and that flowery set belonged to our grandmamma. Those little biddy ones were my first pair," Trey said, pointing to a miniature pair. His hand gently touched a silver pair that looked like they'd been hung up right after the wearer took them off. "These belonged to our dad."

Cadence didn't know what to say, so she just nodded her head sympathetically.

"I think that's enough of the professor's history class for one day," Trent said, grinning. "You'll have to forgive him. While some of us have normal hobbies like football, he spends hours studying history and looking for old spurs."

Trey shot Trent a cool glare, but motioned for he and Cadence to precede him out of the room.

Going back to the entry area, on the other side of the small partial wall was a large open gathering room, visible from the kitchen and dining area, complete with a big fireplace, sofas and several comfy looking chairs. From the gathering room, doors opened out onto a large patio where a barbecue and several pieces of outdoor furniture sat in what seemed like an open courtyard. She noticed there was even a fire pit with curved benches built around it. With the wings of the house flanking it, the view from the courtyard looked out toward a pond and the rolling hills that would be golden with wheat in the summer.

Wandering through the patio area to the end of the south wing, Trent opened a door and stepped back to let Cadence and Trey precede him inside. There were five bedrooms as well as a large bathroom in this section of the house.

"This is where Trent and I get our beauty rest," Trey said with a grin as they walked down the hall back toward the main area of the house. "Travis will sleep here, too, when he's home. And we have two guest rooms in this section with private baths. Trent and I share the big bathroom here." He pointed to a large bathroom, across the hall from the office.

Walking back through the great room and kitchen area, they entered the north wing, where Cadence would stay. Trey moved her things into a spacious room located just steps down the hall from the kitchen. Two large windows flanked a patio door that opened to the courtyard. A rocking chair sat beneath one of the windows and a comfy looking queen-sized bed was topped by an intricate hand-stitched quilt. A chest of drawers with a matching birds-eye maple dresser had surely been crafted a century or so before. Running her hand over the beautiful wood, she watched as Trey stepped over to a door that opened to a nice-sized closet. Cadence was also thrilled to discover she had her own private bathroom.

"Will this room work for you?" Trey asked.

"It is wonderful and more than adequate," Cadence said, knowing that every piece of furniture in the house was nicer than any she'd ever owned. "Thank you for this opportunity. I hope my work will be satisfactory."

"Miss Greer," Trent said, a teasing gleam twinkling in his eye, "If the pie I ate last night is an example of your work, then we'll get along just fine."

The three of them laughed and continued on their tour. Across from Cadence's room was a laundry room with a large washer and dryer with wall-mounted rods for hanging damp clothes. A deep sink sat in a solid counter top and an ironing board rested beneath a set of tall shelves.

Next to the laundry room there was a small guest room with a private bath. A few steps down the hall brought them to a door that opened into a master suite. The room was massive and felt sadly forsaken.

The suite included a fireplace with what was once a sitting area, large windows and French doors that opened out to the courtyard. A chest of drawers and dresser with an ornately carved mirror matched the over-sized king bed. Opening another door, Trey turned on the light in an expansive bathroom with double sinks, a deep garden tub and a walk-in shower. There was also a large walk-in closet.

No art hung on the walls, no quilt topped the bed, nothing in the room was warm or welcoming.

"This was Mom and Dad's room," Trey explained. "When Mom moved to town, she took most of the things from this room with her and none of us felt like doing any redecorating. When Mom comes out to visit, she stays in one of the guest rooms. She says too many memories live in here."

Cadence could almost feel Denni's pain and loss in the room.

"I'm very sorry about your father. Aunt Viv said he was a wonderful man," Cadence said, sincerity adding softness to her voice.

Trey and Trent both looked at her.

"Thank you, Cadence," Trent finally said. "Our dad was one of a kind."

As they walked back out to the hall, Trey reverently closed the door.

"Now, Miss Greer," Trey said as they walked her back toward her room. "We don't expect anything fancy for breakfast but we like to eat at 6:30 each morning. Is that going to be too early for you?"

"Not at all," Cadence said, stopping in the door to her room. "What about dinner tonight?"

"We'll make do with sandwiches or something. You are welcome to make yourself whatever you want or we can make a sandwich for you," Trey said, standing in the hall, smiling warmly at his newest employee.

When Cadence's fresh, womanly scent surrounded him, Trey knew without a doubt he needed to get out more around the female portion of the population. The woman standing looking at him with gold flecks swimming in her eyes was making his heart pound and his shirt collar feel uncomfortably tight.

"Nonsense," Cadence replied. "Give me a few minutes to settle in and I'll whip up something simple."

"Miss Greer, we don't expect you to cook for us tonight," Trey said, taking a step toward her. Placing his hand on her shoulder, he felt an electrical jolt race up his arm and explode through his chest. "Really, you can just relax this evening."

"No. It's fine. I really want to make dinner. I promise it will be simple and easy," Cadence said, surprised she could speak at all. The fire racing from Trey's fingers all the way to her toes was enough to completely addle her ability to think, let alone speak.

"You do know you're stubborn, don't you Miss Greer?" Trey teased, taking a step back toward the kitchen.

"So I've been told on more than one occasion. I'll have dinner ready at 6," Cadence said, stepping into her room, and then turning back. "And thank you for this opportunity. I very much appreciate it."

"It's us who should be thanking you, Cadence," Trent said, backing toward the kitchen. "I'm already dreaming about another piece of your good pie."

As Trent turned the corner into the kitchen, Trey watched a blush highlight Cadence's cheeks.

"Are you sure you don't need anything, Miss Greer?"

"No, I'm fine. I do appreciate you putting your trust in me," Cadence said, humbled that these two men would take her in, give her a job and trust her in their lovely home. They didn't know anything about her, and yet they were willing to give her a chance.

"See you in a bit, Miss Greer," Trey said, walking back to the kitchen and anticipating something good to eat for dinner. Tonight it would just be the three of them. Tomorrow it would be interesting to see how Miss Fancy Pants Greer was going to handle seven hungry men first thing in the morning.

Chapter Four

Just because something doesn't do what you planned it to do doesn't mean it's useless.

Thomas Edison

Cadence was dreaming she was lost in a night fog. She couldn't get out of it and the only thing that was penetrating the all-consuming darkness was an annoying beeping. Struggling to find her way out of her dreams, she sat up with a gasp and slapped her hand on the alarm.

Her eyelids felt heavy, as if each one was being held closed by a five-pound weight, as she struggled to come awake. Cadence had always been an early riser, using the morning hours to catch up on housework, exercise or pay bills. She often arrived home late after work, exhausted with no time to get things done in the evenings.

But the stress of the last few weeks had finally caught up with her and all she wanted to do was sleep. The bed in her room was about the most comfortable thing she'd ever slept on and rolling out of it at 5 a.m. was just not something she wanted to do.

Remembering she would have a kitchen full of starving men in an hour and a half, she quickly hopped out of bed, jumped in the shower and got ready to face the day.

Pulling her damp hair back into a loose ponytail, she didn't take time to dry it. The natural wave escaped the confines of her hair band with tendrils curling around her face. Hurrying to make herself presentable, she brushed on a quick layer of mascara, applied a bit of lip gloss and dressed in jeans with a soft cotton blouse and a pair of ballet flats.

Walking into the kitchen, all seemed quiet, so she turned on the lights, put on the coffee and got down to the business of making breakfast.

While she worked, she thought about the strange turns and twists her life had suddenly taken. A month ago if someone had told her she'd be standing in the kitchen of a sprawling ranch house in Grass Valley, Oregon, making breakfast for seven single cowboys, she would have told them they'd lost the ability to think with any degree of sanity.

Although she was a business professional and excelled at her job with Neil, Cadence had always loved to bake and cook. Right out of high school, she toyed with the idea of becoming a chef, but after taking several courses and doing a month-long internship at a restaurant, she decided she didn't really like the idea of working all the hours required by that profession. That, and the fact she was terrible at the waitressing end of things.

She was glad her love of food was going to be put to good use.

By the time Trent and Trey came in the back door, Cadence had set the table for seven and was finishing up breakfast preparations.

"Good morning, Miss Greer," Trey said as he washed up at the kitchen sink. "Did you sleep well?"

"Yes, I did. Thank you," Cadence said as she flipped another pancake. "The bed is absolutely wonderful. It was hard to get up this morning."

"Well, as good as it smells in here this morning, I'm glad you did," Trent teased as he poured himself a cup of coffee.

Trey looked around the kitchen and admired the set table. His stomach grumbled at the smell of the food.

"Why are there only seven places at the table, Miss Greer?" he asked as he counted them a second time.

"I wouldn't think of eating with you men," Cadence said, adding another pancake to the growing stack on a platter.

"Don't be ridiculous," Trent said, pulling another plate out of the cupboard and picking up another set of silverware. "Of course you'll eat with us."

"But I don't want to intrude," Cadence said. She assumed the men had a routine and she was fairly certain they wouldn't want her to be part of it. She also wasn't convinced she could deal with seven cowboys this early in the morning. Her plan was to put the food on the table and disappear until they finished eating.

"You're kidding, right?" Trey asked, coming up beside her. "You would be the most welcome intrusion I could think of. Please, Miss Greer, join us for breakfast?"

"Fine," Cadence said, wishing Trey would step away from her. He smelled like leather and outdoors and man. She could feel the heat of his body warm beside her and she knew if she turned she'd burn the last pancake to a crisp while she got lost in those intense blue eyes.

Stepping around him, she gathered up the platter of pancakes.

"It will just take me a minute to get everything on the table. What time will the men be in?" Cadence asked as she scooped up a bowl of fluffy scrambled eggs.

"They'll be here as quick as I ring the triangle," Trent said, stepping outside.

Cadence could hear metal hit metal with a homey, almost pleasant ring. Before she could get the thick slices of ham on the table, men began pouring in the back door. They all removed their boots, coats and hats before coming inside. Every last one of them politely smiled and tipped their head or said a word of welcome to her.

When they were all seated around the table, Trey said grace and the men dug in.

"Miss Cadence, may I please have some butter for my pancakes," asked one of the hands, a fresh-faced boy who barely looked old enough to be out of high school.

"Sure, Tommy," Cadence said, starting to get up from the table. "But I melted butter into the syrup before I warmed it up."

Trey motioned her to stay seated and the men passed around the pitcher of syrup.

"I ain't never had warm syrup on my hotcakes before," said another cowboy named Larry. "This is really good, Miss Cadence."

"Thank you," Cadence said, embarrassed by their praise. The way the men were digging into the food and offering up compliments, you'd think they hadn't had a thing to eat in a month of Sundays.

Not much was said during breakfast since the men were much more intent on eating than keeping up a conversation. When all the food was gone, and the last drop of coffee consumed, Trey gave out direction on what he'd like each one of them to work on that day.

Before the men got up from the table, they all thanked Cadence again for a fine meal.

"You are more than welcome," Cadence said, pleased that she had gotten through breakfast and everyone seemed happy. "Please call me Cadence. The Miss seems a little too formal."

"Sure, Miss Cadence, but the boss said…" Tommy started to explain when a thump was heard from the far end of the table where he sat next to Trey. Rubbing his shin, Tommy clammed up and frowned at his boss.

As the hands left the table, they all picked up their plates and carried them to the sink before shuffling out to the mudroom.

Trent and Trey sat at the table discussing their plans for the day while Cadence started cleaning up the kitchen. Bending near Trey to pick up an empty platter, he caught her hand and heat shot up her arm again, like it had the other day in the café. She nearly dropped the dish.

"Please sit down a moment, Miss Greer," Trey asked. When she sank into a chair, he cleared his throat. "Miss Greer, you did a great job on breakfast, but we don't expect you to prepare an elaborate meal every day. You can keep things simple, we don't mind."

"What's simpler than ham, eggs and pancakes?" Cadence asked, confused.

"Oh, well, um," Trey stammered, looking at Trent for some assistance. Trent instead got up from the table and walked out to the mudroom, unable to keep the smirk off his face.

"I just don't want you to overtax yourself. You'll need energy for keeping up the house as well. Being a cook and a housekeeper is a big job and we don't intend for you to work yourself to death. We won't be here for lunch, so you can become familiar with the house and the layout of the place today or do whatever you like." Trey knew he sounded like an overbearing dolt but couldn't seem to keep his mouth shut.

"I realize being out on a ranch is probably a new experience for you so I caution you to stay away from the horses and particularly the bulls. Don't climb over any fences into pens where you see animals. Don't grab ahold of any single-wires stretched over the pole fences because they are hot and you'll get shocked. Don't wander any farther than you can keep the house in sight. Don't step too close to the edge of the pond on the south side. The bank is soft and you'll sink in up to your ears. Don't be afraid of the dogs, they won't bite. Don't stay out in the sun too long. You can still get sunburned as hot as it is and you look like you aren't used to being outside much. And if you hear something rattling, it is probably a snake and you need to get away from it as quickly and as cautiously as possible. We haven't had any around the house for a couple of years, but it never hurts to be careful. Any questions?"

Cadence just looked at him, dumbfounded.

Trey got up from the table and hurried to the kitchen door. "If you run into any problems today, try calling my cell phone. Trent's cell number is on the fridge as well. Have a good day and thanks for the good breakfast."

Cadence let out the breath she hadn't even realized she was holding when Trey walked out the door. She didn't know a thing about living in the country but after Trey's spiel, it was enough to make her think twice about staying. Rattlesnakes? Electric fences? Dangerous bulls? If she wasn't desperate, stubborn and determined, she'd pack her bags and head back to Aunt Viv's. Lucky for the Thompsons she wasn't easily discouraged.

All Trey's warnings didn't bother her nearly as much as the fact that being around him scrambled her thoughts and made her stomach flutter. She would just have to stay far enough out of reach that he couldn't touch her, stand close to her, or come around her with that wonderful scent of his. The last thing she needed was to get her heart and head all tangled up with another man, especially when just a few short weeks ago she was engaged to marry someone she was quickly coming to realize was all wrong for her. It wouldn't do to have feelings like this for any man, even one as fine as Trey Thompson.

><><

Trey could not escape the kitchen fast enough. In his haste to get as far from Miss Cadence Greer as possible, he forgot his gloves and knew he'd regret that mistake before the day was over, but refused to go back to the house to get them. Shoving his hands deep in his pockets, he tried to clear his head before he headed out to work.

When he first walked into the kitchen that morning, he thought for a moment he was seeing a complete stranger, and one that was drawing his interest like she had him tethered on a line.

Only seeing Cadence with her hair pulled into a severe bun, he had no idea how long or lush or wavy her hair would be down, even with it pulled into a ponytail. The curls that drifted around her face made her look all soft and feminine and completely lovely. Her creamy skin, dewy from the shower, was rosy and glowing. When he stepped close to her as she flipped pancakes, her fresh scent nearly buckled his knees.

How was he going to keep his thoughts and feelings in check with her living in his house? What rancher went loopy over his housekeeper, especially a city girl like Cadence?

One thing was for certain, he couldn't do anything foolish to mess up the arrangement. She was about the best cook he'd ever come across and his hired men would hang him from the big old oak in the front yard if he ran her off.

Nope, Trey would keep his thoughts of Miss Cadence Greer firmly in hand so he could keep on enjoying her talents in the kitchen.

><><

Cadence spent the morning deep cleaning the kitchen and dining area. Once she had the windows sparkling and the appliances all shiny, she made herself a salad for lunch and sat with her feet up looking out the big windows of the gathering room across the courtyard at the cattle grazing on a distant hill. Nearly dropping off to sleep, the ringing of the phone brought her wide awake.

Running into the kitchen, she answered a bit out of breath. "Thompson Ranch, may I help you?"

"Well, hello," a female voice on the other line said, sounding a bit surprised. "Is Trent or Trey available?"

"I'm sorry. They are unavailable at the moment. May I take a message?"

"You sure can," the voice said, still sounding pleasant, if somewhat confused. "Please tell them to call their mother."

"I will do that Mrs. Thompson," Cadence said, deciding to introduce herself. "I don't know if your boys told you, but I'm their new housekeeper and cook. My name is Cadence Greer and my Aunt Vivian owns the café in town."

Cadence heard a soft laugh on the other end of the line.

"So those two rascals finally got tired of their own cooking, did they?"

"It would seem so, Mrs. Thompson."

"Oh, goodness, call me Denni. It just makes me feel old to be called Mrs. Thompson. Until one of those boys gets married and makes me a grandma, I refuse to be old!"

Cadence laughed along with her. "Okay, Denni it is."

"Now, don't let them bully you dear, or work you too hard. I used to enjoy the afternoons as my time to do what I wanted. If you play the piano, feel free to make use of the one in the parlor. If you like to sew, one of my old machines is around there somewhere. Trey has a bunch of books you can read in the office. If you haven't found them yet, look behind the door and you'll see the bookcase. Let's see, what else? Oh, the dogs won't bite. They like to get a treat now and then for good behavior and Trent keeps a tin of treats on a shelf in the mud room.

There are a couple of cats that live in the barn. Once in a while I take them out some milk, especially on cold winter days. They'll be your friends for life if you warm it up first. Watch out for Danny. He's a good hand, but a little too fond of the ladies. Just set him straight from the get-go and you won't have any problems."

Cadence found herself smiling and liking Denni Thompson for her straightforward manner.

"Thank you, Denni. I appreciate the information."

"Tell those boys to give their mother a call and remember not to take any of their sass, especially from Trey."

"Yes, Ma'am. I'll be sure and tell them," Cadence said, then added, "And thanks again for the chat. I look forward to meeting you."

"Oh, I expect you will one of these Sundays. If the boys don't come here, then I go to services there with them, and your Aunt Viv goes to our church. Have a good day, dear," Denni said, then disconnected the call before Cadence could say goodbye.

Checking the clock, Cadence decided she had plenty of time before dinner preparations needed to begin. She put a load of laundry in and wandered into the parlor. She hadn't played the piano in years, but decided she would brush the rust off her fingers. She found sheet music in an end table drawer next to the piano and pulled out a few pieces she thought she could play. An hour later, she realized how much she missed creating music and decided to spend her spare time getting reacquainted with playing the piano.

By the time she washed and folded a second load of laundry, Cadence knew it was time to start dinner. Carrying clean clothes toward the north wing, she had no idea what belonged to which cowboy, so she left the clothes sitting in two baskets in the hallway by the bathroom.

Going back to the kitchen, she decided to make one of her favorite chicken dishes for dinner along with chocolate cake for dessert.

She whipped up the cake and punched down the bread dough she had set to rise earlier in the day. Pinching off enough of the bread to make breadsticks for dinner, she rolled out the remaining dough then added sugar, cinnamon and butter, rolled it up in a log, cut slices and made cinnamon rolls. She hoped she could keep the guys out of the rolls long enough to serve them for breakfast tomorrow.

Trent and Trey came trooping in the door at a quarter to six, looking tired and exhausted.

"Hello," Cadence said, barely looking up as she put the final preparations on the meal. "I've got a pot of coffee ready if you want some or I can get you something cold to drink if you prefer."

Trent washed up and took a soda out of the fridge. Trey spent extra time washing up, trying to clean the dirt out of the new blisters he had developed that day without his gloves..

"Maybe you won't forget your gloves tomorrow, boss man," Trent teased as he watched Trey.

Cadence looked up long enough to see Trey shoot Trent a glare.

"Before I forget, your mom called this afternoon and would like one of you to call her back," Cadence said, dishing up each plate individually.

"Thanks, Miss Greer. I'll call her back after dinner," Trey said, standing across the counter from Cadence, watching her work. "You don't need to serve up each plate like a restaurant. Just put it on the table and the men will eat it."

"I know they will, but if they haven't had this before, and they put on too much cheese, it would greatly alter their experience," Cadence said, continuing to dish each plate.

Trent looked over Cadence's shoulder and shrugged at Trey. "Can I help you put the plates on the table?"

"Thank you, Trent. That would be great. Those over there," Cadence nodded toward the far end of the counter, "are ready to go."

"Why don't you go ring the bell, Trey?" Trent said as he carried plates to the table.

As quick as the metal bar clanged on the triangle, men hurried in the mud room door. Cadence worked quickly to dish up their food so it would still be hot.

Trent asked the blessing on the meal and the men spent a moment scrutinizing what was on their plate. After their good breakfast, they'd been looking forward to a tasty dinner. Now they weren't so sure what they were about to eat.

"Miss Greer, might you enlighten us as to the menu selection this evening," Trey asked, attempting to be formal and doing quite well in his efforts.

"Certainly, Mr. Thompson," Cadence said, with an equally cool and formal tone. "You are eating chicken breast sautéed in marsala wine with mushrooms over a bed of spaghetti noodles in browned-butter sauce, topped by finely shredded mizithra cheese. A crisp salad and fresh bread sticks accompany your meal. If you are all good boys and clean your plate, I have chocolate cake for dessert."

"I won't have any problem cleaning mine," Tommy said as he dug in and took a bite. Looking around the table as the rest of them tried to decide if they were going to try it or not, Tommy started to roll his eyes and look like he'd tasted something awful before winking at Cadence. "You guys don't want to eat this. Maybe you better go back to the bunkhouse and open a can of beans."

Trent took a bite of his and smiled his appreciation. Then the rest of them decided to give it a try. Larry didn't like mushrooms, but other than that, they managed to clean their plates, have seconds and still devour large slices of chocolate cake.

"That was some fine cooking, Cadence," said Henry, the oldest member of the crew, as he carried his plate to the sink. "Thank you for another good meal."

Not used to so much praise or attention, Cadence fought the blush that colored her cheeks. "You are most welcome. I like to cook."

"Well, lucky for all of us that you do," said Danny as he leaned close to Cadence when he put his dirty dishes on the counter. Before she could look up, Trey was stepping between them, giving Danny a hard glare that sent him scuttling out the door without a backward glance.

Once the hands cleared out, Trent and Trey helped Cadence clear the table, then she did the dishes. Trey retreated to the office to do some paper work and call their mom while Trent went into the gathering room and turned on the television.

Finished with all she could do in the kitchen, Cadence wandered into the gathering room and sat down in a large rocking chair. Using her toe to set the chair in motion she sat quietly for a while until a commercial came on advertising Halloween. Sitting straight up, she realized she hadn't given a thought to the holiday.

"Trent, do you get any trick-or-treaters out this way?" Cadence asked. Looking over at him she noted he was so relaxed his eyelids looked droopy and his long legs sprawled out in front of him.

"Nah. Not since Mom moved to town," Trent said, rolling his head in her direction. "I guess everyone knows better than to expect us to have something to hand out."

"Oh, okay," Cadence said. She had several weeks to come up with something fun and festive for the cowboys on the ranch to celebrate the holiday.

"Are you and Trey going to The Dalles tomorrow?"

"Yep. It's our Sunday to go see Mom," Trent said, flipping channels. "You're welcome to come with us if you like."

"I think I'll go to church with Aunt Viv and spend the afternoon with her tomorrow, if that is okay?"

"That's fine," Trent said, watching the start of a movie with some interest. "You don't need to cook tomorrow. The hands know Sundays are the cook's day off so they won't expect breakfast or dinner. And don't worry about cooking for Trey or me. We can make do."

"Are you sure? It's no trouble to make something," Cadence offered, while part of her relished the idea of sleeping in and enjoying a quiet breakfast.

"It won't kill Trey to eat cereal for breakfast one day a week," Trent said with a cheeky grin.

"Okay. Although I made cinnamon rolls for breakfast tomorrow. You think that will tide you over?"

Trent shot her a smile of pure appreciation. "I think that will be just fine."

"Great. I think I'll head to bed," Cadence said, getting up from the rocking chair. "Thanks, Trent."

"Thank you, Cadence. That was a great meal. I look forward to more of your menu selections," Trent said, offering her a teasing grin.

><><

Trey spent the evening in his office. After calling Denni and promising to be there in time to take her and Nana to church in the morning, he finished up some paper work, turned on his computer and sent a few emails before he lost the ability to focus. Staring out the window at the darkness, Trey couldn't keep his thoughts from circling around their new cook.

When Danny stepped close to Cadence and gave her a look he'd seen Danny give women a hundred times before, he wanted nothing more than to punch him in the nose. A self-proclaimed ladies man, Danny was one of the best hands they had, but Trey wouldn't tolerate any of his nonsense with Cadence.

He'd promised Viv she wouldn't suffer any heartbreak out at the Triple T and he was a man who kept his word. Although it was going to be hard to hold himself to the same expectations he had of his men.

There was something about this uptight, proper housekeeper that made Trey's heart pound and his palms get all sweaty just thinking about her. If he was 17, he would have said he had a bad case of puppy love. But a 30-year-old weathered rancher? Nah, it couldn't be.

He decided he really needed to think about getting back in the dating circle. It had obviously been way too long since he'd spent time around females who weren't part of his mother's age group. That was probably what this unsettled feeling was every time he came close to Cadence, or thoughts of her started dancing around in his head.

Listening to the quiet from the gathering room, he assumed Trent and Cadence had gone to bed.

Turning off the computer and the desk light, he found Trent asleep in his chair with the television on mute. Nudging his brother's leg, Trent didn't move. Reaching out, Trey gave him a gentle shake.

"Come on, Sleeping Beauty, time for bed," Trey said, giving Trent a more forceful shake.

"You don't have to rattle my teeth loose," Trent said as he slowly opened one eye and yawned. Getting out of his chair, he staggered down the hall still half asleep and tripped over one of the baskets of clothes Cadence left by the bathroom door, banging loudly against the wall as he fell to the floor.

Flipping on a hall light, Trey laughed at Trent sprawled on the floor covered in jeans and shirts.

"What are these doing here?" Trent asked, eyeing the baskets with irritation.

"I'm guessing our new housekeeper didn't know what belonged to whom or where to put things away," Trey said, picking up a basket full of neatly folded socks and underwear. He felt his own cheeks heat thinking of Cadence carefully folding his briefs. Lois always left their underclothes clean but unfolded in a basket on their beds.

"Is everything okay? I heard a big thump," Cadence asked as she rushed around the corner. Taking in Trent on the floor with clean clothes piled around him and Trey holding the other basket, she was smart enough to connect the dots.

"I'm sorry. I forgot to ask about where to put your laundry. I meant to tell you I left the baskets in the hall."

"Not a big deal, Cadence," Trent said, standing up and tossing the clothes in the basket at his feet. Picking it up, he stepped into his room and shut the door.

That left Trey holding a basket of tidy whities, staring at Cadence. She wore a chenille hunter green robe that brought out green and gold flecks in her hazel eyes and her long hair hung loose around her in cascading waves. Trey was glad he was holding a basket full of clothes or he might have given in to the urge to run his hands through all that silky hair.

"I was going to tell you to just leave our clothes in baskets on our beds. We can fold them and put them away" Trey said.

"Nonsense," Cadence said, forcing herself to look Trey in the eye. "I'm perfectly capable of doing your laundry. Just tell me where it goes. I could tell your pants and shirts from Trent's by the length but I wasn't sure on the, um, other things."

Cadence could feel her cheeks heat with embarrassment as she studied the toe of her slipper.

Trey tried to keep from smiling at Cadence's flushed face.

"My shirts all have a black dot on the tag, Trent's all have a blue dot and when Travis gets home, his have red. My socks have the gray heels, Trent's have the gold stitching on the toes and if they don't match either of those, they belong to Travis. The, um, other things in the basket…" Trey felt his own cheeks grow warm. "Trent wears boxers, mine are briefs and we'll worry about Travis's later."

Cadence looked back up at him and offered a shy smile.

"Miss Greer, if you insist on folding our clothes, please leave them on our beds. We can put them away. This is my room," Trey said, pointing to a door directly behind her. "We will strip our own beds and leave the sheets in the laundry room once a week. Is there a day you prefer to wash them?"

"No," Cadence said, slowly backing toward the kitchen. "Any day is fine. Goodnight. I'm glad Trent's fine."

"Goodnight, Miss Greer," Trey said, stepping into the doorway of his room. "I'm sorry we disturbed you."

When Cadence disappeared back around the corner, Trey turned off the hall light and closed his bedroom door behind him. Setting the basket of clothes down, he sank onto his bed and shook his head.

Looking down at his hands, his fingers trembled from the longing to touch Cadence and hold her close.

How could this be?

It had been so long since he'd been on a date he wasn't sure he could even remember when it had happened. Since his father passed away, women had been at the bottom of his list of important things to pursue. Even if he had the time or inclination, he couldn't remember anyone in the past ever having an effect on him like this fancy pants housekeeper.

Sitting down for dinner, he had expected a disaster with her beautifully plated meal. The seven men that regularly sat around the table were used to meat and potatoes. It came as a real surprise when they not only liked her fancy chicken but nearly licked their plates clean.

It was almost as big a surprise as seeing Cadence with all that lovely hair down.

Trey gave himself another mental lecture about how meat and potatoes and that fancy cheese he couldn't even pronounce did not belong together. Just like him and Cadence, two different things from two different worlds.

It would serve him well to remember that.

Chapter Five

Always be planning something.
John A. Schindler

Cadence smiled to herself as she finished up preparations for their Halloween dinner. The Thompson men didn't seem to have any Halloween decorations and she hadn't found time to ask them if there were any in storage, so she carved a few pumpkins, placed battery-operated candles inside and lined them up on the steps outside the mudroom door. She didn't want to worry about catching anything on fire or one of the dogs sniffing too close and burning its nose.

In the time she'd been out on the ranch, she had deep cleaned every room, swept down the outside of the house as high up as she could reach, worked to winterize the flowerbeds that appeared to have been neglected for the last few months and familiarized herself with the sprawling ranch house.

She made the men big, hearty breakfasts then fixed them hot, filling dinners. In between, she had plenty of time for playing the piano, enjoying the outdoors, and searching for Denni's old sewing machine. Trey and Trent sometimes came in to join her for lunch, but more often than not, took a sack lunch with them. They used to throw a sandwich in a bag with chips for their mid-day meal. Once Cadence started making them cookies and special treats for their lunches they could hardly wait until noon to discover what goodies she'd packed for them each day.

Glancing toward the great room from the kitchen, Cadence admired again the beautiful, well-built home. She was thoroughly enjoying it here, even if the house was inhabited by two hunky guys. She knew Trent was her age, but he was quickly becoming more like a brother to her, just like all the hands. Trey was the one who made her thoughts jumble, butterflies float through her stomach and her toes tingle.

Despite her best intentions to never fall for another man, Cadence had a hard time denying her attraction to Trey. What girl in her right mind wouldn't be attracted to the hard-working, good-looking cowboy?

Considering the fact she was still not certain she was in her right mind after agreeing to marry Bill then running off to Grass Valley to lick her wounds, Cadence knew she needed to keep things with Trey on a strictly professional level. That was the rational thing to do.

Planning to be rational was easy. Getting the job done was proving to be a bit of a challenge.

Pulling biscuits out of the oven, she heard the familiar clomp of boots and jingle of spurs at the back door. The biscuits were on the table when the kitchen door opened to a chorus of "Trick or Treat" as Trey and Trent led the hands into the warm kitchen.

"The pumpkins are great, Cadence," Trent said, giving her an approving nod. "Thanks for thinking of them."

"Very festive," Trey added as he washed up and stood at his place at the head of the table. The scents coming from the kitchen were enough to make a grown man weep. When he opened the door, the smell of apples and cinnamon, yeasty dough and rich beef hit him in the face and made his mouth water in anticipation.

Cadence seemed to know the men preferred plain old comfort food so she alternated fixing things like pot pie and meatloaf with veal parmesan and chicken entrées they couldn't pronounce. They were all learning to like new dishes they hadn't tried before because no matter what Cadence fixed, it was always good.

After Cadence sat down at the table, the men took their seats and eagerly passed around bowls of thick beef and vegetable stew, fluffy biscuits and warm honey butter. When they had eaten their fill, some of them told stories of things they had done as "tricks" for Halloween that had them all laughing.

Cadence was just preparing to serve dessert when the doorbell rang.

Trey got up and went to the door, greeted by a little red-headed girl holding a plastic grocery bag. "Trick or Treat," she said, holding out the bag.

Not one usually given to sentimental whims, Trey felt his heart go out to the little girl. She was wrapped like a mummy using toilet paper and her costume was quickly unraveling, trailing behind her. He assumed it was her mother leaning against a beaten up old car, smoking a cigarette.

"Well, who do we have here?" Trey said, hunkering down to her level. He thought he knew who the little girl was, but wanted to make sure he was correct in his assumption. "Before I can give you a treat, you have to at least tell me your name."

"I'm Cass," the little mummy said, pulling a drooping piece of toilet paper from across her face. Her springy red curls shot up between the wraps across her head, making her look a bit deranged.

"Nice to meet you, Cass," Trey said, standing up and motioning to the mother. The little girl was the daughter of Grass Valley's resident drunk and bad girl. "Would you like to come in and get a treat? I'm pretty sure Miss Cadence has something for you."

"Sure," Cass said, putting her tiny hand in his big one. "Who's Miss Dense?"

Trey laughed, sure his prim and proper housekeeper wouldn't appreciate that version of her name.

"Miss Kay-dence," Trey said, over-pronouncing the name, "is my housekeeper and cook."

As he walked into the kitchen, the mother stood at the door, holding her cigarette outside. "Hurry up, Cass. I ain't got all night to drive you around. I've got my own plans, you know."

"Yes, Mommy," Cass said over her shoulder, still gripping Trey's hand tightly. Her little eyes grew wide in wonder as she walked into the kitchen filled with a table full of cowboys and delicious smells.

Cadence was pouring mugs of steaming apple cider when Trey introduced the costumed visitor.

"Hey, everyone, this is Cass. She came to get a treat," Trey looked at Cadence with a raised eyebrow. Cadence nodded her head and turned to look at Cass. It wasn't hard to see the child was hungry, poor and quite likely neglected. Cadence quickly made her a biscuit sandwich with some cold ham. Grabbing a brown lunch bag, she added two apples and a handful of chocolate chip cookies she'd made yesterday afternoon that the men had not yet completely devoured. Closing the bag, she walked over to Cass and put it in her empty grocery sack.

"There is a treat for later," Cadence said, turning back toward the stove before handing the little girl a warm donut covered in cinnamon and sugar. "And here's a treat for right now."

"Oh, thank you," Cass said, holding her donut like it was a golden treasure.

"Go ahead and take a bite, Cass," Trey urged her. "We haven't had ours yet. Is it any good?"

Cass took a big bite, with cinnamon and sugar clinging to her little chin. Her eyes bright with pleasure, she nodded her head and quickly gobbled it down. When Cadence handed her another one, her mother stormed into the kitchen and grabbed her by the shoulder. Cass winced in pain.

"Don't be a pig, Cass. Time to go. Right now!"

"Would you like one?" Cadence asked, holding a donut out toward the mother.

Looking at the donut like it was diseased, the young woman scoffed and shot Cadence a sneer. "I don't think so."

Marching Cass back down the hall, she slammed the door on her way out.

"Did I say or do something wrong?" Cadence looked at Trey with tears in her eyes. "I didn't mean to offend anyone."

"You didn't darlin'. You didn't do anything wrong," Trey reassured her and placed a gentle hand on her shoulder. She felt heat radiate from his hand through her entire upper body. Slowly he pulled his hand away and the warmth settled in his bright eyes. "That poor little girl has got a pretty hard life. I'm glad you snuck in a little something for her to eat later."

"She looked half-starved," Cadence said, returning to the task of pouring mugs of apple cider.

"What kind of costume was that?" Tommy asked as he helped set the mugs on the table. "She looked like she wrestled with a roll of toilet paper and it got the upper hand."

"I'm guessing she probably had to create her own costume and that is the best she could do," Cadence said, worry etching lines across her forehead. "Do you know anything about their family, Trey?

Glad she had called him Trey instead of Mr. Thompson, Trey picked up a platter of donuts while

Cadence carried a second and resumed his seat at the table. It had been ages since they had eaten home-made donuts and if he didn't snag a few, he'd miss out entirely.

Biting into one glazed with maple frosting, he nodded his head.

"Her name is Micki. Her boyfriend joined the military and got sent to Afghanistan about the time she figured out she was pregnant. He must have been a few years older than her, because I think she is about 22. He was only gone a couple months when word came back that he had died over there, leaving Micki to raise the baby alone. Micki grew up in foster care and goodness only knows how she landed here in Grass Valley. She worked for your aunt for a while but with her temper, her stint as a waitress was short-lived. She pumped gas, worked in the antique store and even spent time out at the raceway, but I haven't seen her working anywhere lately."

"Well, is there anything we can do to help her?" Cadence asked, sipping her cider and counting her blessings. As bad as things seemed for her a few weeks ago, she was fortunate to have never experienced anything like little Cass or her mother.

"Micki doesn't take too kindly to help of any kind, as you may have witnessed. I'm surprised she would drive all the way out here for Cass get a treat," Trent said, joining the conversation. "Rumor is she spends most of her time drunk. No one ever sees the little girl. I think she must stay at home alone. Poor kiddo must be about five or so."

Cadence gasped and set her mug down on the table. "That's horrible! Cass is too little to be left to her own defenses," Cadence looked at Trent and then Trey. "Surely there is something we could do, someone who could help?"

"I don't think so," Trey said, biting into another donut. "Viv has tried talking to Micki until she is blue in the face, but it doesn't do any good. This is one thing you can't fix or make better, Miss Greer."

Cadence sat back in her chair, frowning.

All was quiet around the table except for the sounds of contented eating. Even though she made a double batch of donuts, the three left on the platter were about to disappear. Good thing she had left a few hidden for later. She lost her appetite when she watched Micki push Cass out the door.

The men finally left the table, all offering multiple words of gratitude for the good dinner and treat of apple cider and fresh donuts.

Although she didn't say anything further about Cass, Cadence decided to talk to Aunt Viv and see if there was anything that could be done to better the little girl's situation.

With the guys all gone for the afternoon and nothing in the house that needed her attention, Cadence wanted to see if she could find Denni's old sewing machine out in the barn.

The first week of November had arrived with cold temperatures, just like Trent had predicted. Cadence was glad for her warm coat as she walked across the yard toward the barn. Although the sun was shining, it was still nippy outside. Bob and Bonnie, the two dogs, ran around her legs and barked as if to say "come play with us a while." Cadence laughed and gave them both a good rub on their heads.

Pushing open the barn door, she stepped inside then waited a moment for her eyes to adjust to the darkness. The dogs nosed in behind her, sniffing their way across the barn.

Leaving the door open a crack, the smells of horses and hay filled the air. Another somewhat unpleasant scent, one she was coming to recognize as manure, was also present. She supposed that was natural considering she was in a barn.

When she first started doing their laundry, she wondered how Trey and Trent managed to get manure on their jeans on such a regular basis, but it hadn't taken long to figure out it was all part of ranching.

She had to Google some ideas on getting manure out of fabric after the first load of jeans she washed came out looking nearly as dirty as they did when she tossed them in. Cadence felt a little twinge of pride that she was learning and adjusting to this new and completely different way of life.

As a young girl, she wasn't sure what she wanted to be when she grew up. There were so many fascinating possibilities like a chef, a fashion designer, a successful business woman. They all seemed like wonderful careers.

Once she decided the restaurant business wasn't for her, she excelled at her college business classes and graduated with honors. Taking a few jobs that were resume builders, she soon found herself employed at the exclusive law-firm in downtown Seattle working for one of the city's most respected attorneys as his personal assistant. Neil had encouraged her to pursue law school, saying she would make a fine attorney. She was considering it when Bill proposed.

Marrying one of the lawyers who would one day be a partner in the firm seemed like a great next step. Too bad Cadence hadn't stopped to think about the kind of person he was or if she really liked him, let alone loved him.

Now here she was, about as far away from the shiny, sterile offices she was accustomed to as a girl could get, thinking about how clever she was for getting cow poop out of jeans worn by two cowboys she met just a little more than a month ago.

Wandering down the length of stalls, she admired the cleanliness of the barn. Like everything else, the Thompsons seemed to take pride in even the condition of the horse stalls. One of the stalls on the far end of the barn had been made into a bed for the barn cat and her litter of kittens. Stepping inside the stall, Cadence shut the door to keep the dogs out and watched the momma cat. Kneeling in the straw, she waited quietly for the cat to settle down. As bad as she wanted to pet one of the kittens, Cadence kept her hands in her pockets. She thought she heard the barn door close, but by the time she stood up in the stall, she didn't see anything and decided it must have been the dogs.

She left the stall and wandered back down the length of the barn. Opening a door, she found a room full of saddles, bridles and assorted tack. Another door across from it offered a small bathroom, which, to her surprise, appeared to be quite clean. Next to the bathroom door a wooden ladder went up to a loft. Cadence wasn't all that fond of heights, but decided to climb up and see if the storage room was up there.

As she climbed up the ladder, her foot slipped as she reached the top and she flung herself onto the landing. When she did, the ladder tipped backward and fell over.

"Just perfect," Cadence said aloud, wondering how she would get down from her current predicament. While she was stuck up in the loft, she decided she might as well take a look around. She found bags of feed, small pieces of farm equipment and other things she didn't recognize stored neatly around the open area. At one end was a door. When Cadence opened it, a string hung in her face. Giving it a tug, a light clicked on and she could see this was indeed the storage area she had been searching for.

It didn't take long to locate Denni's sewing machine. It didn't look old at all to Cadence. Although she wasn't a fabulous seamstress, she could sew a quilt top and follow simple patterns. She thought about making a warm blanket or a pretty dress for Cass and wondered if Micki would accept them. She would have to wait and see.

Carrying the sewing machine over to where the ladder should have been, she set it down and returned to the storage area. Cadence found several boxes of Christmas decorations, and made a note to have the guys bring those in right after Thanksgiving. She found a few fall decorations and left them piled by the sewing machine. Sitting down on a rickety stool that had seen better days, she studied scrapbooks for Trey, Trent and Travis that highlighted their school days. Although all three boys looked a lot alike, Trey seemed to shoulder more responsibility than the other two. Trent was the most laid-back and Travis looked like a natural-born trouble-maker. While she flipped through the pages, she wondered just how long she'd be stuck up here until someone missed her.

Although the barn was warmer than it was outside, it still had a bit of a chill in the air. With her gloves and scarf in the mudroom at the house, Cadence soon found herself with cold fingers and even colder toes.

She hadn't worn a watch, so she had no idea how much time had passed. She could tell by glancing out the window in the loft that the sun was starting its descent. Wishing now she had left well enough alone and asked Trent or Trey to find the sewing machine, Cadence sat down on the edge of the loft, waiting to be rescued.

Cold and in desperate need of using the bathroom, Cadence paced the length of the loft, swinging her arms and talking to herself. She sang silly songs she made up in her head then launched into singing Christmas carols. She planned out the menu for the next week in her head and vowed to never again climb up a ladder.

Walking every inch of the loft, she again looked to see if there was another way to get down. Other than the possibility of jumping and hoping both legs didn't break, she didn't see any other options, except to wait.

Sitting back down on the edge of the loft, she watched the barn door edge open a bit as one of the dogs came trotting back in. Cadence decided if dogs could smile, this one was wearing a huge grin.

"What are you smiling at? Are you Bob?" Cadence asked. When the dog didn't respond, she tried again. "Is it Bonnie?"

The dog barked in reply, continuing to grin and wag her tail.

"Good girl, Bonnie," Cadence said with a laugh. "I don't suppose you sent Bob to bring home the troops did you?" Bonnie's answer was to bark again and pace by the door.

Soon Bob came charging in the door followed by Trey.

Noticing the ladder on the ground, Trey looked up and saw Cadence sitting on the edge of the loft.

"Cady! You had me worried half to death," Trey blurted out as he set the ladder back in place and held it while Cadence climbed down.

As soon as her feet hit the bottom rung, Trey pulled her into his arms and hugged her tight.

"Good grief, woman. I've been looking for you all afternoon. What in blazes are you doing out here?" Trey asked, continuing to hold her close to him.

He'd gone to the house to see if she wanted to run into town with him and he couldn't find her. Her car was still in the garage, so he knew she hadn't left the place. He checked the barn but the only thing he found inside were the dogs and briefly wondered how they got the door open. Trey made the rounds of the machine sheds and other outbuildings and couldn't find Cadence anywhere.

He thought maybe she'd gone for a walk and went back to the house to wait for her. After more than an hour had passed without her return, he was starting to panic. He was just getting ready to go round up the men so they could all look for her when Bob and Bonnie started barking at the barn door. Bonnie managed to nose the door open and there sat Cadence in the loft.

If something happened to her, he'd be a certified basket case.

Pushing back from him, she ran into the bathroom and slammed the door. Trey stood there confounded until she opened the door and came out looking somewhat embarrassed. Coming to stand in front of him, she cocked her head and smiled. Understanding swept over him and he grinned.

"What did you call me?" Cadence asked, warmed as much by Trey's hug as the name he'd called her. No one had ever called her Cady before. Coming from Trey, the name made her heart pick up tempo and her palms feel sweaty.

"Cady," he said, staring at the toes of his boots, clearly flustered. He hadn't planned to let the nickname he'd been calling her in his head make its way to his lips, but there it was hanging out in the open. Finally he brought his gaze up to meet hers. "I'm tired of calling you Miss Greer and Cadence is just too formal. Would you mind if I call you Cady?"

"I wouldn't mind," Cadence said, barely above a whisper, loving the sound of the name on his lips. "I wouldn't mind if you want to hug me again, either. I'm about half frozen."

Trey laughed. Unsnapping his coat, he pulled her to his chest then wrapped his coat around her, sharing his warmth. He was unprepared for the overwhelming urge to kiss her, to hold her this close forever. Heat wasn't the only thing he was sharing. Trey could feel something else, something unsettling, unfamiliar and unmistakably powerful snapping between the two of them.

Looking above her head to the loft he thought he could see the tip of something setting at the edge.

"What was so important up there that you got yourself trapped for the afternoon?"

"Your mom's sewing machine. She said I could use it if I could find it," Cadence said, staring up into Trey's eyes. "I'm sorry. I didn't mean to get stuck out here and waste the afternoon."

"I'm just glad you're okay," Trey said, rubbing her back. "Let's get you in the house and warmed up."

Cadence would have been happy to stay inside the circle of his arms where warmth unlike anything she'd ever felt before seeped into the very center of her. Breathing in his unique, manly scent, she felt languid and weak.

Trey kept his arm around her shoulders as they walked back to the house. Once they were inside, he built a fire in the gathering room and made Cadence a cup of hot tea. Motioning her to sit down on the hearth, he watched her sip the sweet, hot brew and close her eyes, warming herself by the crackling fire.

"Will you promise me to not go climbing up anywhere again unless one of us is around to rescue you," Trey asked, sitting down on the floor in front of her.

Cadence nodded her head, although she wanted to say no. She thought she'd climb every ladder on the ranch if it meant Trey would pull her into his arms and hold her close like he had in the barn. She had never in her life felt so secure and cherished as she had when he opened his coat and shared his warmth with her.

When Trey placed his hand on her knee, Cadence felt her nerve endings dance to attention.

Melting into Trey's aquamarine eyes, she could barely concentrate enough to hold onto her mug let alone answer him when we asked her a question.

"What was that?" she asked, pulling herself back to reality instead of swimming leisurely laps in the heated pools of those wonderful blue eyes.

"I said not to worry about dinner tonight. We'll make do with leftovers," Trey said, starting to get up.

Cadence looked at him like he'd grown a second head.

"What leftovers? You guys eat every last crumb at every meal. There isn't ever anything left over," Cadence started to stand up, but Trey pushed her back down.

Trey grinned and patted his well-defined abdomen. "That must be why I'm putting on a little weight."

Cadence didn't think he could possibly be serious. Before moving onto this ranch full of hard-working men, she thought physiques like that existed only on gym trainers or in Hollywood.

Not that she'd seen much since she'd been here, but when Trey wore a T-shirt, it was pretty easy to let her imagination run wild. When he held her close today, she didn't think her imagination was too far from removed from the muscle-filled truth.

Gazing into the flames, Cadence cleared her throat, trying to also clear her mind of any lingering images of Trey's physique.

"I don't think you have put on any weight. If anything you'll be losing it fussing over me so. Honestly, Trey, I'm fine. I'll get dinner started, although it might be a little late."

Trey reached out and cupped her chin, turning her to look at him. "If you are going to be a pill and insist on cooking then I'll help you."

Resigning herself to meeting him halfway, she again nodded her head. Finishing her tea, she stood up and pointed toward the kitchen. "Lead the way, boss man."

><><

Trey helped Cadence fry up a big pan of hamburger seasoned with onions, salt, pepper and a bit of chili powder. She warmed up tortilla shells, shredded cheese and chopped tomatoes and lettuce.

Dinner was ready and on the table right on time when the six other men came in the back door. While Trey was setting the table, Cadence whipped up a double batch of flan and had it baking in the oven. Served warm, it would finish off their taco night in fine style.

After they ate and the men left for the evening, Cadence sat at the kitchen table making a shopping list while Trent sat at one end of the table with piles of newspaper on the floor around him as he applied a coat of waterproof sealant to his and Trey's boots.

"You have any boots that need sealed?" Trent asked as he rubbed the gel into a boot.

"Just my hiking boots. Do you know if you can put sealant on them?" Cadence said, continuing to work on her list.

"Sure. I'll do them next. Do you own a pair of snow boots?" Trent questioned, stopping his rubbing to look at Cadence.

"Actually, I don't. It wasn't something I needed in Seattle. I lived three blocks from the office where I worked and if the weather was bad enough to need snow boots, it was a good bet the office would be closed anyway."

"Well, you might want to think of getting a pair if you are going to be here through the winter," Trent advised, continuing to rub the boot, then setting it down to dry on a newspaper along the row of boots he had already finished.

"Thanks, I'll think about it."

"Think about what," Trey asked as he came in the back door toting the sewing machine and the fall decorations she had found. Placing everything on the table, he went back out to the mudroom to remove his coat before closing the door.

"Getting some winter boots. Cadence doesn't have any," Trent said, continuing his work without looking up.

Cadence glared at him like he was a tattle-tale.

"I'll get some if you think it is completely necessary," Cadence said, standing up to examine the sewing machine.

"Oh, it will be necessary," Trey said, pouring a cup of hot water and stirring in a packet of chocolate. He motioned to Trent who shook his head. Cadence didn't even notice him as she started moving dials and turning knobs on the sewing machine.

"Cady, did you hear me?" Trey asked sitting down at the table and watching her. "You need to get some boots."

"Yes, I heard you. Boots," she muttered, distracted by all the features on the sewing machine.

Trent leaned over and flicked Trey on the leg then mouthed "Cady?"

Trey shot him a steely glare and shook his head, hoping his brother would keep his big mouth shut.

"So, I'm going to run into Madras tomorrow to get some supplies since I didn't make it into town today," Trey said, watching Cadence. "I seemed to be too busy rescuing damsels in distress."

Cadence finally glanced at Trey and blushed, looking chagrined. Sitting back down by her shopping list, she continued adding items.

"Would you like to go with me, Cady?" Trey asked, hoping she would say yes. He knew it was probably not the smartest thing in the world to want her to go with him, but after hugging her this afternoon, he couldn't seem to keep his thoughts on anything except her. "You could get your groceries and see some new country on the way there."

"Are you sure you wouldn't mind me tagging along?" she asked, looking up from her growing list.

"I'd enjoy the company," Trey said. He heard Trent snort and chose to not acknowledge the sound. "Why don't we plan to leave in the morning after I get the chores done and you get everything set to rights after breakfast? How does that sound?"

"Sounds like a plan," Cadence said, wondering how far it was to Madras. She wasn't sure she could spend too much time trapped in a car with Trey and still manage to maintain her composure. He seemed to have that effect on her. Looking at Trent, she asked "Will you be going along, too."

Trent looked up with a devilish grin. "I don't think so. That is one trip my big brother can manage all on his own."

><><

After Cadence said goodnight and went off to her room, Trent started needling Trey.

"What's all this Cady business, mister boss-man?" Trent asked, plopping down across from Trey in the great room.

"What Cady business?" Trey said, feigning ignorance.

"I heard you call her Cady. When did that start?" Trent leaned forward with his elbows on his knees. After Trey took over the leadership role of their family and ranch when their father died, Trent gave up hope of his brother ever finding a wife, or even going out on a date. He was always too laser focused on work.

To see a spark of romantic interest in Trey for their housekeeper was nothing short of a miracle.

"Maybe it isn't any of your business." Trey looked intently at the television as he flipped through channels.

Grabbing the remote and turning off the TV, Trent studied his brother closely.

"It absolutely isn't any of my business, but you better tell me anyway or I'll pester you until you do."

"You are every bit as bad as the old cronies Mom hangs around," Trey said, getting up from his chair and going to stand by the fireplace. "I came in this afternoon to see if Cadence wanted to go with me to town but I couldn't find her anywhere. By the time another hour had passed, I was getting pretty worried. I was just heading out to find you, when I noticed the dogs carrying on by the barn door. She climbed up in the loft and the ladder tipped over. She'd been stuck out there all afternoon. When I saw her sitting in the loft, pretty as you please, I just blurted out the name Cady and she didn't seem to mind. Personally, I like it a whole lot better than Cadence. Not so stuffy or formal."

"Right," Trent said, nodding his head and grinning like the Cheshire Cat. "And what about the warning Viv gave you. She told you she nearly got married just before she moved here. You really think she is ready to be in a relationship, out here in the sticks, with a salt-of-the-earth cowboy?"

"Whoa, there, man. You are getting the cart way before this horse. I haven't even asked her on a date," Trey said, running his hand through his thick hair. "I've probably got about a snowball's chance in the Sahara with her, so don't get carried away. Besides, she is our housekeeper and cook. How would that look to suddenly show an interest in her? I wouldn't want to damage her reputation."

"Sure, bro," Trent agreed, still grinning. "That's quite noble of you."

Trey looked at his brother, ready to punch him until he saw the teasing gleam in his eye. Instead he jumped up and put him in a headlock and the two of them wrestled their way down the hall.

Chapter Six

*Without leaps of imagination, or dreaming,
we lose the excitement of possibilities.
Dreaming, after all, is a form of planning.*
Gloria Steinem

Cadence was wiping down the counters when Trey hustled in the back door and said he'd be ready to go in about thirty minutes. Tossing the dishrag in the sink, Cadence ran into her room and plugged in her curling iron. Glad she had already showered, she applied another coat of mascara, adding a hint of blush to her cheeks then carefully combed and curled her hair.

Pulling on slacks and a sweater, she slipped on a pair of heels, grabbed her long wool coat and purse and gave herself a spritz of perfume as she hustled out her bedroom and into the kitchen. Trey was standing at the sink, finishing a glass of water when he turned around and nearly dropped his glass.

"Cady, you look… nice," he said, trying to act nonchalant and failing miserably. Her royal blue sweater brought out the blue and gold in her eyes, her cheeks glowed pink and her lovely dark brown hair fell in long curls down her shoulders and around her face. She wore black slacks with heels and carried a fancy black coat. She looked like she was ready for a lunch date in Portland more than a trip to the feed store in Madras.

Cadence was having trouble focusing on anything except Trey. He cleaned up really well. She started her assessment at his feet with his shiny boots, working her way up his neatly creased Wranglers to the crisp cotton shirt that exactly matched the color of his eyes. He had shaved and his cheeks looked fresh and taut while his sun-streaked golden hair had quickly been combed into place. Although cut short in length, little waves started to break free and curl around his forehead.

Gracious, she didn't know if she could handle an entire day alone with Trey. He was one handsome cowboy.

"You don't look so bad yourself," she managed to say when he took her coat from her and held it so she could slip it on. "Are you ready to go?"

"Yes, Ma'am. I even warmed up my truck," Trey said as they walked into the mudroom and he pulled on a newer looking coat and his good black Stetson.

As they drove down the long drive-way and turned south onto Highway 97, Cady sat quietly, inhaling the scent of Trey's after shave. His truck smelled of leather, and a little of horse, and a lot of him. She thought if that smell could be bottled, the women she knew in Seattle would pay a small fortune for it.

"You're quiet. What are you thinking?" Trey asked, enjoying the sight of her with her hair down, dressed up and smelling so nice. She must have a bottle of something called "after the storm" because that was what she smelled like - the crisp, fresh, slightly sweet air right after a gentle summer rain.

Cadence blushed, hoping Trey couldn't read her thoughts. If he could, she would absolutely die of embarrassment. Her thoughts had been consumed with wondering what he'd look like without that shirt on and if his cheeks would feel as smooth under her lips as they appeared to be.

Trey smiled, wondering what had caused the blush on Cady's cheeks to deepen. Whatever it was, it sure made for a pretty pink hue. Almost as pretty as those pink lips of hers. Would she smack him into next Thursday if he leaned over and gave her a kiss?

"Trey! Watch out!" Cadence gasped as he swerved across his lane.

Pulling his attention back to his driving, he decided it best to keep his thoughts on business and not dreaming about the very attractive woman sitting a few feet across from him in his pickup. Good thing there wasn't much traffic this morning, or he could have been in big trouble.

Deciding to keep both their thoughts occupied, he started describing the area to Cadence, giving her some of the local history and talking about the families who had settled the area.

"Well, I wondered why the towns are so close together," she said as they drove past Shaniko. "It makes sense that it was for the purpose of wagon travel to space the towns nine or so miles apart."

"Yep," Trey said as they headed southwest across the desert. "At one point in time, Shaniko was known as the wool capital of the world. In 1900, it was a shipping center for wool, wheat, cattle and sheep production that covered a 20,000 square mile area."

"What happened to the town?" Cadence asked, intrigued by not only the name, but the history of Shaniko.

"Another rail line diverted traffic and a flood took out part of the tracks and that was all she wrote," Trey said, looking across the desert. He knew some people might think the landscape boring, but he loved seeing the fields of winter wheat give way to rolling hills of sagebrush and scattered juniper, along with the craggy rocks that reached up to touch the blue sky.

Glancing over at Cadence, he wondered if she missed the big city. It was quite a change to go from skyscrapers to scraping manure off your boots.

"Do you miss it?" Trey said, not meaning to voice his thoughts.

"Miss what?" Cadence asked, turning her gaze from the passing scenery to Trey.

"The big city? The people, the traffic, the buildings, the noise? All of it?"

Cadence laughed. She hadn't realized how tired she was of the gray skies, the noise, the constant press of crowds, the smells that rolled in off the water. Out here where the air was clear and unpolluted, where you could stand and see for miles, the city just seemed loud and dirty and depressing.

Taking an internal inventory, she suddenly wondered where that thought had come from. Especially since she'd never been more than an hour or two drive from Seattle. Up until she moved to Grass Valley, she didn't even know blue skies, clear air and miles of unbroken land existed.

"Honestly, Trey, I don't miss much about the city," she said staring out the window. "I might miss some of the conveniences like shopping malls and Starbucks, but for the most part, I don't miss it or the life I had there."

Trey reached over and squeezed her hand, sending a jolt skittering up her arm. Trying to stay calm, she didn't move and let him be the one to break contact.

"I'm glad to hear that," he said, grinning. "I hope your new employer treats you well and has made you feel welcome."

"For the most part," Cadence said, keeping a somber look on her face. "The boss-man can be somewhat overbearing and he's been known to ride the crew a little hard, but I think I can handle him."

"Is that so?" Trey asked, chuckling.

"Yep, boss-man, that's so."

Trey and Cadence didn't seem to have any problem finding things to talk about during their two-hour drive to Madras. It was close to 11 a.m. when Trey pulled into the feed store. He jumped out of the truck and hurried around to open Cadence's door for her. She was surprised at his nice manners. Bill had never opened the door for her. One more thing to add to the growing list of all the reasons he was a blight to mankind.

Walking in the door of the store, Cadence was unprepared for the variety of items offered. One side of the store carried clothing and footwear for the entire family. Behind that, she could see saddles and tack. There were gardening supplies, irrigating supplies, a section of hardware, lumber supplies and feed. In the center of the store near the cash registers was an island of gift items that caught her attention. With Christmas just a little more than six weeks away, it wasn't too early to start some shopping.

Seeing her eyes drawn to the festive display, Trey lightly squeezed Cadence's arm and smiled.

"Take it all in, Cady. It will take me a while to get the feed order filled. I'll find you when I'm ready to go," Trey said, walking backward toward the feed area. "Make sure you look at some winter boots."

Cadence nodded her head and took off her coat, holding it over her arm. She browsed through the gift section and found a few things she thought would make fun Christmas presents. Picking up a basket by the front door, she added her selections then wandered over toward the clothes.

She was impressed with the variety of styles and sizes. They had everything to outfit a rodeo queen to a farmer's wife. Looking through a rack of blouses, she found one that she knew she had to have and added it to her basket. She used to shop at least once a week in Seattle, mostly going to clearance sales, but it was fun to buy something just because she liked it and thought it was pretty, not because it would look good at the office or impress a hot-shot attorney.

Strolling toward the boot section, she had no idea what to look for. Everything looked heavy and clunky. She was staring at the overwhelming choices, when she heard a voice at her side.

"Something I can help you with, hon?"

Cadence turned to look into the face of an older woman wearing a blouse cut too low and jeans too tight, but she had on a great pair of cowboy boots. According to the name tag, her name was Bette.

"I was told I needed to purchase a pair of winter boots. I've never had any before and I'm not sure what to look for," Cadence explained.

"Well, will you be outside riding in the boots, or feeding, or what type of work will you be doing?" Bette asked.

"I'm not exactly sure," Cadence said.

"Huh," Bette said, looking at Cadence like she was one card shy of a full deck. She moved down the aisle of boots and picked up a pair that didn't look quite so heavy. "What size do you wear?"

Cadence gave her the size and Bette pulled out a pair, loosening the laces. Cadence sat down on a bench and took off her heels. Before she could slip on a boot, Bette shook her head and hustled around the corner. She came back with a pair of thick socks in her hand.

"You can't try on boots wearing nylons, hon. That just ain't gonna work." Pulling apart the package she handed Cadence the socks and watched her tug them on. "Now you can try them on."

Cadence put on the boots and was surprised at how well they fit and how warm and toasty her toes felt. Bette gave her some pointers on how they should feel and Cadence thought she made a good selection. The boots were waterproof and supposed to have a special lining to keep her toes warm down to 15 below zero.

Cadence didn't bother informing Bette if it was that cold, the only place her boots would be was parked by the back door because there was no way she'd be outside. Looking at the available options, Cadence decided she liked the black ones she tried on best.

"Hon, while you're trying on boots, come over here," Bette said, pulling out a boot box and handing it to Cadence.

Sitting back down on the bench, Cadence opened the box to find a beautiful pair of cowboy boots. Inhaling the delicious scent of leather, she ran her hand over the boots, admiring the handiwork. Somehow it didn't surprise her that the tall shafts were the exact color of Trey's eyes.

"You getting ready to cowgirl up on me?" Trey asked as he walked up beside her and looked in the box.

"Well, if it isn't Trey Thompson, drug in from the hills," Bette said, giving his arm a friendly pat.

"How are you, Bette? You keeping that husband of yours out of trouble?" Trey asked, watching Cadence study the boots.

"You know it," Bette said, taking a boot out of the box and removing the cardboard and paper from inside it. "Now, what brings you in today?"

"Just the usual. I needed some feed and supplies," Trey said, nodding toward Cadence. "And Cady needed some boots. She is taking over as our new housekeeper and chef extraordinaire."

"Take a look at her boots and see if they pass muster, then," Bette said, handing him the box with Cadence's snow boots.

"These will work just fine," Trey said, closing the box then hunkering down in front of Cadence. "Do you like these boots, Cady?"

"Oh, I was just looking at them. I don't need a pair of cowboy boots," she said, setting the boot Bette had removed back in the box and closing the lid.

"I beg to differ," Trey said, opening the lid and taking the boot back out. He handed the second to Bette for her to remove the cardboard and paper stuffing while he slid the other on Cady's foot. "Now give that a tug and see what you think."

Cadence thought she might pass out if Trey didn't stand up and take a step back from her. This close she could see flecks of light and dark blue swimming in his eyes, smell his after shave, and feel his warmth. The desire to kiss his full lips was about to engulf her.

Instead of giving in, she yanked on the boot and wiggled her foot. She might have liked the blouse she picked out earlier, but she was in love with the boots.

Taking the second boot from Bette, she quickly tugged it on and then stood up, walking up and down the aisle getting used to the feel of the boots and loving them.

Trey looked at Bette and smiled, nodding his head.

"You've got pretty good taste for a city girl," Trey said as Cadence looked down at her boots. "Those are a pair of authentic buckaroo boots, complete with the fancy stitched saddle vamp."

Sitting down, Cadence pulled them off and put them back in the box. Tugging off the thick socks, she slid on her heels. If she bought those cowboy boots, every time she wore them she would think of Trey and the feelings he stirred deep inside her. She just couldn't make herself suffer through that kind of torment.

"I'll just get the winter boots today, Bette, and the socks. I'd like three pairs of the socks."

Standing up, she jammed the winter boot box into the basket she was carrying, picked up her coat and purse and faced Trey as Bette handed her two more packages of the warm socks.

"As soon as I purchase these, I'll be ready to go."

"What about the other boots?" Trey asked, hoping she'd give in and get them. He could see how much she wanted them. It couldn't have been written across her face any more clearly if she'd taken a marker to her cheek.

"I believe I'll pass on those today."

"Are you sure, Cady?" Trey asked, picking up the boot box and taking a step toward her. "Are you positively sure?"

"Positive," Cadence said, giving the box one more longing glance. "If you'll excuse me, I'll pay for these and meet you at the door."

Trey turned to Bette and smiled.

"Say, Bette, don't suppose you'd add these on to my feed bill while I find a place to hide them in the truck while she's checking out?" Trey asked as they walked toward the side door.

"Be happy to, Trey," Bette said with a conspiring smile. "Do you want them gift-wrapped?"

"Nope," Trey laughed. "I won't be able to wait that long to give them to her."

Bette gave him a shove out the door and went to add up his bill. When he came back in she had it ready for him to sign and he slid his debit card across the counter.

He walked up to the front door just as Cadence slipped her coat back on and picked up her bags.

"Ready to go?" Trey asked, taking the bags from her hands.

"I believe so," Cadence said, back to being formal and polite.

"Something wrong, Cady?" Trey asked as he held her door for her and put her bags in the back seat.

"No. I'm just a little hungry, I guess," Cadence fibbed, sad that she had to leave behind the boots she wanted so badly, frightened by the new feelings she was experiencing just being around Trey.

"I think we can remedy that problem," Trey said. Driving through town, he pulled into the parking lot of a nice little Italian restaurant.

Ushering Cadence inside, he kept his hand at the small of her back and waited until she slid into the booth before he removed his hat and sat down. His fingers felt like they were on fire the entire time he touched her and he wondered if she felt it, too.

Browsing through the menu, Cadence was pleasantly surprised by the delicious selections. It was going to be hard to choose.

"See anything you like?" Trey asked, flipping through his menu.

"Several things. Have you eaten here before?" Cadence asked, narrowing down her options.

"A few times," Trey said. "Usually I grab a hamburger to go on the way back home."

Glancing up from the menu, Cadence realized her coming along was doubling the time of Trey's trip. They still had to go to the grocery store.

"I'm sorry, I just realized bringing me along has added a lot of wasted time to your day."

"Cady," Trey turned his warm blue gaze on her face, waiting for her to look at him, which she did reluctantly. "Spending the day with you has got to be the best time I've ever wasted. If I wanted to make this a quick trip, I wouldn't have asked you along. I'm not in any hurry, so just enjoy yourself."

"Whatever you say, boss-man," Cadence said, feeling relieved. If it was Bill, he would have been reminding her how dragging a female along was always a time-consuming, annoying waste of time. Once again, she was glad Bill was no longer a part of her life.

Cadence ordered the spinach manicotti while Trey chose grilled pork chops. From the Italian seasoned salad to the soft breadsticks, the entire meal was wonderful. Cadence couldn't complain about the company, either.

After lunch, they went to the grocery store, each of them taking a cart and filling it from Cadence's long list. Once they had the groceries loaded in the pickup, Trey made her go back inside with him to return the carts and Cadence found herself standing at an authentic Starbucks counter, located inside the grocery store. Inhaling the heady scent of rich coffee, Cadence ordered a cinnamon dolce latte while Trey ordered a caramel macchiato.

"If you so much as even hint to the guys I drink this sissified coffee, you'll be looking for a new place to work, darlin'. Got it?" Trey teased as they walked toward the pickup with the steaming cups of coffee.

"Got it," Cadence said with a smile.

The next afternoon, Cadence was digging through a box of patterns she found in the parlor closet when she heard boots stamping at the back door. The kitchen door clicked shut, so she set down the box and headed toward the kitchen. She turned the corner and bumped right into Trey.

"Cady," he said, grabbing her arms to steady her. "Sorry, I was just looking for you."

"What can I do for you?' she asked, taking a step back.

"Well, nothing, really," Trey said, swirling the toe of his sock in a circle in front of him, acting like he was a kid about to be scolded. "I was hoping… well, um, I had some time this afternoon and thought maybe you might want to learn to ride."

"Ride?" Cadence asked in disbelief. "You mean like a horse? That kind of ride?"

"Yeah," Trey said, with a laugh. "Unless you prefer to ride a ladder."

"No, thank you, Mr. Thompson."

"No? To the horse or the ladder?"

"Both."

"But Cady, I think you'd enjoy riding a horse. Have you ever tried?"

"No."

"So…" Trey gave her an encouraging smile. "Put on your coat and let's give it a whirl."

When Cadence continued to stare at him like he'd lost all his sense, he decided to treat her like he would one of the skittish colts he worked with. He relaxed his stance, gently rubbed her arm and spoke softly.

"I promise I won't let anything happen to you, Cady. You'll be safe with me. I promise."

Cadence didn't know how to tell Trey he'd broken his promise before he ever got her to the door. She wasn't safe with him. Not at all. With him rubbing his hand so gently up and down her arm, he was about to send her over the edge of reason.

That was why she couldn't let him teach her to ride. She was just about to burst wanting to learn to ride a horse, but not from Trey. Spending the day with him yesterday was wonderful until they got back home and she returned to being the employee and he returned to being her boss. She couldn't let that professional distance be breached.

"Please, Cady," Trey pleaded, giving her a smile he hoped would melt her reserve. "Just one afternoon? If you hate it, I promise I won't ever ask you again."

Closing her eyes and chewing on her lip, Cadence knew she shouldn't give in, but she had no willpower left to deny his request.

"Fine. I'll go," she said, opening her eyes to find Trey beaming a smile at her that made her feel weak in the knees.

"Put on warm gloves, and a hat, and your hiking boots," Trey said. "They'll work fine for learning. When you're ready, come meet me at the barn."

An hour later, Cadence was riding one of the mares around the corral, laughing at the pure joy of being on the back of a horse. Trey said she was a natural. Cadence knew that was pushing it a bit far but she did love the experience. Exhilarating was the best word she could think of to describe it. She didn't know when she'd felt so vibrantly alive, despite the cold.

><><

Trey had mush for brains. He would freely admit it.

If he had any sense at all, he would keep far away from Cadence Greer and maintain a professional level of separation with his employee.

Only he couldn't think of her as Cadence Greer, the uptight business professional who was cool and aloof, not to mention one of the best cooks to ever set foot in a kitchen.

At night when he closed his eyes, she was Cady. With the glorious dark hair, sparkling hazel eyes, rosy cheeks and kissable lips.

As she cantered the horse around the corral, the sound of her laugher and the look of happiness on her face were going to be permanently emblazoned on his heart and in his head. He didn't know how it had happened, but in one afternoon of teaching her to ride, she chipped right through the shield he'd been keeping around his heart since his dad died.

Trey knew he was in way too deep with his emotions and there was no hope of recovery.

Despite his best intentions, he had fallen in love with Cady.

Chapter Seven

*For the happiest life, days should be rigorously planned,
nights left open to chance.*
Mignon McLaughlin

"Aunt Viv, I had no idea riding was so exhilaratingly wonderful," Cadence said, sitting in the café, sipping tea with her aunt one afternoon.

"I'm glad you're enjoying it honey," Viv said, passing Cadence a plate of cookies.

"It's beyond enjoyment, Aunt Viv," Cadence said, not sure how to explain her feelings. "I feel like I've gone from living in black and white to bright, beautiful color. I had no idea life could be so full, exciting and amazing. I finally feel alive. Does that make any sense?"

"It sure, does, honey, and I'm glad to hear it," Viv said with a knowing smile. If she didn't know better, she was fairly certain part of Cadence's joy was coming from Trey. She might not have realized it yet, but Cadence was falling for that boy like water running downhill. "So they are treating you well and you enjoy the work?"

"Absolutely. Trey and Trent couldn't be nicer and the hands are all polite. I finally get to put my cooking classes to good use and do something I enjoy. And to answer your next question, no, I don't miss the city, at least not much. I do miss Neil and a few of my friends, but I wouldn't want to go back. I like it here."

Viv beamed a huge smile and gave Cadence's arm a loving pat.

"Well, if you'd listened to me years ago, you could've been living the good life all along. But no, you didn't want to come visit your old auntie in the middle of hickville," Viv teased.

"If you had made it perfectly clear what I was missing out on, I'd have come a lot sooner," Cadence said with a saucy grin.

Noticing a red head bobbing beneath the windows at the back of the restaurant, Cadence lowered her voice.

"What do you know about a sweet little red-headed girl named Cass?" Cadence asked, nodding her head toward the back of the café.

"She comes most every day to see if I have any scraps. She tells me they are for a stray cat, but I think what I send home with her is all she and that worthless mother of hers have to eat. I found her digging in the garbage one day and that about sent me over the brink. After that, I told her to come in the afternoon and I'd keep the good scraps inside for her. So I save leftovers from breakfast and dinner the night before and send home with her. She usually doesn't come in if she thinks there is someone else here. Let's see what she does today."

Cadence took a sip of her tea, and pretended not to notice Cass peeking in the window. Apparently she decided Cadence was a friend rather than a foe because she opened the door and came running over to their table and sat down next to Viv.

"How are you today sweetie-pie?" Viv asked, giving the little girl a hug.

"I'm fine, Miss Viv? How are you?" Cass asked, hungrily eyeing the plate of cookies.

Cadence slid the cookies toward the little girl and smiled.

"Would you like a cookie, Cass?"

Reaching out her hand, she snatched a cookie and gobbled it up. Cadence went into the kitchen and returned with a glass of milk, setting it by Cass.

"You better have some milk with your cookies. You need something to wash them down," Cadence said, trying to look serious.

"Yep. I guess I better drink it all," Cass said, taking a huge gulp before snatching another cookie.

"That's right, you better drink it all," Viv said, giving Cadence a wink.

Looking at Cadence, a smile lit Cass's face when she recognized her.

"You're the lady who gave me a trick or treat. You're Miss Dense?"

"Cadence, that's right," Cadence said, trying not to laugh. "But some of my friends call me Cady. Why don't you call me that instead?"

"That's a pretty name," Cass said, taking another cookie. "I want to grow up to be pretty like you but my hair is the wrong color."

"I think you'll be much prettier than me," Cadence said, reaching out to ruffle the little girl's red curls. "Not everyone has beautiful curly red hair like you."

"My daddy did. That's what my mommy said. She says I remind her too much of him. That's why she drinks that smelly stuff and sleeps a lot."

Giving Cadence a knowing look, Viv hugged the little girl.

"Anytime you need something or get scared, you come right here and get me," Viv said, turning Cass's little face to look into hers.

"Okay, Miss Viv," Cass said, standing up and taking one more cookie for the road. "Do you have any scraps today?"

"You bet I do, kiddo," Viv said. "They are in the box right back there on the counter. You can get it and come right back."

Cass ran into the kitchen and was soon back with the box.

Cadence couldn't help but notice the child's threadbare coat that was a size too small, the lack of gloves or a hat, and pants with holes in the knees. The child would freeze if they had much of a winter, and the men at the Triple T were predicting it would be a cold one.

Swallowing back her tears, Cadence waited while Viv gave Cass another hug before asking if she could give her a hug as well.

Cadence gently hugged the little girl, then pulled back to find Cass looking at her.

"You smell so nice, Miss Cady," Cass said, staring at her new friend with big, bright eyes.

Cadence impulsively grabbed her scarf and wrapped it around Cass's neck and over her ears.

"Thank you for that most wonderful compliment, Cass. And for that hug," Cadence said, tucking the ends of the scarf into the little girl's coat. "A hug like that deserves a little treat, don't you think Aunt Viv?"

"Absolutely, honey," Viv said, then waved as Cass walked to the door. "You take care of that scarf and don't lose it. You might want to take it off right before you go home."

"Okay, Miss Viv," Cass said as she opened the door. "Thanks for hugging me, Miss Cady. Bye."

They watched as Cass ran across the busy highway and up the street toward her tiny run-down home.

"What can we do for that poor child, Aunt Viv? There must be something," Cadence said, brushing at a tear. "She won't make it through the winter in clothes like that. Doesn't her mother care at all?"

"Unfortunately, the more Micki drinks the less she seems to care. I'm just afraid she'll drink herself right into the grave and leave Cass alone."

"I just feel so helpless. Are you sure there isn't something we can do," Cadence asked looking out the window, unaccustomed to the maternal feelings surging through her.

"Pray, honey, just pray."

><><

A few days before Thanksgiving, Henry came in for dinner complaining that his joints were aching "something fierce" and it was going to snow.

The rest of the crew gave him a bad time and reminded him they rarely had snow before the middle of December.

"You mark my words, you bunch of smarty-pants whippersnappers," Henry said in disgust. "There will be snow on the ground in the morning."

After cleaning up the dinner dishes, Cadence went into the parlor where she had set up the sewing machine and was working on making a simple pieced quilt in hopes of giving it to Cass. She found a bunch of fabric scraps in a box and Denni told her to do whatever she wanted with them.

After that first phone call, Denni called once a week to get Cadence's update on what was happening at the ranch since her boys tended to leave out the details a woman preferred to hear. They talked about horses, cattle, fences and feed. She wanted to hear about the cardinals that were nesting in the tree by the mud room, the way the mums around the front porch were still blooming, and how a squirrel was driving the dogs mad as it packed in nuts for the winter. The details about home the boys didn't notice. Cadence enjoyed speaking with Denni and found they had many things in common. They liked several of the same authors, enjoyed crafts and sewing, and they both played the piano.

Denni was planning to join them for Thanksgiving dinner, along with her mother, and Cadence had been busy for days baking and finalizing menu plans. She wanted everything to be perfect for Trey's mom and grandmother.

As she stitched the quilt, she kept one eye looking out the window, watching for snow. Unable to keep focused on the square she was sewing, Cadence finally turned off the machine and light. Stepping into the great room where the guys were watching a football game on TV, she bid them goodnight, then went to her room.

Turning on her laptop, she realized she hadn't checked her messages for a while and spent some time responding to friends, Neil, and a message from her mom. Looking up a few recipes, she tugged out her hair band and ran her fingers through the waves, letting it fall down her back. Glancing at the clock, she didn't realize it was so late. Shutting off the computer, she jumped when a knock sounded at her door.

"Come in," she called, not certain which of the Thompson men would be knocking this late at night.

Trey opened the door and stood leaning against the frame. He had to take a minute to catch his breath and chase his thoughts back together. Cady sat on the bed with the computer on her lap, her hair falling around her like a silk curtain, backlit by the bedside lamp.

She was so beautiful. He felt his mouth go dry and his heart begin to gallop. Remembering the reason for disturbing her, he offered her an enticing smile.

"I was wondering if I could talk you into riding with me." Trey asked hesitantly.

"Sure," Cadence said, surprised Trey would knock on her door to ask her that before going to bed. "I should have time tomorrow to go with you."

"Not tomorrow, Cady. Now. Would you go riding with me now?" Trey was hoping like everything she would say yes.

"Now? But it's late and cold and we've both got a lot to do tomorrow."

"I know all that, but look outside."

Cadence stood up and opened her patio door. Soft, feathery snowflakes drifted down. The whole world seemed to be blanketed in a special kind of quiet reserved for the first snowfall of the season. Holding out her hand, she caught a few flakes and watched them quickly melt in her palm.

"Trey, it's lovely," Cadence said, grinning over her shoulder at him. Glancing back outside, she decided to throw caution to the wind and go for a ride. How many opportunities would she have to do something like this?

"Does that mean you'll go?" Trey asked, stepping away from the doorframe and walking into the room.

"I'll go," Cadence said, unable to resist the urge to lose herself in Trey's eyes.

"I was prepared to bribe you if need be," Trey said, handing her a box wrapped in plain brown paper.

Tearing off the paper, Cadence gasped to see a boot box. Tossing it on the bed, she whipped it open and nearly jumped up and down in her excitement.

She threw her arms around Trey and gave him a tight hug.

"I can't believe you bought these, but thank you so much," Cadence said taking the boots out of the box and admiring them. "I'll pay you back."

"These are a gift, Cady. No pay back is necessary. Watching you smile when you ride is all the payment I need," Trey said, stuffing his hands in his pockets to keep from giving in to his desire to hold her. Or kiss her. Or both. He wouldn't mind if she threw her arms around him again for another hug, either.

"Put on your warm socks and you might want to add a few layers of clothes. It's cold out there. Make sure to cover up your ears and bring your gloves. I'll meet you outside in a few minutes."

"Yes, mother," Cadence said with an impish grin that shot straight to Trey's heart.

When Trey saw it start to snow, he couldn't wait for Trent to go to bed so he could put his plan into action. He wasn't an expert on romance, but he thought riding in the moonlight with big feathery flakes of snow falling gently down had to be right up there at the top of the list. It took him a good five minutes of standing in the hallway giving himself a mental pep talk before he could bring himself to knock on Cady's door. He was glad he'd worked up the courage to do it.

Running to the barn, he saddled his horse, Powder, as well as Sasha, the mare Cady had been riding. She and Sasha seemed to have hit it off and got along well.

He walked the horses to the back step just as Cadence came outside. She was bundled up from head to toe, wearing her jeans inside her new boots and smiling at him like he was her hero.

Holding Sasha's reins until Cadence was settled in the saddle, he handed them to her then mounted Powder. He led them down a narrow path along the ridgeline. When they topped the rise, he stopped and turned back so they could see the moon and snow reflected in the water of the pond. Cadence was sure she had never seen anything quite so beautiful. She knew she would never forget this night and was grateful to Trey for creating the memory for her.

Tilting her head back with her face to the sky, big fat flakes drifted onto her cheeks and eyelashes. Blinking, she laughed then stuck out her tongue to catch snowflakes.

Trey watched her, mesmerized. Where was his tightly laced Miss Greer? She seemed to have completely disappeared the minute she pulled on those turquoise boots. The desire to kiss her was about to take over his good sense as he watched snowflakes melt into all the thick dark hair she'd left down in her haste to come outside. He couldn't get enough of Cady and her joy in such simple things that he often took for granted.

"Come on, boss-man. Aren't you even going to try to catch a snowflake on your tongue?" Cadence teased, her face glowing in the moonlight.

"Some of us are too grown-up for such silliness," he said, striving to come off as reserved and sophisticated. It was difficult to accomplish when he was incapable of wiping the grin off his face.

"Right," Cadence said, sticking her tongue out again. "Since I'm the one who is usually the grown-up around here, that means you have to do it."

"Maybe I don't like the taste of snow," Trey said, glancing up at the sky.

"Are you serious?" Cadence said, staring at him in disbelief. "You don't like the taste of snow? Circle this day in red on the calendar. I've now officially heard everything."

Trey laughed and stuck out his tongue at her, catching a snowflake in the process.

"That was very mature, mister boss-man."

"Just following your fine example, Cady."

They sat in silence and watched the snow for a few more minutes before Trey decided they better head back home. Slowly picking their way along the ridge line, Trey pulled Powder close to Sasha and tugged them both to a stop. Cadence looked at him and he gave in to the longing to taste her lips.

Tipping back his hat, he pulled off a glove then reached over and cupped her chin. Leaning down, he pressed his lips to hers, surprised by the warmth and sweetness he found. Shocked that Cady didn't pull back or slap him across the face, Trey deepened the kiss and felt her respond. Ready to pull her from the saddle into his arms, Trey remembered they were not in the best place for him to get carried away by his amorous feelings. Touching his forehead to hers, he kissed her nose, brushed her lips again and tugged on his glove.

They rode the rest of the way to the house in silence.

Cadence wasn't sure what just happened, but whatever it was, she felt like she'd swallowed a whole bucket of butterflies. Her entire body tingled and the only thing she could think of was that in all the times she'd been kissed in her 27 years, nothing had prepared her for the touch of Trey's lips on hers. She'd like to repeat the process and give it more thought, but the way he was quietly riding back to the barn, she was pretty sure that wasn't an option. How could he be so calm and collected when it was taking all her concentration just to stay seated on Sasha?

Trey rode up to the barn and dismounted. Cady followed suit and he took Sasha's reins.

"Go on up to the house, Cady," he said in a rumbling voice as he led the horses inside. "No need for you to stay out in the cold."

Following him in the barn, she ignored him and led Sasha to her stall, tugged off her saddle and blanket, then started to brush her down.

Pleased that Cady had stayed with him instead of going back to the house, Trey finished brushing Powder, gave the horses a little measure of grain then closed their stalls. He took Cady's hand as he turned off the barn light and closed the door.

Walking across the now-white yard, their footprints leaving tracks in the snow, Cadence wasn't sure what was spinning around in Trey's handsome head. She wondered what had made him grow so quiet. Maybe he hadn't enjoyed the ride or the kiss. That thought nearly made her stumble on the back steps.

Coming in the mudroom door, Trey took off his boots, hung up his coat and hat then turned to watch Cady struggle to use the boot jack.

Standing behind her, he put a hand on her thigh and moved her foot into the proper position. Cadence was sure he could feel her leg begin to tremble at his touch.

"Just like that, darlin'," he said his breath warm and soft by her ear.

Goose bumps popped out on her neck and sprang up on her arms, but Cadence removed the other boot then slowly stepped aside and took off her coat.

Trey tugged the band from her head that covered her ears and dug both hands into her snow-dampened hair. Pulling her to his chest, he groaned as he buried his face in her hair and inhaled the fresh scent that was solely Cady.

Cadence, surprised by the intensity of the emotions racing through her, slipped her hands around Trey's back and held him close. Where her lips rested against his neck, she could feel his pulse thrumming rapidly.

When the stubble of his jaw brushed her cheek, she raised her head and felt herself go under in the turbulent waves of his amazing eyes. Longing and something more, something Cadence couldn't quite describe, created a scorching look of heat that warmed her from head to toe.

"Cady," he whispered before lowering his lips to hers. This kiss was gentle, soft, loving.

Cadence ran her hands up his muscled arms and across his broad shoulders, twining her fingers together at the back of his neck.

Groaning again, Trey put his hands to the small of her back and drew her closer to him. This time his kiss was demanding and urgent. Cadence would have collapsed at his feet if Trey hadn't been holding her up. She held nothing back as she returned the kiss.

Trey scooped her into his arms and carried her inside, kissing her all the way to her bedroom door. Coming up for air, he suddenly realized where they were and what was about to happen.

Setting her carefully on her feet, he took a step back and looked genuinely contrite. Drawing in a ragged breath, he ran a hand through his hair before looking into her face.

"My apologies, Cady," Trey said, trying to ignore the feelings still plowing through him. "I had no right to do that and I'm sorry."

Trying to compose herself, Cadence leaned against the door frame for support. She had never been swept off her feet before. Never been held that closely in a man's arms. Never wanted so badly for a kiss to last forever. Taking a deep breath, she couldn't believe she had let things go so far. She knew better than that.

"I'm sorry as well," she said, in a whisper. "I... um... shouldn't have let things get so carried away."

"Cady, I..." Trey took a step toward her, reaching out for her hand.

Instead, Cadence took a step back, into the safety of her room. Using the door as a shield she started to close it. She looked at Trey, his eyes still filled with wanting.

"Thank you for the ride, Trey," Cadence said, her knees trembling behind the door. "It's something I'll remember always. Goodnight."

Trey watched as Cady closed the door before he went into the kitchen and sat at the counter staring at nothing. He finally warmed up a mug of milk and added a packet of hot chocolate mix. Stirring the drink, he observed Trent as he wandered in to the kitchen, his short brown hair standing up on end.

"What are you doing, bro? Haven't you gone to bed yet?" Trent asked, getting himself a glass of water.

"Nope," Trey said, sipping his chocolate.

"Some reason you are still up?" Trent asked sitting down beside him with a big yawn.

"Yep."

"Want to elaborate on that?"

"Nope."

"You okay?" Trent asked, getting a bit concerned about Trey's one syllable responses.

"Nope."

"Anything I can do?"

"Nope."

"Does this involve a certain female that you've taken a shine to?" Trent stood up and put his empty glass in the dishwasher.

"Maybe."

"Ah, now we are getting somewhere," Trent said, leaning against the counter as Trey sipped his chocolate. Thunder had settled onto his brother's forehead and he was wound up tighter than an eight-day clock.

"You are up in the middle of the night drinking chocolate, looking like you're ready to punch something. Your hair is wet and the vein in your neck is about to explode. You have the look of a man who's been kissing a girl, and kissing her quite thoroughly no doubt, and all I can get out of you is a maybe. There's no maybe about it, man, you've got it bad."

Trey shot his brother a glare that would have sent lesser men running for the door.

"Go to bed, Trent," Trey said, finishing off his chocolate and putting the mug in the dishwasher.

"But, bro…"

Trey gave him a shove toward their rooms.

"Just drop it," Trey said as they walked down the hall.

Trey went in his room and closed the door but Trent stood in the hall thinking for a few minutes before returning to bed. There was no doubt about it. His brother was a goner.

Chapter Eight

Plans are only good intentions unless they immediately degenerate into hard work.

Peter F. Drucker

Thanksgiving Day arrived along with a bright blue sky filled with warm sunshine. The snow from a few days before had melted and the temperature was now above freezing.

Worried about Denni and her mother driving from The Dalles if the roads were bad, Cadence was glad for the sunny day. Aunt Viv and Uncle Joe had also been invited to join them, since the café was closed for the holiday. Trey had personally invited Micki and Cass, but the only response he received was a rickety door being slammed in his face.

Cadence had managed to avoid Trey since their moonlight ride. Or as much as you can avoid someone you share a home with, feed twice a day, and fold their clean underwear. She supposed it would be better to think in terms of managing to not be alone with Trey. At the end of the day, she stayed in the parlor with the sewing machine and ignored the men. Trent watched TV while Trey hid in his office. The arrangement seemed to be working well.

Mostly.

If Cadence could just get her perfidious heart to follow her orders instead of wanting to be near Trey. She had never been swept off her feet before and the wonder of that experience haunted her not only at night, but persisted throughout the day as well.

But the last thing she needed, Cadence reminded herself for the ninety-eighth time, was to get entangled with a man again. Even if Trey was all man... warm, strong, virile and magnificent.

Shaking her head, hoping to derail the direction her thoughts were headed, Cadence attempted to focus on the napkins she was folding and artfully arranging at each place setting.

Glancing at the table, Cadence was quite pleased with how festive it looked. Trent managed to find a few stalks of wheat and brought them in yesterday. Cadence whipped together a centerpiece using the wheat, some pumpkin-colored candles and a smattering of leaves.

The turkey was done, the rolls were nearly finished, potatoes were mashed, gravy was made and a variety of side dishes and salads were ready to be devoured. In addition to traditional pumpkin pie, Cadence made a gingerbread trifle with pumpkin pudding, an apple pie she planned to serve with caramel sauce, and a pan of turtle brownies. She knew Denni and Viv were both bringing a few things as well. She hoped the table could hold all of the food.

She was slathering butter over the tops of the rolls when the back door opened and Denni came inside followed by a woman who looked just like her, only older. This must be the Thompson's darling Nana.

Rinsing off her hands and wiping them dry, Cadence turned to greet the women.

"Hello, Denni," she said, taking the dishes out of Denni's hands and placing them on the counter. "I'm so glad the roads were good for you today."

"Me, too," Denni said as she took off her coat while Cadence helped Nana with hers. Taking both coats, she smiled at Cadence. "I want you to meet my mother, Ester Nordon. Mama, this is Cadence Greer."

Taking the older woman's hand in hers, Cadence smiled.

"It's so nice to meet you Mrs. Nordon. Your grandsons speak so highly of you," Cadence looked into the sweet face of the older woman and was surprised by the brilliant blue of her eyes. Trey must have inherited his eye color straight from his grandmother.

"Just call me, Nana, dear," Nana said, looking around the kitchen with approval. Cadence cleaned up the dishes as she went and kept the counters wiped down so everything looked neat and orderly. "My grandsons have told me you are quite the chef so I'm looking forward to eating my fill of your cooking today."

Cadence blushed and Denni squeezed her shoulders.

"I'm sure whatever you made is going to be delish," Denni said, walking to the table. "Doesn't the table look pretty, Mama? Goodness, Cadence, you must have been working non-stop for days to get all this done."

"I enjoyed doing it," Cadence said, placing rolls in a cloth-lined basket and bringing it to the table. She wouldn't admit it, but throwing herself into Thanksgiving preparations was the only thing that kept her from replaying the other night with Trey over and over in her mind. The thoughts flitted through with enough frequency to drive her daft as it was.

Cadence turned to see Aunt Viv and Uncle Joe pull up outside.

"Looks like everyone's here, I'll go ring the bell," Cadence said, wiping her hands on her apron.

"Do you mind if I do?" Denni asked, as she pulled open the door.

"Not at all," Cadence said with a smile. "Your two boys wouldn't stay out of my way, so I banished them to the bunkhouse earlier this morning."

Denni laughed. "They know that routine well. Lois and I used to do the same thing. It's kind of nice to have the quiet in the house before the storm."

Stepping outside, Denni rang the bell as she called hello to Viv and Joe.

It didn't take long for the house to be filled with the sound of happy, hungry people ready for a good meal. Much to everyone's surprise, Viv and Joe brought Cass with them. The little girl was wearing a new dress and shoes and was positively beaming.

Kneeling down in front of the little redhead, Cadence gave her a warm hug.

"Cass, I'm so glad you could come today. I love your dress."

"Thanks, Cady," Cass said, running her hand up and down the navy blue sailor dress. "Miss Viv said it's a Thanksgiving present. I've never had a Thanksgiving present before. Have you?"

"I haven't before today," Cadence said, walking to the table with Cass's hand in hers.

"What did you get?" Cass said, looking up at Cadence with big eyes.

Cadence leaned down and tapped the little girl on her pert nose. "You."

Cass giggled and threw her arms around Cadence, making a lump form in her throat that was hard to swallow down.

Trey came into the room and noticed Cass. After giving Cadence a shocked look, he came over and picked up the little girl, embracing her in a welcoming hug.

"Look at you, Miss Cass, all spiffed up and ready for the holiday. I'm glad you could come to our house for dinner."

"Me, too," Cass said, throwing her thin little arms around his neck. "Thank you for letting me come."

"Anytime," Trey said, carrying the little girl around the table and setting her down next to his chair. The poor little thing wasn't any bigger than a minute. He planned to make sure she ate her fill and then some.

Once everyone was seated around the table, Trey asked the blessing. The room soon filled with the sounds of good natured teasing, compliments on the food, discussions about farming, ranching, and the community. Cadence took it all in. She wasn't used to being around so many people, especially those who clearly cared for and about each other. The few gatherings she had attended with Bill's large extended family were more like opportunities to one-up each other.

Later, while Viv and Denni were helping with the dishes, Cadence asked how Cass was able to come for dinner.

"She was pounding on the door of the house bright and early this morning, so excited she couldn't stand still," Viv said. "She had a note in her hand from her mother that basically said she didn't care what we did with Cass today as long as she stayed out of her hair. I bought that dress and the shoes for her the last time I was in The Dalles and hoped to figure out a way to give them to her for Christmas. Today seemed like a good day to let her have a present. The child stunk to high-heaven, so I gave her a bath, washed her hair. Thank goodness she doesn't have lice. I gave her new undies and everything to wear today. I had her wear one of my sweaters instead of that ratty old coat. I threw all her stuff in the washer this morning, so it will at least be clean when she changes this evening. I just hope I can talk her into leaving her dress and shoes at my house. I don't think Micki would take kindly to seeing the new outfit."

"It's just a crying shame," Denni said, watching Cass sleeping on Trey's lap. She'd climbed up there after dinner and fell asleep. No one had the heart to wake her to move her, so they just let her be. Trey didn't seem to mind, which really surprised his mother. "She is such a sweet little thing, and bright, too. Shouldn't she be in school?"

"I found out she is 5," Viv said. "So technically, she could be in kindergarten, but Micki won't send her. Next year, I don't see how she can refuse. You'd think as much as she hates having Cass around, she'd want her at school part of the day."

"Won't she be behind the other kids when she does go to school?" Cadence asked, drying the last dish and putting it away.

"She's a sharp cookie, she'll catch on fast," Viv said. "I've been teaching her the alphabet and her numbers when she comes in for her afternoon food run. Even though it is just a few minutes a day, she is making progress."

"It breaks my heart to see her suffer because of her mother's stubbornness," Denni said, leaning against the counter, amazed at how quickly Trey took to the little girl. He'd never been a person who went out of his way to be around kids, so she was surprised at the attention he gave little Cass. Maybe he was finally getting ready to settle down. Hope for future grandchildren sprang up anew in her heart.

As though he sensed her watching him, Trey looked into the kitchen and smiled, first at his mother then at Cadence. Shrugging his shoulders, he raised an eyebrow and turned his attention back to the ballgame.

Cadence felt her knees start to wobble and sank down onto a barstool at the counter. If she wasn't already half in love with Trey before, her silly heart was doing back flips watching the tender way he cared for little Cass today.

A look passed between Denni and Viv, but both women were smart enough to keep their comments to themselves.

When Cass woke up from her nap, she slowly opened her eyes, studied the room and took a moment to remember where she was before looking up into the face of the cowboy who was holding her.

"Hi," she said, rubbing a little hand across her eyes.

"Hi, Cass," Trey said, helping her sit up and rubbing her back gently. "Did you have a good nap?"

"Yep. I had a happy dream."

"A happy dream, huh? What was your happy dream about?"

"I dreamed I got to stay here forever with you and Cady and never be hungry anymore."

Trey felt like a large spoon of mashed potatoes had lodged itself in his throat. How did you respond to a statement like that? While he was trying to swallow down his emotion, Cadence came to the rescue.

Walking up to the recliner where Trey sat with Cass, she held out her arms and picked up the little girl, snuggling her close.

"Did you have a good nap, sweetie-pie?"

"Yep. I did," Cass said, patting her hands on Cadence's cheeks.

"I'm glad," Cadence said, rocking from side to side holding Cass close. She absolutely loved the feel of Cass in her arms, even if the little girl was frightfully small for her age. "Would you like a snack?"

"Yes, please," Cass said, her eyes lighting up as they walked into the kitchen where an array of desserts lined the counter.

After selecting a cookie and a piece of cake, Cadence set Cass on a bar stool with her treats and a big glass of milk.

The men wandered in and decided they could all go for a second round of dessert. After that, everyone went home except for Denni, Nana, Joe, Viv and Cass.

Cadence didn't know who suggested it, but it was quickly decided they needed to send Cass home with a paper chain to count down the days until Christmas. A search through the house revealed nothing except white printer paper and a roll of plain brown paper, neither of which would make a festive chain for the little girl.

Taking a minute to think, Cadence asked Trey if she could use his computer, since it was hooked to the printer. He logged in and stood behind her while she Googled websites for Christmas paper and soon they had a pile of printed paper with everything from Santa to jolly snowmen.

Bringing glue and a few pairs of scissors to the table, everyone helped Cass make her very first paper chain. They put on thirty-one rings, so she could take one off every day, starting tomorrow. There were arguments if they should have a ring for Christmas Day or if the final one should be Christmas Eve. It was agreed to add the extra one to give Cass one more to unfold.

They had so much fun making one, a second one was assembled and Cadence hung it along the curtain rod above the kitchen sink.

When Viv and Joe were ready to leave, Cass pulled on her borrowed sweater and threw both arms around Trey's legs. He picked her up, kissed her cheek and thanked her for coming.

Watching Cadence get all teary-eyed, he passed the little girl over for her to kiss and hug before Trent took a turn and carried her out to the car.

Trying to lighten the mood, Denni started talking about all the sales she wanted to hit in Portland early the next morning for the Black Friday specials. Turning to Cadence, she gave her a once over and said, "Would you want to come with me, Cadence? It's a lot of fun and for some reason, I can't find anyone willing to get up that early and go with me."

"Oh, I don't think so Denni. By the time I get breakfast ready and drive to The Dalles, you'll have missed half the sales," Cadence said, loading the last of the dessert dishes in the dishwasher. "I appreciate the invitation, though."

"Well, maybe we can sweet talk your slave-driving boss into letting you have a day off. You could come spend the night at my house and we could take off early in the morning," Denni said, lifting a raised eyebrow at Trey.

Trey nodded his head at his mother. He didn't know exactly what she was up to, but he was pretty sure he wasn't going to like it.

"I reckon we can rustle up our own breakfast. I think we've got a few options for things to eat," Trey said, waving his arm toward the counter, still full of desserts.

"Yeah, we can manage tomorrow, Cady," Trent said. "Go with Mom and have fun. You haven't taken a full day off since you came."

"Are you sure?" Cadence asked, trying not to get too excited about the prospect of going shopping in the big city. Her mother hated to shop and most of her girlfriends didn't like to get up that early or deal with the crowds, so Cadence rarely indulged in the Black Friday experience.

"Absolutely," Trey said, taking the dishrag out of her hand. "Go pack your bag and hit the road, darlin'."

Cadence didn't waste any time in gathering up an overnight bag and clothes for shopping. Dropping her things by the back door, she helped Nana put on her coat while Trey held Denni's.

Trent ran out and started both Denni's and Cadence's car while Trey packed out the dishes his mom and grandma had brought. Cadence also filled several containers with leftovers for them to take home and enjoy.

Walking the women out to their cars, Trey let his grandmother take his arm, while Denni hooked her arm through Trent's. Cadence followed along behind carrying her bag. Trent had pulled her car up behind his mom's, so she tossed her bag in the backseat and started to open the driver's door when Trey stepped beside her. With him standing so close, she could see his eyes go from calm blue to a stormy sea.

Holding the door open for her, he waited until she was buckled in then leaned down and pecked her check.

"Have fun, Cady," Trey said, intently watching her face. "After that fine meal today, you deserve a little time off."

"Thanks, Trey," Cadence said, placing a gloved hand on his cheek and giving it a pat. "And don't eat cake for breakfast."

Trey laughed and shut her door. Running up to his mom's car, he kissed Nana's cheek and told them to drive careful.

><><

Cadence didn't know when she had ever had so much fun shopping, laughed so hard or had such a pleasant day.

She and Denni got up at an hour so early Cadence wasn't convinced it was technically Friday. They hurried to get ready and were on the road by 3:30 a.m. Denni pulled into the parking lot at Clackamas Town Center a few minutes before 5 and they hustled to get in line at one of Denni's favorite stores.

Pushed along in the rush of the crowd, Denni grabbed Cadence's hand and tugged her in the direction of the bargains she was hunting. Denni had a long list of things she was shopping for while Cadence had just a few things on her list.

She was unprepared for all the great sales and found herself buying more than she had planned.

Coming across the children's section in a huge department store, Cadence couldn't stop herself from buying a few things for Cass. Denni found her there and got caught up in the fun. By the time they were done, they had an entire wardrobe, right down to a frilly green Christmas dress picked out for Cass.

"How are we going to convince Micki to let her keep all this?" Cadence asked as they loaded up the trunk of Denni's car.

"I don't' know, but we'll worry about that later," Denni said, stuffing another bag into the already full trunk. "We couldn't just walk by those sales, though. Who ever heard of coats marked down to $10?"

Shopping their way through several more stores, Denni talked Cadence into buying a few things for herself including a teal satin dress she was sure she would never wear.

"I know it doesn't seem practical, Cady, but that is the whole point," Denni said, studying her as she came out of the dressing room. "But you have to buy it. It was made just for you. I bet if you read the tag it will say 'please hold for Cadence Greer.' Just get it, honey."

"If you say so," Cadence said with a smile as she returned to the dressing room.

Between Trey and Cass calling her Cady in front of everyone multiple times yesterday, it seemed the name had stuck. When she mentioned it to Aunt Viv, she patted her back and said "you need a new name for the new life you are carving out here. Cady is perfect."

Cadence felt different, too. She felt more like a Cady - someone ready for fun and adventure instead of being so professional and uptight. Maybe that was part of the reason she was taking such pleasure in shopping today. She wasn't even attempting to be professional and aloof. She was just enjoying her time with Denni.

Although they had met a few times and spoke on the phone every week, Cadence was surprised how well the two of them got along. Denni was funny, kind and warm.

She made Cadence feel like a friend or a daughter and for that she was most grateful.

Denni had a few more gift she wanted to buy and when Cadence was sure they couldn't fit one more thing in the car, they stopped for lunch at a quaint little tea shop where they had slices of quiche and spicy tea.

Walking back to the car, Denni smiled at Cadence. "Ready for round two?"

Cadence's head shot up and she looked over the top of the car at Denni, not sure if she was teasing or serious. Denni laughed and got in the car.

Two hours later, Cadence was sighing in pleasure at Denni's idea of round two.

Denni drove to a spa where she insisted on treating for a full experience of pedicures with foot massages and relaxing facials. Denni talked Cadence into getting her hair cut at the salon next door. Realizing it had been months since she'd had anything done with her hair, Cadence was glad to have it trimmed into beautiful wavy layers around her face and down her back.

Driving home mid-afternoon, Denni reached over and squeezed Cadence's hand.

"Thanks for spending the day with me, Cady. I had a grand time."

"Thank you for inviting me and allowing me to spend the night," Cadence said, sincerely. "I have never had so much fun shopping before and the spa was beyond wonderful. I had no idea what round two meant, but thank you for the opportunity to find out."

Denni smiled and sent Cadence a wink.

"It was my pleasure. I enjoyed having someone to shop with who could keep up with me. Nana never enjoyed it all that much and now the experience just wears her out thinking about it. With no daughters of my own, my boys would rather be forced to run through town naked than be dragged to a mall the day after Thanksgiving. It was so much fun to get to know you better. I'm really glad Trey and Trent hired you."

"I'm glad they did, too," Cadence said with a grin. "Otherwise I'd have missed out on this fabulous shopping experience."

"Speaking of Trey," Denni said, throwing out some bait she hoped Cadence would catch. "What do you think of him? Do you like working for him?"

"You raised fine men," Cadence said, wondering where Denni was headed with her questions. "He and Trent are both very polite and kind and surprisingly neat. There isn't a lot of work to being their housekeeper."

"Well, I'm glad to hear that," Denni said with a nod. "Lois and I tried to train those boys to behave like gentleman. Most of the time they make their mama proud. I noticed Trey seems to be quite taken with you."

"Oh," Cadence said, trying to stay noncommittal as she caught on to where the conversation was leading. Maybe she could veer Denni off track. "I noticed he was very taken with little Cass. How do you suppose she can be such a sweet little thing considering her home life?"

"I don't know, but she is something special," Denni agreed. "I was surprised to see how easily Trey handled her yesterday. He's never spent much time around kids or showed any interest in them. Something has definitely changed in that son of mine. What do you suppose brought that all about?"

"I couldn't say," Cadence said, looking out the window and thinking the car suddenly felt stifling. She leaned her cheek against the window's cool glass and watched the scenery fly by as they headed back toward The Dalles.

"Couldn't say or won't say?" Denni teased, noticing Cadence's cheeks turn pink. Patting her leg, Denni grinned. "I'll quit my digging expedition for today. Now, you've got to tell me how you made that wonderful caramel sauce for the pie yesterday."

><><

Driving through Grass Valley, Cadence decided to make a quick stop at Viv's Café before driving back to the Triple T. Pulling into a parking space, she walked inside and had just tugged off her gloves, when Cass came tearing across the street and in the door, right into Cadence.

Tears streamed down her little face and she held the shredded remnants of her Christmas paper chain in her cold fingers.

Kneeling down, Cadence pulled her close and let her sob.

"What is it, sweetie-pie? What's wrong?" Cadence asked, picking her up and carrying her to a booth. Sitting down, she held the little girl on her lap and grabbed some paper napkins to wipe off the tears and swipe at her nose.

"Mommy found my paper chain and said it was stupid," Cass said between sobs. "Then she tore it up and threw it at me. Why is she so mean, Cady? Why's my mommy mean to me?"

Cadence had all she could do not to cry right along with Cass. Pulling her close and rocking her back and forth in the booth, she caught Aunt Viv's eye who came out with a mug of hot chocolate and a plate of cookies for Cass.

Wiping up the tears again, Cadence pulled off Cass's coat and stood her up before she stood and removed her own coat, then sat back in the booth, pulling Cass next to her.

"Here, honey, you eat these cookies and drink this hot chocolate. It will make you feel better," Viv said, bringing

Cadence a cup of tea and pouring herself a cup of coffee. "Let's see that paper chain of yours."

Cass placed a wadded up mess on the table and Viv carefully tried to find some way to salvage it. It was beyond repair.

Seeing the ball of paper and the tears ready to spill over in Cass's eyes again, Cadence put her arm around the little girl and kissed the top of her head.

"Tell you what, sweetie-pie, why don't we share my paper chain. I'll bring it in here to the café and you can come take the links off for me, because I won't be able to come every day to do it. How would that be?"

"Really? You'd share yours with me?" Cass looked up at her with a disbelieving stare.

"Absolutely," Cadence said, trying to sound serious. "You'd be doing me a big favor. With all those big men at my house, I get so busy cooking and cleaning for them I might forget to take off a link and Christmas will sneak up on me. This way you can help me stay on track."

"Okay," Cass said, taking a sip of her warm chocolate. Viv and Cadence could see the appreciation in the little girl's eyes as she savored the treat.

"I can't bring it in today, but if I have it here tomorrow, will that be okay?"

"Yep. I'll take off a link when I come to get scraps, right Miss Viv?"

"Right you are, honey," Viv said.

Suddenly a thought struck Cass and she sat up straight in the booth. "What about Sunday. You aren't open on Sunday."

"How about if you come in the afternoon Sunday like you usually do? I'll be here just in time for you to take off a link. How does that sound?"

"Great!" Cass said, eating another cookie and wearing a smile.

Finishing up her treat, Viv packed up a box of "scraps" and sent Cass home. Watching her run across the road, Cadence felt tears sting her eyes. She turned to her aunt, anger straightening her spine.

"How could Micki do something so mean? Cass is just a baby. How could her mother be so cruel?" Cadence asked, knowing her aunt wouldn't have an answer.

"I don't know, honey, but some people have hurts too big to handle on their own and when they don't let God help them, they do things they normally wouldn't. Micki isn't a bad person she just doesn't know how to get past Frank dying."

Cadence tried not to judge Micki, but it was so hard when Cass bore the brunt of her mother's pain and anger.

"Did you have fun today with Denni?" Viv asked, giving her an odd look. "I just noticed you got your hair cut. It looks lovely."

Dragging her thoughts back from Cass, Cadence smiled.

"I had a blast. Denni is so fun and I had no idea you could get so many great deals that early in the morning," Cadence said. She told Viv about some of the things she purchased for Cass and herself. "We had lunch at a tea shop and then went to a spa. It was beyond marvelous. Have you ever gone to a spa?"

"Nope," Viv said, taking a sip of her coffee.

"We will definitely have to do something about that one of these days," Cadence said, already making plans in her head to take her aunt for an indulgent experience.

"Now, don't go getting any ideas. Maybe in the spring," Viv said, looking over her coffee cup.

Cadence glanced at the clock on the wall and decided she better get home or dinner would be late.

"I've got to get home or the boys will be eating leftovers for dinner, provided they didn't clean them up for breakfast," Cadence said, pulling on her coat and gloves.

Viv walked her to the door and kissed her cheek.

"You look real pretty, honey. Having a day to play in the city did you a world of good."

"Thanks, Aunt Viv. I'll see you tomorrow."

Cadence hurried home and had barely stopped the car when Trent jogged over from the barn and Trey came out of the house.

"We started to think Mom had kidnapped you," Trent teased, grabbing an armful of bags.

"Did you have a fun day?" Trey asked, admiring the color in her cheeks and the way her hair tumbled around her shoulders. Before he could stop himself, he brushed a lock back from her face and put it behind her ear. "I like your haircut. It looks nice and so do you. "

Cadence couldn't believe he actually noticed.

"Thanks. I had a great time. Your mom was so much fun and quite the shopper."

"Glad to hear it," Trey said, holding open the mud room door for her as she led the way into the kitchen.

Trent piled bags on the kitchen table and headed out for another load.

"Did you two buy out the stores?" Trey teased, placing more bags on the table.

"Almost," Cadence said with a grin. "I'll have to show you what we found for Cass."

Trey's eyes softened at the mention of the little girl. When Trent came back in with her overnight bag and the last of her purchases, she told them what had happened that afternoon.

"Short of kidnapping her, I don't know what else to do," Trey said. "She's already been turned in to the department of human services more times than you could count. If a caseworker shows up to investigate, Micki cleans up her act long enough to convince them nothing is wrong and the cycle starts all over again."

"So how are you going to give Cass these things? Micki won't let her keep them," Trent said, bringing up a point they all knew to be true.

"I don't know, but your mom and I decided to worry about those details later. We just couldn't keep from buying her a few things."

Trent and Trey smiled, knowing their mother on a shopping excursion was a force to be reckoned with.

Plopping down on barstools, Trent and Trey hung their hats from their knees and looked at Cadence expectantly.

"Well, let's start the show and tell," Trent said.

"Show and tell?" Cadence asked, taking off her dress coat and looking at the Thompson brothers.

"Mom used to pile everything on the table and would show us all the great deals she got, except the stuff she bought for us, of course. She would hide those things in the back of the parlor closet which we would find at some point before Christmas and know everything we were getting."

"You two are pathetic." Cadence looked at them and shook her head. "And ornery. I think Santa should stiff you this year, for being naughty little boys."

Trey laughed and waved his hand at the table.

"Let's see what you got, darlin'."

Cadence showed them the clothes she bought for Cass along with a few storybooks. She passed around the gifts she bought for Viv and Joe and her parents, and the sign she bought for Neil for his cabin. She didn't show them her dress or the gifts she'd picked up for them. When she was done, they helped her pack everything back to her room including the bags of gift wrap, ribbon and tags. She thought she'd use the guest room across the hall as a gift-wrapping station. She didn't think Trent or Trey would mind and they could use it as well, if they had anything they wanted to wrap.

Stashing the gifts in her closet, Cadence pulled out the teal dress and held it against her as she looked in the mirror. It was fancy and lovely and completely impractical for life in Grass Valley. But she loved it and hoped she'd find some special reason to wear it.

Hanging it in the closet, she quickly changed into jeans and a sweatshirt before returning to the kitchen, ready to make dinner.

Trent and Trey were sitting at the table, reading the paper.

"So, what sounds good for dinner to you guys?" Cadence asked, pulling an apron over her head and tying the strings in back.

"Nothing," Trent said, not looking up from the sports page.

"Pardon?" Cadence said, sure she heard him wrong.

"Nothing, Cady," Trey said, looking over the top of the paper.

Stepping around to the table, she put a cool hand on Trent's forehead.

"No fever, you aren't flushed. Are you two sick?" she asked, concerned.

"You better check my forehead, too," Trey said, trying to look ill. He felt fine until Cady's skin connected with his. Her hand definitely caused a fever where it settled on his head, and searing heat flooded through him. Grabbing her hand and kissing her palm, he leaned back in the chair and grinned.

"We're just fine, darlin'. We may have over-indulged in the leftovers today, though."

Cadence snatched her hand back from Trey and marched to the fridge. She opened the door and was surprised to see the twosome had worked their way through a considerable amount of food.

"Is there anything you two didn't eat?" she asked, hoping to see a little remorse on their faces. None was forthcoming.

"Broccoli," Trey said, returning to reading his paper. "We left the broccoli alone."

She had been planning on using some of the leftovers to make dinner for the hands. Now she'd have to whip up something else.

"I can see the wheels spinning and the only person you need to worry about feeding tonight is you," Trey added. "The hands have the rest of the weekend off and goodness only knows what kind of trouble they've gone off to find. They'll be back for breakfast Monday."

Cadence poured herself a glass of milk and sat at the table, picking up the lifestyle section. "Good to know. Do you two want your usual breakfast tomorrow?"

"No, Ma'am," Trent said, as he turned the page. "I'm not sure I'll want to eat anything for a few days."

"What exactly did you two eat?" Cadence asked.

"I told you, everything except the broccoli," Trey said.

"Seriously?" Cadence couldn't believe they could be that juvenile.

Trey leaned forward, his arms on the table, hands folded in front of him. He couldn't keep a twinkle from sparkling in his eye.

"Here it is, Cady. You told me no cake for breakfast, so we each had two pieces of pie and some of that layered pumpkin stuff you made, which, by the way, was really good. Then we had a snack of brownies and some of the cookies Nana left behind. For lunch we made sandwiches with the left-over turkey, piled on potatoes, gravy, dressing, sweet potatoes, and even had a spoon or two of the salad so we could say we ate our vegetables. We had another snack this afternoon with the cake we couldn't have for breakfast and some of that caramel sauce you made stirred into the vanilla ice cream. That was way beyond awesome. Just before you came home, we went through the same routine as lunch but used ham instead of the turkey. We are stuffed. Full. Gorged, even."

Cadence was laughing by this time and Trent had the grace to blush.

"You two are complete pigs," Cadence said, drinking her milk. "Can't you control yourselves at all around food? Do I need to enroll you in some overeater's anonymous program?"

"Now see here," Trey said, snapping upright in his chair, which produced a groan from his full stomach. "We've never had this much good food left unprotected in the house before. Lois and Mom wouldn't let us get away with snitching whatever we wanted and you weren't here to stop us. Besides, you are a better cook than both of them put together."

"So what you're saying is the two of you need a babysitter to dole out your meals," Cadence teased.

Trey shot her a glare and moved from the table to his recliner in the great room. Trent followed, flopping down on the couch and stretching out with a groan.

"If we fall asleep here, just turn out the light and throw a blanket on us," Trent said.

Cadence laughed and went off to the parlor to sew. She had no idea grown men could act like such ill behaved children, or maybe it was just the Thompson boys.

Chapter Nine

It takes as much energy to wish as it does to plan.
Eleanor Roosevelt

"Just what do you think you are doing?" Trey asked as he walked into the barn and caught Cadence climbing up the loft ladder.

Startled, Cadence would have fallen if Trey hadn't been right behind her and held her steady with his hand pressed to her back and his face against her fanny.

"I … um.." Cadence clutched the ladder, unable to think with Trey's hand hot on her back. She thought it might burn a hole right through her sweater.

"You what?" Trey asked, enjoying the view in front of him way more than he should.

"I wanted to get down the Christmas decorations today and I couldn't find you or Trent to help me," Cadence said, tugging her thoughts back together as she stepped down off the ladder.

"What did I tell you about going up into the loft when you were by yourself?" Trey was slightly annoyed that she hadn't taken his warning seriously. Cadence didn't even have on a coat. Just some soft sweater thing that felt wonderful beneath his hands.

Pig-headed, insane, stubborn woman.

"Not to do it, but…"

"No buts, Miss Greer, except your very cute one standing down here while I bring the stuff down. Got it?"

Trey asked as he hurried up the ladder and turned to look down at her.

"Got it," Cadence said, somewhat ashamed to have been caught disobeying a direct order as well as studying his retreating form as he shinnied up the ladder.

Trey could be pretty bossy when he wanted to be and right now was one of those times. Cadence was all set to get irritated over his high-handed man-ways when she realized what he had said about her posterior. That immediately dissolved any anger she was building.

When Trey leaned over the top with a box and handed it to her, she sent him a dazzling smile that nearly made him lean too far over the edge and lose his balance.

"Confounded woman," Trey muttered to himself as he pulled box after box out of the storage room. "Thinks she can smile and make everything fine. Dang if she isn't right."

It didn't take long for Trey to hand the boxes down, close up the storage room and hustle down the ladder. He wasn't going to tell Cadence, but the day he found her stranded up there, he'd personally nailed the ladder to the wall with spikes so big, it would take Paul Bunyan to yank it loose. He assumed if there was something Cady wanted up there, she wouldn't stand around waiting for him or Trent to fetch it for her. As annoying as it was, he had to admire her spunk.

Seeing Trent in the machine shed, Trey hollered at him to come help pack the boxes into the house. The two men packed boxes in while Cadence unpacked the treasures inside. When the plunder covered the table and the kitchen counters, she asked them if they had any preference where decorations were placed. They didn't really care, so they told her to do whatever she pleased. Leaving a box of decorations in the mudroom for the tree they still needed to get, they hauled the rest of the empty boxes back out to the barn.

Cadence spent the entire morning decking the halls and enjoying the wonderful decorations the Thompson family had obviously collected over the years. Unable to stop herself, she called Denni and asked her thoughts on where to place the fat snowman or how she usually displayed the group of carolers.

Denni was thrilled Cadence had thought to call and took her on a holiday stroll down the Thompson family's memory lane.

"I should have invited you to come out to help," Cadence said, as she draped fake pine boughs above the fireplace mantle in the great room.

"Maybe we can plan it for next year, honey," Denni said. "I'm not sure I would have had the energy to help you today after our full day of shopping."

Cadence told her about Trent and Trey getting a little carried away with the leftovers which had Denni laughing hysterically.

"Tell them no more treats until Christmas if they can't behave any better than that."

"Will do, Denni," Cadence said with a laugh. "I better get this finished up. Stop by next week when you come for church and see if I did okay with the decorating."

"I will," Denni said. "And I'll bring Nana along. She so enjoyed meeting you."

"I enjoyed meeting her and spending time with you yesterday. Thanks again, Denni."

After hanging up, Cadence fixed herself a turkey salad for lunch, finished the decorating then went into her room and brought out a Christmas music box that had been in her family for years and years. Her dad said his grandfather purchased it as a wedding gift for his bride. Placing it in the great room on the big coffee table, Cadence stood back and admired her morning's work. Everything looked festive and lovely.

Taking a deep breath, she realized the house even smelled like Christmas from the sachets Denni had tucked into the storage boxes.

Putting on her coat and boots, Cadence took down the paper chain over the kitchen sink and went out to start her car, surprised to find it had started snowing.

Turning onto the highway, the snow turned to sleet and the road looked icy.

Cadence had never driven on bad roads, but supposed she would have to learn how if she planned to spend the winter in Grass Valley. She'd heard enough talk to know they had real winters with wind, ice and snow storms. It looked like she was about to get first-hand experience with the snow and ice.

Gingerly driving the few miles into town, Cadence had a greater appreciation for the four-wheel drive gas-guzzling pickups most people in the county seemed to drive. Her car, while handy to zip around and run errands, was not the easiest thing to maneuver on slick roads. Coming into town, she slowed down and applied the brakes to pull into the parking lot at Viv's Café.

Instead of stopping, though, her car began to slide and fishtailed across both lanes of traffic. Knowing she was going to die when the semi truck that was bearing down on her slammed into her out-of-control car, Cadence sent a prayer heavenward as the Cruiser slid off the road and came to rest just inches from the café.

Holding the steering wheel in a death grip, Cadence took a deep breath then another before she opened her eyes. Turning her head, she found herself staring into Trey's ocean eyes, shooting hot blue sparks at her through the window.

Opening her door, she barely had time to unfasten her seat belt before Trey grabbed her out of the car and pulled her into a tight hug.

"Are you crazy, woman?" Trey hollered, hugging her tighter. "Do you have a death wish? Are you trying to get yourself killed?"

"No," Cadence whispered, clinging to him. After her wild ride, her pulse was hammering and her knees had all the strength of a strand of over-cooked spaghetti.

"Well, only a crazy fool would drive your car on ice-covered roads," Trey said, rubbing his hands comfortingly across her back and up and down her arms.

"Trey, I…" Cadence felt tears sting the backs of her eyes and a lump fill her throat.

Seeing the tears forming, Trey planted a kiss on her that had Aunt Viv and every patron in the café pressing their noses to the glass to get a better look.

"I'm sorry. I didn't mean to yell," Trey said, his lips close to her ear. "I lost 10 years off my lifespan when I saw you slide in front of that semi. Please, next time you need to come to town and the roads are bad, take one of our trucks or find someone to drive you."

Cadence still couldn't speak. She was in shock over her near-accident, dazed by Trey's yelling, and emotionally train-wrecked from that kiss. Looking up, she noticed the faces in the café window intently watching.

Her face flushed five shades of red and she buried her head against Trey's broad chest.

"I'm going to go home and pack and you'll never see me again," she said, without looking up.

Trey stiffened and jerked his head up, sure he had misheard Cadence.

"I can't face anyone again after all that. I'm too embarrassed to be seen in town again."

Trey's heart resumed beating after her announcement caused it to temporarily stop. He laughed and hugged her again.

"Cady, we've all slid around on the ice before and you don't have any experience driving in it. As for our kiss, don't let it bother you. I'm sure it isn't the first time they've seen people kiss in public and I know it won't be the last."

"How do you know? Do people often stand out in front of the café kissing?" she asked.

"Nope."

"But…"

Trey pulled her close and kissed her again, a light, teasing kiss then shot her a wicked grin as he closed her car door and escorted her inside the café.

Speechless, Cadence just let him drag her inside, take off her coat and nudge her into a booth where her cheeks felt like they were aflame.

Taking off his hat and coat, Trey sat across from her and smiled.

Viv came over and sat down beside Cadence, putting her arm around her and giving her a squeeze.

"Honey, you about scared me half to death," Viv said, swiping at her eyes. "Someone was watching over you and that little car of yours for sure and certain, or you'd be decorating the grill of that truck."

Viv turned to Trey and shot him a reproving glare.

"And you, Casanova," Viv said, shaking her finger under his nose. "Who gave you permission to go smooching my niece like that in public?"

Trey looked somewhat chastened, although instead of saying anything he shot Viv a wink.

Suddenly, Cadence sat up and started to push Viv out of the way.

"Someone needs to go get Cass," she said, her voice panicked. "She shouldn't be running across the road on this ice."

"I'll go get her," Trey said, grabbing his coat and hat and hustling out the door. He carefully walked across the highway then hot-footed it up the street toward Micki's house. He soon returned, carrying Cass, who was glowing with happiness and chatting a mile a minute.

Cadence retrieved the paper chain from the car, along with a little present for Cass. She was settled next to Viv with a cup of tea by the time Trey came back in with the little girl.

"Look who I found rolling in the snow," Trey teased as he set Cass down in the booth and slid in beside her.

"I wasn't rolling in the snow," Cass said with a giggle. "I couldn't walk on the street. It made my feet slipper-slide."

"I bet it did," Cadence said. "It made my whole car slipper-slide."

"It did?" Cass asked, taking a bite of a cookie.

"Yep, and everybody watched it, didn't they Miss Viv?" Trey teased.

"They watched something, that's for sure," Viv said, still frowning at Trey.

Cass chatted away, enjoying her afternoon treat. Cadence handed her the paper chain and she took off two, one for Friday and one for today, and then helped Viv hang it by the counter where she could reach it.

She came back to the table and gave Cadence a hug.

"Thank you for sharing your chain with me, Cady," she said, holding tight to Cadence's neck.

"You are so welcome, sweetie-pie," Cadence said, removing a small box from her coat pocket and handing it to Cass.

"Is this a present? For me?" Cass asked, her blue eyes growing wide.

"Yes it is. Just for you," Cadence said, pulling her onto her lap. "Go ahead, open it up."

Cass opened the box to find a little snow globe with a moon and stars inside. She shook it and watched the snowflakes dance around the inside of the glass ball.

"When you feel sad, Cass, I want you to hold this in your hand and remember that we love you all the way to the moon and back again," Cadence said, giving the little girl another hug.

"That much?" Cass said, turning to look at Cadence.

"That much and more," Cadence said, tapping Cass on the nose and kissing her cheek. Tamping down her emotions, she set Cass on her feet and stood up. "Now, let's get you bundled up and Trey will help you home."

Cadence helped her put on her coat and wrapped the scarf around her head. Viv handed Trey Cass's daily box of "scraps" while Cass carefully put the snow globe in her pocket and zipped it shut.

"Bye, Cass. Stay off the ice and promise not to cross the highway if the road is slick," Viv said as she walked Trey and Cass to the door.

"I promise, Miss Viv. Bye, Cady," Cass waved as Trey picked her up and carried her across the street and back toward home.

"I think I better head for home, too" Cadence said, putting her coat on.

"Are you sure you should, honey? It is getting worse out there instead of better."

"I know, Aunt Viv, but I have to learn how to drive in this at some point and my first lesson was to not forcefully apply the brake," Cadence said as she pulled on her gloves and zipped up her coat. "See, I'm learning already. I'll be fine."

Cadence gave her aunt a kiss and went out to her car. Thankfully, no traffic was coming so she carefully pulled onto the road and headed toward the Triple T. She made it just fine to their road and started slowing down long before she needed to make the turn. Rather than touch the brakes, she was able to coast into the turn and only slid a little before the car straightened out and she drove the rest of the way to the house without any problem.

><><

Trey stomped his boots before he went back into the café. It was really starting to cool down and the road looked worse than before. That was when he noticed Cadence's car was gone. Pulling open the café door, he saw Viv behind the counter.

"Cady didn't try to drive herself home, did she?" Trey asked, unable to comprehend that she would do something so stupid.

"That's what she said she was doing," Viv said as she wiped down the counter.

"Durn fool, woman. Is she bent on killing herself today?" Trey said as he stomped to the door.

Since they were the only ones in the café, Viv hollered out at him.

"Just cool your spurs a minute there cowboy."

Trey stopped and turned to look at her. Coming around the counter, Viv marched right up to him and shook her finger in his face.

"You and I both know every gossiping tongue in a fifty-mile radius will be talking about the kiss you gave our girl in front of God and everybody. What exactly are your intentions toward my niece?"

Slumping down on a barstool, Trey took off his hat and ran his hand through his hair.

"I'm not exactly sure myself."

"Well, what kind of answer is that?" Viv asked, sitting down beside him. "Either you have feelings for her or you don't."

"Oh, I've got plenty of feelings for her," Trey said. "I just don't know if she feels the same. You said she came here because she got left at the altar. I don't want to be someone she takes an interest in because she is on the rebound."

Viv laughed, actually laughed, at him.

"Cadence never loved that half-wit she nearly married. She was infatuated with his position, impressed by his fancy talk, dazzled by his success, but she never loved him," Viv said, a knowing look on her face. "I kind of get the idea she has more than a passing interest in a certain cowboy round these parts."

Trey's head snapped up and a look of raw jealousy crossed his face.

"Who? Who's she been seeing?"

Viv laughed again. "No one, you big dolt. It's you. Whether she knows it or admits it, she's in love with you."

Trey let out a sigh. "I hear a 'but' in there, Viv. Spit it out."

"She thinks she can't trust her own judgment because of her past experience. The two situations couldn't be any more different, but she is going to have to tell you that story herself. If you want my niece, you are going to have to figure out a way to convince her that she's in love with you. She isn't going to allow herself the luxury of admitting she's head over heels for one Trey Thompson without a little coaxing."

"Really, Viv? You think she's really in love with me?" Trey asked, surprised and thrilled.

"I guess you're going to have to figure that one out for yourself, cowboy. Now get out of here and make sure she made it home in one piece. And, no funny business."

Trey gave Viv's cheek a quick peck and hustled to the door. "Thanks, Viv. No funny business."

><><

Trey kept watch as he drove home, half expecting to see Cady's car in the bar ditch, but when he didn't see her or any signs of her having an accident, he turned down their lane and breathed a sigh of relief.

He drove into Moro earlier to take care of a few errands and was on his way back home when he watched Cady's car slide across the highway and into the path of the oncoming semi. That her car slid back out of the way was nothing short of a miracle. He felt like he was witnessing the entire thing in slow motion as he waited for the truck to smash into her little PT Cruiser.

Trey knew at that moment he would do anything in his power to protect Cady and keep her safe.

Despite his best intentions of not getting involved, his heart and head were already all wrapped up in Miss Fancy Pants Greer.

Pulling up at the house, he sauntered in the back door, calmly removed his hat, coat and boots, and came into the kitchen. The sights and smells that greeted him hit Trey with a pang of nostalgia.

Cadence put out all his family's old Christmas decorations exactly like their mother used to. Soft white lights glowed from the great room mantle, entwined with pieces of fake greenery. He could smell the bayberry scent that seemed to cling to the oldest decorations along with the spicy cinnamon smell that floated around some of the newer pieces. A fire blazed in the big fireplace and candles glowed from the kitchen table.

Everything looked festive, wonderful and homey.

Trey didn't realize how much he had missed all the trappings of the holidays in the years since his mother moved out. He and his brothers usually went to her house in town for Christmas so she and Nana didn't have to drive out to the ranch. Maybe this year, they could have a big family holiday here again. Somehow with Cadence under his roof, family seemed to be more important than ever.

Hearing laughter and music from down the hall, Trey followed the sound to find Trent sitting in the parlor listening to Cady play a rousing rendition of *Deck the Halls* on the piano.

"Hey, bro," Trent said as Trey came in the room and carefully sat on one of the antique chairs. All three Thompson boys had been warned to play nice in this room full of old antiques and family treasures. "Did you know Cady could play?"

"Somehow it doesn't surprise me," Trey said, leaning back in the chair. "She seems to be able to do just about anything she sets her mind to."

Cadence's fingers fumbled on the keys at Trey's praise and she gave him a look of surprise over her shoulder. He just grinned and nodded for her to continue.

She played a few more carols, listening as Trey and Trent recalled past Christmas celebrations and family traditions.

"Remember how Dad used to put on the Santa suit every year for the school Christmas program?" Trent asked.

"He made a great Santa. No one has quite been able to fulfill the role, especially of going door to door on Christmas Eve," Trey said.

"Door to door? What's that mean?" Trent asked.

"You didn't know?" Trey said, smiling as he looked at his brother. "Dad was the guy who went around to some of the neighbor's homes pretending to be Santa. You remember from when you were little, Santa would come to the door Christmas Eve and we'd sit on his lap and tell him what we wanted and then he'd tell us to be good, give us a candy cane and leave. What we asked for was always under the tree the next morning."

"That was Dad?" Trent said, looking a little teary eyed. "I can't believe I didn't know. How did you find out?"

"I drove him around the last couple years he did it," Trey said, recalling the wonderful time he spent with his dad.

"Doesn't anyone else carry on the tradition?" Cadence asked from the piano, where she played softly.

"They've tried. The kids just have a hard time accepting someone else as Santa," Trey said, looking thoughtful.

"Maybe you should be Santa this year," Cadence said, looking directly at Trey. "From the photos I've seen, you look the most like your father and I saw the suit in the boxes this morning. Why don't you play Santa?"

"I… um… I don't," Trey spluttered.

"I think that's a great idea," Trent said, coming out of his chair. "Where did you say the suit was?"

"In one of the boxes in storage. If you dig it out, I'll make sure it gets cleaned. We may need to make some repairs to it or get some new padding. Trey will need to practice wearing it and laughing and…"

"Just hold your horses, both of you. I never said I'd be Santa," Trey said, not liking the way they planned everything out like he wasn't in the room. They couldn't force him to play the jolly old elf.

"Come on, bro," Trent said, kicking at Trey's foot playfully. "Cady's right, you do look the most like Dad and you're the closest to his size. I'm too tall to pull it off and Travis isn't home. Why not see how the suit fits before you say no?"

"Because, first I'll try on the suit, followed by the beard and hat and before I know what has happened, you two will have me standing down at the café waving to tourist and passing out candy canes."

"That's not a bad idea," Cadence said, trying not to smile. "I bet Aunt Viv would reserve a booth just for you and everyone could come in and sit on your lap and tell you what they want for Christmas."

Trent broke out laughing and Cadence giggled. Trey felt a smile tug at the corners of his mouth.

"I know when I'm licked. Find the suit, get it cleaned, and then we'll go from there."

><><

"Nana, just once could you let me win?" Trent asked his grandmother as she whipped him at another round of Scrabble.

Nana smiled, her eyes sparkling. "Now, what would that teach you if I let you win? You'll work harder to best me the next time we play."

"Sure, Nana," Trent said. "You trick me into thinking I'm finally going to beat you and then you shoot me down. Every time!"

Nana laughed, along with Denni and Trey. "There's always next time."

Trent helped Nana up and on with her coat then offered to drive her home. She lived in a nice retirement center not far from Denni's home, which made it convenient for everyone. Nana didn't need much assistance yet and liked her independence, and Denni could keep a close eye on her without encroaching on Nana's freedom.

While Trent was gone, Trey helped Denni wash up the lunch dishes.

"Son, I don't know when I've enjoyed a day more than Friday. That Cady of yours is something pretty special," Denni said, washing dishes and handing them to Trey to dry.

"She's not my Cady, Mom," Trey said, frantically trying to think of a way to bring this conversation to an end before it started.

Denni raised her eyebrow in a look that said she wasn't at all convinced.

"Is that so?"

"Yep."

"She's just your employee."

"Yep."

"And a good cook."

"Yep."

"And a great housekeeper."

"Yep."

"And the girl you're in love with."

"Yep," Trey said, wishing he could snatch the word back. His mother always did know how to get the truth out of him.

"Thought so," Denni said smugly as she washed the last dish and handed it to Trey. Drying off her hands, she sat down at the table and studied him. "She's a lovely girl, honey. Sweet, caring, funny, smart and hard-working. I got the idea she is more than a little bit interested in you. So what's the problem?"

"The problem is that less than two months ago, she was left at the altar by some jerk and Viv told me to take it slow and easy. She said Cady doesn't trust her own judgment and it will take a while for her to come around to the idea of loving someone again."

"How do you know she loved the guy?"

"Well, wouldn't you have to be in love to accept a proposal and plan a wedding?"

"Maybe," Denni said. "Maybe not. Maybe she was in love with the idea of being in love. Regardless of all that, Trey, how do you feel? Do you love her?"

"I do, Mom. More every day," Trey said, tracing a pattern on the tablecloth and thinking this conversation was some form of parental torture.

"Do you think it is the smartest thing to be living under the same roof, considering your feelings?"

"Probably not, but no one ever said I was the smartest Thompson. And as difficult as it may be to believe, I can behave like a gentleman. My mother taught me well," Trey said with a grin. "Trent is around and the hands are there.

It isn't like we're living across the hall from each other. Besides, I don't know that I could rest at all if Cady wasn't there."

Denni smiled and patted his hand. "You've got it bad, baby. Nearly as bad as your daddy had it for me when we got married."

Before she could tell him the story, Trent walked in the door, flicking water off his hat.

"Starting to rain, bro, let's hit the road," Trent said, standing just inside the door to keep from getting Denni's floor wet.

Pulling on his coat and hat, Trey gave his mother a hug.

"Thanks for the talk, Mom. Maybe we can finish that story another day," Trey whispered in her ear before kissing her cheek.

Denni laid her hand on his cheek and smiled. "You bet, son."

Trent gave her a bear hug before the two brothers jumped in the truck and headed toward Grass Valley.

Driving home, the roads were starting to get slick, but nothing like the ice storm they had the day before. Trent drove while Trey got lost in his own thoughts.

"How's Cady like Sasha?" Trent asked as they turned off the freeway onto Highway 97.

"Just fine," Trey said, turning his attention from the window to his brother. "They seem to hit it off well and Sasha is so gentle, Cady is safe riding her."

"Even during midnight rides in the snow?" Trent asked with a devilish grin. He'd waited years to be able to find a sore spot he could tease Trey about and Cady was it.

"Excuse me?" Trey asked, feeling his irritation rise. Was there anything that happened at the ranch that wasn't open for discussion or speculation? Did his brother know everything he did?

"You heard me, man. Fess up. You bought Cady those boots and took her on a ride in the snow, didn't you?"

"Well, what if I did? No harm in that," Trey said, noticing the temperature in the truck seemed to be getting uncomfortably toasty.

"Nope, no harm in that at all. Or kissing her silly out in the mudroom," Trent goaded him. "Not a bit of harm in that."

"What! How... How could you possibly know that?" Trey could feel the vein in his neck start to throb. He might just have a stroke before they got home.

Trent laughed and playfully punched Trey on the arm.

"I was up getting a drink and saw you two by the back door. I was trying to be quiet and unnoticed. I didn't intend to see anything, but you put her in a lip lock before I could sneak back to my room."

"Is nothing sacred around you?" Trey asked, fuming and mortified.

"Not that involves you," Trent said, still grinning. "You know, I get the distinct feeling that Cady might like you back, just a little bit. Why don't you just marry the girl and make both of you happy?"

"Who said anything about marriage?" Trey ground out. "No one said anything about marriage."

"Let me spell it out for you, bro. Boy meets girl. Boy falls in love with girl. Girl falls in love with boy. Boy asks girl to marry him. Girl says yes. Happily ever after. The end."

"It isn't that simple," Trey said, letting out a deep sigh.

"Why not?" Trent asked.

"It just isn't," Trey said, staring out the window again. "It's complicated."

"The only thing I see that is complicated is the amount of time and effort you are both putting into

143

pretending you don't have feelings for each other," Trent said, as he slowed down to drive through Moro. "Maybe you could take her on a real date and then go from there. What do you think of that idea?"

"That might be one of your better ones," Trey said, showing the faintest hint of a smile.

"There you go then. Plan something for Friday night, take her out and see how you feel after that," Trent said. "And don't forget to ask her out. Don't demand a date, ask nicely."

Trey laughed. "When did you get so wise in the ways of courting women?"

"Wouldn't you like to know?"

Chapter Ten

A good plan violently executed now
is better than a perfect plan executed next week.
George S. Patton

By Wednesday evening, Trey was grouchy, on edge, and ready to punch his brother right in the nose. He still hadn't gotten around to asking Cady for a date, and wasn't exactly sure how to go about it. They'd been busy on the ranch so he hadn't had any time to spend alone with her. He hadn't even had time to give her riding lessons this week.

Cady had been working equally as hard making candy and holiday treats and carefully hiding them away. He and Trent decided to wait until the next time she went to visit Viv and see if they could find the stash. She nearly had a revolt when she set out a small plate last night after dinner with just enough fudge each of them could have two pieces.

"Miss Cady, can't we please have another piece?" Tommy begged "I ain't ever had something that melted in my mouth like that before. Please."

Cadence laughed and patted Tommy on the back as she walked past his chair.

"Nope, I don't want you to over indulge."

Groans followed her into the kitchen with more pleading for just one more taste.

She promised them if they all behaved, she'd have something special for them tonight as well.

Trey stepped into the mudroom and hung up his hat and coat before taking off his boots. Stepping into the kitchen, the delicious smells of roasted meat mixed with the scent of cinnamon and apples. Light twinkled from the candles Cady placed on the table as well as the little white lights that danced among the greenery draped over the top of the big china cupboard.

The house looked, smelled and felt like a home. When Cady turned from the sink where she was rinsing vegetables and smiled at him, Trey felt warmth fill his insides. He could get used to this in a hurry, especially if Cady was part of the package.

"Evening, Cady," he said, coming to stand beside her where he inhaled her fresh scent. Her hair was pulled up in a ponytail and he longed to press his lips along the column of her slender neck. Instead he looked over her shoulder at the broccoli in her hand. "You're not going to make me eat broccoli are you?"

"I can't make you eat or do anything," Cadence said with a grin. "But I am making a broccoli salad for dinner tonight."

Purposefully leaning closer to her, he inhaled then leaned against the sink. "Something sure smells good in here."

Cadence gave him a sideways glance and took a step away as she cut up broccoli and cauliflower into a big bowl. Adding roasted pecans and dried cranberries, she poured on some ranch dressing and gave everything a good stir to mix it up.

Walking to the table, she set down the bowl and looked back at Trey, who was still leaning against the sink watching her. Cadence thought it was completely unfair that he could look so good after a hard day of work.

Trey's bright blue eyes glimmered, his bronzed skin glowed from being outdoors, his short hair curled into finger-tempting waves around his forehead and that square jaw practically begged to be kissed. Standing with his legs crossed in front of him and his elbows resting behind him on the edge of the counter, his pose accentuated the breadth of his shoulders, the definition of his chest and the fact that his perfect fitting Wranglers outlined every muscle in his thighs.

How was she supposed to be able to focus on serving dinner with him in the kitchen?

"I left the mail on your desk," she said, coming back around the counter and peeking in the oven door. "It looks like you and Trent got quite a stack of Christmas cards. Do you plan to send any out?"

Trey didn't answer her immediately. He had been too lost in his thoughts of asking her out on a date. He was going to have to bite the bullet and do it tonight or Friday would be here and gone.

"Pardon?" he finally asked.

"I said you received a bunch of Christmas cards today. Do you plan to send any in return?" Cadence brought two pans of popovers out of the oven and poked the tops with a fork, letting the steam escape.

"I hadn't given it any thought. Mom usually sends out cards, but if they are coming here to us, then we probably need to send some in return."

"Would you like some help?"

"That would be great. Could you help me pick out some cards, maybe write a letter from both Trent and I that we could stick inside?"

"Sure," Cadence said, placing a large covered dish on the counter. "I'd be happy to help you."

Trey walked over to the round dish and started to touch it. It looked like a squatty-shaped flower pot with a lid.

"Don't touch that!" Cadence yelled when she saw Trey's hand hovering near the handle.

Trey jerked his hand back and looked at her in surprise.

"It's hot, you'll burn your fingers," she said, stepping next to him with a platter and a serving fork. Using a pot holder, she lifted the lid and revealed a pork roast, cooked to perfection. Digging in a fork to lift out the roast, she slid it on the platter.

"What is that thing?" Trey said, studying the dish. Made of terra cotta, the bottom half was glazed while the top was not.

"It's a special baker," Cadence explained, turning to pick up a carving knife and expertly slicing the roast. "You soak the lid in water for about 15-20 minutes. Then you put the meat inside, season it up, put on the lid, stuff it in a cold oven, turn on the heat and bake for a couple of hours until the meat is done. The lid releases the water while it bakes, steaming the meat while it cooks."

"Where did you get it?" Trey asking, knowing his mom or Lois never used it.

"It's mine. I've had it for a while. I always use it when I make pork roast," she said.

Suddenly, she laughed as a memory came to her.

"What's so funny?" Trey asked, carrying the platter of meat to the table while she scooped up the contents of a saucepan into a bowl and dropped in a big dollop of butter, stirring until it melted.

"The first time I used this baker, I was so excited to try it out. I got in too big of a hurry and forgot to remove the plastic pad they stick in the meat packages to absorb all the blood and juice. When I took it out of the oven, the entire thing was black, the meat was black and I thought I had just ruined my new baking dish. I cut the outside off the meat and the juice just ran out. I was going to throw it away, but my dad insisted on eating it. It was the best pork roast we'd ever had to that point. Thinking I'd have to throw the dish out, I put it in the sink to soak with a little soapy water while we ate dinner. When I got around to doing the dishes, the black had soaked off and the pan looked almost as good as new."

"I can't believe Miss Fancy Pants Greer would do something like that," Trey laughed. "So the meat is really that good?"

"You'll soon have an opportunity to find out for yourself," Cadence said, setting a bowl of what looked like deformed pasta on the table. "Why don't you go ring the bell for dinner?"

The men were soon seated around the table, filling up on pork, fried apples, popovers, broccoli salad and spaetzle.

"What did you say this stuff was again, Cady?" Trent asked as he dished up a second helping.

"Spaetzle," Cady said. "It's German, kind of like pasta made with milk, eggs and flour. Then I add a little bit of butter and salt."

"It's pretty good for fancy-pants food," Trey teased, taking his third helping of pork roast. The meat was so tender and juicy, he thought it could rival a prime steak.

Leaning back in his chair, Henry patted his expanding middle and sighed. "Another great meal, Miss Cady. You sure know your way around the kitchen."

"Thank you, Henry. I enjoy cooking and baking."

"Speaking of baking, do we get our special treat tonight like you promised," Larry asked, snatching the last popover.

"Have I ever let you boys down yet?" Cadence asked with a saucy grin.

"No, Ma'am," Rex said, cleaning up the last of the fried apples.

Cadence cleared the table and the men brought their dirty dishes into the kitchen. Tommy helped her load the dishwasher and hand wash what wouldn't fit. This gave everyone time for their dinner to settle while they anticipated dessert.

Coming to the table, Cadence set down a cake plate holding a huge popcorn cake.

"That's your big surprise?" Trey said, looking at the popcorn in disappointment. He was hoping for something chocolate and gooey, like more fudge.

"Have you ever had popcorn cake?" Cadence asked as she started cutting slices.

"Can't say that I have," Trey said, still not convinced it was going to be that good. After all, it was popcorn.

Cadence passed around the plates of the sticky treat. Popcorn, melted marshmallows, peanuts and gumdrops, stirred together and pressed into an angel-food cake pan were a special treat her mother made during the holidays. Cadence fondly recalled how much they all enjoyed eating it and sharing it with friends.

After a few bites, the men were licking marshmallow off their fingers and asking for more.

"That wasn't too bad" Trey said with a grin. "What's up for tomorrow's treat?"

"Who says you get a treat every night?" Cadence asked, looking at Trey with a motherly scowl on her face. "I don't think you fully appreciate my culinary efforts so tomorrow I might just make you tuna sandwiches and leave you with a bag of chips."

Seven heads shot up to see if she was serious or teasing. When she winked at Tommy, they released a collective sigh of relief. Cadence's cooking was always good, but it was exceptional with the extra effort she put in the closer the Christmas holiday approached.

When the hired hands passed by the house in the middle of the day, the delicious, homey smells of something baking made them wish they could knock at the back door, begging for a taste. They all knew that would not be tolerated.

Trey made it perfectly clear the day Cadence came to the ranch that unless there was an emergency, other than meals they were to stay away from Cadence. No one was to get any funny ideas regarding romance or courting. She was there to cook and clean and that was it. Even Danny seemed to heed Trey's warning. Now, after a couple months of her good food and friendly welcome each morning and evening, there wasn't a man among them that wouldn't do anything for her. Especially if she kept making them Christmas treats.

Going into the kitchen and coming back with a notepad and a pen, Cadence handed it to Tommy, who was sitting next to her.

"What's this for?" Tommy asked.

"I want each one of you to write down your favorite meal and your favorite dessert. If it is possible, I'll rotate them into the menu. How does that sound?"

"Like heaven," Henry said, already deciding what he would write down.

By the time they were done passing the list around, the men were grinning from ear to ear, envisioning a future meal with all their favorite foods.

As they filed out the door for the evening, Henry stopped to pat Cadence on the shoulder and kiss her cheek.

"I'm done convinced you're an angel, Miss Cady. Thank you."

Henry made her blush, but she gave him a quick hug before he left.

Trent got up and announced he was going to the bunkhouse to play cards with Rex and Danny for a while.

Trey went into his office and Cadence, tired after a busy day, decided to sit in the gathering room and put her feet up a while. She watched a Christmas movie, then turned off the TV and admired the twinkle of the holiday lights along with the crackling fire. Scooting off the couch, she knelt by the coffee table and wound her Christmas music box. She listened to it play through once and started to turn the key on it again when she felt a warm presence sink down on the floor beside her. From the electricity shooting through her where his arm and leg brushed hers, she knew without looking it was Trey.

"Is that yours?" Trey asked as she finished winding the box. It featured a couple skating on a pond on a decorative stand. It wasn't anything overly fancy, but the fact it was a family heirloom made it extra special to Cadence.

"Yes. The family lore is that my great-grandfather bought it for my great-grandmother as a wedding gift. They married January 1, 1927. They had one son who survived past infancy. My grandfather inherited this music box and passed it down to my father, his only child, who gave it to me," Cady explained, watching the figures twirl across the ice in a close embrace.

"It must be really special to you," Trey said taking her hand in his, intertwining their fingers. Trey was glad he had investigated the faint music he could hear from the office, otherwise he would have missed this opportunity to ask her out. He was having a hard time pushing the words through his lips, though, distracted by the way the firelight danced through her dark hair and cast shadows on her smooth cheeks. "What song does it play?" he finally asked when the song ended and the figures came to a halt.

"*The Merry Widow Waltz*. There are a few different versions of the lyrics, but my grandpa used to sing one to me that I liked better than the others."

"Would you sing it for me?" Trey asked. He had listened in rapt pleasure to her singing Christmas carols when she thought no one was around. Although he knew Cady would never perform on stage, she did have a voice that he greatly enjoyed hearing.

"Oh, I don't think so," Cadence said, her cheeks flushing in the firelight. "I'm not that good of a singer."

"Please?" Trey coaxed, rubbing his thumb in circles on the back of her hand.

Cadence released her breath and wound the music box one more time. As the tinny music started, Cadence added her sultry alto to the tune.

"Lovers often hum this soft and sweet refrain,
Even after youth and laughter cease to reign -
It recalls a night
When hearts were unrestrained -
With the dawn that night was gone but love remained."

Trey was literally spellbound as Cadence sang the last notes. He wanted to be the figurine on the ice, holding Cady in a lover's embrace as they skated around a pond without a care in the world. Leaning over, he softly kissed her warm lips, once again amazed by the sweetness he found there. Pulling back, he looked at Cady, watching the gold flecks in her eyes spark in the muted light.

"That is quite a song, Cady," Trey said, thinking about the words she just sang. He longed for a night of unrestrained love with the beautiful girl sitting next to him. He knew he wouldn't go that far, especially knowing one night would never be enough when he wanted a thousand of them.

Cadence was unaware of anything except Trey and the wonderful feel of his lips on hers. When he pulled back, she looked into his bright turquoise eyes and felt herself pulled into their brilliant depths. The firelight made a golden frame around him and she wished that she and Trey could be the couple skating on the ice, lost in each other.

Trey couldn't have said when he pulled Cady onto his lap. Or when he tugged the band from her braid, loosened the strands, and buried his hands in the thick waves. Or when he began kissing her with a fervor that knocked all rational thought from his head. All he knew was that having Cady in his arms felt so right. There had never been, and would never be, anyone who could fill them so completely and perfectly as his Cady.

The feelings Trey was arousing in Cadence were beyond anything she had ever felt, ever dreamed of feeling. Maybe it helped that it was close to Christmas, that the firelight was warm and inviting, that she'd just sung him what she always thought to be a romantic song. Whatever it was, Cadence knew she had fallen for this tough yet gentle cowboy with a depth and intensity that frightened her senseless.

Yanking a big pillow from the couch, Trey tossed it on the floor and then gently placed Cady so her head rested on it. Her hair spilled all around, nearly driving him wild. He looked into her eyes, wide and dark with emotion, and kissed her deeply, heedless of where it might lead.

"Cady, darlin', what are you doing to me?" Trey rumbled, as he stretched out beside her, trailing hot kisses along her jaw and down her neck. When he reached her neckline, he undid the top button of her blouse and let a kiss linger there.

As much as she was enjoying it, Cadence knew she had to put a stop to things before they went too far. The kiss Trey had just placed on her chest left her skin hot and singed, yet wanting more. Placing a hand on either side of Trey's head, she pulled his face up so she could look in his eyes.

"Trey, this can't go any farther. Please."

Trey rolled onto his side and let out a deep breath, then another.

"I'm sorry. I didn't mean to get quite so carried away. Again." Trey smiled at Cady and her insides fluttered with warmth. Sitting up, he pulled her beside him. "You seem to have that effect on me."

Cadence smiled and brushed at the hair that fell across Trey's forehead. He took her hand and pressed a kiss to her palm, then held it to his heart.

"I don't want to rush you if you aren't ready, but would you go out on a date with me Friday?" Trey asked quietly, afraid she would say no.

"A date? You mean like go out to dinner and leave the ranch kind of date?" Cadence asked in disbelief.

Trey laughed and shifted so he could hold her in his arms as they watched the fire burn down.

"Yep, a real date just like that. There's a nice restaurant in The Dalles right on the river and there's a movie theater. Will you go out with me Friday?"

"Yes, I'll go out with you," Cadence said, already looking forward to a date with Trey. "But what about feeding the crew dinner?"

"They can fend for themselves," Trey said, fighting the urge to nibble her ear.

"That wouldn't be right. I'll think of something I can leave for them."

"Great, I'll pick you up at 5 p.m. sharp. Got it?" Trey teased.

"Got it, boss-man."

Trey gave up fighting the urge and had just taken her earlobe captive with his teeth when they heard the mudroom door close. Jumping up off the floor, Trey pulled up Cadence then tossed the pillow back on the couch.

Cadence looked like a deer caught in the headlights as Trent stomped in the back door.

Turning on the kitchen lights, he got down a glass and poured in some milk before he noticed the two of them standing in the darkened room.

"Everything okay?" he asked, sitting down at the counter as Cadence and Trey walked into the kitchen.

"Just fine," Cadence said, hoping the fire in her cheeks would die down. She opened the cupboard where the baking pans were stored and took out a plastic container. Popping the top, she set it in front of Trent, hoping to distract him.

The distraction worked as he smiled and fished out an oatmeal cookie with cranberries, white chocolate chips and macadamia nuts.

Not to be left out, Trey poured a glass of milk and sat beside his brother, eating his share of the cookies.

"You've been holding out on us," Trey teased as he took another cookie.

"Knowing the two of you have no restraint, I have to hide the goodies," she said with a jaunty grin. "I'll trust you not to eat the whole container before morning. Goodnight."

Trey wanted so badly to walk Cady to her room and give her just one more kiss, but instead he wished her goodnight. When she reached the hallway and looked back at him, he winked and she smiled.

Things were going better than he planned, if he could just keep a tight rein on his own runaway feelings.

"So, I get the idea I may have interrupted something," Trent said, finishing up his milk, but not showing any interest in moving from his spot at the counter.

"Nope."

"You're not going to start that again. Did you suck it up and ask her out?" Trent felt like he was on a fishing expedition and the big mouth bass was not biting.

"I may have gotten around to it."

"And judging by her red cheeks and redder face, she must have said yes."

"Yep."

"And?"

"We're going to The Dalles Friday for dinner and a movie. You yahoos are on your own for the evening."

"I think we can handle it." Trent slapped Trey's back and grinned broadly. "Now where are you taking her? What have you got planned? Did you order some flowers for her?"

Trey looked at his brother and shook his head. "Why don't you apply some of this match-making effort to getting Miss Lindsay to go out on a date with you? You don't seem to have a problem dating every other female in a 30-mile radius."

Trent clammed up and glared at Trey. "I was just trying to help. No need to get personal."

Trey laughed and stood up. "Right, bro. No need at all."

><><

Cadence hustled through her house cleaning, laundry and chores Friday morning. After eating a quick lunch, she got out the big slow-cooker and put in dinner, made dessert, and changed her mind for the eighteenth time on what she was going to wear for her date with Trey.

She finally called Denni to ask her about the restaurant. Denni assured her it was the nicest place in town and she should wear her new teal dress. Cadence wasn't sure about the wisdom of over-dressing, but decided she was in the mood to wear something a little fancy.

After taking a long, hot shower, she gave herself ample time to style her hair, apply a little extra makeup and get dressed. Sliding into the satin dress, she loved the way the simple, classic cut glided over her curves and elongated her figure. Putting on her highest pair of black heels, she added the string of pearls that had belonged to her grandmother and decided she looked as good as she possibly could.

Picking up a small black handbag and her black dress coat, she carried them to the kitchen and left them on a barstool at the counter. Looking at her watch, she had ten minutes before Trey said he'd be ready to go.

Calling Tommy on his cell phone, he answered and came running in from the barn.

"Wow, Cady, you look amazing. You'll make Trey's eyes pop right out of his head."

Cadence laughed. "I seriously doubt that, but thank you for the compliment."

"Is everything ready?" Tommy asked, looking around the kitchen.

"Yes, and I appreciate you helping me out," Cadence said. Tommy's request for a meal had been home-made chicken and noodles with hot rolls, creamed corn and peach pie. He was getting everything he wanted for dinner tonight.

"The chicken and noodles will be ready right at six. You can serve right out of the pot if you want. And remember to share with the others. If you like them, I promise to make them again," Cadence smiled at him and patted his arm.

"Okay," Tommy said, his stomach already growling in anticipation of the meal ahead. "What else."

"The rolls are ready to go in the oven. Just put them in for about 10 minutes to get them hot. The butter dish and some jam are already on the table. The corn is in a dish in the fridge. Just nuke it for a couple minutes, stir, then nuke it for another minute."

"That sounds simple enough," Tommy said, noticing the table was already set.

Cadence pointed toward two dish towel covered mounds in the corner. "There is your peach pie, but remember you really do have to share. And there's some vanilla ice cream in the freezer to go with it."

"Ah, come on, Cady," Tommy said with a grin. "I could eat them both before dinner and no one would even know the difference."

"You'd know, I'd know and Trent already saw me making the pies earlier. Your evil plan won't work."

"A man's got to try, doesn't he?"

Cadence laughed and took a foil-covered paper plate out of the pantry and handed it to Tommy.

"This is for helping out this evening."

Tommy peeled back the foil to find an assortment of fudge, toffee and rocky road candy, all for him.

Laughing at his look of surprise, she gave his back a pat.

"Those, Tommy boy, you don't have to share."

Tommy kissed her cheek then popped a piece of fudge into his mouth.

"Is the help getting fresh with you, Miss Greer?" Trey asked as he strolled into the kitchen, looking like he had stepped out of the fashion pages of a western magazine.

Cadence grasped the counter to keep her weakened knees from completely giving out on her.

Trey wore new Wranglers, freshly pressed, with a turquoise blue button-down shirt, a western-cut black sports coat and shiny black boots. His spicy aftershave drifted around her in an enticing cloud and she longed to reach out and run her hand down his just-shaved jaw.

"I was helping Cady with dinner. She put me in charge of the kitchen tonight," Tommy tried to explain around the piece of chocolate in his mouth.

Trey nudged him in the ribs and smiled.

"I know, Tommy. Enjoy your treat and make sure everyone tows the line while we're gone."

Breathing a sigh of relief at his boss's teasing, Tommy nodded his head.

"Are you ready to go?"

"As ready as I'll ever be," she said, slipping her arms into her coat sleeves while Trey held it for her. She picked up her handbag, wrapped a black chenille scarf around her neck and fished black leather gloves out of her pockets.

"Enjoy your dinner, Tommy," she called as Trey ushered her out the back door, setting his black Stetson on his head as they passed through the mudroom.

It snowed the day before and the ground still had a light covering. Trey looked from her to his truck and back at her high heels. Shaking his head, he picked her up and carried her to the passenger door, which she pulled open. Gently setting her inside, he waited until she buckled herself in before closing the door and running around to the other side.

"That was quite chivalrous of you," Cadence said with a warm smile. She didn't think she could have been more surprised if Trey had thrown down his coat for her to walk on.

"Anything for you, milady. You look quite ravishing this evening."

Cadence blushed as he drove down the long driveway toward the highway.

Trey thought Cadence always looked pretty, but tonight she looked positively beautiful. Her hair was loosely piled at the back of her head, with curls escaping down her neck and surrounding her face. Her skin glowed with a rosy blush on the apple of each cheek and her lips were so kissable he felt the need to clamp his own together to keep from stealing one.

He itched to feel the cool satin of her dress beneath his hands. It brought out a green sparkle in her eyes while gliding flawlessly over her inviting curves, making her look tall and voluptuous.

Then there were her shoes. The heels Cady wore were probably going to drive him into some fatal form of distraction before the evening was through. Taking a deep breath, he inhaled her luscious scent.

He still couldn't believe they were going out on a date.

They drove in companionable silence for a while, listening to a holiday station, then Cadence asked him about some of the small town history of the area and they chatted like old friends all the way to the restaurant.

Although Trey said it was on the river, Cadence was not prepared at all for the breathtaking view from their window table as it looked out at the water. The grounds around the restaurant were highlighted with white lights and a smattering of snow, making everything seem lovely and magical, especially as they looked out at the water. The dinner was superb and Cadence was enjoying eating someone else's cooking for a change.

After dinner, they went to the theater to see what movies were playing and what time they started. The one they decided to see didn't start for 45 minutes, so Cadence suggested running by Denni's house for a minute.

Trey thought it was a terrible idea, but agreed without argument. Five minutes later, he was holding open Cady's door and leading her up the steps to his mother's home.

Giving a quick wrap on the door, Trey opened it and stuck his head inside.

"Mom, you home?"

"Trey?" Denni called. "I'm in the kitchen, come on back."

Trey held Cadence's hand as they walked through the living room and back to the small kitchen. Denni was busily stirring a batch of hot syrup that would soon be peanut brittle.

"Well, hello you two," Denni said with a beaming smile as they stepped near the stove. "Out for a night on the town?"

Trey took Cadence's coat and left it over a kitchen chair along with his sports coat.

"We went out for dinner and are planning to go to the movies, but had a little time to kill. What are you going to do with the peanut brittle?"

"Nana wanted some and I thought it would be nice for her to be able to share it with some of her friends at the center," Denni said, stirring vigorously.

Glancing over at Cadence, Denni smiled warmly. "You look absolutely lovely, Cady. That dress is fabulous."

"Thanks, Denni," Cadence said with a grin. "You may have mentioned it before."

"Well, it was simply made for you," Denni added with a wink at Trey. "Don't you think so, Trey? Wouldn't you say it is the perfect dress for Cady?"

"Mother," Trey ground out in warning under his breath, drawing out every letter to sound like a six-syllable word. He wouldn't admit that he had all he could do to keep his hands off the dress and Cady. The satin was even smoother than he imagined, although not as cool as he expected. Her body heat warmed both the fabric and Trey each time he touched her.

Taking the hint, Denni asked Trey to fetch the pan she had in the freezer while Cadence dumped peanuts into the skillet at Denni's request. The syrupy concoction quickly turned from pale tan to brown. Cady and Trey stood back when Denni dumped the candy in the pan and smoothed it out with a spoon.

"Whew! I'm always glad when it is in the pan and not burnt. It can go south pretty quickly."

"I'm impressed," Cadence said. "I can't make peanut brittle to save my life."

"You're kidding, right?" Trey asked. He was convinced there wasn't anything under the sun Cadence couldn't make.

"Nope. I can't make peanut brittle, cheese soufflé or an edible tuna casserole."

Denni laughed. "Well, since the men could care less about soufflé or tuna casserole, I think your job is secure. Anytime you want peanut brittle, I'm more than happy to make a batch. Or I could teach you how."

"I think the ability to make peanut brittle is a missing link in my DNA. Both my grandmothers tried to teach me, my mom, Aunt Viv and two of my friends," Cadence said. "I am a peanut brittle making failure."

"Be that as it may, you should have tasted the fudge she made the other day, Mom. It was so good it literally melted in your mouth," Trey said, wishing the peanut brittle would cool fast enough he could snag a piece.

"If I knew we were coming to see you, I could have brought you and Nana some treats," Cadence said, studying Trey as he watched the peanut brittle. For a 30-year-old man who successfully managed a large ranch, he could sure behave like a naughty little boy sometimes.

"That's okay, honey. We'll be out there one of these Sundays and get a sample then."

Looking at his watch, Trey held out Cadence's coat for her to slip on, signaling it was time to get going. Pulling on his sports coat, he kissed Denni's cheek and steered Cadence toward the door.

They made it to the movie in plenty of time and Trey ordered a large popcorn and Dr. Pepper. Cadence ordered a bottle of water and they settled in to watch the movie.

The comedy was a great diversion from the tension that had been building between them since Wednesday when the out-of-control kisses they shared took their emotional and physical attraction to a whole new level. While she snitched his popcorn and stole sips of his pop, Trey kept one eye on the movie and one on her.

Driving home, they chatted about ranch work, the hands, when Trey thought Travis might be home, and shared memories of past holiday seasons. Cadence could tell Trey still missed his father immensely. Even though she hadn't been really close to her parents, she at least knew if she needed them, they were available.

With all her grandparents gone, her parents in Mexico and no siblings or family except for Aunt Viv and Uncle Joe, Cadence was glad to be part of the sometimes rowdy Thompson household. It made her feel connected and part of a family.

"Have you ever had a white Christmas, Cady?" Trey asked as they neared home.

"No, can't say that I have. They were usually gray, quite often raining."

"That sounds miserable and depressing. How do you expect Santa to bring presents in that?"

Cadence laughed.

"Since I never woke up Christmas morning stiffed, I assume he made it through our coastal weather just fine."

"What about reindeer? Have you ever seen reindeer?"

"No, silly man. Where would I see reindeer? I may have lived north of here, but it wasn't exactly at the North Pole."

Trey grinned. "No malls ever had reindeer with their fake Santas?"

"Not live reindeer. I didn't like going to see the mall Santas. They always smelled funny and I knew they weren't the real one anyway," Cadence said with a lift of her chin. "Speaking of Santa, did Trent find the suit yet? We better get a move on if we're going to have you ready for the Christmas program."

"I never said I'd do it," Trey reminded her. He knew the night of the program he would be wearing the red suit and sporting a big smile if for no other reason than to make Cady happy.

"I know you didn't agree, but you will."

"What makes you so all fired sure?"

"I just know."

"How?" Trey asked as they drove up to the house. Trey parked not as close to the back door as he could have, looking forward to carrying Cadence inside. "How could you possibly know I'll do it when I told you and that brick-headed brother of mine I don't want to?"

"Because you're a good man and because it will mean so much to the kids."

Trey didn't know what to say because Cadence's eyes had grown wide and teary.

Shutting off his truck, he hurried around to the passenger side and opened her door. She started to slide out but he quickly put his hands around her back and beneath her knees, pulling her to his chest.

"Oh, I forgot about the snow."

"That's okay," Trey said, kicking the pickup door closed as he carried her to the mudroom. She leaned over and opened the door and he carried her inside before setting her down. Scraping his boots on the mat, they walked into the kitchen where Trey took off his sports coat and helped Cadence remove her coat and scarf.

She went to the cupboard and took down mugs, making them both some hot chocolate. Sitting down at the counter, she noticed the kitchen was spotless. Tommy did a good job of keeping order while they were gone. Trent left the light on in the kitchen, but other than that, the house was dark and quiet.

"Want me to see if I can find a piece of pie for you or some cookies?" Cady asked, leaning back in the bar stool and crossing one very attractive leg over the other.

"Nah. I'm fine," Trey lied. He was anything but fine. Trying to ogle Cady's legs without being obvious, he wondered, and not for the first time that evening, how she could walk in such high heels. They were about the sexiest thing he'd ever seen in Grass Valley. He assumed they must be something from her law office days. The tiny yet practical part of him still capable of reasonable thought wished she'd worn cowboy boots or even her hiking shoes instead. Those heels drew his attention to her legs which then traveled up her skirt which traveled higher and sent a signal to his brain that was about to give him a short-circuit.

Trey was a church going man. He lived his faith. At least he tried, even after one very tempting female moved into his house. He knew his thoughts weren't ones he should be having but blast if Cady wasn't completely under his skin, in his heart and tap dancing around in his head.

While Cady sat sipping her chocolate, Trey wondered what she would do if he reached over and ran a hand up her shapely calf. Slap him? Dump her chocolate in his lap? Shove him off the stool?

He was about ready to find out when Trent wandered in the kitchen, looking half asleep with his hair pinwheeling around his head, his robe partially tied and his plaid pajama bottom twisted around one leg. Shaking his leg as he walked, he opened his eyes wide enough to notice Trey and Cady sitting at the counter.

"Sorry, you two," he said, starting to back out of the room.

Cadence motioned him forward and smiled.

"You're fine, Trent. I was just heading to bed," Cadence slipped off the stool, carried her mug to the sink and rinsed it, then picked up her coat and purse. Before she went down the hall, she gave Trey's cheek a kiss and whispered, "Thanks for a wonderful evening."

Trey watched her sway down the hall and turn the corner into the north wing.

Pouring a glass of milk and finding the left over pie in the fridge, Trent sat down on Cadence's vacated stool.

"I'm really sorry, bro. I didn't realize you two were back yet."

Trey glared at Trent. Maybe he should be grateful for the interruption. Divine intervention? Trey looked heavenward and raised his eyebrows.

Slapping Trent on the back, he stood up and smiled.

"It's fine, man," Trey picked up a fork and took a big bite of pie. "Where did she get peaches for this pie? It tastes just like summer in a flaky crust."

"I know," Trent said, eating faster so Trey wouldn't get more than his fair share.

Chapter Eleven

*Choose your friends with caution; plan your future
with purpose, and frame your life with faith.*
Thomas S. Monson

The next morning as Cadence pulled cinnamon
muffins out of the oven, Trey walked into the kitchen
wearing a huge smile.

Snaking his hands out to span her waist, he spun
Cadence around and planted a searing kiss on her lips
before she had time to blink.

Stepping back, he noticed she had a smudge of flour
on one cheek and cinnamon smeared on her apron, but she
looked and smelled wonderful to him.

"What have you got planned today, darlin'?" Trey
asked, picking up a pot holder and taking the pan of
muffins from her hand before she dropped them. She
blinked at him and didn't say anything.

Cadence was taken completely by surprise by Trey's
kiss. Although she knew they were progressing in their
relationship, she had no idea he would greet her like that
this morning. She entirely liked the idea of it happening
every morning.

"Huh, what?" she finally asked, coming back down to
earth.

"Now don't you sound all courtroom professional?"
Trey teased. "I asked what you have planned today."

"Well, I was going to wash all the sheets today and I thought maybe I should clean up in Travis' room. Didn't you say you thought he would be home in a week or so?"

"So nothing that couldn't wait until next week to worry about. Perfect."

"Perfect for what?" Cadence asked, putting the muffins into a cloth lined basket and folding the cloth over the top of the pile to keep them warm.

"For what I have planned today. After breakfast, put on your hiking boots and bundle up. You might want to pack a bag with some water bottles and snacks, since we've got about a two hour drive."

"Drive? Drive where?" Cadence said as she put butter on the table and poured orange juice in glasses.

"That is for me to know and you to find out. The roads are clear, the sun is supposed to shine today and I'm in the mood for a little holiday fun. So what do you say?"

Trey stepped behind her, putting his arms around her waist, gently tugging Cadence back against him.

"Say yes, Cady," he whispered in her ear, his breath warm on her neck, causing her insides to heat and turn molten. "You know you want to."

"Yes," she whispered, unable to make the word "no" form on her lips.

"Be ready to go by 8:30. Just so you know we will be around other people, but you don't need to dress fancy."

"Well, isn't that informative," Cadence muttered as she pulled a potato and ham casserole from the oven.

Trey disappeared shortly after breakfast in his pickup. Cadence didn't have time to give his vague itinerary too much thought. She hurried to do the dishes, clean up the kitchen and put a roast in the slow cooker, which she set on low. Whatever they did today, at least she wouldn't have to worry about dinner. It would be ready when they got home.

Hustling into her room, she braided her hair, letting a few tendrils curl around her face. She layered on another coat of mascara, changed into a white turtleneck with a dark red sweater, put on her heavy socks and boots, spritzed on perfume and grabbed her purse.

Glancing at the kitchen clock it was nearly 8:30. She glanced outside to see Trey pull up at the back door, leaving the truck running. Before he could come in, Trent rushed into the kitchen, dressed in what the guys called their "town clothes."

"Ready for some fun, Cady?" he asked, taking the bag with the snacks from her and setting it on a stool in the mudroom. He held her coat for her then slipped on his own coat and hat before grabbing the snack bag.

"Are you going, too?"

"You bet. I wouldn't miss this for anything."

"And what would 'this' be, exactly?" Cadence asked as she pulled on her gloves and preceded him out the back door.

"Wait and see," Trent teased, holding open the back seat pickup door for her.

Looking into the pickup, Cadence smiled in surprise. Sitting on the other side, buckled into a booster seat was Cass.

"Well, sweetie-pie, what a wonderful surprise to see you."

"Hi, Cady. Trey said he was taking us on a Christmas adventure today. Isn't it awesome?" Cass was so excited, her feet couldn't be still.

"It is awesome, Cass" Cadence said as she sat down and buckled herself in. When Trey looked back at her, she mouthed "thank you" to him and smiled. He winked and put the pickup in gear.

"All aboard the Polar Express bound for Redmond," Trey called out as they drove down the driveway.

Cass and Cadence kept up a conversation in the back seat while Trent and Trey talked ranching and farming from the front.

Cadence passed around water bottles and granola bars part way there. Cass asked to stop at the rest area, but other than the one pit-stop they made good time. It was a quarter to eleven when they rolled into Redmond. Trey drove out of town heading east then turned in at a farm set back off the highway. Glancing at the sign Cadence was shocked to read "Reindeer Ranch."

Hardly able to contain her own excitement, she turned to help Cass out of her booster seat.

"Miss Cass, I do believe Trey and Trent have planned an extra special surprise for us."

Cass was trying not to wiggle but she was so excited to get to go somewhere new and see something different. She could barely hold herself still long enough for Cadence to unfasten the strap. When she did, Cass flew out the door Trey had opened and looked around in wide-eyed surprise.

"Are those Santa's reindeer?" she asked, as Trey held her hand and walked toward the reindeer pen. Trent opened Cadence's door and gave her an arm as they came around the pickup, following Cass and Trey.

"What a wonderful treat for her you two planned," Cadence said quietly to Trent. "She'll remember this day as long as she lives.

"Well, the story I heard was that Cass wasn't the only one who had never seen a live reindeer. You don't think Trey and I could just let that go by, do you?" Trent grinned down at her as they stood at the fence and watched the reindeer.

An hour later, they drove back into Redmond and headed south to Bend where Trey pulled up at a Red Robin restaurant. They wandered inside and were quickly seated. Cass didn't know what to think.

"I've never been in a fancy place like this before," Cass said looking around as she sipped her milk.

Trey, Trent and Cadence all looked at each other, their hearts hurting for Cass. The little girl was so sweet and well-behaved, despite her questionable upbringing. All three adults enjoyed her enthusiasm and excitement as she looked at the reindeer and listened to their funny grunts.

After placing their orders, Cadence took Cass to the restroom to freshen up, where the little girl talked about how clean and pretty everything was. Cadence had all she could do not to cry, and instead focused on keeping a happy smile plastered on her face.

Coming back to the table, Trent and Trey both teased Cass and made her laugh. She picked up crayons and colored on her placemat and looked around, trying to take in everything at once. Trey reached under the table and gave Cadence's hand a squeeze, letting her know how Cass was getting to him, too.

Cass cleaned up her hamburger and fries then finished off part of Cadence's fries as well.

Paying for lunch, Trey suggested they check out the mall, since they were already in town. Taking Cass inside, the little girl was overwhelmed by all the sights and sounds. Walking over to the area where a mall Santa was stationed, Trent asked if Cass wanted to sit on Santa's lap. She cocked her head and watched a few of the kids in line taking turns, then decided she was a little scared.

"If you want to go, Cass, I'll hold your hand and stand with you the whole time," Cadence said, smiling warmly at the little girl.

"Promise?" Cass asked, taking a tentative step toward the line.

"I promise," Cadence said. She nodded her head to Trent and Trey and quietly whispered, "This could take a while, why don't you two go wander instead of standing here."

The men walked off with promises to be back soon and Cadence waited with Cass in the slowly moving line.

Cadence was surprised when she got in the pickup at the ranch to not only find Cass in the backseat, but see her dressed in clothes that weren't rags. Trey said he called Viv early that morning with his plan and she hustled over to the church's donation closet to round up some decent clothes for the little girl. When Trey picked her up, Cass was clean, dressed in new-to-her clothes that fit reasonably well and holding a note written by her mother giving her permission to spend the day with them. Maybe Micki was coming around, Cadence mused. She had let the little girl spend quite a bit of time with them recently.

Inching forward in the line, Cass was quiet, watching the other kids as they took turns sitting on Santa's lap. Bending down, Cadence asked Cass if she knew what she was going to ask for.

"Yep. But it's a secret," Cass said, wiggling off one foot to the other, holding tight to Cadence's hand.

"You can tell me, can't you?" Cadence asked.

"Nope. Not Trey or Trent or Miss Viv. If I tell, then it won't come true."

"I see," Cadence said, wondering what the little girl could possibly want that was such a big secret she couldn't tell any of them.

They were next in line to see Santa when Cadence saw Trey and Trent return. She gave them a small wave then turned her attention back to Cass who was fidgeting so much it made Cadence think of the saying "ants in your pants." Cass certainly seemed to have half an ant hill in hers.

When Santa's helper said it was her turn, Cass squeezed Cadence's fingers so tight, she was sure she would lose all circulation in them.

She walked Cass up to Santa before Cass let go of her hand and climbed up on his lap. Santa handed her a candy cane and asked what she wanted for Christmas. She whispered something in the direction of his ear. Santa turned and pointed to Cadence and Cass nodded her head. Then Santa gave Cass a reassuring pat on the back and set her on her feet before sending her on her way.

Cass grabbed Cadence's hand and tugged her toward Trey and Trent.

"Did you see me on Santa's lap?" she asked, nearly dancing a jig as she ran up to the men.

Trey picked her up and gave her a hug. "We sure did. Did you have fun talking to Santa?"

"Yep. He's going to bring me the present I asked for."

"Is that right," Trent asked. "What did you ask for?"

"Can't tell," Cass said, shaking her head.

"She won't tell me either," Cadence said, joining the conversation.

"Well, I guess we'll have to wait and see what Santa Claus brings, won't we?" Trey said, wondering how in the world they would find out what the little girl wanted and get it for her. Maybe Viv would have an idea.

Trey took them to a few more shopping spots before deciding they better hit the road. Stopping in Madras for gas, he bought everyone peppermint ice cream cones for the trip home.

Cass fell asleep as soon as she gobbled up the last of her cone, her rosebud mouth opened slightly with soft little puffs of breath escaping.

A thoughtful silence fell over the group as they drove to Grass Valley.

They all rode with Trey to take Cass home. Cadence unbuckled her and helped her pull on her gloves and scarf before Trey picked her up and carried her to the door.

Setting her on the step, Cass waved and smiled before going inside. They could hear Micki start screaming as Cass shut the door.

Brushing at the tears she couldn't keep from falling, Cadence stared out the window on the way back out to the ranch. Pulling up at the back door, they all seemed lost in their thoughts. Gathering up their purchases, the threesome walked in the house, quiet and somber.

Cadence finally went over to Trent and stood on tiptoe to pull his head down enough so she could kiss his cheek. She turned to Trey and kissed his as well.

"Thank you both for a lovely, wonderful day. You gave Cass and me a day of special memories."

"Our pleasure, Cady," Trey said, putting his hand around her waist and pulling her back against him. "Sorry it didn't end on a better note."

"Nothing we can do about that, but pray," Trent said, wandering off to his room with his purchases in hand.

Turning around, Cadence gave Trey a warm hug and another kiss on the cheek.

"Thank you for what you did, today, Trey. I just wish I could think of something more I could do to help Cass," Cadence said.

"As Nana always says, hem your thoughts in faith and finish them with prayer."

Chapter Twelve

*To wear your heart on your sleeve isn't a very good plan;
you should wear it inside, where it functions best.*
Margaret Thatcher

Monday morning, Trent came in carrying the plastic storage tub containing the Santa Claus suit. He and Cadence took all the pieces out, checking for anything that needed repaired. It all looked to be in good shape.

Trent promised to drop it off at the cleaners in The Dalles when he ran in later that day to help Nana with some errands. Hopefully, it would be ready to bring home with him by the time he was ready to make the return trip. If not, Denni would bring it with her when she came Sunday.

Cadence was keeping very busy with her regular cooking and cleaning duties as well as making a special treat every day for the men. She also worked on Christmas projects. She finished the quilt she was making Cass along with a matching pillow sham that afternoon. Done in pinks, whites and greens, it was soft, pretty and definitely made for a little girl.

Feeling in particularly high spirits, she decided to make Trent's requested dinner of choice.

When the men came in, they were surprised to see a red and white picnic cloth covering the table and the smell of barbecue filling the air.

"Miss Cady, what's on the menu tonight?" Rex asked as he stood next to his chair at the table.

"You'll soon see," she said, bringing heaping bowls and platters to the table. The men enjoyed a feast of barbecued ribs, baked beans, potato salad and cornbread. While Trent had included watermelon on the list, it was impossible to get anything that tasted good this time of year, so she substituted a mixed fruit salad. Dessert was a raspberry cream cake. When Trent took a bite he closed his eyes in rapture and sighed.

"This may be the best thing I've ever eaten, Cady."

Cadence blushed although she sent him a warm smile. "You say that at least once a week, Trent."

Everyone laughed, but Trent begged a second piece of cake and when only one was left, he hoarded it, as well.

"Are you sure you had enough cake, bro?" Trey said with a teasing smile. He had eaten two pieces himself, thoroughly enjoying the treat.

As the men brought their plates to the sink and prepared to leave, Cadence asked them to all come back in an hour.

She quickly finished up the dishes then started cooking something on the stovetop. When the guys returned, she had a pan of taffy ready for pulling. She inspected each set of hands, made them slather on butter and set all seven of them to pulling taffy. As they pulled, she added red and green food coloring. Laughing and trying to snitch bites of the hot candy, it was a fun evening wrapped up in good cheer and good company.

The men had just left for a second time that night when the phone rang. Cadence answered only to find Aunt Viv on the other end of the line.

"Cady, there is a PTA meeting tomorrow night to discuss the Christmas program at the school. If Trey is going to play Santa, I really think he should attend. Can you let him know to be there at seven? You can come, too, if you want. They need some volunteers to help get the treat bags ready and what not."

"Sure, Aunt Viv, I'll let him know. Thanks for the call." Cadence disconnected and turned back to the mess in the kitchen.

"What did Viv need, Cady?" Trey asked, still trying to scrub the red food coloring from the taffy off his hands, while he sucked on a piece of the candy.

"She said the PTA meeting tomorrow is to discuss the Christmas program and Santa. She thought you should probably attend."

"I think all three of us should go," Trent said, helping Cadence pack the candy into two containers, one for red and one for green. "That way Trey can't back out on us."

"I still haven't said I'll be Santa. You two are getting way ahead of things," Trey said, leaning against the counter and drying his hands.

Cadence just smiled at him and shook her head.

After a quick dinner of chili, green salad and hot bread, Cadence, Trey and Trent drove into the school just in time for the PTA meeting. Held in one of the classrooms, the adults looked pretty funny sitting on the tiny chairs. Trent, especially, was having a time of it with his extra long legs.

He didn't seem to mind when Lindsay Pierce sat next to him and smiled.

Trey nudged Cadence with his elbow and nodded his head at Trent before giving her a wink. Cadence smiled back and wished there was a way she could push Trent's chair closer to Lindsay's. From what she had heard and observed, Trent had been carrying a torch for the teacher since she arrived in the community three years ago. She didn't know if it was a lack of interest on Lindsay's part or

178

a lack of effort on Trent's, but they just didn't seem to be able to even take the first step of going out on a date.

It was a pity. Cadence didn't think Trent would come across too many lovely girls who were close to six-foot tall living in Sherman County.

As the meeting began, she sat up and paid attention to the information that was shared. Before it was all said and done, she had volunteered to help Viv fill up the treat bags and it had been unanimously agreed that Trey should play Santa.

Trey was unusually quiet on the drive back home while Trent and Cadence discussed the meeting, the school, the teachers and the upcoming program. Trent found himself roped into helping a couple of the other men in attendance construct a winter scene for the play that would be performed the night of the Christmas program. Cadence and Trent had come up with some fun ideas before Trey pulled up at the back door.

Going inside, Trent went to the office to Google some ideas for holiday sets, leaving Trey and Cadence in the kitchen. She made herself a cup of spicy tea and sat down at the counter. Trey poured a glass of milk and sat beside her, still quiet.

"You're going to have to be a lot more jovial if you are going to be a proper Santa" Cadence said, giving Trey a teasing smile.

When he didn't respond, she placed her hand on top of his and gave it a squeeze.

"Something wrong, Trey? You've been awfully quiet this evening."

Trey kissed the back of her hand and let out a sigh.

"I'm not convinced I'll be the best Santa for the kids, Cady. I want them to have fun and enjoy their time with Santa. I'm just not sure I'm the right person for the job."

Cadence took a sip of her tea. "Well, from what everyone says, you look and sound the most like your father and all the kids, including you and your brothers, thought he was the real deal."

"I know, but it's more than that."

"Like what?"

"For lack of a better way to describe it, my dad just seemed to have that special holiday magic. He could make each and every kid feel special. I don't think I can live up to that kind of reputation or expectation."

"If the job you've been doing making Cass feel special is any indication of what you are capable of, I think you'll be just fine."

"Really? You don't think I'll send the kids home in tears, crying for the real Santa?"

"Nope," Cadence said, sending Trey a mischievous grin. "But you better practice your 'ho ho hos' and being jolly."

"I can think of something else I need to practice."

"What's that?"

Trey grabbed her around the waist and pulled her onto his lap, tickling her sides.

"Letting sweet little girls sit on my lap and whisper their wishes in my ear."

><><

Stopping to visit Viv after driving into The Dalles for groceries and household supplies, Cadence was enjoying a cup of coffee while they discussed the upcoming Christmas program.

They were deciding if they should stick with the traditional orange and peanuts in the treat sacks or go with something more updated when Cass came in the door sobbing.

Flinging herself at Cadence, she seemed to be gasping for breath.

"Cass, what's wrong, sweetheart?" Cadence asked pulling the little girl onto her lap.

"My mommy won't wake up. I shook her and shook her and she won't wake up," Cass said, a haunted look in the blue eyes she turned trustingly to Cadence. "She slept all day yesterday and last night and today and she won't wake up. Please, make her wake up, Cady."

Viv ran to the phone and called Joe to run up to Micki's house while she pulled on her coat.

"Stay here with Cass, Cady."

Cass continued to sob so Cadence held her, rocking her back and forth and humming softly.

"It's okay, sweetie. Everything will be okay."

"But what if my mommy doesn't ever wake up? What if she stays asleep like she said my daddy is sleeping? She said she wanted to sleep forever, just like him."

"Oh, baby," Cadence said, holding Cass close. Cadence bit the inside of her own cheek to keep from crying.

Viv came hurrying in the door, looked at Cadence and sadly shook her head. Taking off her coat, she sank into the booth across from Cadence and took a deep breath.

"Cass, your mommy did go to sleep and, honey, she isn't going to wake up again. I'm so sorry, sweetie, but I promise we'll take good care of you, so don't you worry."

"No," Cass screamed and struggled to get out of Cadence's arms. Cadence knew if she let her go, she'd run back up the street to her mother's dead body and cry over the woman who couldn't bring herself to love her daughter more than her shattered dreams.

Cadence held her tight, even when Cass kicked and hit at her, crying huge racking sobs that shook her little body. Finally spent, Cass slumped against Cadence and held on to her sweater with both tiny hands tightly fisted. Her sobs turned to hiccups and she finally fell into an exhausted sleep.

Brushing the hair back from her face, Cadence stared at the fragile child in her arms and felt a part of her heart break for this poor child who had never really known a mother's love.

"What are we going to do?" Cadence asked, softly. "Trey said both Micki and her boyfriend were foster kids. Did either of them have any family?"

"Not that anyone can find. Believe me, if there had been a suitable relative to send Cass to, DHS would have done it a long time ago. Joe called the sheriff. He'll be out as quick as he can. They'll probably want to talk to Cass and then they'll pack her up and ship her off to a foster home."

"No," Cadence blurted out. "I won't let them."

Surprised by her outburst, Viv just looked at her. "Well, what exactly do you propose to do?"

"I don't know, but I know she's too sweet and good to be dumped into a cycle of more neglect and foster homes. She needs a real home, with people who love her."

"Then take her home yourself," Viv said, looking Cadence square in the face. "If you feel that strongly about this, take care of her, Cady. It's been plain from the start she loves you."

"I don't know anything about raising a child. I don't even have a home. I'm nothing more than a cook and housekeeper at the Triple T," Cadence said. Maternal feelings that had been dormant deep inside her suddenly burst into full bloom. She didn't know anything about raising a child, didn't have a clue where to begin, but she knew she loved the one asleep in her arms like she was her own. "Who in their right mind would let me keep her?"

"Anyone with eyes in their head can see how much you care for the child. Besides, I think Trey is mighty attached to this little girl as well."

"But Aunt Viv, we aren't an approved foster home. They'll never let her stay with us. Two bachelors and a single woman? How unconventional is that?"

"I'd say it's a whole lot better than what she's had for the first five years of her life."

"But I can't just waltz in the door and announce to Trey and Trent that they've got a little house guest for an unknown amount of time. I can't possibly do that."

"You're right. You can't. But I can," Viv said, picking up the phone and dialing the ranch. When she didn't get an answer, she tried Trey's cell phone. From the one-sided conversation, Cadence assumed he must have answered.

Viv didn't give him any details, just saying that Cass needed a place to sleep and Cadence would fill him in on the details later. Hanging up, she smiled at Cadence.

Cadence was considering what her aunt said when the sheriff walked in the café door. Tipping his hat, he came and stood beside the booth where they were seated.

"Thanks for the call, Viv. The coroner will give us a report, but I'd guess she died sometime in the last 12 hours. That her girl?" the sheriff asked, pointing to Cass.

"Yes, sir," Cadence answered, feeling oddly protective. Those maternal instincts kicked into over drive, sending Cadence on the defensive to keep Cass safe and secure.

"We'll have to take her to a foster home, have DHS come run the drill. From what I hear, she's a sweet little thing. Hate to see her get lost in the system."

Cadence turned to Viv and raised an eyebrow.

"Now, sheriff, don't you think it would be a better idea to send her home with someone she knows, someone who cares about her? We don't want to traumatize the poor child any more than what has already been done. Don't you think you could bend the rules a bit, just this once?"

The sheriff looked at Viv like she'd lost her mind.

"Cadence, my niece here, has struck up a special relationship with Cass, along with her boss, Trey Thompson. She'd take Cass out to the ranch and keep her for a few days, until we can all figure out what would be best for the little girl. Doesn't that sound like a great plan?"

"I don't know, Viv, there are rules and regulations and …"

"Oh, hogwash! You know the only two certified foster homes in the county are both full to the brim with wild juveniles. Would you really want to send this little angel there, knowing what she'd have to deal with?"

"Viv, I don't like it any more than you do, but I have reports I have to file, regulations that stipulate…" The sheriff took a deep breath and ran his hand through his already mussed hair. Looking at Cadence he nodded toward the door. "Go on, take her home. I'll be out later to talk to her and we'll decide what to do from there."

Cadence shot the sheriff a beaming smile that tugged a grin from the corners of his mouth. Scooting out of the booth, the sheriff took Cass from her, carrying her outside while Cadence put on her coat and hurried out the door.

"Take her home, Cady," Viv said, giving Cadence a warm hug. "Feed her a good dinner, give her a bath and let her know how much you love her. That's what she needs most right now."

"Thanks, Aunt Viv," Cadence said, kissing her aunt's cheek as the sheriff carefully placed the still sleeping girl on the backseat of Trent's pickup. Trey and Trent both had insisted Cadence leave her car in the garage until winter had come and gone, and taught her how to drive a manual transmission.

Starting the truck, she waved to both Viv and the sheriff before pulling out on the highway and heading toward the ranch with Cass.

Pulling up at the mudroom door, Cadence lifted a sleeping Cass and carried her inside, laying her gently down on the couch in the great room. Pulling a fleece blanket off the end of a chair, she covered the little girl, brushed her hair back from her face and put a soft kiss on her forehead.

Going to the kitchen, Cadence slumped onto a bar stool, put her head down on the counter and wept.

She heard the kitchen door open and close but didn't lift her head. When strong arms lifted her up and pulled her close, she buried her face into Trey's chest and cried out all the pain and anger she had been feeling on behalf of little Cass.

"It's okay, darlin'. It's going to be okay," Trey said soothingly as he rubbed his hands across her back. "It will all be okay, Cady, girl. Everything will be just fine."

Trey let her cry until she didn't have any tears left, continuing to hold her. When she finally lifted her head, he handed her a napkin from the basket on the counter and she wiped at her face, noticing his soaked shirt front.

"I'm sorry," she said, picking up a dish towel and dabbing at his shirt. "I didn't mean to get you all wet."

"Don't worry about it," Trey said, keeping her in his arms. "Can you tell me what happened?"

Taking in a deep breath, Cadence shared with Trey what she knew.

"I'm sorry to bring her out here Trey, but I didn't know what else to do. Aunt Viv can't keep her with the café to run and I just couldn't let them take her to foster care right now."

"It's fine, Cady. I'm pretty fond of the little sweetheart myself. I'd hate to see her get lost in the system but do you think they'll let us keep her for any length of time?"

Cadence didn't know what tomorrow would bring, but she couldn't help but smile with love and admiration in her eyes when Trey asked if she thought they would let "us" keep her. She was so grateful that he wanted to help shelter and protect Cass.

"What will Trent say? Will he mind her being here for a while if we can work it out for her to stay?"

"After the trip to see the reindeer, I think he'd do anything he can for Cass. She's got us both wrapped around her little finger," Trey said, taking Cadence's hand and kissing her fingers. "She's not the only female with that particular talent."

Leaning into Trey, Cadence wrapped her arms around him and gave him a warm hug.

"Thank you, Trey," she said, kissing his cheek and looking into his eyes.

"For what, darlin'?" he asked, watching the gold flecks in her eyes glow brightly.

"For being you."

><><

When the sheriff arrived that evening, Cadence had a game plan in place. She drew on what legal knowledge she had and hoped she could convince the sheriff to leave Cass with them, at least for a while.

"Hello, sheriff," Trey said, shaking the hand of the man he had known his entire life. They had gone to school together, played sports alongside one another, fought over Bree Lynn Bates when they were in high school and remained good friends.

"Trey," the sheriff said, coming inside and sitting down at the counter. "Sorry to be making a visit under these circumstances."

Trent and Cass sat watching a Christmas special in the great room. He kept her interested in the show and oblivious to anything going on in the kitchen.

Setting a steaming cup of coffee in front of the sheriff along with a slice of chocolate cream pie, Cadence stood next to Trey. Moving her hand close to his, he grabbed it and gave her a reassuring squeeze.

"What can you tell us? What happened? What's going to happen to Cass?" Trey asked.

"It looks like Micki simply drank herself to death. The autopsy report should be finished in a few days, but I don't think there will be any surprises. As to what is going to happen, I'm not sure. Micki was in the foster system from the time she was just a toddler. Her boyfriend wasn't any better. We've got a lead on a woman who may turn out to be Micki's sister, but nothing definite yet and that brings us to another problem."

The sheriff looked toward the great room and Trey nodded his head that it was okay to keep talking.

"I need to take Cass and leave her in foster care. She'll be processed into the system and they'll try to place her in a good home. I really hate to see her end up being shuffled from one home to another, especially at the holidays, but not too many of them have openings and none of them are willing to do long-term care."

"What if a home became available that wanted her indefinitely?" Trey asked.

"That would be wonderful, but I can't just leave her anywhere. A caseworker will be heading out tomorrow to pick her up and get her settled somewhere," the sheriff said, taking a bite of his pie and nodding appreciatively at Cadence.

"If this home was to be approved for foster care, then would it be an option for Cass to stay here?" Cadence asked.

"Sure, but the problem is that this house and the adults in it aren't certified, licensed or even approved for foster care."

"What can we do to fix that in the next 24 hours?" Trey said, looking intently at his friend.

The sheriff glanced up from his pie. "Are you serious?"

"Haven't ever been more serious in my life," Trey said, sending a quick glance to Cadence, who nodded her head in agreement. "We want to keep Cass here, at least through the holidays."

"One or all of you could apply to be foster parents. You could have a caseworker come visit, go through the certification process, and fill out all the required paperwork. Usually takes a month or two, depending on how things go."

"So we could keep Cass while we're getting certified?" Cadence asked, hopeful of what his answer would be.

"I don't think it works like that. Certification first, child second," the sheriff said, finishing off his pie and coffee. "That was excellent pie, by the way."

"Thank you," Cadence said, offering the sheriff a beaming smile. "Do you have children, sheriff?"

"Nope. Not married, yet," he said, eyeing Cadence with interest before noticing Trey's glare. "Just haven't found the right lady."

"Despite that, I'm sure you can see the need to give Cass some stability. Trey and I have spent quite a bit of time with her in the past month or so and she knows us well. Wouldn't it be better for the child to stay in an environment where she feels safe and secure, where the people genuinely care for her, where she can flourish and grow under their loving support? Wouldn't that be better than carting her off to a strange home where she's just one more mouth to feed and one more little body to look after? I know not all homes are like that, but tell me the truth, is there a foster home you can think of that isn't already full this time of year?"

"No. They are all pretty full. And yes, it would be better for her to stay here, but you are going to have to convince DHS of that."

Trey leaned across the counter and grinned at his friend. "Who better to convince them than our very own sheriff? You could put in a good word for us. Shoot, you could even give a personal reference. You've known me since we were old enough to walk. Come on. What do you say? Help make a little girl's Christmas merry."

Letting out an exasperated sigh, the sheriff shook his head in defeat. "Fine. I will call DHS, talk to the caseworker, ask her to speed up the certification process and recommend she leave the child here. That is all I can do. Now, if it would be okay with the two of you, I need to ask Cass a few questions. You can sit with her. I basically need a statement from her and to find out if she can remember when Micki died."

"Let's go sit in the front room," Trey said, holding Cadence's hand as they walked into the room.

Cass looked up when they came into the room and ran over to Trey. Picking her up, Trey sat down on the recliner and smiled warmly at the little girl.

"Cass, my friend has come to ask you a few questions about your mommy. He's a nice man and is trying to help, so you just tell him what you remember, okay?"

"Okay," Cass said, leaning into Trey's warmth and wiggling her feet where they dangled over his leg. The sheriff joined Trent on the couch while Cadence sat in the big rocking chair.

The sheriff asked a few questions, wrote down Cass's comments, smiling at her and trying to be encouraging. It didn't take long to figure out that Micki had yelled at her the morning before she died. Cass watched TV, went to the café, ate the "scraps" Viv sent home, watched more TV, tried to wake up Micki then tucked herself into bed. She tried again to wake up Micki the next morning, but got no response. She watched more TV before deciding her mommy needed to wake up. Trying several times to get Micki up with no response, she became frightened and ran across the road to get help.

Closing his notebook, the sheriff walked over to where Cass sat on Trey's lap and hunkered down so he was face to face with her.

"Thanks, Cass, for sharing what you remember with me. It's a big help." He handed her a bright pink lollipop, nodded to Trey and Cadence then walked out with Trent.

Sucking on her treat, Cass was quiet. Finally she looked up at Trey and patted his cheek.

"Who's going to take care of me," her big blue eyes started to fill with tears.

"Don't you worry about any of that, honey," Trey said. "You just leave it up to me and Cady."

"Okay," Cass said, with the trust of a small child. Despite her upbringing, Trey found it unbelievable how innocent and sweet the little girl seemed. She certainly knew how to tug on his heart strings, though, especially when she fell asleep in his arms with the lollipop still in her mouth.

"She must be completely exhausted," Cadence said as she carefully pulled the candy from Cass's mouth. "Just put her here on the couch for a nap. She'll be fine for few minutes."

Lightly covering the little girl with a blanket, Cadence turned off the TV, then she and Trey returned to the kitchen. They decided to make the guest room across the hall from Cadence little-girl friendly and moved out any family heirlooms or things they'd hate to see accidentally broken. Cadence got out the quilt she had been saving for Cass and put it on the bed along with the pillow sham she'd made for her. She also pulled out some of the clothes she'd purchased for the little girl for Christmas and laid them on the bed.

While she finished getting the bedroom ready for Cass, Trey went online to see if he could find information about becoming a foster parent and gathered some helpful details. Trent joined them as they were sitting down at the table to go over the process when the phone rang.

Trent jumped up to grab it on the second ring.

"Triple T, this is Trent."

"Trent? It's Travis. Happy Holidays!"

"Trav! I can hardly hear you. When are you coming home?"

"I … won't… be … home… Christmas."

Travis sounded like he was shouting through a windstorm.

"What?" Trent shouted back.

"Won't… be … home… Christmas."

"Aw, man. We were looking forward to having you here. When will you be able to make it home?"

"Soon… Gotta go."

Then the line went dead.

"From your yelling I'm guessing that was Trav, and he isn't coming home for Christmas," Trey said, looking up with a frown.

"You got that right," Trent said with a sigh as he sat down. "I was really looking forward to having him home this year. With the changes around here, it just seems more like old times."

"Yeah, it does," Trey said, absently watching Cadence. "It certainly does."

After they studied the information Trey had found, Cadence announced her plans to give Cass the best bath she ever had.

"I don't suppose there is a hairdresser in Grass Valley?" Cadence asked.

"No, there isn't one in town, but there is a barber here on the ranch. Rex trims up all of our hair. We could send him in to see what he can do for Cass," Trey said.

"That would be great," Cadence said, relieved. She wanted Cass to look her best when the caseworker came tomorrow and she didn't know if the little girl had ever had her hair properly trimmed. It grew long in some spots, short in others like it had been hacked with a dull butter knife. If it wasn't so curly, it would have looked like a complete disaster instead of just a lopsided mess. "Do you think he'd cut it tonight. I could have her clean in about thirty minutes."

Trey nodded his head and Trent started out the door for the bunkhouse.

When Rex tapped on the back door and came in half an hour later, Cass was sitting at the counter, wearing a new pair of flannel pajamas, eating a cookie with a glass of milk.

"Hello, Miss Cass," Rex said, sitting down at the counter beside her. "Do you remember me from dinner earlier?"

"Yep," Cass said, swinging her feet where they hung from the barstool. "You ate a piece of chocolate pie and Mr. Henry took away your second piece cause he said Cady made it special for him."

"My, you have a good memory," Rex said, sending Cadence a wink. "Are you ready to play beauty parlor?"

"Sure. I haven't played that game before. Is it like playing spa? That's the game Cady and I played. She filled the bathtub with lots of pretty bubbles and I got to splash and swirl in the tub and everything."

"You did?" Rex said, taking a cookie off the plate Cadence passed to him. "That sounds like fun."

"It was, til Cady made me scrub between my toes and behind my ears and everywhere."

Rex laughed. "She's a hard taskmaster."

"What's a tackmadder?"

"Someone who helps you keep doing what you are supposed to be doing," Rex said, trying not to smirk.

"Is she your tackmadder?" Cass asked, staring up at Rex with a thoughtful expression on her little face.

"You bet. She keeps all of us in line, including Mr. Trent and Mr. Trey."

"That's good," Cass said, taking another cookie. Cadence thought the child was a bottomless pit with all the food she had stowed away at dinner. She hoped she would eventually be full and see that she didn't have to worry about going hungry anymore.

"You bet it's good." Rex said, standing up and pulling a pair of barber shears and a comb from his pocket.

"Where do you want to do this, Cady? It might make a bit of a mess and I sure wouldn't want to leave hair where it could get in the food."

Cadence laughed. "Right you are. Let's take a bar stool out to the mudroom. I can put down a plastic tablecloth and then I'll drape a sheet around her. That should catch most of the clippings. I can bring in extra light if you need it."

Rex helped Cadence clear a spot for the stool then went to work. Cadence stood back and watched him clip, comb and trim. In no time at all, he had Cass's hair evenly cut. When he made the final snip, Cass looked adorable with a layered bob that just brushed her shoulders and a few curly bangs across her forehead. Removing the sheet, Cadence picked up Cass and held her in front of the small mirror hanging near the hat rack in the mudroom. Looking into the glass, Cass's eyes grew huge and she reached out a finger to touch the mirror.

"Is that really me?"

"It really is you."

"But I look like a real little girl with pretty hair and new clothes and everything," Cass said, bursting into tears as she threw her arms around Cadence's neck. Patting her back, Cadence rocked from side to side, whispering soothing words. When Cass quit sobbing, she looked at Rex and held out her arms to him.

"Thank you for making my hair pretty, Mr. Rex," Cass said, giving him a tight hug around his neck.

Rex was as tough a cowboy as they came, but even he was having a problem talking around the lump in his throat.

"You come see me anytime you need a haircut." Setting her down in the kitchen, he and Cadence made short work of the mess. Rex went back out to the bunkhouse with a handful of cookies as payment for his barbering efforts.

Trent and Trey were both in the office, discussing plans for the next day's work.

Escorting Cass through the office door, both men looked up and smiled.

"I heard you were playing beauty parlor. Let's see that new haircut of yours," Trey said, picking Cass up and setting her on top of the desk.

Cocking her head to one side, Cass studied Trey.

"Do you like it?" she asked, her blue eyes shining brightly.

"You bet I do, honey," Trey said, kissing her cheek. "You look like a princess, and smell like one, too."

"Cady gave me a bath and let me use some of her fumes. She always smells nice," Cass said.

"That she does," Trey said, picking Cass up and tickling her sides.

Later that evening as Cadence showed Cass her new room and helped her get ready for bed, the little girl couldn't stop talking about her new clothes and hair and being squeaky clean. Cadence thought she would never settle down when she told her the quilt on the bed was just for her to keep forever.

Throwing her thin little arms around Cadence's neck, she squeezed tight.

"Are you magical?" Cass asked, kissing Cadence's cheek.

"No, I'm not, sweetie-pie."

"But you do lots of good things and make everything all pretty and nice," Cass said, rubbing her hand over the top of her quilt. "You must be a fairy."

"Maybe she's one of Santa's helpers," a warm voice rumbled from the hallway.

Cass and Cadence both turned to see Trey leaning against the door. Cass held out her arms to Trey and he picked her up and swung her around before setting her back on the bed.

"Do you work for Santa?" Cass asked Cadence, her eyes wide with curiosity.

"I guess I do," Cass said, winking at Trey over Cass's head. She might not work for the North Pole Santa, but she was definitely on the payroll of Grass Valley's newest jolly old elf.

Trey grinned and gave Cass a kiss on her head.

"Are you ready to go to sleep?" he asked, sitting down on the opposite side of the bed from where Cadence sat.

"I guess," Cass said, her lip starting to pout. "I'll wake up tomorrow, won't I? I don't want to sleep forever like my mommy and daddy."

"Oh, honey," Cadence said, picking her up and holding her close while Trey put a hand on her back. "You will wake up tomorrow and the next day and the next day. I promise."

"You won't let anything happen to me?" Cass asked, still sounding a little frightened.

"No, we won't," Trey said, softly, reassuringly. What did you say to a 5-year-old who had just lost a mother who never cared enough about her to be a real parent? "We promise as long as you are here with us to take very good care of you."

195

"Okay," Cass said.

Tucking her under the covers, Cadence kissed her cheek again and picked up a storybook.

"So what bedtime tale are you reading tonight?" Trey asked with a smile. He had no idea how to take care of a child, but Cady seemed to know a thing or two about it. He decided to just follow her lead.

"*Humphrey's First Christmas*," Cadence said. "It's the story of one of the camels that carried the wise men to see baby Jesus. Have you ever seen a camel, Cass?"

"Nope, but I bet they aren't as nice as Powder," Cass said, already partial to Trey's horse.

Trey had led her around the corral for a bit before dinner in hopes of keeping her distracted from what had happened to her mother. It worked better than he expected.

"Well, let's hear this story about the Christmas camel," Trey said, settling in to watch both the females who had swept in and taken over his heart.

Cadence was only half-way through the story when Cass's eyes drifted shut and her breath came out in soft little puffs. She looked so sweet nestled into the warm bed, her cheeks rosy, and her hair shining in the glow of the bedside lamp.

Trying not to cry, Cadence couldn't keep a tear from running down her cheek as she thought about how resilient and strong this delicate little girl was. Despite everything that had happened in the past 24 hours, the only time she had cried since they brought her home was when she'd been overwhelmed with gratitude. How could such a little thing offer such a big example of humble dignity?

Seeing the lone tear roll down Cadence's cheek, Trey reached across the bed and softly brushed it away. Her eyes caught and held his, tugging him into a place of warmth and wanting. Carefully rising from the bed, they turned off the lamp, plugged in a night light and left Cass's door open just a crack.

Out in the hallway, Trey engulfed Cadence in his embrace, resting his chin on her head. She wrapped her arms around him and absorbed his strength and vitality.

They both wanted to avoid thinking about what the next day would bring. Too much of their happiness rested on what the case worker would decide.

"How can she be so sweet? So unspoiled by what her life has been?" Cadence whispered through the emotion threatening to choke her.

"I don't know, Cady. Maybe Micki tried to be a parent more than we think," he said, rubbing his hands comfortingly across her back. "I've never been a big kid person, but that little girl in there marched right into my heart the same way she marched in here with her toilet paper costume. You'd have to be the worst kind of cold-hearted fool to not care for her."

"What will we do if they take her away? I just can't bear the thought of what could happen to her."

"Let's not borrow trouble. After we meet the caseworker tomorrow and hear what she has to say, maybe we'll be pleasantly surprised. I can't see any reason she wouldn't approve all of us as fit foster parents. Besides, it has got to be a plus that there are three adults in the house to watch after one little-bitty girl."

"Are you always so positive and confident?" Cadence asked with the faintest hint of a smile forming on her lips.

"Why not? It's better than sitting around thinking the world's gonna end every time you turn around," Trey said. "How did you get experience taking care of kids? You seem to know what you're doing with her."

"I used to babysit evenings and summers to make extra money for college. Several of our neighbors had kids when I was growing up and I never lacked for babysitting jobs."

"Well, you might have to teach Trent and me a thing or two about taking care of kids. We don't know the first thing about caring for human offspring although we do pretty well with the four-legged variety."

"You seem to have a natural talent for it. Relating to kids, I mean," Cadence said, giving him such a warm smile, he got lost in it momentarily.

Leaning against the frame of her bedroom door he gave her a kiss that took her mind completely off Cass and everything else, except what was being shared between them right at that moment.

When she could catch her breath, she stared at him, longing written all over her face, heat filling her cheeks.

"What was that for?"

"To keep you thinking on the positive," Trey said, as he sauntered back toward the kitchen. Turning before he reached the end of the hallway, he gave her a teasing grin. "It's not right to fret so much this close to Christmas, darlin'. Believe in a little holiday magic."

Chapter Thirteen

In difficult and hopeless situations
the boldest plans are the safest.

Titus Livy

The case worker called early the next morning to ask for directions and told them to expect her around 10 a.m.

Cadence rushed around cleaning an already spotless house, made Cass take another bath and dressed her in the dress and shoes Viv had bought her for Thanksgiving. Viv arrived after breakfast that morning with a box full of things from Micki's she thought the little girl should have. She brought the clothes that still had some wear in them, including Cass's Thanksgiving outfit. She also drug along the paper chain from the café which Cass insisted go back over the kitchen curtain rod.

While Viv was helping Cass take off that day's paper chain, Cadence hurried to her bedroom and changed into a pair of navy dress slacks, low heels and a lavender cashmere sweater before pulling her hair up into a loose bun.

Coming back into the kitchen, Viv gave her an encouraging hug then headed back to town. Cadence couldn't focus on anything, instead fidgeting and fussing with the holiday decorations, waiting for the case worker to arrive.

Trey and Trent weren't fairing much better. The two of them took showers after they finished the morning chores, put on freshly pressed jeans and shirts along with polished boots. They both carefully combed their hair instead of their usual slap-dash attempt at taming it and now sat in the great room with Cass where she looked through a book about the ABCs.

All three of the adults kept an eye on the clock and the closer it got to ten, the more antsy they became.

Cadence went into the kitchen and made a fresh pot of coffee, prepared a tray with cups, sugar and creamer, and added a plate of raspberry coffee cake left over from breakfast. She was arranging the tray on the coffee table when the doorbell rang.

Trey jumped up and hurried to the door while Cadence and Trent looked at each other and gave Cass another once over. Cadence quickly ran a hand over Cass's curls to make sure all was in place then stood to greet the case worker with a smile.

"Hello, Mrs. Bisbee," Cadence said, extending her hand to the middle-aged woman who bustled in the door.

"Miss Greer," she said, taking Cadence's hand in a firm handshake. "It's nice to meet you. Please call me Barbara. And this must be the other Mr. Thompson. Trent."

Trent shook her hand and motioned for her to take a seat.

She chose to sit next to Cass. Watching the little girl watch her, she offered a warm smile.

"And you must be Cass. How do you do?"

"Fine," Cass said, with a shy smile.

They chatted for a few minutes and Barbara asked them all several questions, while taking notes. Filling out paperwork, she had them sign copies, and then asked to speak to Cass alone.

Cadence, Trey and Trent retreated to the kitchen.

"What do you suppose she's asking her," Trent said, leaning against the sink.

"Who knows? I didn't know anyone could have so many questions," Trey said. "And some of them were a bit personal."

"A bit?" Cadence whispered hotly. "I think asking if I was having 'intimate relations' with either of you exceeds a bit more than personal. And thank you, Trent, for clarifying that I have 'gone sweet' on your brother."

"Just doing what I can," Trent said, not looking remorseful in the least.

"Well, what if ..." Cadence cut off her thought in mid sentence as Barbara came into the kitchen, holding Cass's hand.

"We had a wonderful little chat and Cass tells me that she loves staying here. I think that can be arranged at least through the holiday season," Barbara said, watching the three adults sigh in relief. "We don't usually push through the paperwork quite so quickly, but the sheriff gave you all a glowing recommendation, the house is perfect, you all obviously care about this child and she, quite frankly, adores all of you. So for now, we will come out weekly to monitor how things are progressing. Once the paperwork is finalized, you'll receive notification of your certification."

"That's wonderful, Barbara," Cadence said, pulling Cass to her and giving the little girl a hug.

"I'll keep in touch and if you have any questions, I'm always available by phone. I left copies of my card on the coffee table along with a copy of the paperwork process. If there are no further questions, I'll be on my way."

Trey retrieved Barbara's coat and helped her put it on while Trent volunteered to walk her out.

As soon as the door shut behind her, Trey tugged both of his girls into his arms and gave them a jubilant hug.

Cadence had all she could do not to do a dance. Trey didn't seem to have any problem giving in to his desire as he swept up Cass and did a few fancy steps around the great room.

When Trent came back in he gave Cadence a hug and high-fived Trey, then snatched Cass into his arms and tossed her into the air.

"Looks like you are stuck here with us for a while, Cass. What do you think of that?"

"Yeah," the little girl said, patting Trent's face before kissing his cheek.

The hands were checking in one by one asking how things had gone. Cadence decided to fix them all lunch so they could share the news together.

That night after they had finished the camel story, listened to Cass's bedtime prayers and tucked her in for the night, Trey left Cadence in the great room working on Christmas cards with Trent while he went to try on the Santa suit. He hadn't had time since it came back from the cleaners to see how it fit.

Standing in front of the mirror, he thought he made an altogether sorry spectacle. Where Santa should be round and jolly, Trent was muscular and trim. Even with the padded belly strapped on, he still didn't look very Santa like. Sticking his head around the corner at the end of the hall, he called to Cadence.

"Cady, can you come here a minute, please?"

Going back to his room, he again gave himself a critical look in the mirror, not happy at what he was seeing.

"Trey?" Cadence asked, peeking into his room. "What did…"

Seeing him in the Santa suit, she burst out laughing.

"What's so funny?" Trey asked, turning to look at her with a scowl.

"You and that suit…" She was laughing so hard she couldn't even stand and sank down on a corner of his bed.

Trey had on the entire suit from plush red hat to red velvet pants. Instead of looking jovial and fun he was starting to look mad and more than a little intimidating. The wig was bunched up on one side, the beard was on crooked and if she wasn't mistaken, Cadence thought he might have the stomach pad on upside down which would explain why it looked so ridiculous. The pants fit him well and with his black cowboy boots on, they should work fine.

"I'm sorry, Trey, it just looks a little... humorous," she said, reaching up to take off the hat and wig, then the beard. "Take off the jacket and let's try this again."

He pulled off the wide black belt, unbuttoned the jacket then removed it. While he did that, Cadence was busy fluffing the hair of the wig and straightening it out, then finger combing the beard.

When she turned around to look at Trey, she sucked in her breath.

"Oh," was all she could say, as her eyes roved over Trey's upper anatomy. He was wearing a white tank-style undershirt that accented every firm, impressive muscle in his shoulders, arms and chest. If that wasn't bad enough, the red suspenders of the pants drew vertical lines across those rippling muscles that Cadence couldn't help but follow both up and down and back up again.

Trey, watching her eyes get wide and stormy, was quite pleased at his ability to ruffle her feathers, even if it was unintentional. Not caring at this moment if he looked like an elf on steroids, he was feeling quite smug that Cady was obviously attracted to him. He wasn't all that experienced when it came to wooing women, but he assumed her intense perusal coupled with her inability to say anything was probably a good sign.

Unable to stop himself, Trey placed his hands on his lean hips, drawing up his muscles in a way he hoped showed them off to his best advantage.

"What do you think, Cady?" he asked with a devilish gleam in his eye.

"Huh? Think? What?" Cadence asked, trying to bring herself back to reality. Blinking her eyes, she focused on the stomach pad Trey had put on upside down. Walking up to him, she gave the elastic band running over his shoulder a firm snap.

"Ow! What was that for?" Trey said, jumping back from her.

"You've got this thing on upside down. Turn it around and let's see what it looks like."

Cadence busied herself with the beard again while Trey took off the pad, turned it over and slipped it back on. He then pulled on the jacket and buttoned it and put the belt back on.

"Okay, does this look better?" he asked, noticing in the mirror that it looked much more Santa-like, even without the beard and hat.

"Much better. You don't look so deformed now," Cadence teased, putting the beard, wig and hat on Trey. She tugged the hat to a jaunty angle, then stepped back to give him a critical once-over.

"I think you'll do."

Trey looked in the mirror and was surprised to see Santa staring back at him. A young looking Santa with extremely bright eyes, but Santa none-the-less.

"Not too bad," Trey agreed. "Now I guess I better work on practicing my ho-ho-hos."

"No time like the present," Cadence said, sitting down on the one chair in Trey's room. "Let's hear it."

"I don't think so," Trey said, suddenly feeling exposed and vulnerable. It was one thing to do it for the kids at the program. But it was something else entirely to have Cady sit there and watch him.

"Don't tell me big, bad, tough, take-no-prisoners Trey Thompson is scared to say ho, ho, ho," Cadence teased.

"I'm not scared," Trey said, getting annoyed.

"Then let 'er rip."

"No."

"Come on, Trey, don't be a baby. You've got to practice. The program is coming right up."

"I'm not a baby and I'll practice when I'm good and ready."

"Is that so?" Cadence said, getting up from the chair and placing her hands on her hips, shooting him a determined look. Stepping directly in front of Trey, she stood toe to toe with him, refusing to back down.

"Yes, that's so," Trey snapped, breathing in her fresh scent and wanting to kiss her so badly his lips tingled.

"Maybe you need an incentive," Cadence said, switching tactics.

"What kind of an incentive?" Trey asked, wondering what was flying through Cady's head. He hoped it involved relieving his need to kiss her. Repeatedly.

"How about a kiss? If I kiss Santa, would that help?" Cadence asked as she glanced sideways at him with a flirty smile.

"Maybe," Trey growled. "But I think two kisses would work better."

"My goodness, Santa is a greedy little elf, isn't he?" Cadence teased.

Reaching up she pulled Trey's head down and planted a kiss on one bearded cheek, then the other.

"I'm not sure I like kissing a man with a beard," she said, taking a step back. "Now, let's hear it, Santa."

"Those weren't real kisses," Trey said, shaking his head in disappointment. "You can do better than that."

"Here's the deal," Cadence said, enjoying their banter and being close to Trey. "One kiss before and one kiss after. Got it?"

"Got it," Trey said, bringing his lips to Cadence's in a kiss that made her so dizzy, she clung to Trey's coat for support. When he raised his head and released her, she took a weak-kneed step back and sat down on the bed.

Bemused, she smiled. "Proceed, Santa."

"Ho, ho, ho," Trey said without much enthusiasm.

"That was pathetic," Cadence said. "Even I could do better than that. Give it some gusto, put some jolly in there."

"Ho, Ho, Ho," Trey said, doing a little better, but not really trying very hard.

"You are seriously wasting my time, now," Cadence said, getting up and starting toward the door. Trey caught her by the arm and pulled her to him before dropping her into a dip and kissing her thoroughly. When he raised her back up, he let out a perfect "Ho! Ho! Ho!"

"Now, that's more like it," Cadence said with a huge smile.

"I think Santa deserves a little reward," Trey said, lowering her into another dip. He was just going in for a kiss when Trent cleared his throat at the door. Still holding Cadence bent over his arm, Trey and Cadence both looked up at Trent. The end of the Santa hat dangled over one of Cadence's eyes and she batted at it while her cheeks flushed with embarrassment.

"I wondered what you two were up to. Guess I really didn't want to know," Trent said with a laugh and walked away.

Trey stole a quick kiss then pulled Cadence upright.

"I think that is my cue to leave," Cadence said, tugging her twisted sweater back into place. She'd never had so much fun with a man before or felt so carefree as she did around Trey.

"Be careful, Cady," Trey said, running his hands up and down her sides.

She looked up at him, confused.

"I think you've just about let all those tight stays loose. You let your hair down, learned to laugh and have a little fun. At this rate, I can't wait to see what happens next." Trey's hot blue eyes bore into hers with an intensity that made her catch her breath.

Leaning into him, she pulled down his beard and kissed him with all the longing and passion he had stirred inside her. When she thought she would explode from the wonder of it all, she stepped back and let his beard go with a snap.

Turning, she ran out of the room with Trey's yelp following her into the great room. Half-surprised he didn't chase her, she giggled as she sank down onto a chair.

As she sat there addressing Christmas cards, she couldn't help but think about Trey. Even though she had only known him for two and a half months, she felt like she had loved him for a lifetime.

That thought caught her entirely off guard. Sitting there with her writing pen between her teeth, she wondered how she could have thought she was in love with Bill. She realized she had never loved him and was grateful their relationship ended when and how it did. Thanks to being dumped by good ol' Bill, she found her way here to the Triple T, Trey, and Cass. How full and challenging and amazing her life had become. Being jilted was the nicest thing Bill had ever done for her.

If it wasn't for him, she would never have had the opportunity to meet and fall in love with that fine cowboy in the other room.

Chapter Fourteen

*To achieve great things, two things are needed;
a plan, and not quite enough time.*
Leonard Bernstein

The weekend passed quickly. A snow storm blew in and covered the ground in white once again, although today the sun was shining and would likely melt the snow before long.

Trey took Cass with him for the morning. She was enthralled with the horses and hardly knew what to think when Trey asked if she'd like to go for a ride with him while he checked fences. Cadence made sure Cass had on plenty of layers of clothes along with the new coat and snow boots she had purchased for her the day after Thanksgiving.

Watching the little girl run out the door holding tight to Trey's big hand caused Cadence's heart to do somersaults. She had pictured herself being a mother someday, but not in such an unconventional manner. Although she and Trey hadn't yet spoken of love, she felt their bond growing to include little Cass in the center of it all.

Rolling out pie crust and listening to Christmas carols, Cadence was interrupted from her musings by the ringing of the phone. Brushing off her hands on a dish towel, she grabbed the phone on the third ring.

"Thompson Ranch, may I help you?" she asked politely.

"Cadence? This is Barbara with DHS."

"Hi, Barbara. How are you today?"

"I'm fine, Cadence, but I have some news I'd rather not have to share," Barbara said, sounding distressed.

Cadence sank onto a barstool, waiting for Barbara to drop the bomb. "Go on."

"We found Micki's sister. She lives in Portland and has decided she wants to keep Cass,"

Cadence felt all the air rush out of her. "I thought there was no known family."

"There wasn't at the time of Micki's death, but we have to search every avenue, and we did. And found the sister."

"So what can we do? We want to keep Cass here. I don't think I'd be speaking out of turn to say we'd all like to keep her permanently."

"If that is how you really feel, you could file for custody. If Micki's sister contests it, you could end up in a drawn out battle."

Cadence didn't want to drag Cass through that.

"Would she be a good mother to her? Would she love her and care for her, Barbara?"

"Honestly, I don't know. From what we've dug up, you and the Thompsons would be a much more stable choice for Cass, but the law most often rules on the side of blood relations."

Cadence sucked back a sigh.

"Cadence, as much as I hate to ask, Marcy would like to meet Cass tomorrow. Can you bring her to my office? I figure that is a good half-way point and also neutral ground to you both."

"What time would you like us there?"

"Let's say 11 a.m."

"We'll be there," Cadence said, feeling numb and sad.

"Cadence, I shouldn't tell you this and it is completely off the record, but if you really want to keep Cass, I suggest speaking to an attorney right away and seeing what can be done. Until any further decisions are made, I am recommending Cass stay in your home. I've pushed to get the certification rushed through, so if this does go to court, you should be a licensed foster home by then."

"Thank you, Barbara. I appreciate your help. See you tomorrow."

Hanging up the phone, Cadence couldn't move, shocked by the news that Micki had a sister. Cadence's worst fear was that Marcy would be a replica of Micki and Cass would be right back in a terrible situation. Releasing the sigh she held in earlier, Cadence went back to her pie making, wondering how she would break this news to Trey and Trent.

><><

Planning to take Cass by herself to the appointment, Cadence was surprised when both Trey and Trent decided to join them.

"Mind if we tag along, ladies," Trey asked as he opened the pickup door for Cadence while Trent buckled Cass into her booster seat.

"Not at all," Cadence said, taking Trey's hand as she climbed in the pickup. He kissed her cheek before shutting her door and sliding in the front seat.

Cass chattered away on the drive to The Dalles, but the three adults were barely able to provide answers to her questions, lost in their worries about losing the little girl.

"Where we going, Cady?" Cass asked.

"We are going to visit Barbara. Remember the nice lady who came to the house the other day? We are going to visit her," Cadence explained.

"Will she ask more questions?" Cass asked, looking out the window as they pulled off the freeway into town.

"She might," Cadence said. "But you're very good at answering questions, aren't you?"

"Yep. I tell it like it is," Cass said, making even Trey smile.

"Now, where did you hear that phrase?" Cadence asked as they pulled into the parking lot at the DHS office.

"Miss Viv," Cass replied.

"That figures," Trey muttered under his breath.

Helping Cass out of her booster seat, Trent took her hand and started to the door followed by a somber Trey and Cadence. Trey kept his hand at the small of Cadence's back, needing the reassurance of touching her as much as she needed to feel his warmth, even through her coat.

Going in the door, Cadence told the receptionist they had an appointment to see Barbara. They didn't wait long until they were escorted to a conference room. Barbara soon came in, wearing a friendly smile.

"Good morning, everyone. Cadence, I didn't expect you to bring the troops," Barbara said, looking at the Thompson brothers who sat wearing matching scowls.

"They wouldn't let me leave without them," Cadence said, mustering a grin.

"Here is how this will work," Barbara said. "Once Marcy arrives, I will bring her in and introduce her to all of you. I'll give you a few minutes to chit chat and see how she interacts with Cass then I'll take them to my office for some observations before I bring Cass back to you. One thing I want to make clear is that regardless of what happens with Marcy today, Cass will be going home with you."

Cadence and Trey let out a sigh of relief and Trent smiled at Cass where she sat beside him.

A receptionist knocked on the door and let Barbara know Marcy had arrived.

When Barbara escorted her into the room, Trey thought it was like seeing Micki brought back to life. She and Marcy could have been identical twins.

When Cass looked up, she yelled, "Mommy!" and launched herself at Marcy. Marcy awkwardly pushed Cass away without offering the child any warmth or comfort.

"I ain't your mother, kid. I'm her sister," Marcy said, looking at her choice of empty seats and plopping down next to Trent. A cloud of cheap perfume followed her around the table along with disapproving glances from Trey and Trent. Dressed in a super-short skirt with spiked boots and a low cut blouse, Marcy didn't exactly look like the maternal type. Especially when seated across the table from Cadence who was wearing black dress pants, a berry silk blouse and a black cardigan sweater. Her grandmother's pearls encircled her neck, giving her a look not completely unlike that of June Cleaver, especially with her hair pulled back in a chignon.

Left standing alone by her aunt, Cass ran to Cadence and climbed on her lap, burying her face against her blouse.

"She looks like my mommy," Cass whispered, sneaking a glance across the table.

"I know, sweetie," Cadence said, rubbing her back.

"So you the do-gooders who's been taking care of Micki's kid?" Marcy asked, swinging the leg she had crossed over the other while she snapped her gum.

"The Thompsons and Miss Greer have given Cass exemplary care," Barbara stated, feeling annoyed that she even had to call this meeting. If it was up to her, she'd place Cass with Trey and Cady and leave them to a happily ever after. Unfortunately, the law dictated she follow procedure. Even when it included stirring up what most likely would be trouble.

"How much you making to keep her?" Marcy asked, looking at Cadence.

"Pardon?" Cadence asked, so taken aback by the question, she couldn't even process it.

"You know, how much does the state give you to take care of her?" Marcy asked, then turned to Barbara. "She will be getting social security benefits won't she?"

Trey and Trent both turned to look at Marcy with undisguised loathing on their faces. Cadence could see the vein throbbing in Trey's neck and the hand that wasn't holding hers was now clenched in a fist. She squeezed his hand. Before either of the men could say anything, Barbara spoke up.

"She will receive benefits, eventually. The Thompsons have not received, nor asked for any financial assistance in providing care for Cass."

"Oh, so you guys are probably rich," Marcy said, leering at Trent. "Sexy-hot cowboys with lots of money, isn't that just typical."

Cadence was ready to grab Cass and leave. If it meant going on the run to protect her from Marcy, Cadence thought she would do it.

"Miss Gianotti, why don't you come with me to my office and I'll give you a few minutes to get to know your niece," Barbara said, standing up and taking Cass by the hand.

Cass looked unsure and pulled back toward Cadence. Patting her back, Cadence set her down and kissed her cheek. "Go on with Miss Barbara, honey. We'll be right here waiting for you."

"You want to wait on me, too?" Marcy asked as she ran a red-painted nail across Trent's shoulder as she walked by. As she went out the door, he shuddered.

"That woman is a disgusting, unholy mess," Trent said, getting up from the table and pacing the room.

"They can't possibly think she would make a fit guardian for Cass," Cadence said, looking to Trey for reassurance. "Can they?"

"I don't know that they'll think she is fit, but she definitely is blood," Trey observed. How anyone with eyes in their head could turn their sweet little Cass over to a woman like Marcy was beyond his ability to comprehend. But he knew exactly the same thing happened to other kids every day.

It wasn't long until Barbara was back, leading Cass by the hand. Cass looked a little wary, but was busy sucking on the candy cane in her other hand. Looking at them, Barbara shook her head as Cass ran over to Trey and he picked her up, kissing her cheek.

"Why don't you go with Trent to the truck, honey?" Trey said, handing Cass to his brother. "We'll be out in just a minute."

When Trent left the room with Cass, Barbara sat down and motioned for Trey to do the same. "Marcy said she definitely wants Cass. I don't think it is a good idea or in the child's best interest. While she says she is employed, I have yet to make verification of that and I don't know that her current housing situation will work for a child. Cass seems to be a bit frightened by her, and I honestly can't say that I blame her. She doesn't show any instincts for connecting with or caring for the child, however, she is Cass's aunt. I asked her to think about what she wants to do overnight, so when she calls me tomorrow, I'll let you know her decision. I sincerely hope she will reconsider. If she decides to push this, and you decide to fight her, I'd say based on what I saw today, you'd have a fair chance of gaining custody."

Trey nodded his head and squeezed Cadence's hand.

"However, you will need to make a choice as to exactly who is going to take custody. The biggest obstacle I could see is that Cadence is your employee, not a wife or even a fiancée. What happens if she leaves to go work somewhere else? If the judge is going to grant custody, you'll have to decide which one of you takes it. You need to have a united front on this issue."

Cadence looked near tears and Trey felt like his collar had just gotten two sizes too tight.

Marriage? He wasn't ready to settle down. Sure, he was in love with Cadence, but marriage and a lifetime commitment were miles away from being infatuated with his beautiful housekeeper. As much as he wanted to keep Cass, he wasn't sure he was ready to get married just to gain custody. When he got married, he wanted it to be because he couldn't live a day longer without making the woman he loved his.

Casting a glance Cadence's direction, he took in her classic beauty, her grace, warmth, and innate goodness. He thought about the kisses they had shared and how perfect it felt to hold her in his arms. How frustrated, strong, happy, and fully alive she made him feel.

Maybe marriage wasn't such a bad idea after all.

Standing up, Trey pulled Cadence to her feet, helped her on with her coat, and took her hand again.

"Thank you, Barbara. We'll wait to hear from you tomorrow," Trey said, escorting Cadence out the door to the pickup. Half-way across the parking lot, he bent near her ear and whispered, "Don't worry, darlin'. This will all work out just fine."

Cadence hoped, to the depths of her being, that he was right.

><><

Shanna Hatfield

Barbara called mid-morning the following day. Trey stuck around the house, waiting for the call to come in. He and Cadence sat in the office with the phone on speaker so they both could hear what she had to say.

"She says she wants to move forward and has a friend who knows a lawyer who will help her get custody. I don't know how far she will take this, but I strongly suggest you find an attorney and prepare to go to court. I am going to try to get the judge to bump this case up so we can get this settled before Christmas. If Cass has to be moved, doing it before the holiday will be easier on her in the long run, than after."

Cadence felt her heart fall to the floor. She had hoped, at the very least, to be able to spend one Christmas with Cass, making it special for her. Now they might not even have that long. It was little more than a week to Christmas Eve.

"I'm so sorry. If I could make all the paperwork and procedures disappear, I'd pretend I'd never heard of Cass and leave her with you," Barbara said, her sigh carrying across the phone.

"We appreciate that, Barbara. Please let us know if you hear any more news or have information we should be made aware of," Trey said, noticing the tears glistening in Cadence's eyes.

Disconnecting the call, he walked around the desk pulled Cadence to her feet and wrapped his arms around her, willing her to draw some strength from him. She looked like she didn't have any left.

Soaking up the warmth and comfort Trey offered, Cadence buried her face against his chest breathing in his scent that was becoming all too familiar to her. Resting there a few minutes, she stood back, straightened her spine, and picked up the phone.

"Who are you calling?" Trey asked, leaning against the desk.

216

"My former employer. If anyone can help us, he is the man for the job. He is one of the top attorney's in Seattle and has connections all over the country," Cadence said, waiting for someone to answer the phone.

"Neil Dumont's office. May I help you?"

"Yes, I'd like to speak with Mr. Dumont, please."

"May I say who is calling?"

"Just tell him it's Cadence."

After a brief pause, Neil picked up the line. "Cadence! How are things in the middle nowhere? How's that cowboy of yours?"

"Things are fine and I've already told you that which you keep referring to as mine is not. At least not yet."

"Well, to what do I owe the pleasure of this call?" Neil asked, wanting to get to the point because he knew Cadence wouldn't call him at work without a good reason.

"I need your help," Cadence said, then explained the situation with Cass.

"Sounds to me like the sister is perhaps just digging for gold and hopes the Thompsons will provide it in the form of a payoff."

"I hadn't thought of that," Cadence said, seeing how that would make sense, though, considering Marcy's comments from the day before.

"You need an attorney who can push this through quickly, can show her as an unfit parent and make sure the judge awards you custody. I'm assuming you are the one who will be doing the filing?"

"We haven't really progressed with that discussion. Don't you think the Thompsons would be a better choice?"

"Not necessarily. They've got the funding, but you are the mother figure. You know, the ideal would be if you and your cowboy would get married, or at least engaged and file for joint custody. That would really be a help to the case."

"Neil, I don't' see that being an option. At all."

"Well, think about it," Neil teased. Cadence could hear him scratching down some notes. "How far are you from Portland?"

"A couple hours. Why?"

"I've got a friend there who owes me a favor or two. He might be willing to take your case. Let me check in with him and I'll get back to you later."

"That sounds great. Thanks, Neil. I knew I could count on you," Cadence said, grateful for any help Neil could provide.

"You're welcome. And Cadence?"

"Yes?"

"If you try a little harder, I bet that cowboy of yours wouldn't have too hard of a time popping the question."

"Goodbye, Neil."

Cadence disconnected the call with a blush riding her cheeks. Although Trey couldn't hear what Neil said, Cadence felt her face flame from Neil's comments. If Trey didn't love her enough to want to marry her, there wasn't a thing she could do about it.

Trey grinned at her flushed face.

"I don't know what he said, but it put some mighty high color in those cheeks of yours. If they are going to be that rosy, you might as well come out and ride with me for a while."

Cadence shook her head and started to walk out of the office. Trey grabbed her hand and pulled her back against him, wrapping his arms around her waist and holding her close against his chest. "What's got you so worked up, darlin'?"

"Just you never mind. Neil is calling a friend and will get back to us soon with a name," Cadence said, enjoying resting against Trey and being in his arms. Turning around so she could see his face, she kissed his cheek then walked out of the room.

><><

Neil called right after lunch and let Cadence know he had a friend who would be more than happy to take on their case. He wanted to meet with them the next day in Portland. Neil gave her the phone number and address, and told her to call and confirm the appointment.

"How can I thank you, Neil?" Cadence asked as she wrote down the information.

"By having a wonderful rest of forever, Cadence. Or shall I call you Cady? I think it seems to fit you much better these days. You sound so much more relaxed and happy since you moved out there and found yourself a cowboy. So when are you going to convince him that you are the girl for him?

"Neil," Cadence said with a disapproving tone to her voice. "You and I both know I'm not the best judge of character when it comes to men. I don't want to rush into anything."

"Nonsense," Neil argued. "I had these Thompsons checked out and they are about as upstanding as citizens can get. I hear they are all quite good looking and they have to be bighearted to want to keep Cass. I'm assuming Trey isn't dumb or blind, so he has quite likely noticed all that you have to offer. The only time you exhibited poor judgment was with Bill. And considering the fact that he is closer to a snake than a man, I don't think that one should count."

Cadence laughed. "Well, you might be correct on that one account."

"I know for a fact I'm right. So you just need to convince yourself and the cowboy," Neil said with a laugh. "Give my friend Peter a call and keep me posted."

"I will. Thanks again, Neil. It means a lot to me."

Hanging up, Cadence called Peter Hanson and confirmed the appointment for 10 a.m. the next morning.

When Trey popped in a bit later, she let him know about Neil's friend and what time they needed to be in

Portland. They decided they would get up early and be on the road by 6 a.m. It was a two and a half-hour drive and Trey wanted plenty of time to find Mr. Hanson's office. He figured if they had time to kill, they could go get a cup of coffee or some breakfast.

Cadence made a big batch of blueberry muffins and a slow cooker full of hashbrown casserole for the men to eat for breakfast before she went to bed.

The next morning, she dressed in a black power suit with a bright blue silk chemise, a pair of black heels and pinned her hair into a neat, no-nonsense French twist. Putting on mascara and a spritz of perfume, she snapped on a silver watch, picked up her black wool coat and purse, and hurried out of her bedroom.

She quietly opened Cass's bedroom door, crossed the room and dropped a light kiss on the little girl's forehead before rushing into the kitchen.

Trent had promised to keep an eye on Cass and would take her in to visit Aunt Viv for lunch. Cadence hoped after their meeting, Trey would be game to do a little Christmas shopping.

Pouring two travel mugs full of hot coffee, Cadence looked out the kitchen window to see Trey stop his truck close to the back door. Pulling on her coat, she hustled outside, carefully slid her way down the back steps and right into Trey's arms.

"If you'd hold your horses a minute, I was coming to help you to the truck," he said with a grin in his voice. It was still too dark outside for her to fully see his face, although the flash of white teeth illuminated by the porch light helped convince her of his smile.

"I'm perfectly capable of maneuvering the few steps to your vehicle," Cadence said, sounding like the formal, professional woman who had first arrived at the ranch. Trey turned loose of her and she took two steps before she started sliding in her high heels. Grasping her arms before she fell, Trey pulled her to him, turned her around and stuck his hands inside her coat. Running his fingers up and down her sides, he gave her a light squeeze.

"What are you doing?" she asked, sounding annoyed. If her hands hadn't been full of coffee, she would have smacked him. Now was not the time or the place for Trey to be stirring her emotions into a roiling mess. How could he not know that every touch of his hand made her insides quiver and her thoughts jumble? She needed to stay cool-headed and focused.

"Just checking to see if you laced those stays back up and pulled 'em too tight."

Cadence laughed in spite of her decision to remain serious and in business mode until after the meeting.

"No, I did not. And I've never worn stays, for your information. They went out ages ago, if you have any notion of fashion history." Cadence accepted his help in climbing in the pickup and buckled her seat belt while he shut her door.

"I've got a notion about quite a few things and half of them you probably don't want to hear right this moment," Trey teased as they drove down the driveway.

Cadence shot him a warning glare. "Do you think you could possibly focus on the matter at hand this morning? If I'm going to get through this without turning into a sobbing heap of useless female, you better just leave me and my uptight self alone."

Trey remained silent for a while, taking the opportunity to study Cadence. While she had relaxed and learned to have fun in the past several weeks, he could see she used that cool, aloof persona to maintain a certain level of distance and professionalism. It was, in a sense, like a coat of armor, protecting her from getting close enough to anything to get hurt. Or attached. Or involved. The fact that she had set it aside completely with him spoke volumes to his heart. He suddenly wondered if she let the guy who jilted her make a dent in that armor.

"Cady, can I ask you something?"

She shot him a wary glance, but finally nodded her head.

"Viv said the reason you came to Grass Valley was because you were engaged and the guy left you at the altar. Did you... do you love him?" Trey asked, half afraid of what her response would be. What if she was still in love with the guy? What if she wasn't interested in a future with him?

"No," Cadence whispered. Wondering what had brought Trey to this line of questioning. She supposed he would ask at some point, she just didn't think today would be the day for this conversation. "No, I didn't love him."

"Then what made you decide to marry him? Why would you plan to marry someone if you didn't love them?"

"I wanted..." Cadence released a sigh. This wasn't going to be easy to explain, especially since she had just recently worked through her real reasons for wanting to marry Bill. "Bill was the young hot-shot attorney at the office when I started working for Neil. He had it all - looks, money, position, charm. When he turned his attention toward me, I was flattered. I wasn't anybody, just Neil's assistant. I grew up in a hard-working middle class home. I didn't have any advantages. I wasn't the prettiest girl in the office or the smartest or the most popular. I still don't know why he was interested in me in the first place."

"I've got a few ideas," Trey muttered to himself. Who wouldn't want to be with Cady? She was beautiful, intelligent, exciting and sweet just to name a few of the dozen words he could think of to describe her.

"Bill kept asking me on dates, for lunch, to coffee and I continued to turn him down. That went on for about a year. Although there wasn't any policy against it, I just thought it wasn't a good idea to date anyone who worked in the office. I should have listened to my instincts," Cadence said. Looking over at Trey, she knew that although she wouldn't want to go through a similar experience, the end result of it was worth the pain and trouble if it meant being at the Triple T.

"I finally gave in and went on a date with him. We dated casually for quite a while then this past spring Bill seemed to get more intense about our relationship. He proposed in July and wanted to get married right away. I agreed and planned a beautiful fall ceremony. He ran off with his secretary the week before our wedding. Neil was the one who broke the news to me. Bill sent out an email to the partners the night before telling them he was taking two weeks off and getting married, to Miss Roberts. I knew I couldn't keep working there when he came back with his new bride, so I packed up that day and left. He'd already talked me into getting rid of my apartment and all of my furniture. Essentially homeless and unemployed, Aunt Viv offered to take me in until I could figure out what to do, and you know the rest of the story."

Trey stretched across the seat, captured her hand and gave it a squeeze.

"I'm so sorry, darlin'. No one should have to go through something like that, especially not you."

"Don't go feeling sorry for me, Trey. I made my choices, and had to face the consequences. I realized shortly after arriving in Grass Valley that I didn't love Bill. If I had, it would have hurt more. In a way, I think I was relieved. The person most important to Bill is himself and I know that would never have changed, only gotten worse. I was an idiot for getting involved with him and an even bigger one for thinking I could marry him. I loved his prestige and position, his popularity and his charm, but I never, ever loved him. Believe me, if the opportunity should arise for me to marry, the only reason it will happen is because I am head over heels in love with the man."

Trey was glad to hear that, because he planned to be the one holding Cady's hand when she said "I do."

"You got any prospects on that head over heels thing?" Trey teased.

"Maybe," Cadence said, feeling more relaxed now that she had shared her story with Trey. She was also a bit punchy with only a jolt of coffee in her system. "There are quite a few eligible bachelors out at the Triple T."

Trey stiffened. If any of the hands had been sniffing around Cady, he'd fire them all. He felt Cadence put a hand on his thigh and give it a light pat.

"But their boss-man is the only one of interest."

Trey relaxed and pulled her hand to his lips, placing a warm kiss on her palm. "It's not nice to tease me like that, you know."

"I know," Cadence said, leaning over to give him a quick kiss on the cheek. "But it's fun."

><><

The meeting with Peter Hanson went very well. Trey, and especially Cadence, was impressed with his level of knowledge, and both liked him immediately. By the time they wrapped up their meeting, he assured them he would do his best to get the case before a judge without delay. He would keep them posted and let them know when to show up in court.

"We may run into a small problem, though," Peter said.

Trey and Cadence sat waiting for him to continue. He had sounded so sure that things would go along smoothly and there shouldn't be any problem gaining custody of Cass.

"Although it isn't uncommon for a single person or domestic partners to adopt a child, it would help things along if you two were together or in some way committed to each other. Just think about it."

Cadence's cheeks were bright with color and Trey knew he would choke as his ever-tightening collar threatened to cut off his air supply.

Seeing their discomfort, Peter laughed and walked them to the door.

"I'll be in touch as soon as I have any news."

Shaking both their hands, he returned to his office and left them at the elevator.

Cadence made a big show of buttoning her coat, pulling on her gloves and knotting her scarf around her neck. Trey watched the numbers on the elevator with his hands in his pockets.

When they reached the ground floor, Trey automatically put his hand to the small of Cadence's back and guided her to the parked pickup. Assisting her inside, Trey started the truck and drove to Washington Square Mall.

Parking the pickup in a space that was as close to the door as they could get, which was near the far end of a row, Trey smiled and offered her his arm. She took it with a nod and then walked inside to do some Christmas shopping. Cadence had already given Cass most of the things she purchased the day she shopped with Denni.

She and Trey bought more clothes, a few toys and some storybooks for the little girl. They found a fuzzy red Christmas stocking and had fun selecting little gifts and treats to fill it. When they finished with that, Trey asked Cadence if she'd like to shop on her own for a while and meet him at the Cheesecake Factory for lunch in an hour. She agreed and they split up.

Cadence bought a few more family gifts then wandered the mall trying to think of something more to purchase for Trey. She had ordered a gift for him off eBay a couple weeks ago, but she really wanted to find a few other things for him. She felt guilty that so much of his time in recent weeks had been spent with her and now with Cass. She knew he was a very busy man and so many people depended on his direction and leadership. She wasn't sorry for the time spent with him, just the impact it could have on the ranch.

When she'd voiced those concerns to Trey a few days ago, he had assured her Trent was capable of managing things without him and it was their slow season anyway. As hard as the Thompsons and the hired help all worked, she wasn't sure she wanted to see what their busy season looked like. Then again, she very much hoped to be right in the middle of it all when next summer's harvest time rolled around. She couldn't picture life anywhere other than at the Triple T, right beside Trey.

Sighing, she stared in the window of a jewelry store at a display of wedding bands and engagement rings. She knew Trey cared for her, but she wondered if he loved her the way she was coming to love him. Only time would tell.

She thought back to her engagement to Bill. When he had proposed it was at a fancy restaurant where he publicly got down on one knee, effectively preventing her from saying no and causing an even bigger scene. The ring he gave her was one she hated. Allergic to gold, Bill knew that and purchased a solid gold band highlighted by a two carat traditional round diamond circled by smaller diamonds.

She thought it was large and gaudy and hadn't particularly looked forward to wearing it every day for the rest of her life. It made the skin on her finger raw and sore, yet he insisted she wear it whenever they went out together. Yet another sign she chose to ignore that Bill was all wrong for her. That ring was one thing she had been glad to take off her finger and leave in an envelope on his desk the day she left the law firm.

Never having had the opportunity to shop for an engagement ring, she was surprised at the variety of choices.

Just for fun, she went in the store and asked if she could see a few of the rings. One in particular caught her eye. The band was silver and wide, a sensible choice for a busy ranch wife, with beautiful diamonds lining the inside of the band. The ring was lovely, elegant and simple. Amazingly, it fit her hand like it had been made with her in mind. Smiling, Cadence thanked the clerk, handed back the ring, and returned to her shopping and musings.

After Peter's comments this morning about her and Trey being a couple, along with their teasing each other on the drive to Portland, she couldn't seem to stop mulling over the idea of becoming Trey's bride.

Trey happened to see Cadence go into the jewelry store, wondering what she was up to. He waited a moment then looked in the store window. He spotted Cady looking at rings.

Smiling to himself, he wondered if Peter's comments had gotten her thinking of matrimony. It was certainly all he could think of right now. He would marry Cady tomorrow if he thought she'd say yes. After their talk this morning, he was going to do his best to make sure she was loopy in love with him before he popped the question. He didn't want there to be any doubts at all on her part. He just hoped it wouldn't take too long for her to get to that point.

As for him, he'd fallen in love with her the day she dumped ice water all down him at the café. She had taken their house and made it feel like a home again, chasing away the shadows left behind by the death of his father. Cady made them all feel special, cared for, and loved.

He hadn't expected to fall in love. Certainly wasn't planning on it. Had even tried to tell himself he couldn't let it happen. But, he could no more deny his feelings for Cady than he could fly over the moon.

Watching her through the glass, he saw her pay attention to one particular ring, which she tried on with a wistful look then handed back to the clerk. She smiled, picked up her bags and headed toward the door. Trey ducked around the corner and waited until Cadence walked by before hurrying into the store and up to the sales clerk that had waited on Cady.

"Excuse me," Trey said, turning the full power of his smile and charm on the sales girl.

She glanced his direction then did a double take. It wasn't every day she got to wait on a drop-dead gorgeous cowboy with electrifying blue eyes. "May I help you, sir?"

"The woman who just left, the one who was looking at rings, can you show me what ring she tried on?"

"Certainly, sir," the girl said, her voice sounding a bit deflated and her smile not quite as bright. She placed the engagement ring on a velvet covered display pad. "This is the one."

"Isn't that interesting," Trey said, unable to hide his grin. He picked up the ring and looked at it. The diamonds glistened in the light. "You're sure this was the one? Not a gold ring?"

"Absolutely certain, sir. She mentioned that she is allergic to gold," the clerk said, giving him a cool look that dared him to question her response. "And this ring fit her perfectly."

"Can you tell me what size this is?" he asked, much to the girl's surprise.

"Yes, sir," she said, with a genuine smile and gave him the size.

He continued thumbing the ring and finally set it back down. "Do you make customized rings?"

Taken somewhat by surprise, the sales clerk assured him they had one of the most talented craftsmen in the city in their employ and he just happened to be in the store. Sitting down with him, Trey listened to what he had to share, took down some information and thanked him for his assistance.

Leaving the store, Trey looked at his watch and hustled to meet Cadence for lunch. When he rounded the corner, he saw her standing outside the Cheesecake Factory, several bags resting at her feet.

Coming up to her, he kissed her cheek and started to pick up the bags. Cadence snatched two before he could see what they were.

"No peeking in these," she said with a grin as he gathered the rest of the bags and held the door open for her.

Enjoying a leisurely lunch, they decided they couldn't leave without dessert. Trey ordered a chocolate coconut cream cheesecake while Cady enjoyed a pumpkin cheesecake. As Trey savored the first bite, Cadence laughed at him.

"Is it really that good, Trey?" she teased.

"Yep. I have a thing for chocolate and coconut, and beautiful housekeepers."

Cadence blushed, and changed the subject.

"Are you ready for the Christmas program? Have you been practicing sounding like Santa?"

"I'll be ready by the program. I've been practicing but something is missing," Trey said, trying to look and sound serious.

"Oh? What's that," Cadence said, taking another bite of her own delicious cheesecake.

"A sweet little gal to sit on my lap and whisper wishes in my ear." Trey shot her a smile that nearly made her drop her fork, especially when the hot gleam in his eyes brought a warm spark to her own. "Want to volunteer?"

"No. Since I won't be helping you with that, I suggest you get busy practicing on your own."

"Come on, Cady," he urged as he finished up his dessert. "You wouldn't want the kids to be disappointed, would you?"

Her raised eyebrow let him know she still wasn't falling for his ploy. Finishing her dessert, she excused herself to the restroom.

Trey watched her walk away, enjoying seeing her dressed for battle in her black suit, blue top and black heels. He had no idea how she managed to walk through the mall in those shoes, but the way they highlighted her shapely calves and made her hips sway, he was glad she hadn't thought to bring a pair of sensible shoes to change into.

He always assumed when he found the girl of his dreams, she'd be a country girl who didn't own or care about having expensive suits, silk blouses or high heels. Watching Cady had changed his mind. Maybe this whole citified thing had some good points.

Cadence studied Trey as she walked back to the table. He had dressed in newer Wranglers with a white shirt, a charcoal gray western cut sports jacket and a burgundy silk tie. Of course, he ditched the tie and unbuttoned the top two buttons of his shirt as soon as they left Peter's office. She thought that just added to his rugged appeal, particularly with his polished black boots and black Stetson.

As much as it annoyed her to admit it, she felt pangs of jealousy every time a woman glanced appreciatively his direction. She wanted to grab his arm and yell "He's mine!" but she didn't have right to a claim any more than any other female.

"Ready to go?" Cadence asked as she approached the table.

"Yep. I've got one more stop to make and then we can head for home," Trey said as he held her coat for her. His hands lingered on her shoulders and he pressed a light squeeze to them before he stepped back.

Picking up their purchases, they were soon on the road heading out of town. Trey pulled into a tree lot in The Dalles on the way home and, with Cady's help, selected a large noble fir tree. Cadence was nearly bouncing with excitement as they pulled back out onto I-84 toward home.

"Can we decorate it tonight?" she asked.

"I don't see why not," Trey said, enjoying the pleased look on her face. "You can ask the hands to join us if you want."

"That would be fun," Cadence said, already planning a special treat to go along with the tree trimming. "Do they usually help?"

"No. We haven't had a tree in the house since dad died. Mom puts up a small tree and we spend Christmas day there with her and Nana." Trey took her hand and squeezed it lightly. "Thank you for bringing Christmas back to the ranch house, Cady. We're all excited about celebrating at home this year."

Cadence nodded her head and blushed in pleasure. She hadn't done much in comparison to what Trey had done for her. He gave her a job when she needed one, provided a roof over her head that was nicer than any she'd ever had while making her feel needed and important. He was ready to do whatever it took to rescue the little girl who had captured both their hearts. On top of all that, he had shown her what an amazing, wonderful thing true love could be.

She knew without a doubt she loved, and was in love with, Timothy Andrew Thompson III. Head over heels in love.

Chapter Fifteen

To accomplish great things, we must not only act,
but also dream; not only plan, but also believe.
Anatole France

Christmas carols played softly in the background and a crackling fire added ambience that evening to the great room as everyone gathered around the towering fir tree to decorate it.

Cadence made a huge pot of hot chocolate along with a batch of seven layer bars and a heaping bowl of popcorn for everyone to snack on.

Male laughter filled the room as the hands, Trey and Trent all helped decorate the tree. Cass had never had a Christmas tree before and was quite taken with the wonder of it all. Attempting to direct the men in some semblance of order, Cadence quickly gave up and let them have their fun. They all took turns lifting Cass to place an ornament here or a candy cane there.

Accepting the fact this would not be a perfectly decorated tree, Cadence decided it didn't matter if there were multiple decorations hanging from one branch or some smaller ornaments were on bottom branches while bigger ones sat near the top of the tree. The important thing was that it was being decorated amidst much laughter and joy with love and friendship.

When they were finished, they turned off all the lights except for those twinkling from the tree and sat back to enjoy the cozy atmosphere. Sipping hot chocolate, Cadence discovered Danny could play the harmonica quite well and soon they were singing a rousing rendition of *O Christmas Tree,* followed by *Deck the Halls* and *Jingle Bells.*

Someone started singing the *12 days of Christmas* and the guys began substituting ranch items for traditional words. Finishing up the crazy song, they were laughing so hard, they could barely sing.

Cass was growing sleepy, resting her head against Trey's chest as he held her in the rocker, close to the fragrant tree.

"Sing us a song, Cady," Trey asked, catching her eye and looking at her imploringly.

Somewhat embarrassed to sing solo in front of everyone, she shook her head.

Raising her head, Cass looked at Cadence and smiled. "Please, Cady? You sing me pretty songs at bedtime."

Knowing she was beat, Cadence took a deep breath and began to sing *What Child Is This.* The room grew oddly quiet and still as she sang, the only other sound coming from the pop of logs on the fire. The song seemed quite appropriate considering it was a special child that had brought them all together in this room this evening. When she finished, Henry swiped at his nose with his red bandana and muttered something about being allergic to trees.

It was the perfect way to end the evening and the men quietly filed out the door to the bunkhouse. Trey picked up Cass who had fallen asleep and carried her to her room where Cadence tucked her into bed.

Trent and Trey picked up the mugs from the hot chocolate and carried them to the kitchen.

When Cadence returned, the kitchen was clean and there wasn't anything left for her to do, so she wandered into the great room where Trent watched TV and Trey sat reading some paperwork.

"Thanks for cleaning up for me," Cadence said, sinking down in the rocker. "You do know that is my job don't you? I wouldn't want to get into trouble with the boss-man."

Trent winked at her while Trey gave her an indulgent look before returning to his papers. Cadence sat back and was lulled into a state of peaceful serenity as she sat listening to the holiday comedy Trent was watching while she studied the lights twinkling brightly on the tree. Tucking her feet up in the chair, she pulled a chenille throw over herself and watched the lights soften with blurry edges, the sounds grow distant. A feeling of tranquility settled over her much like a cozy blanket.

Looking up from his paperwork, Trey noticed Cadence sleeping in the rocker. He started to say something, but Trent put his fingers to his lips and nodded her direction, as if to say "let her sleep."

Trey nodded and remained silent. Instead of returning to the paperwork, he sat and watched Cadence bathed in the light from the fire. Fine, feathery shadows swept across her cheeks from her long eyelashes and her lips looked as rosy and appealing as he'd ever seen them. She was snuggled up under the blanket and looked so relaxed with her guard completely down, he felt the now-familiar urge to protect her and provide for her tugging at his heart.

The way her head was cocked against the chair, he knew if she stayed in that position too long she'd get up with a crick in her neck. Standing, he walked to the chair and thought about waking her. Instead, he carefully set aside the throw, hooked his hands beneath her knees and around her back, pulling her to his chest. She roused long enough to whisper his name which brought a smile to his face and warmth flooding through him.

Carrying her to her room, he placed her on the bed, brushing his lips to hers in a soft kiss. She stirred and opened her eyes, realizing she was no longer staring at the lights on the tree.

"Trey?" she asked, adjusting her eyes to the darkness of her room. Trey hadn't bothered to turn on a light, instead relying on the moonlight gliding in soft beams through her window.

"Yeah, darlin'?" he rumbled, realizing it was a bad idea to not only carry her to her bedroom, but to sit next to her on the bed. He had no desire at all to get up and leave. Ever.

"I was dreaming you carried me off and kissed me, but I guess that was real," she said, resting against the pile of pillows on the bed.

"It was real," he said, his voice low and raspy. "Just as real as this."

Trey leaned over and kissed her, gently at first. The intensity of his desire for this lovely, generous woman quickly chased away his good sense and they were soon locked in a kiss that was strong, wild and demanding.

When Trey finally pulled back, he rested his forehead against hers. "Once again, I'm sorry, Cady. I shouldn't have done that."

"I know," Cadence whispered, taking a deep breath. "But I'm glad you did. Now you better get out of here while we still have a lick of sense to split between us."

Trey kissed her on the nose and chuckled as he backed out the door. Standing in the doorway, outlined by the light coming from the kitchen, he fought his desires back to where he could keep them tightly reined. "Goodnight, Cady. Thanks for today and for the song. It was beautiful. Just like you."

With that he turned and left, leaving Cady feeling oddly alone and more than a little afraid of her feelings. She had never felt anything with the intensity created just by being near Trey. His touches nearly undid all her sense or ability to reason. Until everything was settled with Cass, she thought it would be best if they could put their romance on the backburner and focus on doing what was best for the little girl.

Keeping Trey at arm's length might just prove to be a bigger job than Cadence could handle.

Coming into the kitchen the next morning to start breakfast, Cadence smelled the scent of the tree. Trent or Trey must have plugged it in already that morning because the lights were twinkling in the early-morning darkness.

Flipping on the kitchen lights, Cadence couldn't help but laugh when she looked up to see mistletoe hanging above the mudroom door and kitchen sink. On further inspection, she found bunches of it hanging above the table and counter, and she could see a bunch dangling from the ceiling light in the great room.

She had to assume that was Trey's contribution to the holiday decorations.

Smiling to herself, she hurried to ready breakfast. Dropping the last of the waffle batter in the waffle maker, she heard the door open and close. Not looking up, she felt warm breath on her neck while Trey's voice rumbled in her ear.

"Morning, Cady. Notice anything different this morning?"

"Yes, I did," she said, flipping the waffle, still not looking up. "It seems to be a lot colder out this morning."

Trey took her by the shoulders and spun her around to see a teasing grin on her face.

"You wouldn't be funnin' me now, would you?"

"Possibly." Cadence turned back to breakfast preparations.

"Then you must pay a fine for messing with the boss."

"Oh, and what will that fine be, mister boss-man?" Cadence dished up the last waffle and carried the platter to the table. She turned around to get the syrup out of the microwave and found herself enfolded in Trey's arms.

"A kiss."

Cadence pecked his cheek and pulled back.

"That won't do," Trey growled.

Cadence offered a quick kiss to his lips.

"You can do better than that, darlin'."

"Trey, the guys will be in here any minute," she said, putting her hands against his chest, which was a mistake on her part. She could feel his taut muscles beneath her hands and the heat from his eyes drew her like a cozy fire on a sub-zero day. Releasing a sigh, she pulled his head down and gave him a kiss that made them both stagger for breath when it ended. Trey was swooping in for another round when the door opened and the hands poured in.

Cadence jumped a step back, her cheeks a rosy shade of red, as she hustled to finish setting breakfast on the table.

The mistletoe did not go unnoticed by the rest of the men. Before they left for the day, each and every one of them had delivered a kiss on the cheek to both Cadence and Cass.

"How come missytoes means you have to kiss somebody?" Cass asked as she sat at the counter drying a bowl for Cadence.

Cadence laughed. "Mistletoe is a part of holiday traditions and legends. That's why people hang it up and kiss under it during Christmas."

"What's a legend?"

Drying her hands, Cadence took the bowl from Cass, put it away then sat down and looked at the little girl with a smile. "A legend is a story that has been passed down for years and years. The legend of mistletoe is that a magical woman had a son and a bad man killed him with an arrow made from mistletoe. Some magic brought him back to life and the mother decided that from then on mistletoe would represent love and people meeting under it would kiss."

"Do I have to kiss anybody?" Cass asked, not sure she liked all the stubbly cheeks that had brushed hers that morning.

"No, you do not. But the guys were just having fun with you this morning."

"Some of them have scratchy faces," Cass said, rubbing her cheek. "Except Trey and Trent and Tommy. Their cheeks are smooth. Trey's smelled the best."

Out of the mouths of babes, Cadence thought. It was hard for her to get the scent of Trey's spicy aftershave out of her nose let alone out of her head. Even little Cass noticed how good he smelled.

Picking up Cass, Cadence swung her around a few steps, making the little girl giggle, then took her into the great room where they worked on learning the alphabet and reading. Cadence was concerned Cass was far behind other kids her age, but she was a bright little thing and a quick learner.

Mid-morning Trey and Trent came in to warm up and have a cup of coffee. Opening and closing cupboards, they both seemed to be intently searching for something.

"May I help you gentlemen?" Cadence called from the great room.

"We know you've got cookies hidden somewhere, Cady," Trey said, continuing to search. "Can we please have a few?"

Cass ran into the kitchen, followed by Cadence who shook her head as she pulled a tin of cookies from one of the cupboards. She had learned not to leave the treats stashed in the same place two days in a row or they would all be gone. The men had absolutely no control when it came to sweets.

Sinking down at the counter on barstools, Trey and Trent munched on sugar cookies with their coffee, while Cadence poured Cass a glass of milk and gave her a cookie as well. Cass climbed up between Trey and Trent and settled in to enjoy her treat. A few weeks ago she was painfully thin and malnourished. In the short time she had lived with them, her skin had a rosy glow and she was starting to fill out. Cadence was thrilled to see her flourishing in their care.

Cadence was putting another load of jeans in the washer when the phone rang. Trey answered and was surprised to find their attorney on the line.

"Mr. Hansen, what can we do for you today?" Trey asked.

"Just call me Peter, Trey. I was calling to let you and Cadence know you'll be appearing before a judge a week from today to fight for custody of Cass. It looks like her aunt is planning to go ahead and pursue gaining custody. I spoke with your case worker and she is willing to testify on your behalf. Do you have anyone else that would be a witness? Someone non-related would be helpful, but family will work if you can't find anyone else. Neil is sending me a written statement I'll enter on behalf of Cadence."

Trey gave him a few names of people they could contact then asked him to hold while he went to the office phone where he could speak without Cass overhearing the conversation.

"Peter, sorry about making you wait, but I didn't want Cass to overhear. She won't have to appear in court, will she? Cady and I would prefer to keep her out of the mess."

"She shouldn't have to, but it will really depend on how things go. The judge might ask to have her brought in at some point, but I'm hoping it won't go that far. Do you have someone who wouldn't mind waiting with her outside the courtroom during the hearing?"

"I think my mom would be available. If not, we can certainly find someone. Is there anything else we need to know or have prepared?"

Peter went over the basics and Trey wrote down some notes.

"Did you and Cadence give anymore thought to what I said about getting engaged?" Peter asked with a teasing lilt to his voice.

"Well, um…"Trey sighed and ran his hand through his hair. "Here's the thing, Peter. I love Cady and I plan to ask her to marry me. I want to wait until after the custody hearing because I don't want her to think, even for a minute, the reason I'm asking is to up our chances at keeping Cass. I know it would help the cause if we were engaged, but I just can't do that to Cady."

"I understand," Peter said. "From what I observed, I think she'd say yes without any hesitation. Seriously, though, I don't foresee any problem with Cadence being granted custody. After giving it some thought, I would suggest you both file for joint custody. If that works for you, just let me know and I'll have everything ready to go next week. I'll be emailing you both some information Monday. If you have any questions in the meantime, please give me a call."

"I will. Thank you, Peter. We appreciate your help with this and moving things along so quickly. Cady and I would love to see this settled in time for Christmas."

Trey hung up and returned to the kitchen to find Cadence sitting on his vacated stool drinking a cup of tea and eating a cookie. A tiny bit of frosting clung to her upper lip making Trey wish he could kiss it off. Tamping down the direction of his thoughts, he instead smiled and tipped his head toward the office.

Cadence nodded and gave Cass a pat on the head. "Can you remember what I told you about legends this morning, Cass?"

"Yep," the little girl said, helping herself to another cookie.

"Can you tell the story to Trent? I bet he'd love to hear all about mistletoe."

Cass turned her big blue eyes to Trent. "Missytoes gets hunged up so you have to kiss somebody because a magical lady said so. She…"

Trey was trying not to laugh as he walked Cadence to his office and shut the door. Relaying the information from Peter's call, Cadence listened quietly, waiting until Trey was finished speaking to share her thoughts.

"I definitely think we should file for joint custody. Can you let Peter know? And he said Neil was sending a statement, so that is awesome. I don't suppose Aunt Viv would work well to testify since she is a somewhat biased relative."

Trey laughed out loud. "Somewhat biased? Who's any more biased about you than your aunt unless you count any one of the hands, Trent or me?"

Cadence smiled.

"I think we need a fun diversion from what we'll be facing next week, so what do you say to you, Cass, Trent and I going to The Dalles tomorrow? I heard there is going to be a boat light parade on the river and we could have dinner with Mom."

"That sounds fantastic. I know Cass will love it, but what about dinner for the hands?"

"Can't you leave them something in the slow cooker or make sandwiches or let them fend for themselves?"

"I would not feed them sandwiches after working hard all day, but I could put a roast in the slow cooker. What time do you want to leave?"

"Let's leave here about 3:30. That will give us time to visit with mom and enjoy dinner before we watch the parade."

"It's a date," Cadence said, standing up and walking toward the door.

"Does that mean I get to steal a kiss or two and hold your hand?" Trey asked, coming up behind her and placing a kiss on her neck. Heat suddenly shot from where his lips touched her neck all the way to her toes.

Trying to gather her composure, she turned around and gave him a saucy grin.

"Not while Cass is watching. Or Trent. Or your mother. Or anyone else."

"Party pooper," Trey said, wrapping his arms around her waist and pulling her to his chest. "How about you make up for it now?"

"Haven't you had enough kisses this morning?" she asked, hoping Trey would say no. Although he didn't verbalize his response, the way he pressed his lips to hers with urgency and warmth let her know exactly what he was thinking.

Taking a step back, Cadence put hands to her hot cheeks. "I think I better get back to Cass and you better go back outside. Cool off awhile. Think about something besides kissing."

"And missytoes?" Trey asked, garnering a giggle from Cadence.

She stopped in the doorway to look back at him. "Really, Trey, I don't think you needed to hang it quite so liberally throughout the house. What will your mother say?"

"That I'm resourceful and clever," Trey said with a wicked smile, pointing up above Cadence's head where yet another bunch of mistletoe hung from the door frame.

Smiling, she slowly put her arms around his neck. Leaning into him she felt his pulse begin to gallop, matching her own run-away heartbeat. Waiting until the last second, she veered off course and pressed a wet, sloppy kiss on his neck that made him laugh.

"Just so you know Cass is not quite so impressed with all your mistletoe. She said she didn't like all the scratchy cheeks," Cadence said with a grin. "She did say, however, that your cheek was smooth and smelled the best. I think I would have to agree."

Trey raised an eyebrow then bent his head toward her again.

Before he could kiss her or point out more mistletoe, she escaped back to the kitchen. Merciful heavens, did the man have to hang mistletoe everywhere? She'd already found a bunch in the laundry room, another by the front and back door, in the pantry and one above her bedroom door. She wondered when he had found time to hang it all.

She didn't have any more time to contemplate the mistletoe because Barbara showed up to do her weekly report for DHS right before lunch. Cadence invited her to stay and they talked about the hearing set for the next week.

After she left, Cadence bundled up Cass and took her out to the barn for Trey to keep an eye on while she went into town to help Aunt Viv fill the goodie bags for the Christmas program.

Viv and Cadence had plenty of time to talk as they worked on filling the bags. More than Cadence wanted when Viv turned the conversation toward Trey.

"So," Viv said, looking sideways at Cadence with a sly smile. "I get the idea a certain rancher might be a bit smitten with you. Is that correct?"

Glaring at her aunt, Cadence chose to ignore the question. It didn't really slow Viv down.

"Well, come on, girl. You can't hold back on me now. Is he in love with you? Are you in love with him? I know you never loved Bill, but do you love Trey? Do you have any feelings for him?"

Taking a deep breath, Cadence decided Aunt Viv was not going to be distracted or ignored.

"Yes," she said, continuing to stuff bags.

"Yes what?" Viv said, getting annoyed. Why was Cadence being so stubborn in spilling the juicy information she so desperately wanted to know.

"Yes to your questions."

"Well, which one…" Viv said, trying to remember what all she had asked. "He loves you?"

"Yes."

"And you love him?"

Cadence got a dreamy look in her eyes and paused in her work briefly. "Oh, yes, Aunt Viv."

"Well, then, what are you going to do about it?" Viv asked. "You do know men aren't so good at figuring these things out on their own. They usually need a little nudge in the right direction."

"And what direction would that be?" Cadence asked.

"Marriage, my dear girl. Where else would this be leading?"

"Good grief, Aunt Viv. We've barely dated. I've only known him a couple of months. It is entirely too early to be thinking about marriage. Isn't it?" Cadence was hoping her aunt would tell her it wasn't too soon at all. That it was perfectly logical to be thinking about spending forever with someone she didn't even know a few months ago.

"Hogwash," Viv said, smacking her hand on the table. "Sparks flew between the two of you the first day he came in here and saw you. I know you felt it and I could see it in his dazed expression. Quit wasting time, Cady, girl, and go lasso yourself that handsome cowboy."

"Good gracious, Aunt Viv, what kind of girl do you think I am? I certainly won't be…" Cadence searched for the right word then used her aunt's instead, "lassoing him or anyone else."

Viv laughed; thrilled she had accomplished her goal of getting Cadence worked up about Trey. It just proved how much in love her niece was with the head cowpuncher at the Triple T.

Giving Cadence's shoulders a squeeze, Viv smiled broadly. "You're a goner for him, aren't you, honey."

Cadence looked at her aunt in defeat. "Completely and totally gone."

><><

Hustling home, Cadence rushed to get dinner ready, feed the men and spend the evening working on Christmas projects.

All the while, her mind kept wandering to the teasing man with the electrifying blue eyes who had kissed her until she felt like her insides had turned to molten lava that morning. What were his plans for the future? She wondered where he thought all this flirting and kissing was heading.

><><

When the men trooped in for breakfast the next morning, every last one of them had freshly shaved cheeks. Cadence tried to hide her laughter as they took a seat at the table. She was pretty sure Henry's grizzled cheek hadn't been shaved since before Lois retired, but there he sat looking like a plucked chicken.

The men were nearly done eating when Cass wandered out from her room, rubbing sleep from her eyes. She climbed up on Cadence's lap, hugging a floppy toy bunny that Aunt Viv had given her.

"Good morning, sweetie-pie," Cadence said, kissing the top of Cass's head. "Are you ready for breakfast?"

"Yep, I'm right hungry," she said, sounding just like one of the hands. Cadence split open a muffin and buttered it then poured Cass a glass of milk. Adding some scrambled eggs and a few pieces of bacon to a plate, she placed it before Cass.

Trey and Trent discussed plans for the day with the hands and Cadence reminded them they would have to dish up their own dinner that night since they would be gone. Tommy volunteered to be in charge again, in hopes of getting another plate of goodies. Cadence gave him a wink when he said he'd make sure the dishes were done.

"What's got you kissing up to the cook?" Danny teased as they carried their breakfast dishes to the sink.

"Not a thing," Tommy said, his mouth already watering at the thought of the goodies Cadence would leave for him. "I'm just trying to be helpful."

"Right," Danny said, with a doubtful expression covering his face.

Before the men went out the door, Cass stood up on her chair and announced she was ready for "missytoes." Each one of the hands gave her a kiss on the cheek before leaving. Trey was the last in line. After he kissed her rosy little cheek, he picked her up and carried her to the kitchen where he set her down on the counter.

"What do you think, Cass? Does my cheek still smell the best?"

"I don't know," she said, her blue eyes twinkling. "Trent smells good. But I like your kiss the bestest."

Trey laughed and ruffled her mop of curls. Turning to Cadence he kissed her cheek and waggled his eyebrows at her. Leaning close he whispered, "What do you think? Do I kiss the bestest?"

Cadence gave him a playful shove toward the door. "Get out of my kitchen, mister boss-man. You are entirely too conceited for your own good." But the warm smile she gave him took the sting out of her words. He whistled all the way to the barn.

Chapter Sixteen

*I try to learn from the past, but I plan for the future by
focusing exclusively on the present.
That's where the fun is.*

Donald Trump

"Is it time now?" Cass asked for the sixth time in the last fifteen minutes.

Cadence swallowed down an exasperated sigh and smiled at the little girl. When she told her at lunch they were going to town to have dinner with Denni and then watch a parade, Cass got so excited she could barely sit still. After half-heartedly working on her letters and numbers, Cadence gave up and got them both dressed and ready to go.

Dinner was in the slow cooker ready for the hands to dish up when they came in for dinner. Trent was getting dressed and Trey was taking a quick shower.

"We'll be out the door in just a few minutes, sweetie-pie. Why don't you sing me the song you learned this morning?" Cadence said, trying to distract her.

"Which one?" Cass asked, climbing up on a barstool and swiveling the chair back and forth by gripping the counter with her tiny hands.

"The one about the ships," Cadence said, sitting down next to Cass and starting the song. Cass let go of the counter and focused her gaze on Cadence, singing along.

*I saw three ships come sailing in
On Christmas Day, on Christmas Day;
I saw three ships come sailing in
On Christmas Day in the morning.*

*And what was in those ships all three,
On Christmas Day, on Christmas Day?
And what was in those ships all three,
On Christmas Day in the morning?*

Clapping from the dining area made both of them spin around. Trey and Trent stood watching.

"Very nice, ladies," Trey said, walking into the kitchen and picking up Cass. "Since you are singing about ships, I'm guessing you are ready to go see some?"

"Yes!" Cass said, so excited she couldn't keep from wriggling. "I can't wait. I've never seen a ship before."

"Well, let's get your coat and boots on so we can get this show on the road," Trey said, setting her down on a barstool before helping her put on warm insulated boots, coat, hat, scarf and mittens.

Trent ran out to warm up the pickup while Cadence put final preparations on the meal and left Tommy a note with a treasure map to his plate of treats.

By the time they got to The Dalles, Cass had them all singing Christmas carols. Half the time Trey and Trent substituted silly words. Cadence wasn't sure if it was accidental or on purpose, but it certainly made Cass laugh.

Denni was making them dinner at her house then they would all go down to the river to watch the parade.

Going in the house, each of the Thompson boys hugged and kissed their mother. Cadence gave her a warm hug, then Denni bent down to give Cass a hug. Cass squeezed Denni and kissed her cheek.

"Do you have any missytoes?" Cass asked as she looked around the room.

"Missytoes?" Denni asked, confused.

"Mistletoe," Trey whispered in his mother's ear.

"Well, come to think of it, Cass, I don't. Why?" Denni said.

"Trey hunged it all over our house."

"Oh, he did, did he?" Denni said, shooting her son a motherly glare.

"Yep. And I got kissed by everybody. Henry shaved so he wouldn't be so scratchy. I don't like the scratchies."

Trying not to laugh, Denni instead gave Cass a serious nod. "I'm sure you don't."

"Trent and Trey smell the best," Cass said, hanging off of Cadence's hand swinging back and forth as she talked, taking in the Christmas tree and the few packages beneath it. "But Trey gives the best kisses."

"Is that right? We'll isn't that nice," Denni said, smirking at Trey.

"What do you think, Cady?" Denni teased. "Does Trey give the best kisses?"

Cadence flushed five shades of red and busied herself removing Cass's outerwear.

"Yeah, Cady," Trent joined in the teasing. "Does he?"

"I believe I will refrain from providing a response to that particular question," Cadence said, looking right at Trey with a lifted eyebrow.

"Cady, how come your face is all red?" Cass asked in her typical honest and inquisitive fashion.

All the adults, including Cadence, laughed.

Dinner was fun and lighthearted with Denni telling stories about the mischief her boys used to get into, particularly during the holiday season. Cadence felt like she should cover Cass's ears to keep her from getting any wild ideas, but the little girl was so sweet tempered she wasn't really worried about her turning overnight into a Thompson terror.

Trent and Trey did the dishes while the women sat in the living room around the tree. Cass watched a Christmas cartoon while Denni and Cadence chatted about plans for the holidays. Denni was going to come for the Christmas program so she could see Trey as Santa. She and Nana would come Christmas Eve and stay through Christmas Day. She was also planning to drive out for church services tomorrow and come for lunch.

Cadence thoroughly enjoyed visiting with Denni and could see that Trey and Trent inherited their lively, teasing ways from their mother. She was just fun.

Once the dishes were done, they all bundled up and drove down to the river. Although the temperature wasn't terribly cold, it was chilly near the water. Cadence was glad they thought to grab a few fleece blankets before they left the house. She wrapped one around Cass then picked her up and held her close as they waited for the festivities to start.

"Let me take her," Trey said, his voice rumbling in her ear while his warm breath on her neck made her shiver.

With her arms empty, Cadence felt chilled to the bone and quickly wrapped a blanket around herself. Moving closer to Denni, they shared the warmth.

Trent and Trey took turns holding Cass as they watched the parade.

There were quite a few boats, all bedecked in lights. Some were all white, others covered in a dazzling display of color. Many featured lit trees, some had candy canes and gingerbread men made of lights. A few had snowmen. One even had a large fish made of lights that looked like it was jumping over the boat.

The final one featured a waving Santa Claus. Cass waved in return until the boat disappeared from sight.

"Did you see Santa?" Cass asked as they strolled back to the pickup.

"We sure did, sweetie-pie," Cadence said, buckling Cass into her seat. "Was that pretty cool?"

"Yep. It was awesome!"

Laughing, they drove back to Denni's for hot chocolate before heading home. Cass fell asleep before the chocolate was even made. Denni asked if she could keep her for the night. Trey and Cadence decided it would be fine and Denni would bring Cass to church with her in the morning.

On the drive home, the pickup seemed oddly quiet without the little girl's chatter. Cadence sat in the back seat staring into the inky darkness thinking how different her life had become from where she had been just a year ago.

Last December, she and Bill rushed from one holiday party to another. They never spent time with friends. He was too busy schmoozing his next potential client. Cadence hated it. Bill looked at the holidays as a time to expand his client base instead of a celebration of the spirit. Christmas Eve with his parents was a nightmarish formal affair of stuffy people who lost most their inhibitions after their third or fourth trip to the hosted bar. Hung-over, Bill spent Christmas Day at home while Cadence went to church with friends then spent the rest of the day alone.

This year, Cadence mused, would be more like the Rockwell-esque vision of Christmas she had always wanted and never thought she would have.

Arriving home, the house seemed so quiet without Cass's chatter. Trent wandered off to the great room and Trey stole a quick kiss in the kitchen before wishing Cadence a good night.

Falling into bed exhausted, she knew the only visions dancing in her head would be those of Trey and Cass.

Chapter Seventeen

Plans made swiftly and intuitively are likely to have flaws.
Plans made carefully and comprehensively are sure to.
                                    Robert Grudin

Travis Thompson was so happy to be back on American soil he could have wept.

When he flew into Portland that afternoon, he was ready to kiss the pavement outside the terminal. The grumpy crowds and disgruntled travelers weren't having any effect on his excitement. He couldn't even think of words to describe how glad he was to be home.

Well, nearly home.

Taking a taxi to an auto dealership where the Thompsons had done business for years, he bought a new four-wheel drive pickup, loaded up his bags and drove to Clackamas Town Center.

He sat in the food court and ate a sampling of the food he had missed while he was in Iraq. He couldn't think of a better time to come home when all the stores were decked out for the holidays and the sights and smells wrapped around him in a warm welcome.

Looking at his watch, he decided he better get some shopping done before heading home. Since his last phone call to the ranch got cut off, he wasn't sure if Trent understood that he was coming home a week early.

After six years in the service and two tours of duty in Iraq, he was ready to work side by side with his brothers

253

and return to the tranquility of the Triple T Ranch in Grass Valley.

Strolling through the stores, he found gifts for his mother, Nana, Trent and Trey. He wondered if his brothers had found a new housekeeper, but decided if they had, someone surely would have told him. He wasn't looking forward to the three of them sharing cooking duties, but maybe they could talk their mom into coming to spend a few days at the ranch.

The stores were making a last call as Travis left the mall and started the two and a half hour drive toward home.

He would have stopped in The Dalles to see his mother if it hadn't been so late. He knew he would see her tomorrow for church, though, and kept on driving.

It was past midnight when he drove up the drive to the ranch and parked near the back door. All was dark and quiet in the house, except for a light in the kitchen. Bob and Bonnie came running out from their dog house and stopped mid-bark when they recognized him. He ruffled their ears, gave them both warm pats on the head and told them to go back to bed.

Quietly going in the back door, Travis left everything but one small duffle bag in the mudroom, took off his boots and outerwear, and went into the kitchen. The house was warm and inviting with the scent of cinnamon hanging in the air. Travis wondered if his brothers had resorted to burning candles that smelled like food.

Deciding to sleep in the north wing so he wouldn't wake up Trey and Trent, Travis went to the door of the large guest room. Lois, their previous housekeeper, had always used the room across the hall. Travis assumed if a new housekeeper had been hired, she would be set up in the room Lois had vacated.

Opening the door, Travis didn't bother turning on a light. The moon shining through the window provided just enough light he could see a vague outline of the bed. Travis set down his duffle then quietly took off his boots, socks, shirt, and pants, dropping them in a trail on the way to the bed. Lifting the covers, he climbed in and was surprised the sheets felt toasty. A fresh, womanly scent floated around him.

Rolling over he encountered a warm, soft body. Surprised, he let out a gasp at the same time a woman's scream pierced the air. A light flicked on and Travis found himself staring into the face of a very frightened, very lovely young woman.

It took them both a moment to react. Cadence grabbed the sheet and kept screaming while Travis rolled toward the edge of the mattress.

Trying to scramble to his feet, Travis got entangled in the covers, falling out of bed. He was still sprawled on the floor with a blanket holding his feet captive when Trey came barreling into the room followed by Trent.

Holding a baseball bat in a death grip, Trey looked from Cady to the intruder in his camo print briefs, struggling to extricate himself from the twisted blanket and get to his feet. Ready to do him bodily harm, Trey suddenly dropped the bat and grinned.

"Cady, I'd like you to meet my baby brother," Trey said, reaching down to give Travis a hand before engulfing him in a brotherly hug.

Cadence, who had quit screaming with Trey's arrival, was sitting up in bed with her chest heaving, eyes wild and her long, wavy hair mussed into an alluring tousle. Although she had the sheet pulled up to her chin, a thin dark-green spaghetti strap dangled across an exposed creamy shoulder.

Despite his attention being focused on Travis, Trey took note of Cadence's disheveled state. Walking over to the bed, he pulled the strap up on her shoulder and tugged the covers around her.

Trent hugged Travis and the three brothers stood grinning at each other. Travis seemed to realize he was still in his underwear, turned around and quickly pulled on his pants and shirt.

"Dude, what are you doing here?" Trent said, one arm hanging around his younger brother's neck. "I thought you weren't going to make it home for Christmas."

"No. I called to tell you I'd be home a week early. You must not have heard me with all the static on the phone," Travis said, somewhat pleased to have surprised his family. "Now that I've got my pants on, will you introduce me to your lovely house guest?"

Cadence eyed Travis who looked so much like his brothers she could have picked him out of a crowd as a Thompson. He was taller than Trey, but not as tall as Trent, and shared the same broad chest.

Embarrassed at her rumpled state, her cheeks flushed a pretty shade of pink as Trey introduced her.

"Travis, this is our housekeeper and cook, Cadence Greer," Trey said, as Travis shook Cadence's free hand. The other was too busy clutching the blankets up under her chin. "Miss Fancy Pants can cook like nobody's business, but she tends to take herself too seriously, so we call her Cady."

Cadence glared at Trey, irritated and hurt. Was that all she was to him? A housekeeper and cook? Someone to tease? Someone to kiss when he was in the mood?

It would have been nice if Trey had thought to introduce her as his girlfriend, or special friend. Someone other than just an employee. Maybe that was all she really was to him. Anger oozing out of every pore, she pushed it aside and shifted into caretaker mode, pointing toward the door.

"Since we are all awake anyway, why don't I fix a snack and the three of you can visit a bit."

"Are you sure, Cady?" Trey asked as he walked with his brothers out the door.

"I'm sure. I'll be right out," she said coolly, trying to hold back her temper as the three of them disappeared down the hall.

Cadence found the three men sitting at the bar in the kitchen. "What can I make for you, Travis?"

"Don't go to any bother on my account," he said, studying their new housekeeper. She looked too young and pretty to know how to cook.

"I'm happy to make anything you like," Cadence said. Then added with a smile, "Within reason."

Travis laughed. "I'd love a grilled cheese sandwich and tomato soup. If it isn't any trouble."

"That's no trouble at all. But you'll have to settle for canned soup," Cadence said, already getting things out to make the sandwiches.

"That sounds perfect," Travis said with a heart-stopping grin.

"You two want a sandwich?" Cadence asked with a pointed look at Trey.

He wasn't sure what he'd done to get on her bad side, but the cool look she shot him made him squirm in his seat. This wasn't like Cady at all. Maybe she was just upset by waking up to find Travis in her bed. That would certainly surprise anyone.

"Yes, please," Trey said and Trent nodded.

While the cheese was melting on the sandwiches and the soup was heating, Cadence made a pot of hot chocolate and set out a plate full of cookies and candy.

Taking their food and drinks into the front room, Cadence plugged in the tree and sat in the rocker listening to the conversation, sipping on a cup of hot chocolate.

It was easy to see a close bond between the three brothers.

She wondered what it would have been like to grow up with a sibling. Someone she could have shared secrets with or gone on fun adventures. Someone she could sit talking to until the wee hours of the morning.

Feeling her eyes grow heavy, Cadence pushed to her feet and bid the men goodnight. All three of them stood.

Travis stuck out his hand and gave her another handshake. "I'm very sorry, Cady, about coming into your room. I guarantee it will never happen again."

"Simple mistake," Cadence said, with understanding. "It could happen to anyone. I'm just glad you are home. These two were quite disappointed when they thought you weren't going to make it. I know your mother will be thrilled."

"I can't wait to see her tomorrow," Travis said. "Thanks again. I appreciate the food and Trey's right, you are a great cook."

"You are more than welcome. Good night," Cadence said, turning to walk out of the room. Trey stepped behind her and attempted to place a kiss to her cheek. Before he could, she stiffened and hurried away from him back toward her room. Giving his brothers a bewildered look, Trey followed after her. He caught up to her just before she shut the bedroom door.

"What's wrong, darlin'?" Trey asked, stepping into the door to keep her from shutting it in his face. "Did Travis accidentally hurt you?"

"No. Travis wasn't the one who hurt me," Cadence snapped, not looking at Trey, feeling tears sting her eyes. "I'm fine. I am, after all, just the cook and housekeeper."

"Just the cook and housekeeper? What's that supposed to mean?" Trey asked, feeling his irritation grow at Cadence's response. He had no idea what had her all riled up. He really wanted to get back to visiting with his brother, but he wasn't moving until he found out what had her teary-eyed and cross with him. "Why don't you tell me what put a burr under your blanket? We had such a nice evening and you were fine when we went to bed. Are you sure Travis didn't hurt you?"

"I'm positive. Travis did nothing to hurt me. Surprise me, yes, but he didn't hurt me. Someone else took care of that. As to that burr under my blanket, as you put it, I guess you'll have to figure out who put it there."

"Cady, you're not even making sense," Trey said, running his hand through his hair and trying to keep his own temper in check.

"I'm sorry. I guess that is all you can expect from someone who is *just* the cook and housekeeper." Cadence would have slammed her door if Trey hadn't been standing in it. Instead, she turned her back and stepped into the room, trying to blink back the tears that threatened to spill down her cheeks.

"Just the cook and housekeeper? Why do you keep saying that? You know you are more than that to us all, especially to me. Why would you think that is all you are to us? No one thinks that. No one has said... Oh." It suddenly dawned on Trey that was exactly how he had introduced Cady to Travis. As the cook and housekeeper. Not as his girlfriend. Not as the girl he loved. Or the woman he planned to marry. Or the person who made him feel alive in ways he'd never felt before.

No wonder she was mad.

Stepping into the room, Trey wrapped his arms around Cadence. "I'm sorry, Cady. I didn't mean to make it sound like you are just the hired help to Travis. You know you are much, much more than that to me."

"And I would know that how?" Cadence mumbled, her head pressed against his chest.

"Because I... because you... I..." Trey realized although he had thought it hundreds of times in the last few months, he had never once told Cady how he felt. Tipping up her chin with his index finger, he smiled down at her. "Cady, I love you. Before you came along I didn't realize how empty and lonely my life was. You've changed all that. I love you, darlin', with all my heart."

"Oh, Trey," she whispered, tears spilling down her cheeks. "I love you, too."

"Well, that's a very good thing, then," Trey said, lowering his head to hers. "It makes doing this even more special." He placed his lips to hers softly, tenderly. When she ran her hands up his shoulders, he gathered her closer in his arms and kissed her so thoroughly, he wanted nothing more than to keep doing it the remainder of the night.

Breaking apart, she created a breath of space between them and smiled.

"I'm going to bed and you are going back out there to visit with your brother," Cadence said, walking to her bed, straightening the covers and making a shooing motion at Trey with her hands. "Go on, mister boss-man."

Instead of leaving, Trey walked over to the bed and put his hands on her shoulders. Turning her around, he tugged on her robe.

"What are you doing?" Cadence said in surprise, looking over her shoulder at him.

"Tucking you in."

"I think not." Cadence pulled the tie on her robe even tighter. Faster than she could react, Trey reached around her and pulled it loose.

"I think so," he said, shooting her a devil-may-care grin. "I'll turn my head." Trey turned his head to the side and closed his eyes. As soon as the robe loosened in his hands, he popped open his eyes and felt desire slam through him with the force of a run-away team of horses. He had expected Cady to wear prim and proper night gowns or even flannel pajamas, not the lovely little silk number that glided smoothly over her womanly curves.

Her hair was still mussed and her cheeks were once again blushed with pink.

"Cady, you are a temptress in disguise as a cook" Trey growled in her ear, "Do you have any notion how incredibly sexy you look right at this moment?"

Trey ran his finger lightly along the line of her spaghetti strap, igniting little tendrils of fire everywhere his skin made contact with hers. Goosebumps broke out on her arms and she felt a tremor race through her.

Realizing her robe was no longer providing a layer of protection from the cowboy standing behind her in his t-shirt and flannel pajama bottom, Cadence jumped into the bed and yanked the blankets up around her. Trey placed a knee on the bed and tried to tug them down, but Cadence held them in a death grip.

"You're darn lucky my brothers are here or I'd have a very hard time keeping my promise to Viv."

"What promise is that?" Cadence asked, her eyes wide and dark.

Trey could see the pulse pounding in her neck and pressed a hot kiss there. "No funny business." Giving her a wicked smile, he slid off the bed and walked toward the door.

"Sweet dreams, Cady," he said, closing the door behind him. Stopping in the hallway for a moment to let his runaway pulse calm down, Trey decided it was a good thing he'd be up visiting with Trent and Travis for a while. He was going to have a hard time sleeping. He knew when he shut his eyes, he would picture Cady looking tousled and enticing with one thin strap of her satin gown sliding off her shoulder.

It really was perfect timing to have his baby brother home. He needed all the distraction from Cady he could get.

><><

Travis looked at Trey as he came back in the room and grinned. "So that's the way the wind blows."

"What way?" Trey said, a broad smile covering his face.

"You've got it bad for the cook," Travis teased. "About time you fell in love. Trent and I thought you'd end up married to the ranch, a shriveled up old bachelor."

"Huh," Trey said, frowning at his brothers. Shooting Trent an ornery glare, he turned to Travis, "Why don't you ask him how his romance with Miss Lindsay, the school teacher, is progressing?"

Trent sat up and looked annoyed. "No need to get personal, Trey."

"Is that right? Seems to me you don't mind getting personal with my love life."

"That's because it's happening right here under my nose. Besides if you don't want public speculation you shouldn't be kissing Cady in front of the café or hanging mistletoe all over the house or cozying up to her when you think no one is looking. Believe me, bro, we're all watching."

"And what exactly are you seeing," Trey asked, indignant and irritated. Was nothing sacred around the ranch anymore?

"A man in love," Trent said with crooked grin.

Chapter Eighteen

We must let go of the life we have planned,
so as to accept the one that is waiting for us.
Joseph Campbell

Standing in the church vestibule, Cadence waited with the three Thompson boys for their mother to arrive with Cass. She held the little girl's dress and shoes in one hand and her purse in the other.

Travis was busy getting his hand shaken and back slapped by everyone who came in the door. It was obvious Travis had been missed in the small community.

Watching the crowd with interest, Cadence felt Trey's presence behind her. When he placed a hand on her waist, she leaned back into him, enjoying the solid warmth at her back.

Denni came in the door with Cass a few minutes before the service began. When she saw Travis standing next to Trent, she dropped Cass's hand and threw her arms around her youngest son, sobbing with joy and relief.

"My baby's home," she said, to anyone who cared to listen, which was about half the congregation.

Cadence whisked Cass off to the restroom to change her. When they came back, Denni was still hugging Travis fiercely and mopping at her tears.

Trey put a hand to Cadence's back and picked up Cass. They led the way to a pew, followed by Trent, Travis and Denni.

"Who's that?" Cass asked in a loud stage whisper to Cadence when they sat down. "He looks like Trey and Trent."

"That's their brother Travis. He'll be living at our house, too."

"He will?" Cass asked in surprise. "Will he give me horsey rides like Trent? Or read me stories like Trey?"

"Maybe," Cadence said, holding a finger to her lips to signal Cass it was time to be quiet as the service started.

At the end of the service the pastor invited everyone to stay for coffee and cookies to celebrate Travis' return home. Cadence brought a few dozen cookies like she did every Sunday and was glad she hadn't forgotten them with all the hub-bub that had taken place at their house in the last 24 hours.

They stayed until Cass got tired and went to Trey, leaning against his legs and asking to go home. He decided it was time they could all use some lunch. Trent retrieved Cass's booster seat from Denni's car and put it in the pickup then Travis drove Denni to the ranch while the rest of them followed in the pickup.

Giving the appropriate words of praise for Cadence's decorations and how nice the big tree looked in the great room, Denni kept her attention focused on Travis. She hadn't seen him in more than two years. While he hadn't grown in height, his chest had broadened out like Trey's and he was more grown up than she remembered.

Denni didn't know what to do with Travis when Drew died. He seemed to take his father's death harder than the other two boys. Part of that was probably his age, but he acted out, got into trouble and she was at her wits end when he came home and said he was joining the army. Although she dreaded seeing him go, she was glad he had because it turned the troubled boy into a responsible man.

Sitting in the great room with the fire crackling, the tree lights twinkling, the sounds of her boys laughing,

Denni's cup was nearly overflowing. Cass played on the floor by the tree with a set of farm toys that belonged to her boys and Cadence was busy bringing out steaming mugs of cider and a plate of sweet treats.

The house, for the first time in years, felt like home. For that Denni was grateful and knew much of the credit could be given to Cady. She was a hard-worker, honest, strong and just what Trey needed. If only her son would realize it and ask the woman to marry him. You'd think with a child they wanted to keep, he'd get a little more excited about proposing. Maybe she'd have to give him a nudge in the right direction. Then she could get started on Trent. If he didn't ask that pretty school teacher out on a date soon one of the other local yokels would scoop her up.

"You look like the cat that found the cream, Mama," Travis said, giving his mother a boyish smile. "What's got you looking so pleased?"

"Having all my boys together right here where they belong," Denni said with a warm smile. She took Cadence's hand as she walked by and gave it a squeeze. "Thank you, Cady, for making our old house feel like home again."

Cadence blushed. "I didn't do anything, Denni. Just cook and clean."

"And decorate, and add homey touches, and cater to the men around here until they are spoiled so badly they won't be fit for anything," Denni said with a teasing smile.

"Now just hold up there, Mom," Trey said, sitting forward in his chair. "Let's not get carried away. We like things just the way they are and we don't want anyone messing with this deal. Unless, of course, you can find out all the places she hides the cookies and Christmas candy."

"Not happening, cowboy," Cadence said, turning toward the kitchen with a saucy grin, which made everyone laugh.

Travis got down on the floor and showed Cass how to hook the little pieces of farm equipment together.

Watching her push them around, he smiled. "You know, those used to be mine when I was about your age."

"They were?" Cass asked, stopping to look at Travis. She hadn't decided yet if she liked him or not. He was getting an awful lot of the attention today and she had gotten used to most of it being focused on her. "Do you want them back?"

Travis laughed and ruffled her mop of curls. "Nope, Miss Cass, they are yours to keep. But if you ever need help playing with them, you let me know, okay?"

"Okay!" Cass quickly decided the third Thompson brother might not be so bad after all.

After dinner was over and the last dish dried, Denni declared she needed to go home. She had to open the store in the morning and would have a busy week ahead of her. Planning to return Tuesday night in time for the Christmas program, she was also taking time off Thursday so she could sit with Cass at the courthouse.

Walking Denni to the door, Travis escorted her out to her car, which earned him another hug and kiss to his cheek.

A light dusting of snow fell the day of the Christmas program. Cass was so excited about attending the festivities Cadence thought the little girl might explode before it was time to leave.

She chattered all through dinner about the program. It seemed that she had taken herself to it the year before and remembered the other kids having fun and there being treat bags and good things to eat.

The hands were all going as well. Programs at the school were events the entire community turned out to support. Cadence was glad they would all be there. They could help keep Cass occupied when she and Trey disappeared to get him into costume. Lindsay was letting them use her classroom as a dressing room. Trey stashed the costume in Trent's pickup and would get it out after everyone was seated for the program.

Denni met them at the school and hooked her arm through Travis's, still surprised to have him home. Cass ran up to Denni and hugged her legs.

"Are you going to sit by me?" Cass asked, taking Denni's free hand.

"Absolutely," Denni said. She ended up sitting with Travis on one side and Cass on the other. Trent sat on the other side of Cass followed by the hands with Trey and Cadence on the end of the row. Aunt Viv and Uncle Joe were sitting in the row in front of them.

The lights dimmed and the first group of performers took the stage. A handful of kindergarten kids came out wearing paper wings and tinfoil halos. Cadence didn't know how they could look any more angelic. Cass was straining to see, so Trent picked her up and held her on his lap.

The tiny angels sang a rousing rendition of *Away In A Manager*. After the applause died down and they left the stage area, the entire student body joined in to put on a play.

The storyline featured a group of students trying to raise funds for the homeless shelter by wrapping gifts. Everyone was too busy to utilize their services until a kind and understanding Mr. Nicholas paid a visit to the booth. The wrapping paper he "accidentally" left behind turned out to be a magic roll that bestowed the spirit of loving kindness and generosity to all who touched it.

The children did a wonderful job performing while offering a gentle reminder to all attending about the true spirit of the season. Despite the teachers looking a bit harried, they made it through the entire production without incident and all the parents stood clapping at the end.

The children sang through *We Wish You a Merry Christmas* twice before rushing into the audience to find their families.

While the children were taking a bow at the end of the play, Cadence and Trey quietly slipped off to Lindsay's classroom and hurried to get Trey into his costume. A big red velvet sack was filled to overflowing with the goody bags Cadence helped Viv fill the previous week. In addition to the traditional orange and peanuts, they added a few pieces of chocolate candy and a big jingle bell tied with a red ribbon.

Adjusting the tilt of his hat, and fluffing his hair and beard, Cady brought out a tube of glittering lip gloss and touched it to the apple of each cheek.

"You look perfect, Trey," she said, standing back to admire how much he did look like Santa. "If you can just get a little redder in the face, they'll think you are the real deal."

"That won't be hard," Trey said, picking up the sack and tossing it over his shoulder. "Between the heat of this costume and the embarrassment, my face should be glowing by the time we walk in the door."

Hearing the beginning strains of *Here Comes Santa Claus*, Trey started down the hall, about as nervous as he'd ever been in his life.

He didn't know a thing about being Santa Claus and being the center of attention was not terribly high on the list of things he wanted to do. But thanks to Trent and Cady, here he was dressed in a red suit about to walk into a room filled with kids expecting jolly ol' Saint Nick. Sending Cadence a glance, she mouthed "I love you" and blew him a kiss as he turned and walked into the room.

Jiggling the red sack so the bells tinkled merrily, he let out a hearty "Ho! Ho! Ho! Merry Christmas!"

Walking down the middle of the room between the aisles of seats, he waved to the children and headed for the big chair that had been set up front just for him. Settling into the seat, the children all clamored to get in line to see Santa and get their treats.

The teachers came to the rescue and lined them up by age, with the youngest getting in line first.

Cass was practically jiggling off one foot to the other. She was ready to run down and get in line as soon as Santa walked past their seats, but Trent kept his arm around her and told her not to worry, she would get her turn.

Looking up at him with her big blue eyes and perfectly combed curly hair, she smiled and put a tiny hand on his leg. "Will you come with me? I don't want to go by myself."

"Sure he will, Cass," Travis said, goading Trent. "Mom said that is the famous Miss Lindsay keeping the kids in line."

"Hmph," Trent said, standing up with Cass in his arms. Cadence bought her a beautiful blue velvet dress that matched her eyes and made her red hair glisten with gold highlights. She was gaining weight and looking more like a normal little girl - cared for, well-fed, and loved.

Trey was giving it his best as Santa, throwing out jolly laughter at all the appropriate times, passing out goody bags and listening to what all the kids wanted for Christmas. He hoped he could remember all the requests so he could let the parents know if they asked.

Cass was next in line and Trey was especially nervous that she would recognize him. He didn't want to shatter her illusions of Santa Claus and put everything he had into playing up the part.

"Well, who do we have here all dressed up so pretty?" Trey said in a deep voice. "I bet you are Cass. Is that right?"

Cass turned to Trent with huge eyes and said, "Santa knows my name!"

Trent laughed and set her down on Trey's lap. "Of course he does. He's Santa."

Putting his arm around Cass, Trey admired her dress. Cadence had done a great job of dressing her up to look like a big doll complete with white stockings and black patent shoes. "Want to tell me what you want for Christmas, Cass?"

"Yes, but can I whisper it?" Cass asked, looking from Trent to Trey.

"You sure can," Trey said, bending down so she could whisper in his ear. He felt her warm breath on the side of his face.

"I want to stay forever with Trey and Cady. That's all I want this year, Santa. They feed me and take care of me and tell me they love me and are the bestest ever."

Cass threw her arms around Trey and gave him a warm hug before pulling back. It took everything in Trey to swallow down the lump in his throat and pretend to be jolly. He told her she was a good girl and he'd try very hard to make her wish come true. Handing her a treat bag, he helped her down and wished her a Merry Christmas. Trent took her hand and led her back to the row where they had been sitting. Cadence was sitting in Trent's vacated chair and Cass ran to her, climbing on her lap.

"Cady, did you see me with Santa. He's gonna bring me what I wished for. I just know it!"

"That's wonderful, sweetie-pie," Cadence said, smoothing Cass's hair and kissing her on the head. "What did you wish for?"

"I can't tell or it won't come true."

"I see," Cadence said, winking at Trent, who stood in the aisle. "We'll just have to see what Santa leaves under the tree Christmas Eve, won't we?"

"Yep," Cass said with a giggle.

Trey wished Cass had been the last child in line instead of toward the front. Her innocent wish had made his heart hurt. He wanted nothing more than to tell her they would keep her forever. But that was going to be up to a judge to decide, not them.

Returning his focus to the job at hand, Trey dug deep and brought out a jolly "Ho! Ho! Ho!" and continued on with his role of Santa Claus.

When the last of the kids were through the line, Denni walked up to Trey and gave him a hug.

"Your dad would be so proud of you, honey," Denni whispered, brushing at her tears. "So very proud. He couldn't have done it better himself."

Unable to speak, Trey nodded his head and gave his mom a warm hug. Taking her hand, they joined the group of adults and kids feasting on the after-program sweets. Many of those in attendance had brought in punch, cider, and trays of cookies to share after the program.

Cass finally noticed Trey was missing as the crowd began to disperse and people gathered up their coats, tired children and leftover treats. Helping her put on her coat, Cadence took Cass's hand and started outside.

"We can't leave. Trey's lost."

"Oh, he's not lost, sweetie-pie, he had to go take care of something important and he'll meet us at home," Cadence assured her as they headed toward the door. They all gave Denni a hug and kiss goodbye. Travis walked her to her car while Trent ran outside and pulled his pickup up to the door, so Cass wouldn't notice Trey's pickup still parked in the lot. Quickly fastening her into the booster seat, Cadence climbed in beside her while Travis and Trent told jokes and kept her occupied.

Arriving home, Cass ran into the house, calling for Trey. When he didn't answer, she shuffled back to the kitchen and let Cadence help her out of her coat and boots.

"Are you sure he's coming back?" Cass asked, her bottom lip starting to stick out.

"Absolutely," Cadence said, tapping Cass on her button nose. "He'll be here before you know it."

"Who'll be here?" Trey asked as he sauntered in the back door. Cass ran to him and he swooped her up in a hug. "Santa Claus?"

"No. You," Cass said on a giggle as Trey tickled her sides. "I missed you."

"You missed me? Where was I at?"

"Losted."

"I was?" Trey asked, kissing Cass on the cheek and carrying her over to a barstool where he sat down with her on his lap.

"Yep. But Cady said you'd come back," Cass said, putting her little arms around his neck and squeezing tight. "I'm glad."

"I'm glad you're glad," Trey said, feeling his throat tighten as he thought about Cass's Christmas wish.

He hoped and prayed he and Cady would be able to make it come true.

Chapter Nineteen

*Some people are making such thorough plans for rainy
days that they aren't enjoying today's sunshine.*
William Feather

Looking out the kitchen window the next morning,
Cadence watched Trey come toward the house leading
Powder and Sasha by the reins.

Wondering what he was planning, she didn't have to
wait long to find out. Tying the horses to the post by the
back door, he stomped his boots, stepped into the
mudroom, and opened the kitchen door.

Leaning back from the sink so he could see her while
she finished up dishes, she smiled. "What are you up to,
Trey?"

Taking off his cowboy hat, he leaned farther around
the door and gave her a loving smile that made heat pool
in her mid-section, sending delicious spurts of warmth
curling out all the way to her fingers and toes.

"I want today to be special for us and Cass, so I
thought we could take a ride together. What do you say?"

Cadence nodded, feeling emotion fill her throat and
cut off her ability to speak. Today could be the last day
Cass would be with them, depending on what the judge
decided tomorrow. She prayed that he would see they
could provide Cass with all the love and shelter a child
would need, but anything could happen at the hearing.

273

"Let me get Cass," she said quietly, drying her hands on a dish towel.

Breaking a cardinal rule of not walking inside with work boots on, Trey stepped into the kitchen with his spurs jingling, tossed his hat on the counter and gathered Cady in his arms. She could smell his spicy after shave, the scent of horse and hay on his chore coat. The canvas was rough against her cheek, but somehow soothing, too.

"It's alright, darlin'. Everything will work out fine," Trey said, rocking her in his arms and rubbing his hands comfortingly along her back. "No matter what happens, God knows the plan and we just have to follow. Right?"

"Right," Cadence whispered. "But I so want the plan to be for her to stay with us. For Cass to be our little girl."

"I know, Cady, I know. But let's just make the most out of today. Let's make memories today that Cass will keep with her no matter what tomorrow brings."

Taking a deep breath, Cadence again nodded her head and took a step back. Looking up at Trey, staring into those beautiful aquamarine eyes, she saw love, strength and hope reflected there.

"Thank you," she said, placing a warm hand on his cheek.

"For what?" Trey said, turning into her hand and kissing her palm.

"For being you. For loving me. For loving Cass."

"Loving you and that sweet little gal is easy," Trey said with a smile. Turning her around, he popped her bottom with his gloved hand. "Now go get Cass and let's have some fun."

Cass was in the front room watching Sesame Street. Cadence turned off the TV and swung the little girl up in her arms.

"Guess what, Cass?"

"What?" Cass asked, giggling as Cady carried her into the kitchen where Trey stood waiting.

"We're going for a horseback ride. Doesn't that sound like fun?"

"Yipee! I love horsey rides." Cass's grin reached from ear to ear. She had ridden with both Trent and Trey on numerous occasions and chattered for what seemed like hours afterward about how much she enjoyed it.

Trey helped her pull on another pair of socks and her snow boots while Cadence helped Cass put on an extra sweater, her coat, scarf, stocking cap and mittens.

Cadence ran into her room and pulled on a turtleneck under her sweatshirt and put on her thick socks. Hurrying back to the kitchen, Trey was already outside, holding Cass up to pet the horses.

Cadence pulled on her cowboy boots, yanked on her coat, scarf, headband and gloves then hustled out the door.

"Where are we going boss-man?" Cadence asked as she ran a hand along Sasha's nose.

Trey held Sasha still while Cadence mounted, handed her the reins then sat Cass in his saddle. Mounting behind her, he put his arms around the little girl and led them out of the yard.

"I thought we could go down past the pond and over on the north ridge. You can see one of the herds really well from there."

"Yeah," Cass said, wrapping her hands around the saddle horn.

They rode out to where they could see the herd, got off and watched the cattle for a while. Remounting, they circled around the other direction and came up on the back side of the pond on their way to the house.

Along the way, Trey pointed out a small herd of deer, three wild turkeys, and a hawk flying over head.

Cass seemed to love being outside every bit as much as Cadence did. Spending most of her life indoors at a desk, Cadence hadn't realized how wonderful it was to be outside in the sunshine. To be in a place where she could breathe in gloriously clean air, and feel a tug toward heaven in the peacefulness of nature.

Glancing at Cass, she smiled to see the little girl look so at ease in the saddle, so happy and carefree. Not at all like the little girl who had come to them such a short time ago.

"What do you think, Cass?" Cadence asked. "Is this pretty cool?"

"It's wicked!" Cass said, causing both Trey and Cadence to laugh.

Trey looked over his shoulder at Cadence and mouthed "Wicked?" Cadence shrugged and smiled.

They'd been gone almost two hours when they rode up to the barn. Trent and Travis sauntered up as they stopped outside the barn door. Bob and Bonnie ran out and chased each other around, waiting for Cass to get down and play. She and the two dogs had become fast friends.

Trent picked up Cass and set her down while Trey dismounted. Travis offered his hand to Cadence. Whistling, he admired Cadence's boots.

"Those are some real nice cowgirl boots, Cady. Very sharp."

"Thanks, Travis. I'm still getting used to them, but I love them."

"You mean you didn't have them before you moved out here?" Travis asked, loosening the cinch on Sasha's saddle.

"No. They were a gift." Cadence said, rubbing Sasha's nose.

"Or a bribe," Trent said in a stage whisper. Cadence blushed. Trey glared at Trent and Travis laughed.

"Did you know how to ride before you came out here," Travis said, searching for a safe topic. "You ride like a natural."

" Before your brothers hired me, the closest I'd been to a horse was seeing some for rent at the beach when I was on vacation. I don't remember ever petting a dog before, either. I do enjoy riding and the animals, though. At least the animals around here don't have hidden agendas, aren't out to stab you in the back and they let you know exactly what they are thinking, which is more than I can say for many of the two-legged variety I've worked around over the years."

All three men laughed as they finished combing down the horses and turned them loose in the small pasture behind the barn. Cass was having her face thoroughly licked by Bonnie while trying to pet Bob.

Picking her up, Trey walked to the house along with Cadence, Trent and Travis.

Making them a quick lunch of leftover stew with hot French bread and a plate of cookies for dessert, they decided to stay inside for the afternoon and play games.

It didn't take long for the Thompson brothers to construct a fort in the great room out of couch cushions, pillows, blankets and chairs. Trey, Travis and Cass were the good guys and Trent and Cadence were supposed to be the bad guys. They play acted and teased and ended up in a laughing heap in the middle of the floor when the "fort" collapsed.

"I haven't laughed this much in years," Travis said, wiping tears from his eyes as Trey tried to disentangle himself from one of the blankets that had been a fort wall.

"It's a regular riot around here," Trent said, pulling his long legs out from between two chairs. Reaching over, he tweaked Cass's nose. "This little goofball keeps things lively."

"She does at that," Cadence said, standing up and surveying the mess. "I vote for the four of you to set this room back to rights while I make dinner."

Although moans of protest followed her to the kitchen, she could hear Cass giggling and the men laughing. Pretty soon they were settled in watching a

Christmas movie. Cadence listened with one ear while she made what she hoped would be a fun meal for Cass.

When the hands came trooping in the door, they were more subdued than usual. Taking their places at the table, they were surprised to be greeted with smiley faces on their plates made from ketchup and mustard.

Cass came running in from the great room followed by Trey, Trent and Travis. They all sat down and smiled right back at their plates.

Sitting next to Trey, Cass could hardly keep from bouncing in her chair as she waited to eat miniature hamburger sliders, home-made corn dogs, wedge-cut French fries, and veggie sticks as well as macaroni and cheese. A small dish next to each plate held pear halves festooned with cottage cheese, almonds and raisins to look like bunny rabbits nestled on a leaf of lettuce.

"Look at the bunnies," Cass said as she glanced at the plates lined in a row down the table. "Cady, I love bunnies!"

"I know, sweetie-pie," Cadence said, sending Cass a motherly smile. Trey said grace and they all dove in to the fun, albeit kid-themed meal. Conversation was lively around the table.

As it wound down, Cadence asked the hands if they had plans for the evening.

"No, Cady," Henry said. "Are we making more candy?"

"No, but I thought it might be fun to make S'mores around the fire pit. What do you all think?"

"What's snores?" Cass asked, finishing up her bunny salad.

"S'mores," Travis corrected. "Are one of the best things ever and I haven't had one for years. I don't care what the rest of you want to do but count me in."

Cadence smiled at Travis and nodded her head.

"Maybe a few of you could get the fire going. By the time the dishes are cleaned up, we'll be ready to roast some marshmallows."

Tommy and Rex volunteered to help clean up the dinner dishes while the rest ambled outside, built a roaring fire in the pit and swept off the benches that surrounded the fire.

Cadence bundled Cass up, picked up a stack of blankets and went outside. The fire was popping merrily and the men were all in good spirits. Although it was chilly, the air was sharp and crisp.

The sky boasted her best finery, a gown of navy velvet sprinkled with thousands of sparkling diamond stars.

Hurrying back inside, Tommy helped Cadence bring out the makings for the treat as well as a large pot of hot mulled cider and mugs. The men produced an assortment of sticks to toast the marshmallows. Travis and Trey had a contest to see who could make the first S'more. Travis barely beat Trey, then devoured his while Trey let his treat cool just a bit before handing it to Cass.

Biting into the crisp cracker, warm marshmallow and oozing chocolate caused the little girl's eyes to grow wide.

"This is yummy," she said, finishing the rest of the treat in just a few bites. "Can I have more, please?"

"More S'mores?" Trent teased.

Sitting outside long after they had eaten their fill, no one seemed to be in a hurry to go back inside. Trey and Trent kept the fire burning while Cadence held Cass on her lap with a blanket draped over them both.

Danny brought out his harmonica and started to play *Up On The Rooftop.* Everyone joined in the singing. They sang every Christmas carol they could think of, finishing up with *Silent Night.*

The song was a fitting end to their pleasant evening.

Glancing up at the sky, Cadence glimpsed a shooting star and pointed it out to Cass, the others following her finger as she gestured to the streak of light.

"Thanks for a great evening, everyone," Cadence said, setting Cass on her feet and standing up.

"Thank you, Cady. This was one of the nicest evenings I've had in a long while," Travis said, thinking once again how glad he was to be home. Although he had been surprised to return to the ranch to find Trey in love with the housekeeper and trying to gain custody of an orphan, Travis wouldn't trade Cass or Cady for anything. After a few days spent with them, they felt like part of his family.

The hands helped put out the fire, carried things back into the house and bid everyone goodnight. Trey helped Cass take off her outerwear, wiped her nose and sent her to brush her teeth and put on her pajamas.

It was going to be really hard saying goodnight when it could be their last.

Finally, Cass was ready for bed. Trent and Travis both stopped by her room, kissed her cheek and wished her sweet dreams. Cass said her prayers and climbed into bed. Trey stayed in the room, sitting on one side of the bed, listening as Cadence read Cass a story. When she finished Cass was already sleeping, looking just like a little princess with her curly mop of hair, pink cheeks and rosebud mouth.

Trey sent another prayer heavenward that everything would work out for the best and they would have the strength to accept it, whatever it might be.

Chapter Twenty

A wise man fights to win, but he is twice a fool
who has no plan for possible defeat.
Louis L'Amour

Trey and Cadence arrived at the courthouse at 9:30 the next morning. They were due to appear before the judge at 10:30 a.m.

Sitting down on a bench in the foyer, they had just removed their coats when Peter came in, wearing a jaunty red silk tie and a friendly smile. Leading them to a quiet corner, they went over details and waited for their turn in the court room.

Trent and Travis arrived with Cass at 10:15. Trey introduced them and Peter warmly shook their hands. Squatting down, Peter got on eye-level with Cass and shook her little hand.

Cass looked adorable and sweet, dressed in the sailor dress Aunt Viv bought for her for Thanksgiving along with white stockings and black patent Mary Jane shoes. Cadence styled Cass's gleaming hair in ringlets of curls with one side pulled back and held secure with a little white bow.

"Cass, it is nice to meet you. Trey and Cady have told me all about you," Peter said, offering a friendly smile. "I bet you are the same age as my little girl."

"I am?" Cass said, her eyes getting big. "Is she 5?"

"She sure is. Her name is Emily and she likes to read, especially about princesses. Do you like princesses?"

"Oh, yes," Cass said. "I think Cady is a princess."

Peter laughed. "I think you might be right."

Standing up, Peter pulled a few children's books out of the leather satchel in his hand and handed them to Cass.

"Emily and I want you to have these. I hope you enjoy them as much as she does."

Taking the books in one hand and clutching them to her little chest, Cass threw her other arm around Peter's leg and gave him a hug. Looking up she beamed at him. "Thank you, Mr. Peter. Will you tell Emily thank you for me."

"You bet I will," Peter said, smiling warmly as he patted her back.

Before anyone could say anything further, they were called into the courtroom. Aunt Viv and Uncle Joe were there along with the sheriff and Barbara, their case worker from DHS. Denni kept Cass entertained in the foyer.

Marcy had yet to arrive, so they sat waiting for her several minutes. She finally came bustling in the door followed by her attorney who looked like he probably moonlighted in some sort of enterprise of questionable legality. His suit was cheap and shabby, his scuffed shoes squeaked across the floor and his hair looked like he'd survived an unfortunate encounter with a bottle of oil.

Walking in and sitting across from Peter, his hard eyes narrowed and he threw out a "hey" with a short nod of his head.

Marcy looked nothing like she had the day at Barbara's office. Her hair was pulled back into a tight and mostly tidy bun. She wore a button up, conservative blouse, a pair of slacks and flats. The way she continuously tugged at the sleeves and collar led Cadence to believe she had not worn the shirt or anything similar for a very long time, if ever.

Someone had coached Marcy and that fact now settled over Cadence and Trey like a dark cloud. Why else had she temporarily changed except in an effort to get custody of Cass?

"Since everyone is here and accounted for, I'd like to get moving along," the judge said, annoyed at the delay.

Listening to the details presented by both sides, the witnesses and testimony from the three adults filing for custody, the judge sat without showing a flicker of emotion. When all the information had been presented, he considered it for a while before he spoke.

"Based on what has been presented, I still have a few questions I need answered before I grant custody. First of all, Marcy Gianotti, no one has been able to confirm your place of employment. You've provided a name and address, but according to the records, no such place exists. Second, I'm not sure I understand the relationship between Mr. Thompson and Miss Greer, his housekeeper, since they are filing for joint custody. Third, I want to be perfectly clear as to why two strangers would want to provide a home for a child who is no blood relation to them when she has an aunt willing to take her in.

"You people have already tested my patience and gone over your allotted time today, so be back here at 10 a.m. tomorrow with the answers I want. And I'll want to meet with Cass tomorrow before I make a decision so Miss Greer and Mr. Thompson, please make sure she is here promptly at 9:45 a.m. She will remain in your care until a further decision is reached."

With that the judge dismissed them and they all left the courtroom. Walking into the foyer, Denni, who sat with Cass, watched them come out the door and saw Trey shake his head as he held tight to Cadence's hand.

Mindful of the fact there was an audience Marcy rushed over to Cass and wrapped her in a painfully tight hug. Cass struggled to pull away. When Marcy wouldn't let her go, she started to whimper. "Leave me alone," she cried, trying to twist free. "You aren't my mommy. Leave me alone."

Trey swooped in and picked up Cass, holding her close and murmuring to her softly. "It's okay, honey. It's fine. You're not hurt. Everything is just fine."

Cadence placed a loving hand on Cass's back and kissed her cheek.

"Miss Gianotti, I think it best if you leave the child alone for the time being," Barbara said, stepping between her and Cass. "And I need you to give me your employer's name and address again."

Marcy rattled it off then shot a look full of loathing at Cadence before she turned and walked down the hall with her attorney. They sat down on a bench and spoke for a few moments, not noticing Travis standing nearby, pretending to get a pop out of the vending machine.

"You said dressing like Miss Uptight would win me custody in nothing flat. Obviously, that isn't going to work. And what happens when they find out where I really work. That isn't going to fly. I want that social security money, but I'm starting to think this kid isn't worth the fuss and bother. Do you think the hot cowboys would just pay me off?"

"Just shut up Marcy and let me think. First thing we've got to do is keep the nosy case worker from finding out what you really do. Did you have to go and give her the real address?"

"It slipped out," Marcy pouted, as they got up and walked toward the door. "Quit worrying, Jonesy, you said yourself the judges always place kids with family before strangers."

As Marcy and Jonesy walked out the door, Travis began to form a plan. Pulling Trent aside, he asked him to accompany him on an errand and the two of them drove off in Travis's pickup.

The rest of the group decided to go to Denni's for lunch and regroup before driving back home. After eating take-out pizza, the adults sat around the table drinking hot coffee while Cass watched an afternoon cartoon and snacked on milk and cookies.

Peter led the conversation, going over the responses Trey and Cady would offer the judge. Everything they planned to share was true and sincere and he told them that sticking to the facts and presenting the truth would go a lot farther than Marcy's lies and falsehoods.

"Think positive," Peter said, getting up to leave. "The judge is a fair man, even if he seems a little stern. I'm going to head back to Portland and see if I can't dig up a little dirt on Marcy and her attorney. I'll be at the courthouse no later than 9:30 in the morning."

Trey and Cadence walked him to the door and shook his hand. "Thank you for helping us with this. We just want to see Cass somewhere she can continue to thrive and be happy."

"I'm fairly certain that place is with you two. As soon as you receive custody, we'll see about speeding through those adoption papers.

Giving Peter a hug, Cadence stepped back wearing a sincere smile. "Thank you again, Peter. We truly appreciate it."

"That's what I'm here for. Now get some rest and I'll see you in the morning."

Buckling Cass into her booster seat in Trey's pickup, they waved goodbye to Denni and made the long drive home, wondering where Travis and Trent had disappeared.

Filling in Trent on the conversation he overheard between Marcy and Jonesy, Travis wanted to go to Portland and see for himself where Marcy worked. From snatches of conversation he heard, he already knew she lived in a seedier part of Portland.

Programming in the address Marcy had given Barbara into the pickup's GPS system, Travis and Trent weren't all that surprised to be pulling up in front of a business in a somewhat dicey area a few blocks from Lloyd Center Mall. The sign on the outside wall said "Jones Imports and Specialties."

A neon sign wasn't plugged in and it certainly didn't look open for business. Trent ran over and tried the door, finding it locked.

"Isn't that an interesting development?" Trent said, as he got back in the pickup. "I think we should go hang out for a few hours, eat some dinner, and then come back to see what we can find out. What do you think?"

"Great idea," Travis said. "Since we are close to the mall, I've got a bit more Christmas shopping I'd like to finish."

"Let's go then" Trent said, as they pulled back out into traffic.

Calling Trey from the mall, they told him they were shopping and not to wait up for them because they'd probably be late getting in.

It was close to 9 p.m. when they drove back to the business and parked across the street. Both men and women loitered along the sidewalk outside. Leaving their cowboy hats in the pickup so they could blend into the crowd, Trent and Travis walked in the door, somehow not surprised to find themselves in a strip club.

"Well, I guess we know what those imports and specialties are, don't we?" Travis said, looking around the room.

Going to a table in a far corner, they sat down and waited. A scantily clad waitress came over and asked what she could get them. She took their orders and gave them a strange look.

Returning with their drinks, she eyed them suspiciously.

"Anything else I could get you?"

"Actually, there is," Travis said, leaning back in his chair and turning on his charm. He watched the waitress change her body language in response to his inviting smile. She was now leaning toward him, waiting for him to go on. "We heard there is a girl named Marcy that works here who is really something. Is that true?"

"Marcy?" the waitress stood up and huffed impatiently. "She's not half as good as me, sugar, and that is a fact."

"Would you be interested in proving that point?" Travis asked, playing the part of strip club patron for all he was worth.

Before she could answer, Trent asked, "What exactly do you girls do, other than waitressing?"

Shooting him a glare that said she thought he was about the dumbest man she'd ever encountered, the waitress cocked one hip and bent over so her nearly bare chest was just inches from Trent's face. "Anything you want."

"You'll have to forgive my friend. He doesn't get out much," Travis said, reaching over and pulling her onto his lap. She threw an arm around his neck and toyed with his hair. "So you waitress, you strip. What else?"

"On occasion, we might be an escort to one of the gentlemen who frequent our fine establishment," the waitress said.

"And Marcy does that too?" Trent asked, earning another glare.

"Yes. She also has been known to meet guys in the back room for the right price, if you get my meaning."

"We get it," Travis said, looking her over from head to toe and making her smile. "We may want to talk later about some of those unique services you offer."

Standing up, the waitress winked at him and started to walk off. Before she did, Travis grabbed her hand. "Hey, do you know someone named Jonesy?"

The waitress laughed. "Jonesy? He runs this lousy joint when he isn't busy pretending to be an attorney. Something about getting kicked out of law school."

"Thanks for the info."

After the waitress left, Trent looked at Travis in disbelief. "Was all that part of your military training?"

"Well, where else do you think I learned how to act like that," Travis said. "I feel like I need hosed down with disinfectant just from sitting in here. Do you think I really wanted her on my lap? But we got the information we were after."

Trent chuckled.

The two brothers sat waiting. Their patience paid off when they spotted Marcy working tables across the room. As unobtrusively as possible, Trent pulled out his phone and snapped a few photos. Even in the dim light, it was easy to distinguish Marcy's features. On a winning streak, they also saw Jonesy making his way around the tables and snapped a few photos of him. Leaving a tip on the table they hurried out to the pickup and started toward home.

Although exhausted, Trent and Travis were up early the next morning, filling in Trey and Cadence on what they discovered the night before.

"A strip club!" Cadence said in shock. "You two tracked her down in a strip club? I can't believe you went in there. I can't believe she works there."

"We've got her now, darlin'," Trey said, swinging Cadence around in the kitchen, much to her surprise and that of his brothers. Stopping his sashay across the kitchen floor, he turned loose of her and smacked the counter. "What sane judge would award custody to a woman who works in a strip club, lives in a dive, and pretends she is an upstanding citizen?"

"We've even got photos," Trent said, pulling out his cell phone and showing them the photos he took.

"This is awesome," Trey said, slapping both Trent and Travis on the back. "You two are the best."

"I agree," Cadence said, giving them each a kiss on the cheek. "A strip club... I just can't believe it."

Calling Peter as soon as they thought he would be up, Trey filled him in on the news. Trent sent the photos to Peter and they agreed to meet at the courthouse a little early to go over the details of the hearing in light of what these amateur investigators discovered.

Pulling up at the courthouse a few hours later, Cass was chatting up a storm, oblivious that life as she was coming to know and enjoy it could be drastically altered in a few hours, depending on the judge's decision.

Cadence had dressed her up in the blue velvet dress she wore to the Christmas program. She looked sweet and angelic as she walked into the courthouse with them, carrying a little bag with her new princess books from Peter, her stuffed rabbit and a coloring book.

"Is Grammy coming today?" Cass asked as they sat on a bench to wait.

"Grammy?" Cadence asked.

"You know, Trey's mommy, Miss Denni. She told me yesterday I could call her Grammy. I've never had a Grammy before. I like her," Cass said, taking her bunny out of the bag and playing with its floppy ears.

"I think that is real nice, Cass. You call her Grammy all you want," Trey said, sitting down on the other side of Cass. "But she had to work today, so she won't be able to come."

They were only there a few minutes when Peter arrived. Viv and Joe kept Cass busy while Peter, Trey and Cadence talked with Travis and Trent.

Before long, Cass was taken to meet with the judge. She looked frightened, so Cadence gave her a hug and told her to go visit with the nice man and answer all his questions and not to be afraid.

Cass smiled and waved her fingers as she disappeared through a doorway down the hall. The rest of them walked into the courtroom, waiting for the hearing to begin. Marcy and Jonesy showed up just a few minutes before ten, looking smug and confident.

As they took their seats, Trey dropped his hand down to the bench, burrowing between the hem of his gray sports coat and Cadence's navy suit jacket until he found her hand and gave it a gentle squeeze. She squeezed back and rubbed her thumb along his palm. He turned his head ever so slightly, giving her a tender smile.

If it wasn't for this woman with whom he had fallen madly in love, he wouldn't be sitting here fighting for custody of an orphan he barely knew existed six months ago. Now, he couldn't imagine his life without either one of them in it. He wanted more than anything to make their ties to him permanent. Cass's through adoption, and Cadence's through marriage. He had plans, big Christmas plans, and he prayed he'd be able to see them through.

The judge entered the courtroom, holding Cass by the hand. He told her she could sit with anyone she wanted, so she ran over and climbed onto Cadence's lap. She held up a candy cane and said the "nice man" gave it to her.

Giving Cass a warm hug, Cadence looked at the judge, waiting to see if he would have Cass taken out of the court room. He waved his hand at Cass, motioning it was fine for her to stay.

Taking his seat, the judge looked around the room and nodded.

"I'd like to keep this as short and painless as possible, so let's get started. Mr. Thompson, Miss Greer, I'd like to hear from the two of you why you want joint custody of this child. It is my understanding that up until a few months ago, you lived in Seattle Miss Greer and were not acquainted with the child at all. Is that correct?"

"That is correct sir," Cadence said, still holding Cass.

"And Mr. Thompson, you knew of the child, but not the child on a personal level. Is that correct?"

"Yes, sir, that is correct," Trey answered.

"So why do the two of you, who have only known each other a few months, want joint custody of a child you barely know who is of no relation to you at all?"

"Because we love her," Cadence said, hugging Cass.

"What benefit is there to the two of you in gaining custody of this child?"

"The benefit is an endless supply of love, laughter, warm hugs and sticky kisses," Cadence said, trying not to get teary-eyed. "Spilled milk, bed-time stories, getting asked why a hundred times a day, and watching her face light up when she learns something new. The benefit to us is not missing out on all the things we didn't even know we wanted or needed before we met this little girl."

Trey placed a gentle hand on Cass's leg as she swung it back and forth from where she sat on Cadence's lap. Clearing his throat, he said, "Cass is a bright, sweet little girl who just needs a chance to grow into the person God has planned for her to be. We think we can give her a good foundation for that growth. We can provide a happy, healthy, loving home for her. The benefit to us is a very precious gift - the love of a child. We would never take that gift lightly, sir."

The judge took down some notes but didn't say a thing. Finally he raised his head and looked at Cadence.

"Miss Greer, you have known Mr. Thompson for how long?"

"Three months, sir."

"And you have been his housekeeper and cook for how long?"

"Three months, sir."

"And you have been in love with him for how long?"

Cadence blushed, a fiery red, but answered honestly. "Three months, sir."

"I see. And Mr. Thompson, you would say you have known Miss Greer for that same time period as well?"

"Yes, sir."

"And she's been working for you for three months?"

"Yes, sir."

"And how long have you been in love with her?" Trey felt his collar get too tight and sweat trickled down his neck. Swallowing he answered the question.

"Three months, sir."

"And your intentions toward her are honorable?"

"Absolutely, sir."

"And don't you think, if you want to give Cass a stable and loving home, it would be a good idea for the two of you to make a commitment to each other? How can I trust you to be committed to this child you've had in your care for just a few weeks, when you can't commit to each other after a couple months when it is as plain as the nose on your face that the two of you are in love with each other."

"Yes, sir. I mean no, sir," Trey stammered. Peter hadn't exactly warned them the judge would be so direct or personal in regard to their relationship.

"Well, spit it out, son," the judge said, sounding annoyed.

"Yes, sir, Cady and I love each other. Yes, we are capable of making a commitment to each other, but we both felt that taking care of Cass and getting things settled with her took precedence over everything else."

The judge looked at him over his glasses with a frown. If Cadence didn't know better she was sure she saw him offer her a quick wink. But that was impossible. Not with the way he had them rattled, not with that gruff demeanor.

Turning to stare at Marcy he held her gaze until she started to shift uncomfortably.

"Miss Gianotti, were we able to verify your employment?"

"Yes, sir. I believe Mrs. Bisbee, Cass's case worker, spoke with my employer yesterday."

"I see," the judge said, then eyed Barbara. "Mrs. Bisbee, did you speak with her employer yesterday?"

"I did speak with someone at a Jones Imports and Specialties in Portland who confirmed Marcy is employed there. He was not perfectly clear on her duties, though. She has mentioned several times that she is a waitress, but her employer said he runs an import business, so the two pieces of information aren't quite matching up."

"Miss Gianotti, or Mr. Jones, would either of you care to shed light on the subject?"

Neither Marcy or Jonesy were speaking. They sat glaring at each other, wondering how they were going to talk their way out of this tangle of lies.

"I believe I can shed some light on that subject," Peter said, standing up. "Mr. Jones, would you like to join me in front of the judge, please?"

Jonesy reluctantly got up and walked with Peter to the judge's stand. Peter took out his phone, pulled up the photos Trent sent earlier that morning and showed them to Jonesy who turned white.

"I can share these photos or you and Miss Gianotti can drop the act right now and never bother Cass again."

Admitting defeat, Jonesy studied the toes of his scuffed shoes as he said, "Miss Gianotti is withdrawing her request for custody."

"I think that is a very wise decision," the judge said. He then ordered her to sign a statement waiving her custody rights and had it notarized by the county clerk in front of the courtroom full of attendees.

"I hereby grant full custody to Timothy Andrew Thompson and Cadence Vivian Greer," the judge declared. Leaning Trey's direction he motioned him to approach the stand. "And if I were you, I'd get busy putting a ring on that gal's finger. Quit wasting time, boy."

"Yes, sir," Trey said with a crooked grin. "Thank you, sir. You have no idea what this means to us all."

"I think I do. I've got two adopted daughters of my own. Now take those gals of yours out to celebrate and have a Merry Christmas."

"Yes, sir! Thank you, sir!" Trey said, shaking the judge's hand. "Merry Christmas!"

As the courtroom erupted with clapping and cheers, Cass clapped, too.

"Why are we excited, Cady?" Cass asked as Cadence stood up, still holding the little girl in her arms.

"Because the nice judge said you get to stay with Trey and I for a long, long time," Cadence said, giving the little girl a dozen kisses on her cheeks, making her giggle.

"Yipee!" Cass said, putting her arms around Cadence's neck and squeezing tight. "Santa made my wish come true and it isn't even Christmas yet."

"What was your wish, sweetie-pie?"

"To stay with you and Trey forever and ever."

"Really? That is what you wished for Christmas?" Cadence could hardly believe what Cass was saying.

"Yep. I love Christmas and Santa Claus and you!" Cass gave Cadence another hug then leaned out to Trey when he walked up, giving him a hug as well.

"We love you, too, sweetie-pie" Cadence said, hugging them both.

The tapping of the judge's gavel and his booming voice telling them to take their frivolity out of his court room, chased them all out into the foyer.

Cadence noticed Marcy standing by the door, looking hurt and angry. Walking over to her, Cadence put a gentle hand on her arm.

"Marcy, if you ever want to see Cass, I'd be happy to meet you here in The Dalles, or even bring her to Portland. You are her aunt, after all."

"Fat good that does me," Marcy said, shaking off Cadence's hand. "Just take care of the kid, okay?"

"We will, Marcy, and please do think about getting to know Cass."

Marcy shrugged and jerked on her coat, but Cadence could see the sheen of tears in her eyes. As she walked toward the door, she looked back and gave the slightest nod of her head.

"That was pretty big-hearted of you, honey," Aunt Viv said as she put an arm around Cadence. "I'm proud of you, Cady. You've turned out to be quite a woman."

"Thanks, Aunt Viv. If I grow up to be half as wonderful as you, I'll be doing just fine."

"Oh, honey, you know just how to butter me up. I think Joe and I should buy lunch. Let's go celebrate. Besides, we've got lots of plans to make since tomorrow is Christmas Eve and all. We need to..."

Cadence got carried along with her aunt's plans and caught sight of Trent packing Cass. She wore his cowboy hat and Travis was trying to help her stuff her arms into the sleeves of her coat. Trey was attempting to shake Peter's hand while Uncle Joe was slapping him on the back.

Smiling, Cadence felt wrapped up in the chaotic love of this group of family and friends. It was a cozy, comfortable feeling unlike any she had experienced before, but one she hoped to know quite well in the coming years.

Chapter Twenty-One

God has a plan for all of us,
but He expects us to do our share of the work.

Minnie Pearl

If every single person at the Triple T Ranch had been magically transported to the North Pole and left smack-dab in the middle of Santa's toy shop, Cadence didn't think they could have been any more excited than they were Christmas Eve. Even the dogs seemed to pick up on the holiday magic floating in the air.

Cadence had been up long before dawn working on preparing food for Christmas Eve dinner as well as Christmas Day.

The Thompson boys were all three in fine form that morning, joking and teasing, hiding Christmas secrets and running in and out so much that Cadence thought they might as well put a revolving door between the mudroom and the kitchen.

Denni and Nana would arrive after lunch and stay until the day after Christmas. Aunt Viv and Uncle Joe were coming out for dinner tonight and then again for the big Christmas meal tomorrow.

The hands were heading off to spend time with their families. Those who hadn't left yet were wandering in for one last goodbye and another handful of Christmas treats.

Cass, sweet little Cass, could hardly sit still and kept talking about Santa sending her Christmas wish early and how it would be the best Christmas ever.

Sitting her down at the counter, Cadence put Cass to work cutting out gingerbread cookies. They both snitched a piece of dough and giggled.

"Did you and your mom make anything special for Christmas?" Cadence asked, curious if Cass had enjoyed much celebration for the holidays before.

"No. Mommy said she couldn't cook," Cass said, cutting out a gingerbread tree.

"What did you do for Christmas?"

"Mommy slept a lot. And cried a lot. I think she missed my daddy. Is that why she cried?"

"Probably," Cadence said, watching Cass intently work on cutting out cookies for a moment before leaning over and kissing her on the head. Cass looked up with her big blue eyes sparkling. "I love you, sweetie-pie."

"I love you, Cady. Whole bunches."

"Well, I'm ever so glad to hear that," Cadence said. "Shall we get these gingerbread men in the oven and move on to our next project?"

"Yep. We've got lots to do, right?"

"Right you are," Cadence said, removing two cookie sheets from the oven that were finished before popping in two more.

"Why don't the guys help us?" Cass said, pounding down a little mound of leftover dough and cutting out one more gingerbread man.

"That is a very good question," Cadence said. Those three Thompson men were acting like the bunch of hooligans Aunt Viv often accused them of being.

"What's a good question?" Trey asked as he came in the back door yet again.

"Why us womens are doing all the work and you mens are playing," Cass said, putting her hands on her hips just like she had seen Cadence do when she was displeased with something.

Trey choked down a laugh. Stepping back he executed a royal bow with a grand sweep of his hand and offered up his most charming smile. It wasn't lost on either Cadence or Cass. "At your service, milady. Your humble servant is now at your beck and call, at least for the next 45 minutes."

"That is a generous offer, kind sir," Cadence said with a teasing lilt in her voice. "First, you can put the clothes from the washer into the dryer, then you can vacuum the front room, dust, polish the silverware, set the table, sweep out the mudroom, get logs ready to light in the fire and make sure the outside lights are ready to turn on."

"You are a slave driving maniac," Trey said, slumping down beside Cass on a barstool and stealing a piece of cookie dough. "What about you? You got orders for me to follow, too?"

"Yep! You can give me a horsey ride, then we can play fort and then you can read me a story and…"

"I think I need to head back outside for a while," Trey said, standing up from the counter, giving Cadence a wink.

"Before you run off with your tail between your legs, cowboy, come here," Cadence said from her spot across the kitchen where she appeared to be dipping something into a pan on the stove.

Sidling up next to Cadence, Trey breathed deep of her fresh womanly scent that mingled with the spicy smell of gingerbread and the delicious fragrance of chocolate. Putting his arm around her waist, he hugged her gently and kissed her cheek.

"Too bad there isn't some mistletoe over here," he rumbled in her ear.

"Good thing or I'd ruin your chocolates," Cadence whispered, setting another piece of candy on a rack to set up. "Try one of these. Take one from the far end there."

Trey picked up one of the chocolates, not quite certain what he was about to taste. The candy he picked up was still slightly warm and it started melting on his fingers. Putting it into his mouth, his eyes registered both his surprise and pleasure at the creamy coconut filling.

"Cady, darlin', these are like the best thing I've ever had," Trey said, picking up a second piece and finishing it in two bites. He rolled his eyes in a state of bliss. "I don't even want to know how you made them or what they are called, just hide them all for me. Travis will scarf them all down if he finds them. He likes coconut almost as much as I do."

Cadence laughed and kissed his cheek. "You really do need to learn to share, especially with your brothers."

Trey looked wounded and grabbed his chest, making Cass laugh.

"Some things are meant to be shared," Trey said, waving his hand toward the counter covered in gingerbread and sugar cookies.

"Others are meant to be savored…" Trey moved her braid aside and placed a soft kiss on her neck, causing goose bumps to pop out on her arms. "And appreciated by just me." He stole another piece of candy and popped it in his mouth.

The fire in his eyes seemed to grow in direct proportion to the weakness of her knees. If they didn't stop where this was headed Cass would be asking how come they were kissing without any 'missytoes.'

Breaking contact with his hot gaze, she blushed and went back to her chocolates. "I may be able to put a few aside just for you."

"You tease!" Trey playfully swatted her bottom. "You save more than a few for me. Got it?"

"Got it, boss-man," Cadence said, nodding her head toward the door. "Now get out of my kitchen and go find something useful to do until lunch."

><><

When everyone gathered around the table for dinner, Trey was surprised to see it was finally his turn to enjoy his favorite meal - prime rib, twice baked potatoes, green beans with bacon pieces, home-made yeast rolls with berry jam and fried apples. He could barely wait to dig in.

Viv and Denni contributed a few salads and side dishes and the table looked like it might buckle under the weight of all the good food.

Once everyone was seated, Trey asked them to bow their heads and led them in a heartfelt prayer of thanks that ended with, "We thank thee for every gift from thy loving hands, especially for our own precious child, Cass. Please bless this food, bless the hands that prepared it, bless each one gathered around this table and bless our time together. In Jesus name we pray."

Soft whispers of "amen" echoed around the table.

After a jovial meal, they cleaned up the table, put on their coats, loaded up trays of treats and drove into town for the evening church service.

Trey sat next to Cadence, holding her hand with their fingers entwined. At Denni's insistence, she was dressed in the teal satin dress she wore on their first date. It was making her hazel eyes shimmer with flecks of green and gold, while a rosy blush highlighted the curve of her cheeks. Her dark wavy hair was pulled into a loose bun at the back of her head, with plenty of tendrils escaping down her neck and around her face.

She looked so soft, womanly, and wonderful it was all Trey could do to keep his hands to himself. He didn't think holding hands should count against him when he wanted so desperately to hold her.

Cass sat on Trent's lap on the other side of him. He figured she would be run down and fighting to keep her eyes open by now, but she was wide awake and taking everything in.

It was hard to remember that this was a Christmas full of firsts for the little girl. It was like experiencing everything himself the first time just watching her. She didn't seem to take anything for granted, though, and was very good about saying thank you.

As the congregation stood to sing the last song of the service, Cass reached out her arms to him and he took her from Trent, holding her close to his chest. He had no idea his heart could be so full of love it ached in the most wonderful way.

Back at the house, Cadence and Denni set out desserts and made both hot chocolate and coffee. Trey hurried out to the barn where he had stashed the Santa suit along with a special gift for Cass. Hurrying to put it on, he ran around the back side of the house, telling Bob and Bonnie to hush their barking, and gently shook a string of jingle bells.

Everyone in the house was so busy visiting they didn't seem to hear it. He shook it with a little more force and noticed Cadence looking around. He waved to her through the patio door and she smiled. Taking Cass by the shoulders, she turned the little girl around and pointed outside.

Trey sauntered up to the door and Cass ran to push it open.

Before he could get all the way inside, Cass threw both arms around him in a warm hug.

"Oh, Santa, thank you so much for my present," she said, turning big china blue eyes up to his. "You are the bestest."

"Well, thank you, Cass." Trey squatted down so he was on her level. "I knew you'd get your present a little early, so I wanted to bring you something special."

Cass looked confused. "But I already got my present. I don't want to be piggy. Can you give it to a little girl who doesn't have one?"

Trey had to swallow twice before he could speak. This little girl was really something special.

"You don't need to worry about that, Cass," Trey said pulling a box wrapped in snowman paper and tied with a bright red bow out of his big red sack. "But I still want you to have this."

"Thank you," Cass said, taking the box and starting toward the tree with it.

"You can open it now, Cass," Trey said.

"I can?" she asked, surprised.

"Sure you can. Go right ahead."

"I need to wait for Trey," Cass said, looking around for her hero. Trey hadn't planned on her missing him. Cadence came to the rescue.

"He had to run out to the barn, sweetie-pie, so you go ahead," Cadence said.

Cass untied the simple bow and started to carefully tug at the paper.

"Aww, Cass, just rip into it," Trent said, while Travis nodded encouragingly.

Cass grinned and tore away the paper revealing what looked like a small boot box. Setting it down on the coffee table, she opened the lid and yelled, "Yipee! I'm a cowgirl, now!"

Trey had found a tiny pair of cowboy boots the same color as Cady's that were just Cass's size. Grabbing the boots out of the box, Cass had her dress shoes off so fast Cadence wasn't sure where they landed. Hopping on one foot, she was trying to pull on a boot. Trent scooped her up while Travis shoved them on her feet.

"There you go," Travis said, while Trent set her down. "Let's see you two-step in those."

Cass jumped around and twirled while everyone laughed and clapped. She finished by running up to Santa and giving him another big hug.

"Thank you, Santa. I love you."

"I love you, too," Trey said, giving her another hug. "Now, I better be on my way. I've got a lot of houses to visit tonight."

Trey started for the back door but Travis and Trent stood there shaking their heads, pointing toward the fireplace.

"Since I can't reveal all my magic secrets, I need you to close your eyes and count to three, Cass, and I'll disappear up the chimney. Okay?"

"Okay," Cass said, holding her hands over her eyes. "1, 2, 3!"

When Cass opened them, Santa was gone. She spun around a few more times singing "I'm a cowgirl, I'm a cowgirl."

As quick as Cass closed her eyes, Trey ran through the great room, silencing the jingle bells as he went, and tore down the hall to his bedroom. Shucking the costume and stuffing it in his closet, he hurried out the door at the end of the hall, circled around the house and came stomping in the kitchen door.

"Brr. It's cold out there," he said, walking into the great room. "I thought I saw something fly off our roof. Did you guys see anything?"

Cass ran over to him, all smiles. "Santa was here, Trey, and he brought me boots just like Cady's. I'm a cowgirl now."

Picking her up and swinging her around in her frilly green Christmas dress, he kissed her on the top of her head. "You sure are a cowgirl. Those are some boots. And you say Santa was here?"

"Yep."

"And I missed him?"

"Yep."

"Well, how do I always miss out on all the fun?" Trey asked, setting Cass down and claiming a spot next to Cadence.

"You seem to have a talent for it," Cadence said with a twinkle in her eye. She leaned over and whispered "thank you" in his ear.

He nodded and pressed a kiss to her cheek.

Trey was ready for everyone to go to bed, leave, make themselves scarce, and in general disappear. He had plans, big plans, and wanted to be alone with Cady.

"Isn't it about time for Miss Cass to be in bed? She's got a big day tomorrow with presents to open and parades to watch on TV and more good food to eat," Trey said, putting a hand around Cadence's waist and giving her a light squeeze.

"I think it is way past her bedtime. Say goodnight to everyone, honey."

Cass made the rounds and went running off to brush her teeth. She took off her boots long enough to change into her new plaid Christmas pajamas, but then she pulled her boots right back on.

"Cass, you can't sleep with your boots on," Cadence said after Cass finished her bedtime prayers.

"Why?"

"Because it isn't good for your feet and they'll get your sheets dirty and you just shouldn't."

"But the boots aren't dirty. They're brand new," Cass said sticking a foot in Cadence's face. "See?"

Pushing the little foot back down, Cadence shook her head. "Yes, I see. Tell you what, you can sleep with them in your bed, just not on your feet. How about that?"

"Okay," Cass said, lifting a foot and pulling off her boot. Cadence tugged off the other one and Cass cuddled them into her arms like they were a favorite stuffed toy.

"Santa must really love me," Cass said as her eyes got droopy. "He gave me you and Trey and Grammy and Nana and Trent and Travis and all the guys and Aunt Viv and Uncle Joe for Christmas, didn't he?"

"Yes, he did."

"And boots, too. He loves me lots."

"He sure does, and so do I, sweetie-pie," Cadence said, pulling the covers up around Cass as her eyes closed and she drifted to sleep. "Sleep tight, Cass."

Returning to the great room, Cadence found the dessert dishes cleaned up and the great room empty except for Trey. He was leaning over the mantle, stirring the coals of the fire. The only light in the room came from the twinkling lights of the Christmas tree and a few candles set out on the massive coffee table.

Walking into the room, Cadence stood and watched Trey for a moment. Between the custody hearing, the Christmas program, and holiday preparations, they had barely managed more than the briefest of conversations. They certainly hadn't had any time to spend alone or discuss any possible plans for their future, if there were any. Cadence certainly hoped there would be.

Cadence knew, without a doubt, that she loved Trey with all of her being and wanted to spend every single Christmas, right here at the Triple T with him. She might have ignored all the warning signs telling her Bill as a big mistake, but she wasn't turning a blind eye to all the signs that said Trey was the one God had planned for her all along.

She studied the way his muscles rippled through the shirt that matched his magnificent blue eyes, the way the firelight cast a warm glow on his golden head, the way he looked in those Wranglers. Cadence was definitely attracted to Trey. But it went way beyond the physical.

Her heart melted thinking of how he played Santa just for Cass and bought her those cute little boots. Not to mention the way he cared so openly and lovingly for not only Cass, but all his family and friends. He was a good man, a loving man. One Cadence wanted to spend the rest of her life loving.

Slipping up behind him, she circled her hands around his chest and gave him a hug.

"Hi," she whispered.

Setting down the poker, Trey turned and put his arms around her. Gazing into her face, he looked deep in her eyes and found what he was searching for there. Placing his lips to hers, he gently kissed her and took a moment to enjoy having her all to himself. A luxury he would never take for granted in this house full of people.

Having missed spending quiet time with her over the last few hectic days, he deepened the kiss and gathered her closer to him. Running his hands up and down the back of her dress, he enjoyed the silky smooth feel of it against his calloused fingers and imagined her skin would feel much the same way.

Taking a step back, he inhaled a deep breath before they got too carried away.

"Thank you for making my favorite dinner tonight," Trey said. "It was about the best prime rib I've ever had."

"I'm glad you enjoyed it. Sorry it took me so long to get around to making your meal."

"It was well worth the wait," Trey said offering her a seductive smile that was pure male flirtation. "Like a few other things that I fully anticipate being well worth the wait."

Cadence blushed. The things that man said made her feel hot and cold and fuzzy headed all at the same time.

Needing some distraction, she stepped over to the Christmas tree and pulled a package from behind it.

"I wanted to give you your present without an audience and now seems as good a time as any," Cadence said, handing him a package that was beautifully wrapped in blue foil paper covered in a flurry of snowflakes and tied with a white bow.

Trey took her hand and led her to the couch where they both sat down. Untying the ribbon, he opened the package and stared at a plain brown box. He wondered what was inside and gave it a little shake.

"You are really just a little boy in a grown man's body, aren't you?" Cadence teased, enjoying Trey's enthusiasm over his present.

"You know it, darlin'."

Trey removed the lid of the box and pushed aside a layer of white tissue to find a pair of spurs. They were old, of that there was no doubt. Holding them up so he could see them better in the firelight, he noted the simple design that featured a silver heart button on each side of the heel band.

"These are wonderful, Cady, thank you. I'm guessing these are more than a year or two old."

"Actually, they are from the Civil War. There are letters in the box that will give you a little more detail, but I'll tell you the short story," Cadence said, watching Trey as he held the spurs reverently. "I wanted to get you a pair of spurs to go with your collection, but I wanted them to be something special. As unbelievable as it will seem, I found these on eBay. The seller was a direct descendent of the owner of the spurs and had not only the envelope full of letters in the box, but also the personal story.

"There was a southern couple, Tim and Katie, newly married and deeply in love just as the war broke out. He felt it his duty to go fight with his friends and neighbors for a cause he believed in and left his new bride. Hoping her husband would be home for Christmas, Katie commissioned a local silversmith to make this pair of spurs. When she realized Tim wouldn't be home for the holidays, she wrapped them up in a box along with a letter, wrote his name and troop number on the outside and sent them with a neighbor boy who was headed out to battle, asking him to make sure her husband received them. In her letter, she explained that the spurs were made with the hearts on each side in hopes he would feel surrounded by her love every time he put them on. Even though he lost a leg in battle, when he arrived home from the war Tim was wearing one spur and carrying the other. That box contains their letters during the war. They lived a long and happy life together. Their great-great-great-great grandson is apparently the last in their line of descendents wasn't interested in keeping either the spurs or the letters. I was more than happy to take them off his hands."

"Wow, Cady. I don't know what to say," Trey continued studying the spurs. "No one has ever given me a gift quite like this. Thank you."

"I wanted those hearts to be significant for you, too. I hope every time you look at them, you'll feel surrounded by my love."

Setting the spurs and the box on the coffee table, Trey turned to Cadence, wrapping his arms around her and burying his face in her hair.

"Darlin', just seeing you across the room makes me feel things I've never felt before. Your love surrounds me every time I walk in the door. I don't know what I did to deserve you, but I'm so glad you are here."

After another kiss that made Cadence's stomach quiver and her cheeks fill with heat, Trey slid off the couch. Getting down on one knee, he pulled a little box from his pocket. Opening the lid, he held it out to Cadence and smiled.

"I met you just a few short months ago, but I know in my heart you're the one I'm meant to love forever. You fill me up and complete me. You've made this house a home again. I want to spend every day for the rest of my life showing you just how special you are to me. Cady, darlin', will you do me the honor of becoming my wife? Will you marry me?"

"Oh, yes, Trey! Absolutely, yes!" Cadence said, throwing her arms around him while tears rolled down her cheeks.

She felt his breath warm on her neck as he whispered, "I love you so much, Cady. I love you."

Pulling back, he took the ring out of the box and slipped it on her finger. She held it up in the firelight.

"I love you, Trey. The ring is perfect and beautiful," Cadence said, admiring the way the diamonds set into the silver band sparkled in the amber light. Turning her hand, she studied the ring. "What is this shape?"

"It's a copy of a horseshoe nail," Trey said, holding her hand and pointing to the overlapping ends. "Sometimes people use horseshoe nails as temporary rings until they can get the real thing. I liked the way the ends overlap, just like the way our hearts and lives have wrapped around each other."

"Trey, it's wonderful," Cadence said. The ring was so much like the ring she had tried on at the mall, she thought for a moment it was the same one, except for the unique design.

"How did you know I couldn't wear gold?" Cadence asked.

Trey grinned. "I saw you trying on that ring in the mall and after you left the store, I went in and had a little chat with the salesgirl. They have a very talented artist who does their custom work for them and he just happened to be there that day. I showed him what I wanted and he was able to get it done just in time."

Looking at her fiancé of five-minutes, Cadence felt her heart melting into a warm puddle. "You are amazing, Trey, and I'm so blessed to be loved by you. I can't wait to marry you."

Kissing her again, Trey smiled against her mouth, "I can't wait much longer either, so what do you say we start the New Year off right?"

Chapter Twenty-Two

Many people spend more time in planning the
wedding than they do in planning the marriage.
Zig Ziglar

When Trey proposed to Cadence Christmas Eve, he envisioned a tiny wedding with just family members, maybe at the house in the great room with an intimate reception following. He should have known better than to make small plans with his mother and Aunt Viv on the case.

He and Cady went to the courthouse first thing Monday and applied for their marriage license, which sent the rumor mill into overdrive. By that afternoon, he was pretty sure most of Sherman County and parts of the surrounding areas were aware a marriage was being planned for New Year's Day. Trey knew Cadence was pleased they would wed on the same day that her great-grandparents shared their nuptials.

By Tuesday afternoon, the church was reserved, the pastor agreed to perform the ceremony, flowers and cake orders were placed, and Viv kidnapped Cady and Cass to go to Portland to shop for dresses with Denni.

Trey had hardly seen Cadence all week with the fuss and flurry of wedding plans and now, as he stood in front of the church, he was impatient to see his bride.

Smiling, he thought a few secret wedding plans he'd made. First, he had his brothers help him clean and rearrange the furniture in the master bedroom. He bought a new sitting room set to go in front of the fireplace. His mom contributed a wedding ring quilt for the bed with matching shams in the shades of green Cadence seemed to prefer. The bathroom had all new towels and luxurious rugs. He couldn't wait to surprise her with the master suite when they got home.

Since they were getting settled into a family unit with Cass, neither one of them wanted to up and leave on a honeymoon right now. They decided a Valentine's Day escape would be just right. Trey suggested they go to Mexico to visit her parents and Cadence agreed that would be great. What she didn't know was that Trey invited her parents to the wedding and they had arrived last night, hiding out at Viv's. When Cady got ready to walk down the aisle, her dad would be there to give her his arm.

Miss Fancy Pants wasn't the only one who could plan wedding details.

><><

Cadence wasn't nervous like she expected she would be minutes before walking down the aisle to become a rancher's wife.

Even though she knew next to nothing about ranching, Cadence did know she was deeply, truly and irrevocably in love with one handsome, good-hearted cowboy.

Thinking of Trey made her smile.

"What's that look for?" asked her maid of honor, Maria, who arrived two days ago from Seattle. They had been close friends since grade-school. "Don't tell me. You're thinking about that gorgeous fiancé of yours, aren't you?"

Cadence grinned. "Maybe."

"There's no maybe about it, girl. And who could blame you. Those Thompson brothers are something else.

It's a pity they are buried out here in the middle of nowhere. Now, if they were in the city they'd be snatched up so quick their hats would be spinning."

"Which is precisely why I'm grateful Trey is out here in the middle of nowhere so I had a chance to find him first. What do you think, Lindsay?"

Cadence had become friends with the schoolteacher and asked her to stand up as a bridesmaid. Trent and Travis were serving as joint best men so it was decided Travis would escort Maria and Trent would escort Lindsay.

"Think? About what?" Lindsay said, looking dreamy.

"Trent?" Maria asked, with an impish grin.

"Well, I…" Lindsay stammered.

Viv stuck her head in the door. "You girls ready to go?"

"Perfect timing, Viv," Lindsay said, hurrying out the door.

Choosing black and white for her wedding colors, Maria and Lindsay both wore black dresses, carrying bouquets of mixed white flowers.

The music started and Lindsay walked down the aisle followed by Maria. Viv pointed Cass in the right direction with her basket of flowers.

Cass took her job of dropping petals seriously and caused more than one muffled laugh to escape from the crowd, especially with her turquoise cowboy boots peeking out from the bottom of her ruffled white dress.

Cadence had to take a moment to collect herself when she stepped out of the dressing room to see her father standing there. Embracing in a long hug, he kissed her cheek and whispered, "You're beautiful, baby," in her ear, before walking her down the aisle.

Willing her tears to stop, Cadence saw her mother give a small wave from where she sat in the front pew and Cadence waved back.

Turning her attention to the front of the church, Cadence caught her breath to see Trey in his black tux. He was absolutely stunning. His broad shoulders and chest were highlighted by the elegant cut of the jacket and the blue of the vest was the exact shade of his eyes. From the black Stetson on his head to the tips of his polished black boots, he was one fine looking cowboy.

Feeling herself pulled in by the rising tide in Trey's sea-blue eyes, Cadence smiled at her beloved and whispered "thank you" as her father handed her over to her soon-to-be-husband's keeping.

Trey felt his breath catch in his throat when Cadence started down the aisle. She was breathtaking in her white satin gown. He didn't know the formal words to describe how she looked, but the sleeves of lace that hit half-way down her arm, the scalloped edge that came just off her shoulders and across her neckline, and the tight bodice that gave way to a full skirt - it was all perfect for her. The skirt of the gown glistened with beadwork and she wore a short lace train that nestled on top of her head where her hair was piled in an abundance of rich, dark curls. Her grandmother's pearls encircled her neck and she carried a bouquet of all white roses, tied with a white ribbon. When she was almost down the aisle, she paused for just a second to lift her hem ever so slightly and flash Trey a glimpse of her turquoise cowboy boots.

That made him grin from ear to ear. It was her way of saying she was ready to blend their two very different lives into one.

In what seemed like no time at all, they were saying "I do" and the pastor gave Trey permission to kiss the bride, which he did so thoroughly the overflowing congregation began to clap and whistle.

"I think you got the job done, son," the pastor whispered with a wink as Trey straightened back up and took Cadence's hand.

Everyone hurried over to Viv's Café for the reception.

Amid all the well-wishers, Trey found it hard to keep tabs on his bride.

Finally coming up behind her, he put his arms around her and kissed her neck. "Well, Miss Fancy Pants…"

"That's Mrs. Fancy Pants, to you, boss-man," Cadence corrected.

"Mrs. Fancy Pants, how does it feel to be a married woman?"

"Wonderful," Cadence said, leaning back against Trey and absorbing his warmth and strength. "Thank you so much for getting Mom and Dad here. I didn't realize how much I missed them and wanted them to share in today."

Not only had Trey managed to get her parents there, Neil along with Peter and their case worker Barbara had all been invited and joined in the celebration, along with their families. Neil was going to return to Portland and spend a few days with Peter since they were old friends who didn't often get a chance to visit.

"You were busy planning a few surprises of your own this week weren't you?" Cadence asked, placing a warm hand to his cheek. "Thank you, Trey, for giving me a home, making me feel needed, wanted and most of all loved. Thank you for this fabulous day."

"You made the day special, Cady. One I'll remember always."

"And I'll always remember our first Christmas together. If I hadn't already been head-over-heels in love with you, I certainly would have been by the time Christmas Eve rolled around. You made it magical and wonderful beyond anything I could have imagined."

Leaning close to her ear, Trey took a quick nibble. "Maybe it was just the mistletoe doing its thing."

Cadence put her arms around his neck, not caring who saw them kiss.

Just then, Cass ran up and wedged herself between them.

"We're a real family now, aren't we?" Cass asked. Trey picked her up and Cadence gave her a kiss.

"You bet we are, honey," Trey said.

"Yipee! And I've got grandmas and a grandpa and uncles and an aunt. And I get to stay with Aunt Viv tonight, right?"

"Yes, you do."

Cadence's parents wanted to spend a little time getting to know Cass, so Viv volunteered to have her stay at their house for the few nights her parents would be in town. Not only would it give them time to bond, it would also give Trey and Cadence a few days to adjust to being married without a 5-year-old underfoot.

"I'm the luckiest girl, ever," Cass said, trying to hug them both, which made all three of them laugh.

"That you are," Trent agreed as he and Travis walked up and each put an arm around Cadence, squeezing her between them. "And we're the luckiest brothers-in-law, ever. I can't believe you gave us tickets for Christmas to go to the Blazer's game this coming Friday. "

"Yeah, Cady, those center court tickets are impossible to get," Travis said. "I don't know what kind of Christmas miracle you managed, but Trent and I can't wait for the game. This will be awesome."

Cady pointed across the café toward Peter. "You might want to tell Peter thanks. He was a big help in getting the tickets."

"We'll do that, but in case we haven't mentioned it before, we're all so glad to have you as part of our family, officially," Trent said, kissing her cheek.

"We think you're crazy for marrying this old man," Travis teased, pointing at Trey, "but glad just the same."

Trey scowled at them both. They laughed then wandered toward Peter, taking Cass with them.

><><

Travis and Trent decided to drive Denni back to The Dalles and spend the night there with her so Trey and Cadence would have the house to themselves.

Trey pulled his pickup up at the front of the house in the circular drive, instead of parking around back. Cadence gave him an odd look, but didn't say anything when he hurried around the truck, unlocked and opened the house door then hustled back to open her pickup door.

Sweeping her into his arms, he carried her across the threshold and kicked the door closed with his boot.

"Welcome home, Cady." Trey gave her an impassioned kiss that made them both breathless before slowing setting her down.

Still in her wedding gown, Cadence adjusted the full skirt so she could walk and turned toward the kitchen.

"Are you hungry?"

Trey caught her arm before she took a step. His eyes glowed from an inner fire. "Nope. Not for dinner, anyway."

"Oh," Cadence licked her lips that had suddenly gone dry.

"Do you need anything?" Trey asked, as he removed his Stetson and set it on a nearby table. He unpinned her veil with surprising dexterity and laid it next to his hat.

"No," Cadence whispered, watching as Trey removed his tux jacket and vest, along with the black crosstie he had worn around his neck. He unfastened the sleeves of his shirt and let them hang loose.

"Are you sure?" Trey asked, grasping her around the waist, rubbing his hands up and down her sides. Each trip up, he rubbed a little higher until the heat in Cady's eyes sparked into a flame, nearly matching his own.

"I'm sure," she managed to whisper on a ragged breath. Trey was stirring her emotions in a way she'd never felt before and the sensations were overpowering.

Lowering his head, Trey continued letting his hands wander where they willed while he nibbled on her ear then trailed hot kisses down her neck and along each scalloped edge of her gown's bateau neckline.

Cady sighed in pleasure and he felt her tremble. Trey pulled her flush against him, not leaving a breath of space, and drank in the delicious wonder of holding her this close. When his own knees started to feel weak, he stepped back and took her hand in his.

"I want to show you something," he said, leading her toward the north wing hallway. She hesitated at her bedroom door, and Trey grinned, coaxing her to the end of the hall where a bunch of mistletoe hung over the door. Pointing above their heads, Cadence smiled and he kissed her again.

"This is the master bedroom," Cadence said, confused.

"I'm well aware of what room it is and now it's ours," Trey said opening the door. He picked up Cadence and carried her inside. Giving her another kiss, he set her down as she looked around, admiring the amazing transformation that took place in the room.

Tommy and Rex had built a crackling fire in the fireplace, lit a profusion of candles and carried in a large bouquet of fragrant flowers that filled the room with an enticing exotic scent. The forsaken aura that had hung so long in the air was gone, replaced by a warm, inviting atmosphere.

Cadence didn't think a five-star hotel in Seattle could have looked any more romantic or welcoming.

"Trey, it's wonderful," she said, turning around to take in all of the room again. "I think you must have worked some holiday magic in here."

"Quite possibly," Trey rumbled in her ear as he came behind her and placed a kiss on her neck. He fumbled to undo the first of many, many buttons down the back of her gown.

"Why can't you brides be practical and go for snaps, or even a zipper?"

Cadence laughed, some of her fear and tension taking wing and flying away.

"I think it was just last week a love-struck cowboy told me some things are worth waiting for."

"Sounds like an idiot," Trey muttered as he continued working on the buttons. Nearly half-way finished, he was gaining confidence that he might get the dress undone before tomorrow morning.

"I wouldn't call him an idiot, although sometimes he can be a little thick," Cadence teased, shooting him a saucy grin over her shoulder.

"Is that right?" Trey said, stopping with the buttons as he fell into the warmth in her eyes.

"Yep, boss-man, it shore enough is," Cadence said in her best imitation of talking like one of the hands.

Trey chuckled, returning his focus to the buttons. "You sure I can't use my pocket knife and cut this thing off?"

Cadence gasped. "Absolutely not! What if Cass wants to wear it for her wedding someday? Or one of our other kids?"

"Other kids?" Trey asked. "What other kids?"

"Well... I... um..." Cadence stuttered. This was ridiculous. It was just Trey after all. Her husband. Joint parent of Cass. Her soon to be lover.

"So you think you want to make some babies with me?" Trey teased, exceedingly pleased at the idea of the process taking a lot of time and effort.

She swallowed hard, unsettled by a sudden case of nerves and shyness. "Yes, Trey, I think I would like to make babies with you. They would be beautiful. I hope they have your gorgeous eyes and your giving heart."

"And what else?" Trey asked, keeping her distracted as he entered the homestretch on getting the buttons undone.

"Your hair the color of warm honey and your ears, which are perfectly shaped, in case you didn't know," Cadence said, closing her eyes to see him better in her mind. "If they are boys, I hope they have your strong jaw and chin, your wide shoulders and broad chest and your hands. Those hands are calloused and strong, yet they can tenderly comfort a little girl, gently pat a dog or make the knees of your wife go weak."

Trey lifted his head and smiled a slow, lazy smile. "They do?"

"Yes, they do," Cadence whispered, blushing again.

"How does it work exactly?" Trey asked, as he undid the last button. Sticking his hands inside the back of the dress, he pushed at the sleeves with gentle fingers until they slid down Cadence's arms and the dress fell in a satiny pool at her feet.

"Just like that," Cadence whispered, whooshing out the breath she was holding. He watched goose bumps break out on Cadence's skin and felt her tremble. Glancing at what she now wore, Trey couldn't believe what he was seeing.

"Cady, what have you gone and done?" Trey asked, appreciation and surprise coloring his voice.

Cadence stood wearing a strapless white lace corset with matching undics, white stockings with garters and her cowboy boots. Walking in a circle around her taking it all in, Trey felt desire and heat flood his entire being. The ability for rational thought left him about the time her dress hit the floor. This Cady, his Cady, was nothing short of spectacular.

Trey moved behind her again, quickly studying the ties on the back of the corset, figuring out the fastest way to get them undone, short of slicing through them with his pocket knife.

Cadence turned to smile at him with a look he hadn't seen before as the full strength of her feminine powers swept through her. "I believe you once told me I shouldn't wear my stays so tight. Care to help loosen them up?"

"Oh, darlin'," Trey said, scooping her up and carrying her to the bed. He gently laid her down, then stood up and pulled off her boots before kicking off his own. Rolling down her stockings he pulled off one, followed by the other and tossed them aside, kissing a blazing trail of heat down each leg clear to her toes.

Not completely certain her traitorous knees would hold her, Cadence slipped off the bed and untucked Trey's shirt, slowing unfastening each button. Trying to embrace this new experience, her hands shook as she pushed off his shirt and placed fiery kisses across his chest. Trey closed his eyes, lost in the sensations Cady was stirring. Sensations he'd never felt before that were about to push him beyond the point of reason.

Kissing her until he thought he would explode from wanting, he spun her around and began tugging at the corset ties. Before he could get even one loose, Cadence laughed and turned back around.

"Why don't you try the hooks? I think that might be easier." Cadence looked down and Trey followed her gaze to the front of her corset, fastened with a row of tiny hooks. He was sure he would die in his impatience to get them undone. When he finally did and the corset fell away, Trey swept her up in his arms.

"Cady, my beautiful Cady. I love you," he whispered softly against her ear, laying her down once again on the bed.

><><

Watching the last embers of the fire flicker and the light from the candles grow dim, Cadence rolled over in Trey's arms so she could look into the face she had memorized, knowing every curve, every valley, every tiny scar by heart.

"Trey?"

Trey opened his eyes, gazing at the lovely face of his bride. "What, darlin'?"

"How long do you think we'll be married?"

Although surprised by her question, he didn't need long to respond. "At least fifty or sixty years. Why?"

"That might give me enough time to get used to being loved by you," Cadence said, kissing his chin. "If this was all part of your master plan, you done good, cowboy."

Trey laughed and pulled Cadence closer.

"It won't take nearly that long, darlin'," he said, lowering his lips to hers again. "And, no, this was not part of the original plan. Trent and I were just hungry for some good food and you reeled us in with the best apple pie we ever tasted. Loving you wasn't anything I planned, but exactly what I needed. Just like Cass becoming our little girl. Thank goodness someone wiser than me already had a plan in place for the two of us to fall in love."

"It was, as Cass would say, the best plan, ever," Cadence said.

❄❄❄

Here are a few of the recipes Cady made for the Triple T cowboys.

Enjoy!

Chicken & Noodles

1 lb. boneless, skinless chicken breasts
salt and pepper to taste
2 10-3/4 oz. cans cream of chicken soup
1 14-1/2 oz. can chicken broth
16-oz. package of wide egg noodles, cooked

Place chicken in a slow cooker and sprinkled the salt and pepper. Top with both cans of cream of chicken soup, cover and cook on low setting for six hours. Remove chicken from slow cooker and shred. Return chicken to slow cooker and add broth along with the cooked noodles. Mix well, cover and cook on low setting for an additional 30 minutes or until heated through. Serves six.

Apple Pie

6 large firm, tart apples (I like Granny Smith the best)
2/3 cup sugar
2 tbsp. flour
2 tsp. cinnamon
1 tbsp. butter, cut into small pieces and softened
Pie Crust

Preheat the oven to 350 degrees.
Roll out your pie dough and line the bottom of a 9-inch pie pan. You can use pre-made dough or whip up a batch of your own.
Peel, core and thinly slice your apples. Put in a microwave safe bowl and stir in sugar, flour and cinnamon. Let rest about 10 minutes. Microwave a minute at a time, stirring after each setting, until the apples are hot and begin to soften, about 5-7 minutes. Spoon apples into the crust and drop in several pieces of butter. Place the second crust on top, seal the edges and poke in a few air holes with a fork. Slather the rest of the butter over the top of the crust then bake about 35-40 minutes until juices are bubbling and crust is golden brown. If you are worried about the edges of the pie getting too brown, cover them with a strip of foil and remove about 10 minutes before the pie is ready to take out of the oven.
Serve warm with a drizzle of caramel sauce and vanilla ice cream or cinnamon laced whipped cream.

Pie Crust

2 1/2 cups flour
1 tsp. salt
2 tbsp. sugar
1 1/2 sticks cold butter, cut into 1/4 inch slices
1/2 cup vegetable shortening, cut into 4 pieces
1/4 cup cold vodka
1/4 cup cold water

Process 1 1/2 cups flour, salt, and sugar in food processor until combined, about 2 one-second pulses. Add butter and shortening and process until dough just starts to collect in uneven clumps, about 15 seconds (dough will resemble coarse crumbs). Scrape bowl with rubber spatula and redistribute dough evenly around processor blade. Add remaining cup flour and pulse until mixture is evenly distributed around bowl and mass of dough has been broken up. Empty mixture into medium bowl.

If you do not have a food processor, work the dough together with either a fork or pastry cutter until all the flour is mixed in and it is crumbly.

Sprinkle vodka and water over mixture. With a rubber spatula, use folding motion to mix, pressing down on dough until dough is slightly tacky and sticks together. Cover with plastic wrap and refrigerate at least 45 minutes or up to two days.

Generously flour a clean, flat surface and your rolling pin. Divide dough in half and roll out one half, turning dough over between rolls to keep from sticking to counter or surface. Roll to desired thickness then transfer to pie plate.

Popcorn Cake

24 cups of popped popcorn*
1 bag of spiced gum drops
1 1/2 cups of peanuts
1 large bag of mini marshmallows
1/3 cup oil
1/2 cup butter

Mix oil, butter and marshmallows in a large bowl. Microwave at 20-30 second increments, stirring between each set until marshmallows are melted and oil and butter are mixed in well. (It will still look a little oily). Mix in popped popcorn, peanuts and gum drops. Grease hands and press into greased bundt or angel food cake pan. Leave standing at room temperature for an hour or so until cake is set, then slice and serve. You could also press into balls and wrap individually.

* For a fun variation, use colored popcorn kernels.

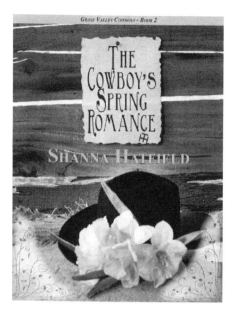

Coming Spring 2012!

The Cowboy's Spring Romance - Trent Thompson has carried a torch for the new schoolteacher since she moved to Grass Valley more than three years ago. Instead of asking her out, he's dated every single female in a 30-mile radius, giving her the impression he's not interested in her at all. Linsday Pierce moved to Grass Valley to teach and quickly fell in love with the small community as well as the delightful people who live there. Everyone welcomes her warmly except for one obnoxious cowboy who goes out of his way to ignore her. Will Trent be able to maintain the pretense when he has to babysit his niece, who happens to be in Lindsay's class? Find out if romance will blossom along with the first flowers of spring.

For more recipes and holiday entertaining tips, download a free copy of *Savvy Holiday Entertaining!*

Savvy Holiday Entertaining gives hosts the information they need to plan ahead, get organized and prepare to have the best holiday season ever! A guide to quick tips, easy ideas, and festive recipes every savvy host needs for a fun holiday. From tips on good enough housekeeping to ideas on menu planning, gift giving and table settings, this book is full of useful ideas. A bonus section offers several simple holiday recipes sure to wow guests.

SHANNA HATFIELD spent 10 years as a newspaper journalist before moving into the field of marketing and public relations. She has a lifelong love of writing, reading and creativity. She and her husband, lovingly referred to as Captain Cavedweller, reside in the Pacific Northwest with their neurotic cat along with a menagerie of wandering wildlife and neighborhood pets.

Shanna loves to hear from readers:

Blog: shannahatfield.com

Facebook: Shanna Hatfield's Page

Twitter: ShannaHatfield

Email: shanna@shannahatfield.com

20515099R00186

Made in the USA
San Bernardino, CA
13 April 2015